Readers love
ANDREW GREY

Fire and Hail

"I absolutely LOVE this series and this newest addition is without a doubt a wonderful welcome."

—Diverse Reader

"Overall, an excellent addition to the Carlisle Cops series and a must read for Andrew Grey fans."

—Jessie G Books

Noble Intentions

"This is a really sweet story. I loved the pacing and the careful revelation of character and motivation."

—Joyfully Jay

"This is a good read for anyone who likes Andrew Grey (come back for this one), and enjoys a quick read with some nobility thrown in. English accents, internet wizards and down-to-earth men—definitely worth picking up."

—Alpha Book Club

The Playmaker

"This is a story for people looking for a nice getaway. It's light, low on angst, has a few hot smexy times, and is lovely in the way that Andrew Grey books always are."

—Open Skye Book Reviews

"Another must read from Andrew Grey."

—Scattered Thoughts and Rogue Words

By Andrew Grey

Accompanied by a Waltz
Between Loathing and Love
Can't Live Without You
Chasing the Dream
Crossing Divides
Dominant Chord
Dutch Treat
Eastern Cowboy
In Search of a Story
Noble Intentions
North to the Future
One Good Deed
Path Not Taken
Planting His Dream
The Playmaker
Saving Faithless Creek
Shared Revelations
Stranded • Taken
Three Fates
(Multiple Author Anthology)
To Have, Hold, and Let Go
Turning the Page
Whipped Cream

HOLIDAY STORIES
Copping a Sweetest Day Feel
Cruise for Christmas
A Lion in Tails
Mariah the Christmas Moose
A Present in Swaddling Clothes
Simple Gifts
Snowbound in Nowhere • Stardust

ART
Legal Artistry • Artistic Appeal
Artistic Pursuits • Legal Tender

BOTTLED UP
The Best Revenge • Bottled Up
Uncorked
An Unexpected Vintage

BRONCO'S BOYS
Inside Out • Upside Down
Backward • Round and Round

THE BULLRIDERS
A Wild Ride • A Daring Ride
A Courageous Ride

BY FIRE
Redemption by Fire
Strengthened by Fire
Burnished by Fire
Heat Under Fire

CARLISLE COPS
Fire and Water • Fire and Ice
Fire and Rain
Fire and Snow • Fire and Hail

CHEMISTRY
Organic Chemistry • Biochemistry
Electrochemistry
Chemistry (Print-Only Anthology)

DREAMSPUN DESIRES
#4 – The Lone Rancher
#28 – Poppy's Secret

EYES OF LOVE
Eyes Only for Me
Eyes Only for You

Published by DREAMSPINNER PRESS
www.dreamspinnerpress.com

By ANDREW GREY

Published by DREAMSPINNER PRESS
www.dreamspinnerpress.com

CHEMISTRY
ANTHOLOGY

ANDREW GREY

Published by
DREAMSPINNER PRESS

5032 Capital Circle SW, Suite 2, PMB# 279, Tallahassee, FL 32305-7886 USA
www.dreamspinnerpress.com

This is a work of fiction. Names, characters, places, and incidents either are the product of author imagination or are used fictitiously, and any resemblance to actual persons, living or dead, business establishments, events, or locales is entirely coincidental.

Cover Art
© 2017 Aaron Anderson.
aaronbydesign55@gmail.com
Cover content is for illustrative purposes only and any person depicted on the cover is a model.

ISBN: 978-1-63533-648-1
Library of Congress Control Number: 2017933585
Published April 2017
v. 1.0

Printed in the United States of America
∞
This paper meets the requirements of
ANSI/NISO Z39.48-1992 (Permanence of Paper).

Table of Contents

ORGANIC CHEMISTRY

ANDREW GREY

Chapter One

"IS IT St. Patrick's Day already?" Gerald, one of Brendon's colleagues, called as they passed each other in the hallway. Brendon stopped and glanced down at his shirt and pants. He was wearing khakis and a green T-shirt—what was wrong with that? Brendon continued walking, actually hurrying toward the department meeting. He was already late because he'd gotten wrapped up in the paper he'd been working on for the past two months, and everything was finally coming together. He hated these meetings because they pulled him away from his work and tended to highlight how he didn't fit in with the rest of the department.

"Nice of you to join us, Dr. Marcus," the chair of the chemistry department, Dr. Nungesser, said as Brendon stepped into the room. All eyes turned to him, and Brendon tried his best to find a seat at the back of the room and disappear. "And a happy St. Patrick's Day to you too," he added, and everyone in the room snickered.

Brendon turned toward the windows that looked out into the hallway of the brand-new science building and suppressed a groan. He needed to remember to look in the mirror before he left the house. Yes, he was wearing a green shirt, like he thought, but why hadn't he noticed the huge shamrock with the dancing leprechaun on the front holding a pint of beer? His cousin had given him the damned thing as a joke, and he'd stuck it in his closet along with everything else.

"Now that Dr. Marcus and his shirt have joined us, we can continue," Dr. Nungesser stated and began to drone on about the various departmental business that was so urgent he had to call the meeting even though they'd discussed the same topics at the past three meetings and nothing ever happened.

Brendon half listened, but spent most of the time running formulas in his head for the paper he desperately wanted to get back to. Everyone else seemed to be listening intently, and Brendon wished he'd remembered to bring a pad and pen with him. It wasn't like he was absentminded, but he'd had a breakthrough, and he knew he'd keep running the formulas over and over until he wrote them down. Until he did, a part of his mind was afraid he'd forget, so the formulas and the arguments around them kept circling, like a plane in a holding pattern.

"Dr. Marcus."

Brendon looked up from where he'd been staring at his shoes. "Yes?" he said calmly.

"Are you paying attention? This isn't class, where you can get the notes from another student," Dr. Nungesser chided snidely.

"Yes, sir," Brendon said softly and continued running his formulas in his head. He was really beginning to get excited. What had begun as a purely academic exercise on his part was turning out to be helpful in explaining why certain isotopes behaved the way they did. It wasn't the total answer, but it was a step, possibly a leap, and Brendon desperately wanted to get back to work.

"Then why don't you enlighten us, since your shoes seem so fascinating?" Dr. Nungesser said. Brendon hadn't even realized where he was looking, and he raised his gaze to Dr. Nungesser's disapproving expression. "It's no secret I didn't want you in my department, and it looks like I was right." Brendon blinked a few times. "So please enlighten us."

"You were explaining about such weighty issues as what the department was going to do as part of the campus's upcoming Halloween charity celebrations. Dr. Gold suggested we create a mad scientist laboratory, which you all agreed was a bit predictable. Dr. Diebus suggested borrowing a skeleton from the biology department and creating an embalming studio, which is a bit more creative," Brendon said as the formulas continued circling in his mind. "You decided to table the decision till next week, and now you're discussing the possible changes to the curriculum for next fall." Brendon stared at Dr. Nungesser as he turned beet red from his chin to his ears, but he barely saw him. The formulas he was working on were definitely more interesting.

"Then let's continue," Dr. Nungesser said after clearing his throat.

"Actually, it might be interesting to recreate Madame Curie's lab for Halloween," Brendon interjected. "Her notebooks are still radioactive, so we could make them glow in the dark, and we could set up some fake Geiger counters that went off after people walked by the samples of radium. Stuff like that." Brendon quieted and heard on a peripheral level the overlapping voices of the other people in the room. They seemed to like his idea, but all Brendon wanted to do was get back to his paper.

The last one of these meetings had gone on for almost two hours, and Brendon was getting itchy as hell.

"Please, if we could get back to the topic of our curriculum," Dr. Nungesser said in an annoyed tone. Someone thrust a pad and pencil in front of him, and Brendon lifted his gaze. Dr. Schurr smiled, and Brendon took the pad and furiously began to scribble down his ideas. By the time he was done, the meeting was over and Brendon had filled pages and pages of the pad with notes and formulas that seemed to have poured from his mind like some sort of computer core dump.

"Brendon," Dr. Schurr said softly as everyone left the meeting. "Can I have a word?"

"Okay," Brendon said as he cradled the pad to his chest like a precious relic. His mind was calmer now. All the information swirling around was now safely on paper, and he could relax. Brendon followed the professor he'd first had as a freshman here at Dickinson, before going on to Cal Tech for his master's and eventually his doctorate. They ended up in Dr. Schurr's office, and he closed the door.

"You shouldn't antagonize Nungesser like that."

"But, Dr. Schurr, I...," Brendon began.

"Call me Frank. You aren't my student any longer. And you have to know that Nungesser will be on you constantly. Why do you think you're teaching all freshman classes? He didn't want you, but the dean did."

Brendon swallowed hard. "I figured it was because I was new," he said, sitting in one of the chairs.

"It has nothing to do with you being new. It's because you're a hell of a lot younger than he is and a world smarter. Nungesser got his doctorate ages ago, and he wheedled his way up to department head. And he'll wheedle you right out the door, whiz kid or not." Frank lifted the carafe off his coffeemaker and poured two mugs before handing one to Brendon. "Although there probably isn't anything you can do about it either."

"But I didn't do anything. He asked me a question, and I answered it." Brendon set the mug on the edge of the desk and showed Frank the pages he'd scribbled during the meeting. "Look at this. I got all the formulas to work out, and even the logic is perfect. I can prove on paper how this entire isotope family will behave under almost any conditions. Now all I need to do is prove it in the lab."

"You'll need Nungesser to sign off on the equipment," Frank said, "and you know he's going to fight you the entire way."

"But this will be good for the university," Brendon said. "It could lead to millions in research grants, and a great deal of prestige that will bring more students here. Isn't that what we're supposed to do?"

Frank took the pad, pulled on a pair of reading glasses, and began flipping through the pages. "You did this during the meeting?"

"I was working on it before the meeting," Brendon said before glancing at the clock on the wall. "Shoot, I gotta go get ready for class."

"Are you going to teach in that?" Frank asked, pointing to his shirt. Brendon shrugged. He didn't have enough time to go home and change. Frank opened his desk drawer and pulled out an old blue polo shirt. "Put this on before you get to class. It's probably a bit big, but you can tuck it in, and at least you won't have the students laughing at you."

"Thanks," Brendon said as he took the shirt and then hurried out the door. He then rushed back in to grab the notepad and darted out again, nearly colliding with a pair of girls, who giggled and then laughed outright when they saw his shirt. Yes, he definitely needed to look in the mirror before he left the house.

Brendon made it to his tiny office and closed the door. He pulled off the offending shirt and shoved it in a bottom drawer before he put on the polo and tucked it in. Then he grabbed his laptop with his class presentations on it, picked up the stack of papers he'd been working on, and left the office, rushing as fast as he dared through the hordes of students. His phone chimed, and he reached to get it out of his pocket.

WHAM! Brendon slammed into what felt like a brick wall and ended up falling backward, skidding along the floor on his butt. His papers and phone went flying, and Brendon sat, stunned, for a few seconds.

"Sorry," the brick wall said, and Brendon blinked a few times as the man reached out a beefy hand to him. "Didn't see you there," the huge man said, and Brendon shied back. He'd spent way too much of his life running from guys like this to react any other way. "Let me help you up," the man said, practically yanking Brendon back onto his feet.

"My papers," Brendon said, thankful the laptop hadn't gone flying along with everything else. The man helped him gather his things, and Brendon retrieved his miraculously undamaged phone.

"I think that's all of it," the man said, and Brendon thanked him and then hurried on to his class. He arrived disheveled and shaken, but thankfully on time. He hooked up his laptop to the network connection and booted it up.

"Hey, Prof, what happened to the dancing leprechaun?" one of the kids in the back of the room asked.

"He bit the dust," Brendon said and began his lecture. He followed the text for the class, but when he had been in school, the best instructors were those who went off the script a bit and added their own insights, so that was how he taught, and before he knew it, the fifty-minute class was over. Of course, students talked to him after class, stopping to ask questions before heading on their way to their next class. Brendon was always grateful he didn't have back-to-back classes, so he hung around until the students had left. Then he gathered his things and headed back to his office.

Once inside, he placed his laptop on his desk, booted it up, and began going through the stack of jumbled papers he'd gathered off the floor. "Where is it?" Brendon asked himself as he sorted through everything. The notepad with everything in it for his paper was gone. He looked everywhere. He hadn't meant to take it with him to class, but he must have grabbed it with the other papers, and when he fell it had gone flying. Brendon shook as he plopped in his chair. He'd put all his ideas in those notes. Since writing them, he hadn't thought about his formulas or how everything fit together, because it was all in his notes. Sure, he could try to replicate the information, but he wasn't in the same place mentally, and it would take hours for him to recreate everything and then check it all over again. He needed those notes. Brendon sorted through his office again, putting everything in its place just to make sure he hadn't missed anything. He hadn't, so he left his office and hurried back to where he'd dropped his papers. Nothing. The hallway sparkled, without any papers or notebook. Then, without any other recourse, he went back to his office and turned to his computer, opened a file, and began to try to remember what it was he'd been thinking.

An hour later, he didn't have much. His frustration was blocking his thought processes, he knew that, but he was so angry at himself. And to make matters worse, the text he'd received that had caused the whole collision earlier was some marketing thing from his service provider. Texting and driving was dangerous, Brendon reminded himself, but he shouldn't walk and text at the same time—it could be detrimental to his research.

A knock sounded on his door, which Brendon ignored at first because he was just starting to make progress. It sounded again, and he reached behind him and opened the door before returning to his typing. "Can I help you?" Brendon asked as he finished getting down one of the ideas he'd had.

"I'm sorry, but I think you dropped this earlier."

Brendon turned to see the huge man he'd collided with in the hall holding the notepad. Brendon nearly snatched it out of his hand and then looked through it.

"Thank you," he said with a relieved sigh. It was all there, and as soon as he saw his writing, the ideas he'd had flooded through his mind once again.

"I found it halfway down the hall, and it took me a while to locate you. I kept looking for a student," he said, and Brendon glanced up to find the man looking him over. "I'm Joshua Horton. And no, I've never heard a who." Brendon looked at him blankly, wondering what he was talking about. "Dr. Seuss, you know."

Brendon shook his head. "Never read any of that stuff."

"No way," Joshua said. "How could you have missed that?"

"When other kids were interested in things like that, my mother was helping me read *Treasure Island*." Brendon put down the notepad. "I'm Brendon Marcus," he said, holding out his hand. "I'm an associate professor of chemistry."

"My friends call me Josh or Freight Train. I'm the new assistant football coach," Josh said as he pumped Brendon's hand hard. When Josh released it, Brendon's hand tingled, and he wondered where that had come from. Maybe Josh had caused nerve damage or something. "Sorry I bumped into you and spilled all your stuff. Did you get everything back?"

"I did now," Brendon said with a smile of relief. "Thanks again. I had a bunch of ideas in there, and it was going to take a lot of time to try to recreate them." Brendon wondered exactly how long he had to chitchat before he could return to his work. Eventually he began to shift in his chair. "Um, I need to get back to work now."

"Okay. I should be going, then," Josh said, and Brendon turned around and returned to his computer, but he didn't hear Josh leave and eventually he turned back around. "Is there something I forgot?" He started to run through the social conventions his mother had taught him.

Brendon never seemed to understand other people. He didn't read facial expressions well, and vocalisms like sarcasm were simply beyond him. Lots of people thought he didn't care, but he did care—he simply didn't understand. Should he have offered Josh coffee? He didn't think so. They really didn't know each other. He reached for his wallet. "Do you need a reward?" He already had his wallet in his hand when Josh touched his arm.

"No," Josh said.

Brendon looked at him, confused. "I need to go back to work, but you're still standing here. Therefore I must have forgotten something, but I can't figure out what it is." Brendon was becoming agitated as he twisted his seat around and stared up at Josh, the Freight Train guy.

"You didn't forget anything, String Bean. I was just trying to figure out how to ask if you might like to get some dinner or something?"

Brendon blinked. "No, thank you. I'm not hungry and I have to finish my work." Brendon turned around to face his computer again. If the man didn't leave now, he didn't know how he could get him to go. He heard nothing from behind him, and for a second he thought Josh might have left, but then he heard laughter. "I don't think I said anything funny," Brendon said, looking over his shoulder.

"I wasn't asking you to get dinner now. I thought I could come back here about five o'clock, and we could walk someplace nearby to get something to eat." Brendon felt Josh place his hand on the back of his chair. "You do eat, don't you?"

"Of course I eat," Brendon said. "Everyone has to eat."

"Then would you have dinner with me tonight?" Josh asked.

"Okay," Brendon said and then turned back around to go to work. "But I don't eat squishy food or fishy food." He began typing. "Or stringy meat." He shivered at the thought of eating any of that stuff. "It all feels funny."

"Okay," Josh agreed. "I'll meet you here at a little after five for a nonsquishy, nonfishy, no-stringy-meat meal." Brendon nodded and continued working. "Okay, I'll see you then," he heard Josh say, but he was already descending into his work and he barely noticed when the door closed. Brendon continued working for about five minutes and then stopped, resting his fingers on the keyboard. He was having dinner with someone. Like, as a friend. Without thinking, he brought up the Internet and began searching for articles on the right social conventions for a situation like that. Did he need to bring a gift? Should he have money to pay? The sources he found said he didn't need to bring anything unless he was going to someone's home for dinner, in which case he should bring something small, but it also said he should be prepared to pay for his own meal. He decided he could handle that, so he went back to his work.

Brendon worked like a fiend. His mind was firing on all cylinders, and with his notes, the ideas formed on the screen as quickly as he could type. For minutes or hours—time had little meaning to him when the ideas were flowing—Brendon worked with his head down, until a knock sounded on his door. He ignored it and continued working, typing like a madman. He was so close, and if he got the last of this down, he'd have it. The knock sounded again, and this time he felt a breeze as his door opened.

"You know I can hear you typing through the door," Josh said, but Brendon didn't speak, he just continued typing furiously.

"Almost…," Brendon said as he kept typing, adding the final formula to his document, "there." Brendon pressed save, then grabbed a flash drive and stuck it into one of the USB ports. After waiting for the computer to register it, Brendon saved the file to the flash drive and then removed it and placed the small memory stick in his backpack. Then he pulled out his keys, unlocked his desk drawer, and pulled out an envelope. From inside the envelope, he pulled out another flash drive and placed it in the computer.

"Don't you think one backup is enough?" Josh asked with a slight chuckle.

Brendon whirled around in his chair. "What if my laptop is stolen and the flash drive gets corrupted? Then I'd have lost all that work." He turned back around and saved the file to the second drive. Then he placed it back in the envelope and put it inside the desk drawer before locking it up. Brendon sighed in relief.

"You're a funny man," Josh said as Brendon closed his laptop and placed it in his bag.

Brendon paused before closing the zipper. "I don't think I said anything funny." Brendon went over the conversation with Josh word for word and couldn't find anything humorous.

"Never mind," Josh said. "Did you still want to go to dinner?"

Brendon tried to remember the last time he'd eaten, and he realized it was probably the cereal he'd had for breakfast. "Yes." He got his jacket and ritually made sure his chair was in position at his desk, his papers were all in their places, his drawer was locked, and even that all his books were on the bookshelf in their proper places, organized by subject and then by author. "We can go now," Brendon said, but when he turned around, he was alone. Josh was so huge it wasn't like he could disappear. "Oh," he said softly.

This had happened before. He was always too smart and got wrapped up too deeply in his own mind and projects. He'd had friends—or, he guessed more accurately, *potential* friends—before, but they'd never worked out. His mama used to say he was too much for most people. Brendon left his office and closed the door, making sure he had his keys in his pocket and his backpack over his shoulder before locking it. "Are you ready to go?" Josh had been leaning against the wall in the hallway, and he pushed off before striding to where Brendon stood.

"I thought you left," Brendon said softly.

"It takes more than you being really anal to get rid of me."

"I'm not anal, I just don't like to forget things, and if I don't do things the right way, I forget stuff," Brendon explained.

"So you're the absentminded professor," Josh said, and Brendon once again stared at him a bit blankly.

"My mind is never absent," Brendon said with a smile, and Josh began to laugh again—a deep, hearty, resonant laugh that Brendon could feel rumble through his body like a big truck did when it went past on the road.

"I didn't mean it that way. I meant you're forgetful," Josh said, and he motioned Brendon down the hall.

"I never forget anything," Brendon explained. "I remember everything I learn and everything that happens to me. For example, I remember that the day before my sixth birthday, my mother made me French toast for breakfast with butter and powdered sugar. I can almost taste that, and the next day she made me blueberry pancakes, but she burned them. The only time I'm ever able to stop remembering everything is if I write it down. Then my mind stops and sort of relaxes. But then I worry that I'll lose what I write down, like today."

"So you always make extra backups," Josh said.

"Yes. Now I can have dinner without the work running through my head the entire time," Brendon said. "I used to lie awake for hours every night with things running through my mind. My mother had the idea for me to write things down, and that helped. Once I stayed awake for three days before she was able to help me."

Josh stopped walking. "So you're really smart," he said.

"Yeah, I guess," Brendon said. He knew he was, but he'd also found out a long time ago that people didn't want to hear about it. In fact, he should probably stop talking about himself. "What do you do? You said you were the new assistant coach. Is that for football?"

"Yeah, how could you tell?" Josh asked.

Brendon stopped walking. "Based upon your size," he said evenly.

Josh laughed again. "You don't understand sarcasm, do you?" Josh asked, and Brendon shook his head as he started walking again.

"I try, but most of it goes over my head. I end up taking most things literally, and that sometimes pisses people off. I don't mean to, but it happens." Brendon figured maybe it happened more than he knew.

"It's okay. I understand now. No sarcasm." Josh smiled and lightly clapped Brendon on the back, causing him to stumble slightly. "Sorry," he said and shoved his hands deep into his pockets. "We're really trying to build up the program, so they created my position to try to add some energy to the offense. We've won our first two games, and the team's working hard."

"Yeah, I know. I was at the first game," Brendon said.

Josh stopped. "You like football?"

"Yes," he answered simply. He wasn't going to explain that he went because the movement of the players fascinated him, as did the way they looked in their uniforms. The way he felt about… that… was something he kept very much to himself, when he allowed himself to think about it at all. He wasn't a social person, so he figured he'd never actually find someone to be with. Not that he didn't want to—he simply didn't know how to go about it.

"That's cool," Josh said, and Brendon faltered for a second.

"It is?" Brendon asked. "I don't think I've ever been cool in my life about anything." They reached the stairs and descended to the first floor, then headed toward the front door.

"Dr. Marcus," Dr. Nungesser said from behind him, and Brendon turned around. "It seems your little outburst in the meeting has taken on a life of its own. The department likes your idea for the Halloween celebration, so I'm putting you in charge of it."

Brendon took a tiny step backward. "No, thank you," he said politely. "I have many other things to do for the next couple of months. But thank you anyway." Brendon turned toward the door to leave.

"I wasn't giving you a choice," Dr. Nungesser said, and Brendon stopped with the door held open, studying the department head's expression, trying to understand it.

Josh growled from next to him, and Dr. Nungesser took a step back.

"I'm sorry, Dr. Nungesser, this is Joshua, the new assistant football coach." They shook hands, and Josh seemed to get bigger and more formidable.

"We'll talk about this more tomorrow," Dr. Nungesser said after the two of them released hands, and Brendon left the building with Josh following right behind.

"What a prick," Josh said. "Who is he, anyway?" Josh strode until he was right next to Brendon, close enough that Brendon could smell his cologne.

"The head of the department. He doesn't like me," Brendon said factually and descended the stairs. He'd gotten to the bottom before he realized Josh was still standing at the top, glaring inside the glass-fronted atrium. After a few moments, Josh joined him. "Where are we going to dinner? I stay away from the places around the campus most of the time."

"Don't worry, I have the perfect place," Josh said and motioned toward the main intersection of campus. "It's just a few blocks." Brendon nodded and walked next to Josh. It didn't take long before he thought he'd figured out where they were going.

"Café Belgie?" Brendon asked, and Josh stopped and smiled.

"Is that okay?" They were standing under one of the many trees that lined the streets in Carlisle.

"I like it there," Brendon said and prepared to continue walking, but Josh just stared at him without moving. Brendon got this jumpy, jittery feeling in his stomach, and at first he thought he must be hungrier than he'd realized, but it didn't feel like that. "Is something wrong?" Brendon looked down at his clothes, wondering if he was dressed right, and he tried to remember if he'd put the green shirt back on. He hadn't, but….

"Brendon, I think you're really cute," Josh told him, and Brendon tilted his head slightly to the side, watching Josh shift from foot to foot. He was nervous, but Brendon wasn't sure why. Josh's breathing was becoming rapid, and he seemed bigger, like when he'd puffed up in front of Dr. Nungesser.

"Are you okay?" Brendon asked, and Josh took his hand. "Are you sure there isn't something wrong?"

"No, there's nothing wrong. But I want to ask you something." Josh moved a little closer. "Can I kiss you?"

Brendon blinked a few times and then looked away. "No one's ever kissed me except my mother, and that was, well, my mother."

"Is that a yes?" Josh asked.

"Okay, but why?" Brendon asked.

"You want me to tell you why I want to kiss you?" Josh asked. "I mean, I'm gay and I think you're really cute, and I thought you were gay too, but maybe I was wrong." Josh backed away.

"Is this a date?" Brendon asked.

"Yes," Josh answered.

"According to the Internet, when you date someone, a kiss is usually expected. It comes at the end of the date, usually, but I don't think quibbling about it is necessarily a—"

Josh lightly cupped Brendon's cheeks and kissed him. Brendon didn't know what to expect from a first kiss, but his head felt swimmy, and Josh's lips tasted a bit like coffee, only better—much, much better. Then the kiss ended.

"Didn't you like it?" Josh asked. "You didn't kiss back."

"Oh," Brendon said, and Josh kissed him again. This time, Brendon moved his lips the way Josh had, and soon Josh had him wrapped in his arms, pressing their bodies together. Brendon felt warm and flushed, his heart was pounding, and everything, well, everything stood up and took notice. A car passed by on the street, and Josh broke the kiss and stepped back. "That was nice," Brendon said with a smile. "Can we do that again?"

"God, you sound like a kid who just ate chocolate for the first time," Josh told him. "And yes, we can do that again, but after we eat."

"Okay," Brendon said, and they walked down the block to the main street of town. They passed the bakery, A Slice of Heaven, and Brendon couldn't help pausing to peer into their windows. "Mama used to tell me I would eat cake at every meal."

"Me too," Josh said. "I'll walk a mile for a slice of chocolate cake." Brendon turned away from the window and saw Josh simply smiling at him. He didn't know quite what the smile meant, but it made him warm inside, and he wanted to believe that smile was for him, but maybe it was for the cake. Then again, maybe after that kiss, or two kisses, to be accurate—and Brendon was all about accuracy—he wasn't wrong, and the smile was for him.

"Should we eat?" Brendon asked, but he made no effort to move. He liked being looked at that way, like he was important and not just some nerdy kid who happened to be smarter than everyone else but made everyone uncomfortable because of it.

"You're hungry, huh?" Josh said.

"I haven't really eaten since breakfast," Brendon said. "I had some crackers at my desk this afternoon."

"Then let's get you fed," Josh said, and he started across the street. Brendon lingered in front of the bakery, wondering why Josh had asked him to dinner and why he was being so nice. Based on his experience, limited as it was, it made him wonder what Josh wanted. The last time someone had befriended him, they'd wanted him to write a paper for them. Brendon had refused, and of course that had been the last he'd ever seen of Timothy. Josh was almost across the street before Brendon pulled himself out of his thoughts and hurried to catch up with him.

"Have you been here a lot?" Brendon asked Josh once they were seated at one of the tables near the large windows overlooking the sidewalk.

"No. This is only my first job out of college, so I haven't had a lot of money to go out. I ate here once a few weeks ago, and I thought it was nice and the food good, so when I saw you this afternoon, I thought of this place."

Brendon squirmed in his chair. "Why?" He wanted to ask Josh what he wanted, but he could hear his mother telling him that wouldn't be polite. He hoped that maybe Josh didn't want anything, but he didn't know, and he hated not knowing things. All day, he dealt with facts and things he could prove. That was where he felt comfortable. Facts, figures, formulas—they didn't lie, and they produced a result he could see and recreate over and over again.

"Why what?"

"Why did you ask me to dinner? What...." He stopped himself before the next question spilled out. "Friendships are built on common interests and hobbies. And it isn't likely we have too many of those other than I watch football sometimes." He kept trying to puzzle it out but he couldn't quite do it. Too many of the variables were missing or unknown, and he couldn't develop the formula for what was happening, let alone solve it.

"Maybe I like cute, smart guys with shaggy blond hair and big blue eyes," Josh said as he leaned a little closer over the table.

"Are you teasing me?" Brendon asked.

"No, I'm saying I thought you were cute and I got one of those feelings I get when I'm around other guys who are gay, so I took a chance," Josh said. Brendon looked at him blankly. "You know, that jittery feeling in your stomach that feels like a dozen butterflies are fluttering in there."

"Is that what that is? I got that feeling when I saw you, but I thought I was hungry," Brendon said and then began arranging his silverware in precise locations around his place, making sure they were all the same exact distance from the edge of the table. After a few seconds, Brendon realized what he was doing and stopped. He didn't want Josh to think he was weird.

"You like everything just so, don't you?" Josh asked.

"Sometimes," Brendon answered, putting his hands in his lap, even though his salad fork was off-kilter just a little bit and he wanted very much to straighten it.

"It's okay. I like certain things just so too," Josh said.

Brendon straightened the fork and checked all the utensils as the server approached their table. Brendon handed the server Josh's glass and his own bread plate. "They have spots on them," he said, and the server hurried away and then brought clean replacements.

"I'm sorry about that," the server said. "I'm Billy, and I'll be taking care of you this evening. Can I start you with drinks? We have a wonderful selection of Belgian beers on tap."

"I'll have a Diet Coke," Brendon said, and Josh ordered some beer that Brendon had never heard of, but the name was now caught in his mind, so later he'd probably Google it. The server told them the specials and pointed out some popular dishes on the menu before leaving to get their drinks.

"So what's your family like?" Josh asked. "Do you have brothers and sisters?"

"I'm an only child. My mother said after having me, she couldn't take the chance on having any more children. I was enough of a handful," Brendon answered, then he sipped from his water glass.

"She really said that to you?" Josh asked, his eyes widening, and this time Brendon was sure Josh was surprised.

"Yes. I had just gotten finished with one of my experiments, and I sort of blew up the pipe under the sink. But I think she was right. I was probably a handful. My mom used to read to me when I was a kid, but she said by the time I was four, I was reading to her. My mom went back to school when I was about seven, and by ten, I was reading some of her textbooks. I finished high school two years later and went to college at twelve, graduated by fifteen, and had a master's and doctorate by twenty-one."

"Where's your mom now?" Josh asked.

"She died when I was fifteen. That's why it took me so long to get my master's." Brendon's stomach clenched slightly when he thought about her, like there was a hole he was trying to fill but never could. "I still had my dad, but it wasn't the same. He had a heart attack two days after I got my doctorate." A lump formed in Brendon's throat that he swallowed away. "Do you have a big family?" Brendon asked, remembering it was better to get the other person to talk.

"A brother and a sister. I'm the youngest. My sister is in her internship for pediatric oncology down in Houston, and my brother went to Harvard and has a position with a big East-Coast law firm." Josh looked down at the table. "I'm sort of the failure of the family. I was always interested in athletics, and my father had hopes of me following in his footsteps and going into sports medicine or orthopedics. Instead, I majored in exercise science. I have everything for premed, but that isn't where my interests are. Dad and I have argued about that for years."

"Why?" Brendon asked. What Josh wanted to do with his life was no one else's business. Brendon discovered his love for chemistry when he was nine years old, and nothing his father or mother could have said or wanted would have caused him to deviate from his path. "My mother and father allowed me to try everything I wanted, including the six months I explored my musical talent," Brendon explained before adding, "I don't have any."

Josh laughed. "You do have a sense of humor," Josh said.

"I do?" Brendon asked. He'd been serious, but made a note to try to do whatever he'd done again, because he liked the sound of Josh's laugh. He admitted to himself if he did make Josh laugh, it would probably be an accident, but a happy one nonetheless. "My dad was disappointed I didn't have any athletic ability. I throw like a girl. But he wanted me to be happy. Isn't that what your dad wants for you?" Brendon asked seriously.

"Yes. But my father thinks he knows what will make me happy," Josh said.

"How can anyone know what will make someone else happy?" Brendon asked. He wanted to learn more about this phenomenon, but then the server returned with their drinks and took their orders. Both Brendon and Josh ordered the steak frites, and Billy left the table. "How can your dad know what you want?" Brendon drank some of his Diet Coke.

"My father thinks he knows everything," Josh said.

"No one can know everything." Brendon paused. "Not even me." He smiled, hoping his little joke had the desired effect. He rarely attempted humor because he didn't get it. But Josh laughed, so Brendon smiled. It was a nice moment, and some of the social awkwardness that seemed to accompany his everyday life slipped away.

They talked nonstop until the server brought their dinners, and then Brendon began to eat. "Geez," Josh said after a few minutes. "I thought I ate fast. You must have been hungry."

Brendon looked up from his plate and nodded. "I need to remember to eat more often." Brendon wondered if Josh wanted to talk, but he returned to his meal, so Brendon finished his. By the time he was done, Brendon was stuffed and a bit sleepy. He'd probably eaten too much, but he didn't really mind.

"Would you like to see our dessert menu?" Billy asked.

Brendon shook his head. "The meal was very good," he said, and Billy smiled at him before leaving the table. He returned a few minutes later and brought the check. Brendon reached for the check, but Josh got it first.

"This is a date, remember? And I asked you," Josh said before pulling out his wallet and placing cash with the check before closing the little folder. Then they got up and Josh thanked Billy as they passed, and Brendon did the same.

On the sidewalk, Josh looked around him and then back at Brendon. "Do you live nearby?"

"On South Street," Brendon answered, and Josh began walking in that direction. It seemed to Brendon that Josh was walking him home, and he found he liked that idea. They continued talking while they walked. Josh asked questions about Brendon's work, and he tried to explain it as simply as he could. It wasn't like he thought Josh was dumb or anything, but what he was doing was very advanced, and most graduate students in chemistry would have had a difficult time keeping up with Brendon's explanation of what he was attempting to prove, let alone someone without advanced degrees in chemistry and chemical engineering. "It's pretty complicated," Brendon said after a few minutes, when even he could tell Josh wasn't understanding what he was trying to say.

"Is there anything you like to do besides work?" Josh asked, and Brendon smiled and nearly skipped a step.

"Yes, and I can show you if you like," Brendon offered as they turned the corner. They walked a few blocks west, back in the direction of the college, until they reached Brendon's small house. Instead of unlocking the front door, though, Brendon led Josh through a passage between Brendon's house and the one next door, to a side gate. He unlocked the gate and pushed it open, then stepped through and flipped on a switch near the back door. Josh walked through and then stopped, his mouth hanging open.

"Did you do all this?"

"Yes."

"But... how long have you worked at the college?"

"Well, this was my mom and dad's house, but neither of them could grow a bean. At first I used the yard for some of my experiments, but after a while, I figured out I had a creative side and I took over. Mom and Dad just let me." Lights led off along the path, and Brendon waited for Josh to take the lead.

"It almost seems like a tunnel of green," Josh said as he cautiously walked down the path. Brendon followed and heard Josh gasp when he reached the main portion of the yard. Lights shone up into the trees and shrubs, and illuminated the flowers. A large patio his father had installed for him years ago was covered with a gazebo his dad had given to his mother shortly before she died. "This is incredible," Josh said as he stood under the gazebo roof, turning slowly. "It's like I stepped into Eden."

Brendon thanked Josh for the compliment and stayed with him as he walked the rest of the way down the path to the back gate. "That leads to the alley," Brendon said, and Josh nodded, continuing to look around.

"You're amazing," Josh said. "This is amazing." Josh had turned around and was walking back toward him. Brendon watched as Josh looked around for a few minutes and then returned to where Brendon waited. He wasn't sure what was going to happen next, but when Josh stepped close to him, Brendon got a pretty good idea. "Do you know what this garden was made for?"

Brendon didn't understand the question and shrugged. He waited for Josh to answer, but instead the larger man leaned closer, lightly cupped Brendon's cheeks in his hands, and then kissed him. The ones they'd shared earlier had been nice, but this one felt deep, like Brendon could feel the kiss with more than his lips and tongue. He didn't know how that was possible, or how he could feel the kiss all the way to his now curling toes, but he did. "Was that a good-night kiss?" Brendon asked when Josh pulled away.

"No. This is," Josh said and then kissed Brendon again. "Or is it this one?" All Brendon could think about at that moment was that at this rate, he'd never get to bed, and then he realized he didn't care.

Chapter Two

JOSH SAT in the coaches' office near the locker room after practice, working on some paperwork Coach Norris, the head coach and an institution at Dickinson, had asked him to handle.

"Well, I don't care what any of you say, if he so much as looks at me funny, I'll beat the crap out of him." Josh recognized the voice as belonging to Lyle Kensington, one of the players. He stood up and stepped out of the coaches' office, then went into the locker room.

"You and what army? The guy's huge," one of the other players said. "Besides, he seems decent."

"Exactly. I am decent," Josh said firmly. "You know, Lyle, you're in college, not high school, and it's time you grew up and started acting like an adult rather than a spoiled teenager."

"I'm a Christian, and…."

Josh had had plenty of that thrown at him in his life. "If you want to act like that, then maybe you'd be happier at Messiah College. You'd feel right at home. But if you're going to stay here, you'll keep that kind of opinion to yourself or you will be looking for another team and another college. That isn't tolerated and you know it," Josh told the player and saw him redden and lower his eyes. All the players had been drilled on the college's diversity policy.

"Is there a problem here?" Coach Norris asked as he came into the locker room. The players scattered fast, and Josh went back into the office to return to the paperwork. "Josh, what was going on out there?" Coach Norris pressed a little later, once the players were gone.

"Nothing I haven't handled before and won't handle again," Josh answered. The head coach knew Josh was gay, and he didn't give a damn as long as Josh did his job and helped the team. "Don't worry about it. They're football players and they're big, pumped up on testosterone, but in some ways, they're barely out of diapers. It's part of our job to help them grow up."

"If you say so," Coach said as he sat down at his desk. "But I won't tolerate any disrespect from any of the players toward anyone."

"I handled it," Josh reiterated, returning to his work. "I'm just about done here."

"Then go on home. I've got some things I want to do," Coach told him. "I'll see you at practice tomorrow."

Josh finished up and left the office, heading out of the athletic center. He lightly jogged across campus until he reached the science center, then took the steps two at a time as he headed up to the building and then again up the stairs and down the hall to Brendon's office. When he'd first tried to locate Brendon to return his notepad, he'd had no idea he was a professor and had been surprised when he'd been directed to one of the faculty offices. Now he knew his adorable Brendon was a genius, but he was funny, too, and to Josh, as cute as they came. There was something about his big blue eyes and blond hair that Josh found irresistible.

Brendon's door was closed as Josh approached, and Josh was about to knock when he heard a raised voice coming from inside. Without waiting, he turned the knob and pushed open the door.

"You will do it because I'm assigning it to you," Brendon's department head was telling him. He couldn't remember the dweeb's name. "Remember, the dean might be in your corner, but as department head, I'm the one who will sign off on your tenure application."

"Brendon," Josh said, keeping his temper in check.

The older man turned toward the door and seemed surprised. Brendon looked upset, and Josh wanted to demand to know what was going on.

"I'll expect the plans on my desk by Monday. I want to win the interdepartmental contest this year, and since this was your big idea—" The dweeb turned on his heel and left. Josh waited until he was gone and then stepped into Brendon's office.

"Are you okay?" Josh asked. Brendon seemed paler than usual.

"Yes," Brendon said.

"What was he threatening you over?"

"The departmental entry in the charity Halloween contest," Brendon said. "I don't understand why it's so important."

"It isn't," Josh said.

"Then why is he doing this?" Brendon asked, looking completely confused, his mouth hanging open a bit, his gaze moving down to the floor. "I never did anything to him. But then I never did anything to any of the bullies, either, and they all thought I had a target on my back."

"That's a good way to look at it. He's another bully." Josh closed the door so anyone passing by wouldn't see Brendon upset.

"But why?" Brendon asked again. Josh was beginning to understand that "why" was one of Brendon's key questions. He really seemed to *need* to know why things happened. Even if there was no logical explanation, he still wanted to know.

"I don't know. Maybe he's threatened by you. You're smarter than he is. Well you're probably smarter than everybody. You're nice, if a bit shy, and he's a douchebag," Josh quipped, and Brendon smiled ever so slightly. Josh stepped closer as Brendon turned back to his computer and began shutting it down. Gently, Josh placed his hands on Brendon's shoulders and massaged lightly. "You know, it's possible that the whole Halloween contest is just a smoke screen and he's using this as an opportunity to exercise control." Brendon shifted, and Josh could see the confusion on his face. "If he can control you, then maybe your successes can be his successes."

Brendon closed his laptop and then unplugged it. "I don't understand," he said. Josh continued massaging Brendon's shoulders, and he was amazed at the amount of tension Brendon was carrying. His muscles were nearly tied in knots. "All this stuff about the way people act, I don't understand it. All I want to do is teach my classes and do my research. That's what I love. I don't care about Nungesser and what he thinks. I don't want anyone to be threatened." Brendon slumped forward. Sure, Brendon was really smart and a college professor, but he was, what, maybe twenty-three years old?

"It's okay. He doesn't really matter," Josh said, and then the conversation he'd overheard in the locker room flashed through his mind. "Has he ever said anything to you about being gay?"

"No," Brendon answered. "The school has a diversity policy. He wouldn't do anything like that."

"Brendon," Josh began gently, "a policy won't change anyone's mind. It just makes them more sneaky in the way they go about things. Does he know you're gay?" Brendon shrugged, and Josh took a deep breath and then released it. "So, are you ready to go?" Brendon nodded, and Josh figured it would probably be best to let this drop. Brendon was getting more upset, and every protective instinct Josh had ever had was screaming right now. They'd had one date a few days before, and already Josh was ready to wring Brendon's boss's neck for giving him grief.

"Can we please go?" Brendon asked, and as he got up, Josh slipped his hands off his shoulders. Brendon packed all his things in his backpack, and then Josh waited while Brendon went through his routine.

"Did you want to go somewhere for dinner? Or if you like, I can cook for you," Josh offered.

"You can cook?" Brendon asked, as if Josh had just offered him the Nobel Prize. "Other than heating things up, I never learned. My mom always said I had better things to do than spend time in the kitchen with her." Brendon once again looked toward the floor.

"You don't have to do that," Josh said, placing two fingers beneath Brendon's chin. "My mom taught all of us to cook. She said she didn't want us to starve."

"Do you want to cook at my house?" Brendon asked. "No one has really used the kitchen in a while, but all the stuff is there. The cabinets are full of everything you could think of."

"Do you have food in the house?" Josh asked, but he thought he already knew the answer. "If you don't, we can stop at the store," he said, and Brendon checked his pockets and the door to his office one more time before they headed down the hall. Josh usually walked to work, but he had driven that morning because the weather had looked threatening. He led Brendon to his car and then drove to the large grocery store nearby. They shopped, Brendon wandering through the store and placing a few things in the cart, while Josh decided what he wanted to cook. Since he wasn't familiar with Brendon's kitchen and what he had, Josh decided on something rather simple and basic: pork roast, mashed potatoes, and beans. Once they had checked out, Josh drove to Brendon's and then followed him into the house.

Brendon explained where things were in the kitchen, and as Josh expected, everything was in its exact place and the only person who could find anything was Brendon. He might not have cooked much, but everything was organized according to Brendon's thought patterns. "How about we make some dinner and I'll give you your first cooking lesson."

"I don't know anything about cooking," Brendon said.

"Think of it like kitchen chemistry and you'll be a natural," Josh told him, and Brendon giggled.

"The last time I did that, I ruined one of Mom's best pans. I was trying to make something so Mom could get the spots out of the living room carpet."

"Did it work?"

"It would have if it hadn't eaten a hole in the pot first and melted part of the stove. Mom didn't allow me in the kitchen after that," Brendon said. "And she never let me have that babysitter again."

Josh roared with laughter. "I promise, no batches of spot remover."

They began working on dinner. Josh asked Brendon to peel the potatoes while he got the meat ready. After a few minutes, Josh looked up at Brendon, who was concentrating fully on peeling the potatoes so precisely he'd peeled exactly one half of one potato. Josh couldn't help laughing. "You're adorable," Josh said. "But you don't have to be so precise." He then showed Brendon how to use the potato peeler, and the process sped up.

Once the potatoes were peeled and cut, Josh placed them in a pan of water on the stove and brought them up to the boil, then added a pinch of salt. He then got the vegetables ready and put the meat in the oven to roast. Soon the entire kitchen smelled of spices and roasting pork. Josh heard Brendon's stomach rumble. "This smells so good," Brendon hummed, stepping closer to the oven door. "Mom used to make this," he whispered and then inhaled again. They sat in the other room and talked while the scent of the roast filled the entire house. After a while Josh got up to check the meat and then returned.

"Can you get out the plates and set the table outside?" Josh asked. "I'll bring the food." Brendon carried the glasses and utensils out to the gazebo.

"I don't eat out here much," Brendon said once they'd sat down. Josh handed him his plate and then set his own at his place.

"I have something to ask you," Josh said as they started eating. "My brother and sister are going to be in town in a few weeks, and my parents are planning a family dinner. I was wondering if you'd like to go with me."

Brendon set down his fork. "You want me to meet your family? What if I say something wrong? I always say things that are wrong."

"You won't say anything wrong. All you need to do is be yourself. That's all anyone can ask," Josh said, and Brendon quivered slightly.

"But what if being myself isn't good enough? I always say things that people don't want to hear because I don't understand what *isn't* being said. I've discovered a lot of human communication is nonverbal, but it's like I didn't get the manual. At least that's how Mama used to describe it." Brendon was really agitated, and at first Josh couldn't understand Brendon's reaction. "I like you, Josh, and I don't want to cause trouble for you."

Damn, where did that *come from?* Brendon was one of the smartest people Josh had ever met, and that was saying a lot, given his family. "Whoever made you feel like you didn't matter was full of crap. You're a lot more than just a smart guy, and people need to see that." Josh stroked Brendon's cheek. "So, yes, I want you to come with me to dinner with my family, and I want you to promise me you'll just be yourself."

"Okay, I promise," Brendon said. That smile was too much to resist, so Josh leaned closer and kissed Brendon. The smaller man practically melted into him, and Josh tightened his embrace as Brendon wriggled and squirmed against him. At first Josh thought he was holding Brendon too tightly, but then he realized Brendon was almost trying to climb him. It was hot as hell.

"Have you ever… done anything?" Josh asked.

"I've done lots of things," Brendon answered, and Josh instantly realized he needed to be more precise.

"Have you ever…" Josh tried to phrase his question properly. "… had sex with anyone?" he whispered.

Brendon shook his head. "You're the first person to really kiss me," he answered, turning a bit red, and then he smiled. "So, no, I've never done the dance with no pants." Brendon began to giggle. "I saw that on television once. Did I use it right?"

"You used it right," Josh said, and then he proceeded to kiss those giggles into little moans and whimpers. He was careful not to take things too quickly. But all he wanted was to cup Brendon's tight little butt in his hands and lift him up until Brendon curled his long legs around him. Then maybe he could find the stairs and take Brendon up to his room and…. Josh broke the kiss and gasped for breath. His cock throbbed in his pants and he needed a few minutes to think. The last thing he wanted to do was ravish Brendon like he was some quick fuck. Brendon deserved better than that. Slowly Josh released him. "I think I better finish dinner now." He desperately needed to do something normal.

"Oh," Brendon said. "Was I kissing wrong?" Josh could almost see Brendon's mind turning as he went over their kiss in his mind, analyzing each second like a slow-motion replay.

"No. You weren't kissing wrong," Josh said. "I just needed to breathe for a few minutes." *To keep from ripping your clothes off right here.* "It was good, believe me." Josh took a deep breath and then released it slowly, trying to will his heart to stop pounding and his dick to go down. Sounds coming from the yard next door reminded him they were still outside. Brendon began clearing the dishes, and Josh helped him carry the things back inside.

Normally, he would have suggested they leave the dishes in the sink and find a comfortable spot on the sofa, but Josh was learning very quickly that Brendon was a creature of habit and routine, so they washed and dried the dishes together. Josh was able to remember where most of the things went, and Brendon put away the rest.

"Would you like something to drink?" Brendon asked once they were done. "I don't want you to go home right away."

"I don't want to go home either," Josh admitted.

"I don't have wine or anything. Would a Diet Coke be okay?" Brendon asked, and he got out a can for himself and then handed Josh another one. He then seemed to remember they might need glasses, rushed to the cupboard, and pulled out two.

"You don't have to rush or feel worried," Josh said, sensing Brendon's agitation.

"I just want to do things right," Brendon said.

"Whatever you do for me is done right, okay?" Josh said as Brendon handed him a glass. "You don't need to be nervous."

Brendon's glass chinked on the counter as he set it down a bit hard. "Yes, I do," Brendon said, clearly agitated.

"Why?" Josh asked, taking a page from Brendon's book.

Brendon glared at him, and Josh wondered what he'd said. "I never had many friends. The other kids thought I was weird because when they were playing baseball, I was trying to explain why the ball did what it did. They rode their bikes up and down the street, and I saw how those wheels explained the concept of inertia. I tried to relate to other kids, but I couldn't. The people I did relate to were adults, but they didn't want to talk scientific theories with a ten-year-old. So I was on my own quite a bit."

"You never had friends your own age?" Josh asked.

Brendon shook his head. "Not really."

"That must have been lonely," Josh continued. No wonder Brendon was so anxious all the time. "I already like you. So just be yourself and don't worry." Josh wasn't sure how much Brendon accepted his answer, but he did seem to relax a bit. Then he picked up his glass again and led Josh through the house to the living room. The furniture was comfortable, if a bit worn, and Josh figured this was Brendon's parents' furniture.

Brendon had said he'd grown up here and this had been his parents' house, so it made sense a lot of the things here had once belonged to his folks. "Was all this your parents'?" Josh asked without sitting down.

"Is that bad?" Brendon countered as he sat in an upholstered chair.

"No. But I want to see the things that are important to you," Josh said, and Brendon jumped to his feet.

"You want to see my lab?" Brendon sounded like he'd won the lottery, and before Josh could answer, Brendon was off, hurrying through the house. Josh set his soda on a coaster next to Brendon's drink and strode as fast as he could to catch up with Brendon. "My dad gave me this space when I was a kid, after I nearly blew up the basement." Brendon continued out the back door and through the yard to the back gate. He pushed it open, and just outside was what looked like a new garage. Brendon unlocked the door and pushed it open, then turned on the lights.

"Dad figured it would be better if I worked out here."

Josh had been expecting something like a mad scientist's lab, but it was a clean garage with counters and cabinets against most of the walls. "Did you blow up the old garage?" Josh teased, and for a few seconds, Brendon stared at him, wide-eyed, then his expression changed.

"You're teasing," he said, almost asking a question.

"Yes. Do you still work out here?"

"No. I don't have the equipment or the near-sterile conditions I need now. But my dad and I built this as a place for me to work without fear I'd blow up the house."

"It sounds like your mom and dad were both very proud of you and supported you," Josh said with a touch of regret. "I never got that from my father. He supported me only if I wanted to do what he wanted me to do." He and his father had rarely seemed to get along when he was a kid. He'd wanted his father's approval, but for him that had always seemed just out of reach.

"My dad didn't really understand me much either," Brendon said. "I know he wanted someone he could teach to play baseball and football. It was my mom who tried to understand me. I don't know if she ever really did, but she really tried." There was more than a hint of sadness in Brendon's voice, and Josh imagined that after his mother's death, Brendon had probably been set adrift emotionally. Maybe he was still drifting.

"Is there some part of the house that you furnished? A place that's special to you?" Josh asked.

"You mean like my rooms?" Brendon asked. "I can show you those." There was definite hesitation in his voice.

"You don't have to show me if you don't want to," Josh said. "I didn't mean to invade your privacy."

"You're not," Brendon said, and Josh noticed that some of Brendon's excitement had faded. "I suppose the lab isn't much to look at."

"It's wonderful. I can just imagine all the ideas you hatched in here," Josh told Brendon as he moved closer. "And while the scientist is a big part of you, I want to understand the real you." Brendon shrugged, and Josh met his gaze. "There's more to you than just the scientist. I already know you're going to be a great chemist; that's a given, as far as I'm concerned." No matter what Brendon's department head might think. To make his point, Josh tugged Brendon close and kissed him. "I'm not kissing the scientist, I'm kissing Brendon."

"Oh," Brendon said. "I think I like the nonscience parts."

"I know I do," Josh whispered, wondering if he was going too fast, but then Brendon initiated a kiss for the first time. Josh just held him close and let Brendon drive for a while. He was a natural, and Josh loved every second. When Brendon broke the kiss, Josh was breathless, and Brendon seemed to be gasping for air. God, Josh wanted more of those kisses. Hell, he wanted more than kisses, but he pushed those ideas out of his head for now.

Brendon turned off the lights and led Josh through the lighted garden and back toward the house. Inside, he turned off the outside lights and then led Josh to the front of the house and up the stairs.

The second floor had a nice landing and small hallway with a number of closed doors. "This is my office. I work in here sometimes when I'm home," Brendon said before pushing open one door. This was what Josh had expected to see: the walls of the plainly painted room were lined with overflowing bookshelves. There were even books stacked on top of the shelves, some nearly to the ceiling. The room looked nothing like the near-obsessive order of Brendon's office at the college or in the rest of the house.

"This is a great room," Josh said as he stepped inside, imagining Brendon sitting at the desk in the center of the room, the light from the now dark windows making his golden hair shine in the sun as he worked. "Have you... of course you've read all these," Josh amended.

"Yes," Brendon admitted. "I don't know why I kept them all. I can remember every word written on every page. Once I've read them I rarely open them a second time unless I want to show them to someone, but there hasn't been anyone to show anything to in a while." Brendon ran his fingers over the spines of some very old-looking books. "These are some my mother got me. I was interested in the history of chemistry, so she found me these." Brendon pulled the book off the shelf and handed it to Josh, who marveled at it. Carefully, he opened the book, but was afraid to actually touch the pages. "It was printed on a printing press, but the rest of the book was illustrated and decorated by hand. Mom would go to great lengths to find me what I needed."

"But this must have cost a fortune," Josh said, handing the book back. He was scared to even look at the date it was printed.

"Mom inherited money from her parents, and she spent a lot of it buying me books and making sure I got to attend all the schools she thought could help me." Brendon held the book in his trembling hand. "Now the books are all I have left of her. I thought about donating them to the college, or even selling them, but I can't, because she gave them to me." Brendon carefully put the book back in the exact spot he'd taken it from.

Josh walked around the shelves, surprised that all the books weren't on science or chemistry. He also saw *Robinson Crusoe, Treasure Island,* and *Les Miserables.* Josh pulled one of the books off the shelf. "I remember this one," he said.

"Me too," Brendon said. "When I wasn't working or reading for school, I used to escape into adventure stories. They were my friends. I could read one of these books in a few hours." Brendon took the book. "I remember 24601," he said quietly. "I think I liked this one best because sometimes I felt like Jean Valjean. He was always a criminal first—no matter what he did, everyone branded him a criminal, even when he saved a little girl and helped people in need. I was always smart, and even when I use my brain to help develop a drug or find a cure for a disease, I'm still just a brainiac freak." Brendon put the book back.

"You're not a freak and you never were," Josh said, pulling Brendon into his arms. "You're just someone who got all the smarts in the world, but never really had a chance to be a kid."

"But I'm too old to be a kid now," Brendon told him.

"You're never too old to be a kid," Josh said, tugging Brendon into a hard kiss. Brendon clung to him, moaning softly into each touch, every kiss.

"Josh," Brendon said softly after breaking the kiss.

"Hey, it's okay," Josh said. "I know you've been alone for a long time."

"And I don't want to be alone anymore," Brendon said, pressing against Josh and kissing him again.

"I know, but this isn't the answer. Not yet," Josh whispered.

"I thought you liked me. I thought maybe this was what you wanted," Brendon said. "I knew I wasn't good enough or handsome enough for you." He looked near tears.

"Hey. It's not any of that," Josh said, taking Brendon's hand. "It isn't that at all. When we do something like that, I want it to be special. You deserve it to be special." Josh hugged Brendon close, cradling his head in his hand before stroking his soft hair. "You've never been with anyone before, and…." Josh had messed everything up. He should have known to take it slower, but he hadn't realized how much pent-up need and loneliness lurked inside Brendon.

"But you don't want me either," Brendon gulped against Josh's chest.

"Oh, but I do. I just want things to be special. Not rushed and not fast," Josh said. "This has to mean something to me, and to you. It has to be more than just convenient." Josh tilted Brendon's head upward so he could gaze into his eyes. "Can you understand that?"

"I guess so," Brendon said, but Josh knew he had no idea what Josh was trying to say. Brendon's eyes only displayed hurt. When Josh released him, Brendon took Josh by the hand and led him out of the office and into another room, which had to be Brendon's bedroom. He knew Brendon was silently begging him to stay, but Josh knew if he did, he wouldn't be able to resist the temptation Brendon was turning out to be. He didn't want to hurt him, either way, but that was exactly what he would be doing.

"This is nice," Josh said as he looked around the room. It had obviously been Brendon's room for quite some time.

A shelf ran along three of the walls about a foot below the ceiling, lined with science-fair ribbons, trophies, certificates, rocks, minerals, figurines, and even a small stuffed bear. The shelves were cluttered, but Josh got the feeling each item had been placed with great care. The rest of the room was rather plain, decorated in solid, masculine colors. The one exception was the bedspread, which looked handmade, and Josh figured it had probably come from Brendon's mother. "Did you pick all this out yourself?"

Brendon nodded slowly. "Yes. Is this what you wanted to see?" he asked softly, like he was afraid to speak.

"Yeah," Josh said as he looked around the room again. The furniture was old and solid. It had been painted, and Josh wondered if that was Brendon's way of updating it. "This is so you."

"What do you mean? This is all my stuff," Brendon said. "Of course it's me."

"I mean this entire room is you. See, you can tell you're smart from all the awards, but also sentimental. You like to be surrounded by familiar comfortable things, and you want things to be in their proper spot," Josh said, and Brendon nodded. "You're also kind and caring," Josh added as he looked at a picture of a tiny squirrel with a bandage on its little leg. "See, this is you, and it's a picture of the whole you. And I like the whole you."

"Why?" Brendon asked. "I'm not that special. If you take away my intelligence—"

"You are who you are, Brendon," Josh said. He wanted to take Brendon in his arms and make him understand what he saw and what he felt, but he was afraid to in case Brendon misunderstood. "You're a scientist, but you're also a teacher, a son, a boyfriend, and so much more."

Brendon paused, blinking at Josh. "I'm your boyfriend? I thought you didn't want…. How can I be your boyfriend?"

Josh sighed. Brendon was as sharp as a tack, but when it came to relationships, he was almost as innocent as a child. "Just because sex is something I think we should wait on for now, doesn't mean I don't want you that way. I do, very much. But I don't want to rush you and make you feel like you have to do something you aren't ready for."

"I know my own mind," Brendon said, his eyes blazing.

"I know you do, but I want to get to know you first. Sex is nice…," Josh said, faltering slightly. "There are things my father and I don't see eye to eye on, but the one thing I've always known is that he loves my mother more than life itself, and the love between them is almost visible. When they're together, they can't seem to keep their eyes off each other. And I want that in my life. So I'm saying that instead of just having sex, I want to wait until it's making love." God, Josh hoped Brendon could understand.

"What's the difference?" Brendon asked.

"Making love engages your heart," Josh explained, and Brendon looked lost. "Trust me," Josh added. Then he said to hell with it, pulling

Brendon into his arms. "I know you like the way you feel when I kiss you, but try to close your eyes and imagine how the kisses would feel if you loved me, if your heart engaged as well as your lips and mouth. I'm not saying I don't like you, because I do, very much. I'm asking you to wait until it means more than just sex. Can you understand that?"

"I think so," Brendon said.

"I know you're a scientist and it's easier to understand things you can see, touch, test, and prove, but this is emotional and it takes place in your heart. Just trust me." Brendon nodded, and Josh kissed him again and then stepped away. "I should probably go home."

"Are you sure?" Brendon asked. "I don't want you to go."

"I don't want to either, but I don't want to tease you or make you feel bad."

Brendon shifted his gaze to his shoes. "I understand," Brendon said, but Josh got the feeling he really didn't understand. And when Brendon wrapped his arms around Josh and rested his head against his chest, Josh felt his fortitude waver.

"You're a minx, you know that?" Josh said, and Brendon hummed softly, holding him tighter.

"Will you stay with me?" Brendon asked, lifting his gaze. For someone who said he didn't understand people, Brendon sure seemed to know how to get under Josh's skin.

"Okay," Josh said, and Brendon closed his huge blue eyes, and they stood together for a while, wrapped in each other's arms.

Eventually, they went back downstairs and watched television. Well, to be accurate, Josh watched a little television while Brendon sat next to him with a pad and pencil, glancing at the images on the screen from time to time as he scribbled and scratched at various formulas. Josh had no idea what they represented, but he did know that whatever Brendon was working on had to be important, so he simply enjoyed having Brendon close.

"I got it!" Brendon said suddenly, jerking away from Josh's side and hurrying out of the room. He didn't come back right away, and after half an hour, Josh wandered through the house to look for him. Eventually he found Brendon up in his office, pounding frantically away at his computer. When Josh walked in, Brendon lifted his gaze from the keyboard and grinned. "I worked out the last formula and I needed to run it through some programs to make sure I was correct, and I am."

Brendon was practically vibrating with excitement, and then slowly that excitement slipped away. "I left you downstairs alone, didn't I?"

"It's okay," Josh said. He hoped someday he'd see that same kind of excitement aimed in his direction.

"I didn't mean to be gone for so long," Brendon said, his cheeks pinking. "I just got this idea and…."

"Hey, it's okay," Josh said and then yawned. He'd been up since very early that morning, and he had an early weight-room session tomorrow he needed to conduct with some of the players before they went to class.

"Are you tired?" Brendon asked as he closed the lid to his laptop and then began turning out the lights in the room. When Brendon joined him near the door, he was yawning as well. "I guess it's later than I thought," Brendon remarked, and Josh almost swore Brendon peeked at him to see if he was angry.

"Come on, let's get to bed or I'll be sleeping through practice. If I did that, the coach would yell at me and I'd probably find myself tied to the goalpost by the players." Josh took Brendon's hand, and they walked quietly toward the bedroom. Josh could feel Brendon's nervousness by his slight clamminess, but he didn't say anything. Josh had promised, and he believed in keeping promises.

"You can use the bathroom first, if you want," Brendon told him and directed Josh just down the hall.

In the small room, he found the basics he'd need and cleaned up as best he could before leaving the room and going back to Brendon's bedroom. He found him already in bed with the covers pulled up to his chin, his blue eyes wide. "What is it?"

Brendon swallowed. "What if you don't like what I look like?"

Josh couldn't help laughing. "You'll look like a guy without his clothes on. I've seen lots of them—big ones, tall ones, thin ones, young ones, old ones. You don't have to cover yourself like you're afraid of me." Josh toed off his shoes and pulled off his socks. Then he tugged his shirt over his head and heard Brendon gasp softly.

"You're gonna squish me," Brendon said, and it took Josh a second to realize Brendon was teasing.

"No squishing, I promise," Josh told him and then opened his pants, turning slightly so the extent of his reaction to Brendon wasn't immediately visible. After folding his clothes and setting them on the chair in the corner, Josh pulled down the covers. Brendon moved over and held his side of the blankets right up under his chin.

"What is it?" Josh asked.

"I'm skinny and pasty," Brendon said, but Josh gently pulled the blankets out of his hands, lowering them until he could see Brendon's chest and little pink nipples. Then Josh climbed under the covers and rolled onto his side, tugging Brendon against him. "Oh," Brendon said, a bit of surprise in his voice, but Josh stayed where he was.

"Is this okay?" Josh asked, not sure how Brendon would react to being held like this.

"Un-huh," Brendon said with a yawn, and then he punched his pillow twice before turning it over and then placing both hands under the pillow. He pressed back against Josh. "Good night," Brendon said, and within minutes he was asleep. That was the last sound out of him other than his soft breathing, and Josh barely moved a muscle the rest of the night.

Chapter Three

BRENDON RARELY slept through the night, at least not that he could remember, yet last night and the two times before that over the past couple of weeks, when Josh had stayed with him, Brendon had slept, really slept, and without formulas running through his head or ideas for the current paper or project he was working on wearing on his mind. He hated getting up, but Josh had early practices, and Brendon found the science building was silent before seven in the morning, so he'd been able to get a lot of the work done on his proposal for proving his hypothesis. He was going to need both computer and lab time to complete his work, and both of those required Nungesser's approval. His idea was sound and he could prove his hypothesis on paper, so getting the resources to complete his work should be a snap, but the head of his department was becoming more and more obstinate. Even Brendon could tell. At just before nine, he put the finishing touches on his proposal and sent it to Nungesser with all the I's dotted and T's crossed.

"How did it go?" Frank asked from Brendon's doorway once Brendon had pressed the send button.

"It's done and in Nungesser's hands," Brendon said.

"You know he's going to deny it," Frank countered, and Brendon sighed. He and Josh had talked about that last night, too, and Josh had warned him.

"But it's a good proposal and the results could be important," Brendon argued.

"I know it is," Frank said as he stepped inside and closed the door. "I could never figure out why Nungesser had it in for you. You're as smart as they come, your students love you, and you help others in the department. Just yesterday you caught an embedded math error in Kraft's cosmological constant paper that would have embarrassed him no end. Yes, he has more work to do because of it, but you took the time to look over his paper." Frank paused.

"Is it because I'm gay?" Brendon asked. Josh thought that had to be it, but Frank shook his head.

"It seems Professor Jardin is getting ready to retire and there's going to be an opening for a full professor. Your name has come up for the position, but he wants Karl Jameson to get the position and Nungesser figures if he can make you look bad, he can move Karl into that spot."

"I don't understand," Brendon said. Department politics and stuff like that made his head spin, and he could never make heads or tails of it anyway.

"You know that next year they're reworking the curriculum, and Nungesser has very definite ideas about what he wants to do. The thing is, the rest of us, including you, disagree with him," Frank said.

Brendon nodded. He hated Nungesser's ideas to add more flashy classes, without real substance, to lure students from other schools into filling their electives. Instead, most of the department felt they should continue to concentrate on the basics, particularly at the undergraduate level. Yes, they needed to modernize, and Brendon believed a science education was good for everyone, but not at the expense of the chemistry students. And even he knew there was only so much money to go around. "If Karl gets the position, then Nungesser will have the clout he needs to make his vision a reality, and you'll be teaching freshman chemistry until the day you die," Frank told him. "Or worse, he'll have you teaching one of those show-and-tell classes that turns science into a sideshow."

"But…," Brendon said. None of this made any sense to him, but he trusted Frank.

"I know you don't get all this political crap, and most of the time I'd say you were lucky, but not this time. See, you're playing into his hands and you don't know it. Nungesser can't really make you run the department entry in the charity Halloween fundraiser, but your refusal gives him ammunition, because he can say you're not a team player and a professor needs to think of the good of the department as well as himself."

"But I'm really busy and my work's important," Brendon explained.

"I know it is, and if you were to get it published and get the accolades for it that it deserves, no one would say anything, but Nungesser will delay until he has you where he wants you."

"So what do I do?" Brendon asked. He hated this sort of thing with a passion. Maybe it was good he didn't understand people, because sometimes they sucked.

"Agree to run the Halloween entry. That would at least take away that line of attack. And if the entry is a winner, all the better, because then you'd have some leverage. Sometimes you have to play the game."

"But what about the stuff with Karl?" Brendon asked.

"Don't worry, I think that will take care of itself," Frank said and then opened the door. "I need to get ready for class, and so do you." Brendon fussed and worried for a few minutes before getting his materials together for the first class of the day.

Once his class was over, Brendon decided to take a walk over to the athletic building to surprise Josh. He always came to see Brendon when he had a few minutes, so Brendon decided it was time to see where Josh worked. He walked across campus, the crisp fall air refreshing, but not too cold yet. Brendon pulled open the door to the athletic center. He consulted the map of the building and headed back toward the coaching offices. He thought he heard Josh's voice coming from one of the rooms, so he poked his head inside. There were weights everywhere, and huge guys were lifting, pressing and pulling, grunting with every movement.

"What do you want, Poindexter?" one of the guys growled after dropping a set of dumbbells with a bang that reverberated through the room.

"That's enough," Josh snapped louder than Brendon had ever heard him speak before. "What are you, twelve?" Josh asked, yelling in the man's face. "Just because people are smaller than you is no reason to pick on them. This isn't the playground, and bullying is never permissible, Rogers." Josh motioned Brendon to come closer, so he cautiously stepped into the weight room. "This is your lucky day, Rogers. Put out your hand." The big guy complied, and Josh motioned for Brendon to take it. "You just got the pleasure of shaking the hand of the smartest person you will ever meet in your life, and you're damn lucky if the professor here—yes, he's a professor—doesn't have you expelled or cost you your scholarship. Now, you apologize to him, and you had better think twice before you open your mouth without engaging that pea-sized brain of yours."

The man bobbed his head up and down. "Yes, Coach," Rogers said, and then he turned to Brendon. "Sorry, Professor," he said, and Brendon acknowledged him before turning to leave the room.

"I'll find you at your office later," Josh said to Brendon, turning away from Rogers and flashing Brendon a smile. Then he turned back to the student. "I think it's time you think about the kind of man you want to be, Rogers. All of you. What kind of men do you want to be?" he asked in a voice that boomed through the room. Brendon didn't hear the answers because the door closed behind him, cutting off the rest.

Brendon took a deep breath and gasped before heading back to the safety of the science building and his office.

BY THE end of the day, Brendon was exhausted, and he wasn't sure he had anything to show for it. Nungesser had looked smug, even to Brendon, when Brendon had told him he'd run the chemistry department's entry in the Halloween charity event. At least some of the other professors had agreed to help, and so had a number of his students. Now all he needed to do was put together a plan and try to execute it in the next few weeks. And to top it off, he was supposed to go to have dinner with Josh and his family. He hurried home, showered, and changed clothes, finishing up just as the doorbell rang. "Come in, Josh," Brendon called from upstairs as he finished buttoning his shirt.

"Are you ready?" Josh called, and then Brendon heard footsteps on the stairs.

"Almost. Do I look okay?" Brendon asked, looking down at himself. No dancing leprechauns, and his shoes matched. He knew his shirt and pants didn't clash. He checked his belt, which was plain leather, so he thought that was okay.

"You look great," Josh said, and Brendon was quickly gathered into Josh's huge arms and first hugged, then kissed. "You always look great to me." Brendon didn't know what to say, but he really didn't care as long as Josh kissed him like that. "You have nothing to worry about. Mom and Dad are going to like you just fine."

"But what if I mess up?" Brendon asked.

"Just be yourself and you'll be fine. Let them get to know you."

"But what if they don't like me?" He'd never met a boyfriend's parents before. He'd never had a boyfriend before, and he didn't want to disappoint Josh. In a lab or in front of a class, where he could talk chemistry, formulas, and theories until he was blue in the face, Brendon was at home and happy. But all this people stuff was almost more than he could take. He hadn't really ever had friends, and he was just beginning to understand what he'd been missing. He didn't want to lose that.

"They won't hate you. My mother is wonderful, and my dad can be forceful, but they're not hateful people. Just driven, sort of like you are when you're working," Josh told him, but the little shakes that ran through him intensified. Josh ran his hands gently up and down Brendon's arms. "If something happens and you aren't comfortable, we'll leave."

"But they're your family," Brendon said.

"And you're a guest. It's their job to make you feel comfortable and welcome. That's part of being a good host. So don't worry about anything. You're going to be fine," Josh said, and then he turned Brendon around, gathering him in his big, warm arms.

"Okay," Brendon agreed, and Josh held him tighter. "I think we'd better go before you squish me."

Josh chuckled. "I promised you no squishing." Brendon chuckled too, and they descended the stairs and left the house once Brendon had gotten a jacket from the closet. The ride to Hershey, where Josh's parents lived, took almost forty minutes, and Brendon spent most of the time trying to keep his nerves in check. Eventually they turned off the main road and wove through neighborhoods of stately homes, until Josh pulled into the driveway of a large home with a circular drive that extended under a portico. Josh parked, and Brendon got out of the car, then waited for Josh to lead the way inside.

Inside the house, Josh led him into a grand foyer with a huge crystal chandelier hanging overhead. Voices drifted in from one of the other rooms. Josh took Brendon's jacket and hung it up in the hall closet and then led Brendon through a forest of rich, dark woodwork toward the voices. When they entered the large living room, everyone stood, and Josh was hugged by a surprisingly small woman. "We've been waiting for you," she said, releasing Josh from the hug. Brendon lingered near the doorway.

"Mom, this is Brendon," Josh said. Brendon was ready to shake hands, because that was the accepted convention, so he was surprised when Josh's mother hugged him as well. "Brendon, this is my mother, Cecile. Everyone calls her Cici."

"Please come in," she said.

"This is my father, Dwight," Josh said.

Brendon shook his hand. "It's nice to meet you, sir," he said, hoping that was right.

"Please, call me Dwight," Josh's father said in a booming voice that almost echoed off the walls. "And this is Joshua's sister, Gloria, and his brother, Reggie." He motioned toward a leather sofa, and Brendon went to sit next to Josh. "Gloria was just telling us about her work with children down in Houston."

"Dad," Gloria interrupted. "Josh just got here. Let's not bore him with all that talk." Even to Brendon she sounded condescending. "What do you do, Brendon?" she asked, and all eyes turned to him.

"I teach chemistry," Brendon said.

"So you teach, that's wonderful," she said, and Brendon glanced at Josh.

"Yes. I currently teach mostly basic classes. But I'm also working on a number of other projects." Brendon turned to Josh, who nodded. "Well, the experiment I'm designing now will explain how specific isotopes behave under certain conditions. It's their molecular structure that guides how they behave, and if I can isolate them and prove exactly how they behave, then I'll be one step closer to actually probing the possible origin of life." Brendon felt some of his unease slip away as he talked about his work. "I have the experiments designed and my proposals written. All I need are the resources and the funding, which I hope to be able to get from the university."

"How long will it take you to prove your theory?" Dwight asked him.

Brendon shrugged. "It's just a small piece of a larger theory and I've worked out everything in my head and then put it all on paper, so all I really need to do is prove that what I believe to be true on paper actually reflects the reality of the greater world." Brendon was almost bouncing, he was so excited.

"Gloria, Brendon is an associate professor at Dickinson," Josh said.

"So is this experiment part of a thesis?" Reggie asked.

"No. It actually builds on some of the work I started on for my dissertation two years ago, but once I finished my doctorate and got hired on at Dickinson, my work has veered off into some new directions that I hadn't foreseen."

"Would you like something to drink, dear?" Cici asked as she motioned toward a bar cart.

"Maybe some water or a diet soda," Brendon said, and she got up, then brought him a glass of ice water and what looked like a beer for Josh.

"How old are you, son?" Dwight asked.

"Twenty-three," Brendon said, and then he sipped from his glass.

"So you earned your doctorate at twenty-one?" Reggie asked, and Brendon nodded slowly, wondering if he'd said something wrong.

"Both your parents must be very proud," Cici said with a large smile.

"They were, yes," Brendon said, and he saw Cici's smile fade. "My mother died a number of years ago, and my dad died just after I got my doctorate."

"You must be brilliant," Dwight said. "What are you doing with Josh?"

"Dwight!" Cici scolded before swatting him on the arm. "That's not a nice or proper thing to say."

"Cici, we all know Josh could have been so much more than a football coach. If he'd applied himself, he could have been just as successful as Gloria and Reggie. Instead, he'll be coaching football for the rest of his life." Dwight turned to Josh.

"Josh does a lot more than coach football," Brendon said, shifting to the edge of his chair. "He's helping teach the players how to be good men, and that's very important. They're all very large, with huge amounts of hormones running through them. They've been taught that might makes right, and Josh teaches them that *right* makes right. He helps them grow up and teaches them that being a man is more than being bigger than someone else. He also helps make sure they don't just play football, but get an education too." Brendon turned to Josh and smiled. Then he wondered if he'd said too much and got quiet, especially when he saw all the other people in the room staring at him. Brendon looked down at his shirt, wondering for a second if the danged dancing leprechaun had suddenly made an appearance.

"He coaches football," Reggie said.

"And he's good at it and it makes him happy. Chemistry makes me happy. I can sit in my office and work for days without taking a break. Sometimes I forget to eat, and it isn't until the numbers begin to swim that I remember to eat. Then I sit back at my desk and start working again. I love what I do, and it makes me happy, especially when I'm working through a formula," Brendon explained. "Josh is the same way about his players. He loves what he does and he's good at it."

"But he could have been so much more," Dwight said.

"Did your father pick your career for you?" Brendon asked Dwight. "My dad wanted me to be a baseball player. The tiny mitt he bought me when I was a baby is still in the house somewhere. But I didn't love sports."

"You watch football," Josh said. "You told me you did."

"I do, but only because the players on the field remind me of chemical compounds and how they interact and react to one another. I watch the game and work through formulas in my head. I know I live, eat, and breathe chemistry and science, just like Josh loves coaching. It's in his blood, and he'd be missing something if he couldn't do it. I'd probably go crazy—well, crazier, anyway—if I couldn't do what I loved." Brendon knew he'd probably said too much and he stopped talking and stared down at his shoes. "I'm sorry if I said too much," Brendon whispered, and then he felt Josh press his hand lightly to his back.

"I think you said something that needed to be said in this house a long time ago," Cici said, and Brendon lifted his gaze. "He's definitely a teacher at heart," Cici added, looking directly at Dwight. "Brendon certainly taught you a thing or two about your son, didn't he?"

"I only want Joshua to be the best he can be," Dwight said.

"I will be, Dad. I'm good at what I do, and someday I'll be promoted to coach and have my own team to manage. And maybe I'll be offered a chance at one of the big-time schools, but that isn't why I do this. I love coaching, seeing a player and helping him work on his weaknesses and build on his strengths, physically and mentally. It's what I do. Build up a group of men and help them work together to accomplish a goal."

"Okay, I know when I've been beaten," Dwight said.

"Good," Cici said, touching Dwight's shoulder as she passed him. "I'm going to bring in the appetizers. I'll be right back."

"You're really a professor?" Reggie asked once she'd left the room.

"Yes. But I could be anything I wanted. All I have to do is read the books," Brendon said. "I remember everything. But I love science."

"Fascinating," Gloria said. "Did that ability develop over time or did you always have it?"

"I think it was always there," Brendon said. "I remember reading my books to my mother when I was about four, and then reading her college textbooks when she was in school."

"Wow," Gloria said.

"Brendon is more than just a memory machine. He puts things together and works them through in his head," Josh said, and when Brendon leaned back on the sofa, Josh leaned against him slightly.

"One of my colleagues is doing some work with memory," Gloria said. "Would you be willing to come down and work with him? The way your mind works would fascinate him and could help advance his research."

"Of course. I could probably arrange to come down during one of my breaks." Brendon shifted and pulled out his wallet, then handed Gloria one of his cards. "Have him contact me at the college and we can make the arrangements." He liked the idea that he could help someone advance their research.

Cici returned to the room with a tray of steaming hors d'oeuvres, plates, and napkins. She sat down, and they all ate and chatted. It had been a long time since Brendon had sat down with a group of people like this and simply talked. What was even nicer was that they all seemed interested in what he had to say and they even understood most of it. He was really enjoying himself. Eventually Cici called them in for dinner, and the conversation continued while they ate, and then after they moved back into the living room. By the time he and Josh were ready to leave, Brendon was nearly talked out. He was also happy and relaxed. Josh got his jacket for him, and Brendon said good-bye to Josh's family, receiving another hug from Josh's mom and an invitation to come back anytime.

"That was really nice," Brendon said as he settled into the passenger seat of Josh's car. "You have a great family." Josh started the car and didn't say anything as he pulled out of the drive and onto the street. "I wasn't nervous at all." Josh still didn't say anything, and Brendon settled back in the seat and let him drive across the metro area and back toward Carlisle. "I really think your family liked me," Brendon said after a while, a smile breaking out on his face. They had liked him, he was sure of it, and Josh's mother had invited him back.

"Yeah, they liked you," Josh said rather churlishly.

"Are you upset?" Brendon asked. He was never sure about these things.

"Maybe you should have been my father's son instead of me," Josh mumbled without looking at him, clenching the steering wheel tightly enough that his knuckles were white in the oncoming headlights.

"You're mad at me?" Brendon asked, but Josh didn't answer. "You're upset because your family liked me?" Josh didn't say anything. "If you didn't want them to like me, then you shouldn't have taken me to meet them." Brendon stared out the windshield. "You know, you're a total butthead." Josh pulled off the freeway onto the surface streets of town. "Why did you take me, anyway? So you could show off the freak to your family? Was all that stuff before we left just bull puckey?" Josh stopped at a traffic signal, and Brendon opened his door and got out of the car, then slammed the door closed and hurried to the sidewalk. He'd rather walk home. "Butthead!" Brendon yelled as the light changed, and after some horn honking, Josh's car moved forward.

Brendon began walking home, his strides purposeful as his anger continued to build. "What did he want? His family to hate me? Jesus, they were nice and we got along. What a butthead!" Brendon yelled out loud as a car passed. His entire frame shook as he thought about it. A car slowed as it approached, and Brendon turned off the main road. He didn't know if it was Josh or not, but he didn't care. All he wanted was to get home behind locked doors so he could immerse himself in his work and formulas and forget about all the things he'd hoped for. He thought he'd made a friend and he'd been hoping he might have found something more. "You're a fool. People don't like you; they never have," Brendon muttered as he continued walking. "I don't fit in anywhere and I never have, so why would I think things would change?" Brendon turned to look over his shoulder and saw nothing but the empty street. He wasn't sure if he was disappointed or not. Part of him wanted Josh to find him and say he was sorry, and another part of him wanted to punch Josh in the nose the next time he saw him.

He kept walking, quickening his pace the closer he got to home. By the time he was on his street, he was nearly jogging, and as he reached his door, he was running. Brendon tugged his keys out of his pocket and unlocked the door, then hurried inside and nearly slammed the door closed. Josh and everyone else could stay out and stay away. Brendon went to hang up his jacket and realized he'd left it in Josh's car. After closing the closet door, Brendon climbed the stairs and went into his office, where he booted up his computer. He sat in his chair and waited for the computer, but once it was ready, he wasn't interested. "Butthead," Brendon said softly as his anger fell away, replaced by hurt. He kept asking himself why Josh had acted that way, but he had no answers. He never did when it came to other people.

He heard knocking on his front door and thought about ignoring it, but he took a deep breath and told himself to get mad again. He descended the stairs and cracked the door open to see Josh standing on his doorstep. "Just give me my jacket and go," Brendon said.

"Brendon, I...."

"Just get my jacket and leave me alone," Brendon said.

"I was hurt, but I shouldn't have taken it out on you," Josh said.

"You bet you shouldn't," Brendon said, opening the door. "I know I don't say the right thing sometimes, but I don't try to hurt people, and that's what you did to me."

"I'm sorry. You didn't do anything, and I'm happy my family liked you. I just wish they liked me like that," Josh said.

"Well, that's no reason to act like a big butthead." Brendon was beginning to really warm up to that term.

"I know. I shouldn't have acted that way," Josh said as he stepped closer to the door. Brendon backed up, not sure he wanted to let Josh inside with him.

"No, you shouldn't have. You hurt me, and I was so happy because your family seemed to like me. All you could worry about was that they didn't like you? They're your family—of course they like you." Brendon backed farther inside the house and began closing the door. "I think I need you to leave now."

"Brendon," Josh said just above a whisper. "I really am sorry. I shouldn't have treated you that way. You deserved better, and I am happy my family liked you. They should have liked you, because you're pretty special."

Brendon stood in the partially open doorway. "You really hurt me," he said softly. "I didn't like it." He also didn't really understand it, and maybe that was why he felt so bad.

"I know and I was wrong," Josh said, and this time when he stepped closer, Brendon didn't back away. "I'm sorry I hurt you and I'm sorry for being so selfish." Josh moved closer and then reached out and pulled Brendon into his arms.

"Why did you do that?" Brendon asked as he rested his head against Josh's chest.

"I was jealous, and I shouldn't have been. I should have been happy you made such a good impression on my family. I won't do that again, I promise," Josh whispered, and Brendon closed his eyes. He sincerely hoped that was true, because he hated fighting. It sucked.

"How do I know?" Brendon asked softly and waited for Josh to answer, but he didn't hear anything. "These things always take me by surprise. I never seem to know when they're going to come at me." Brendon lifted his head off Josh's warm chest. "Do you have any idea what it's like to find out someone is angry with you only when they start yelling? Everyone else seems to understand. There are signs, I know there are, but I always miss them. And people fight over the most stupid things. Your family liked me. That was a good thing, but somehow their liking me became about you. How? I don't know. But you got jealous and then mad at me... see? Stupid." Brendon backed away from Josh. "If anything, your family liking me should have made you happy because we were together, so them liking me meant your social esteem went up because we were together." This made sense to Brendon.

"It's not always that simple," Josh said, and Brendon blinked.

"But why can't it be? Why does everything have to be so muddled?" Brendon asked. "And why get mad at me, anyway? All I did was what you told me to do, and they liked me."

"They didn't *like* you—they loved you. My father hung on your every word through most of dinner, and my mother probably thinks you walk on water."

"No one can walk on water," Brendon said.

"It's a figure of speech. It means she thinks you're dang near perfect," Josh told him as he closed the front door. "And you are. I shouldn't have gotten upset, and you're right: my family liking you has nothing to do with how they feel about me." Josh smiled and tugged Brendon back into his arms. "Did you really mean what you said to my dad about me helping make better men?" Josh leaned forward, and Brendon shivered, but not from cold, as Josh kissed and nibbled his neck.

"You do. I saw it, remember? At the weight room." Brendon tried to say more, but all that came out was a soft moan. "Josh, what are you doing?" He shivered again.

"Making you feel good. Is this okay?" Josh asked, and Brendon hummed his agreement.

"Josh, I want...," Brendon began. He really wasn't sure what he was asking for, or necessarily how to ask for it. All he knew was he hoped now was the time. "Can we?" Brendon's heart raced and his breath came in shallow pants. And his pants were way too tight.

"Do you want to go upstairs?" Josh asked. Then he added, "To your bedroom."

"Yes," Brendon whined, stretching his neck so Josh could.... He gasped softly when Josh licked the skin at the base of his neck. "Don't stop," Brendon moaned softly.

"I won't," Josh mumbled, and then he scooped Brendon off his feet and began to climb the stairs.

"I saw this in a movie once," Brendon giggled as he held Josh around the neck.

"Me too, except you're no Scarlett O'Hara," Josh told him as they reached the top of the stairs. "You're a whole hell of a lot cuter." Josh carried him into the bedroom and set him on the bed, and before Brendon could think what was happening, he was being kissed hard. Josh's shoes thunked to the floor, and Brendon kicked off his own. Once the shoes had joined Josh's, Josh rolled Brendon on the bed until Brendon stared into Josh's eyes. "Remember, I promised no squishing," Josh said and then tugged Brendon down into a hard kiss that stole his breath away.

Brendon gasped when Josh broke the kiss. He heaved a deep breath and looked into Josh's eyes, surprised by what he saw there. He jumped slightly as Josh began fumbling open the buttons on his shirt. "Is this a new shirt?" Josh asked him, and Brendon shook his head.

Buttons went flying, and then Josh shoved the shirt down Brendon's arms. He was about to protest until Josh leaned forward and licked one of his nipples, and Brendon forgot about everything. Josh wrapped his arms around him, and Brendon dropped his head back, thrusting his chest forward for more. When Josh released him, Brendon moaned, but within seconds Josh's shirt was gone and then he pressed his bare skin to Brendon's.

"Josh," Brendon groaned as Josh licked his chest. They'd slept together, but mostly on those nights Josh had held him or lightly stroked his skin—they hadn't done anything like this.

"Is this good?" Josh asked, and Brendon mumbled something. Never in his life could he remember all the parts of his mind focusing on one single thing, one single point. Until this moment, his mind had always been like a multilane superhighway, but right now it felt more like a single-lane country road that led to Josh.

"Don't stop," Brendon groaned.

"I won't, I promise," Josh told him, licking all the way up his chest and throat before capturing Brendon's lips in a searing kiss. "Don't think, just feel," Josh said, and Brendon nodded. He'd stopped thinking a while ago.

Josh shifted him on the bed, until Brendon rested on his back on the bedding. Josh knelt over him, stroking him as they kissed. Josh sucked on his tongue and lips, making small, moaning sounds that Brendon had never heard before. It took him a second to realize some of those sounds were his. Josh made his way back down Brendon's throat and then down his chest, teasing each nipple before kissing down his stomach and licking at the skin just above his belt.

Brendon sucked in his stomach, closed his eyes, and waited. He felt Josh tug on his belt and then open his pants. Brendon kept his eyes closed, afraid if he opened them all this would be a dream.

"You're wonderful," Josh said.

Brendon tried to mutter, "So are you," but it might have been lost in the deep groan that followed when Brendon felt Josh's lips on his cock for the first time.

All the air in his lungs tried to rush out at the same time. "Josh!" he gasped as his cock was taken deep into his lover's amazingly hot mouth. The pressure and pleasure slipped away and then returned. Brendon opened his eyes, shaking as Josh bobbed his head up and down. Brendon placed his hands on Josh's head, twining his fingers in Josh's soft hair, and thrust his hips into the heat. Everything stopped, and Brendon wondered what had happened. Then, slowly, Josh began sucking again, and Brendon could do nothing but enjoy it. He'd seen pictures and watched movies on the Internet, so he knew what Josh was doing, but in his imagination, he'd never thought anything could feel like this—searingly hot, wet, and yet so surprisingly intimate that Josh became the only other person in the universe. "D-don't stop," Brendon gasped, and then Josh did just that.

"You okay?" Josh asked, his eyes twinkling and a massive smile curling his lips upward.

"Yes," Brendon whimpered, and then Josh kissed him sloppily before tugging Brendon's pants off, leaving him naked on the bedding. Brendon had originally felt shy being around Josh without his clothes. He was skinny and pale, and Josh, well, he was anything but, and Brendon had been truly afraid Josh would take a look at him and laugh and that would be the end of his new "boyfriend." But that didn't seem to be the case. Brendon's shyness returned, lingering only until he felt Josh's lips on his skin and heard his small humming moans, and then he forgot all about it. And once Josh sank his lips down his cock and Brendon was sucked into his lover's mouth, he thought of nothing but what Josh was doing to him. The world could come to an end and he wouldn't have known. "That's...." Josh took him deep and whatever Brendon planned to say flew from his head.

He clutched at the bedding, his legs slowly thrumming up and down. "Josh, I'm gonna," Brendon started to say as he rushed toward a release he couldn't stop if he tried. "Josh!" he cried and then clamped his eyes closed, his entire body going rigid as he came down Josh's throat. Brendon felt him swallowing around him and slowly thrust his hips upward, his entire body floating on clouds of endorphins. His mind knew what was making him feel this way, he'd studied it before, but....

Josh pulled his lips away, and Brendon melted into the bedding, breathing hard as Josh lay on the bed next to him, holding him tight. "You know, you're so beautiful when you come," Josh whispered, and Brendon rolled his head on the bedding so he could see him.

"I knew what happened physically when a person reached orgasm, and I've felt it before, because... well, you know... but that was different. That was...." Brendon was at a loss for words. "I mean, I know what's supposed to happen. I've studied it. The endorphins that are released, the physical response, but nothing ever mentioned this."

Josh chuckled and held him tighter. "Do you remember our conversation the first night I stayed? Of course you do," Josh added with a smile once Brendon nodded.

"That's the making love part?" Brendon asked, and Josh leaned close, kissing his neck the way he had before they'd come upstairs.

"Uh-huh," Josh breathed against Brendon's skin, blowing hot air over the spot he'd wetted with his lips and making Brendon shiver with delight.

"Can I do the making love thing to you?" Brendon asked, and Josh grinned.

"It's not what you do, it's what you feel. Making love is how you feel when you're having sex," Josh told him before sucking on his neck once again. "Tomorrow you need to be sure to wear a collared shirt or everyone is going to see my love mark."

"You love me?" Brendon asked very carefully. He figured this might be one of those times when it wasn't a good idea to ask a whole bunch of questions, but the words were out of his mouth almost before he could stop them.

"Yes, I love you," Josh said.

"But... but... we haven't known each other that long. I...." Brendon closed his mouth. It seemed Josh had short-circuited his brain. He wasn't even sure what love was.

"It's okay," Josh said.

Brendon lifted himself onto his elbows. "No, it's not. How do I know if I love you?" Brendon understood what he could see and measure, but this was something different. "I looked it up online, but the answers were really vague."

Brendon thought he was being stupid, but Josh shifted and held him, pressing him close. "Let's say I'm coming over for dinner. Before I get here, do you get anxious and a little sweaty even when the room isn't warm?" Brendon nodded. That happened all the time. "Do you sometimes get what feels like butterflies in your stomach when I'm around?"

"Yes, and when you're going to come over, I want you to get here faster."

"Exactly," Josh said. "Those are some of the physical signs that you're in love. But how do you feel?" Josh placed his hand over Brendon's heart. "In here, how do you feel? What is it you want?" Brendon thought carefully, weighing all the evidence. "It isn't that hard, sweetheart. Just listen to your heart; it knows what it wants."

"I never want you to leave. When you stay the night and then we have to go to work, I want to stay in bed. I never want to stay in bed, but I do when you're here. And sometimes, like just now, I don't think of anything but you. I like not thinking of anything but you," Brendon said. "Does that mean I love you too?"

"Only you can decide what you feel," Josh said, holding him tight. Brendon knew what he felt, but he didn't know how to translate those feelings into words, and what amazed him was that Josh seemed to understand. "You don't have to tell me what I want to hear. That's not what I want from you, ever. You'll figure out how you feel and be able to put it into words when you're ready. Until then, know how I feel about you. That's enough."

Brendon held Josh tight, breathing in the rich scent from his skin. His body reacted right away. He wanted Josh again, and he could feel how Josh wanted him. Brendon squirmed and began tugging at Josh's pants. Josh sighed and then laughed softly before climbing off the bed. Brendon watched as Josh shucked his pants. "Even your butt is tanned," Brendon said, and Josh turned around to give him a good look. "I love your butt dimples," Brendon said, giggling as he stroked the smooth skin of Josh's butt. He felt naughty, and then Josh slowly turned around. His cock was pointing straight up at the ceiling, and Brendon moved closer, crouching on the bed as he gently ran his fingers up and down Josh's length.

Everything about Josh was perfect and in proportion, like a statue. Brendon could hardly believe he was touching another man. He'd touched himself, of course, but this was different, and when Josh hissed softly, he looked up to make sure he wasn't doing something wrong.

"That's so good," Josh moaned, and Brendon stroked harder, Josh's cock like a steel rod wrapped in silk. Brendon moved closer and Josh shifted closer to the bed. Brendon wanted to taste Josh. The way Josh's mouth had felt on him was indelibly etched on his brain, and he wanted to make Josh feel the same way. "Go slow," Josh whispered, and Brendon opened his mouth and slowly sucked Josh's cock in.

The flavor that burst on his tongue was like nothing Brendon had ever experienced—salt, and a touch of sweetness—and he loved it. Brendon sucked harder, wanting to go as deep as Josh had, but he quickly found out he couldn't. "Sorry," Brendon mumbled after backing off.

Josh leaned forward and cupped Brendon's cheeks, then kissed him hard. "Take it easy and go slow. This is your first time, and you need to enjoy it too. This isn't just about me; it's about both of us." Josh stroked his cheeks, and Brendon lowered his head, determined to try again. This time he went much slower, sucking slowly and swirling his tongue around the head of Josh's cock. Josh groaned loudly. "Damn, you're good."

Brendon smiled and relished the sounds he was getting Josh to make. Those noises made him really happy because he was making Josh happy.

Slowly, Josh began moving his hips. Not a lot, but enough that Brendon relaxed his throat and moved with him. "God," Josh kept saying over and over again. Josh ran his hands up and down Brendon's back, and Brendon's cock throbbed. "Roll onto your back," Josh told him, and Brendon let Josh's cock slip from his lips and then rested on the bed. Josh guided his dick back to Brendon's lips, and he sucked him in. Then Josh leaned over him and, mother of God, he sucked him at the same time.

Brendon thought he'd died and gone to heaven. He'd never thought about doing both things at the same time. In a moment of clarity, he realized how sheltered a life he'd led and how much he now wanted everything, all of it, and he wanted it with Josh. He sucked Josh as deeply as he could, and at the same time, Josh sucked him to the root. Without thinking, he grabbed Josh's legs and held on. He'd come not half an hour earlier, but Brendon could already feel his excitement building again, and when he felt Josh lift his legs and then press a finger along his cleft to his opening, he stilled. Brendon wasn't sure he was ready for that, but then Josh began teasing the skin there. The sensation nearly overwhelmed him. Josh thrust into his mouth, and he did the same, coming closer and closer to the edge.

Brendon clamped his eyes closed and sucked hard as Josh pulled him over the edge. Brendon began coming, and then Josh flooded his mouth with his own release. At first, Brendon forgot to swallow, but he quickly caught up and swallowed repeatedly.

Josh moved, slipping his lips from around Brendon as he slowly pulled out of Brendon's mouth. Brendon opened his eyes as the mattress shifted, and then Josh tugged him in, pressing him against his hot skin and bulging muscles. Brendon loved the way Josh felt. Hell, he loved the way he felt when Josh held him, safe and secure, like no one could get to him. That was why he'd been so hurt earlier. "I like how you protect me," Brendon whispered, and Josh held him tighter.

"I know I hurt you, and I'm sorry." Josh kissed him once again. "I can't promise I'll never hurt you again, because I probably will, but I'll try not to."

"Okay, I'll do the same," Brendon said, closing his eyes and letting Josh's warmth form a secure bubble around him.

"Why don't we get comfortable under the covers?" Josh shifted and began pulling down the blankets. Brendon shifted and climbed between the sheets. Josh kissed him and whispered that he'd be right back, and Brendon watched him leave the room, his perfect butt bobbing slightly as he walked. Brendon couldn't help a small giggle of joy as he enjoyed the view.

By the time Josh returned, Brendon had burrowed under the covers, and Josh joined him in bed. Brendon fluffed his pillow and then turned it over so the cool side was up. Then he shifted so he could press his butt and back to Josh, placed his hands under the pillow, and closed his eyes. He was nearly asleep before he realized he hadn't thought about anything or anyone except Josh for hours… and he smiled.

Chapter Four

JOSH APPROACHED Brendon's front door. He could see the light through the second floor window where Brendon had his office. In fact, if he closed his eyes, he could picture Brendon sitting at his desk, typing at his computer, oblivious to the rest of the world. Josh had realized very early that if he wanted any type of relationship with the brilliant scientist, he had to accept there would be times when Brendon's science would be the most important thing in his life. Not always, but Josh knew he had to be prepared to accept that sometimes he wouldn't be the center of Brendon's attention. As Josh knocked on the door and heard no response from inside the house, he began to realize how sometimes that situation would be hard to accept. He knocked again and still didn't hear any response. He knew if he rang the doorbell, Brendon wasn't likely to hear that either. Brendon had been working hard for the past three weeks to complete the draft of his paper, teach his classes, and put together plans for the display for the charity event that was coming up fast. Josh hadn't been able to see him as much as he'd have liked, both because of Brendon's schedule and his own. It was, after all, the height of football season.

He knocked again and then tried the door. It was locked, so he strode down the path between the houses to the back gate. It was open, so Josh went through and then closed the gate behind him. Instead of going directly to the house, he wandered back into the garden. Dry leaves crunched under his feet, and many of the plants that had been so glorious just a few weeks ago were now covered in brown and gold leaves. Fall had definitely arrived, and as a breeze blew through the yard, cutting through Josh's jacket, he shook slightly, as did the leaves littering the ground. It seemed like the garden was shivering too, in anticipation of winter. Josh turned around, walked to the back door, and tested the doorknob to see if it was locked. The door opened and he stepped inside. "Brendon, sweetheart, are you home?" Josh called, but he didn't hear any sort of answer. He closed the door and walked through to the front of the house. "Brendon, it's me," he called up the stairs, and he thought he heard an answer, so he began to climb. "Brendon?"

Muttering reached his ears and got louder as he got closer to the office. Josh heard Brendon typing, or something that sounded more like Brendon typing his keyboard into submission. Josh had heard Brendon type plenty of times, and the sound was often soothing and gentle. This was angry. "Hon, what did that keyboard ever do to you?"

"Stupid Nungesser, that asshole," Brendon snapped and stopped typing. "I want to punch the slimy bastard."

Brendon rarely swore, and certainly not like that. "What happened?" Josh asked as he stepped into Brendon's office.

"Nungesser approved my application for the lab resources I needed," Brendon said.

"That's great," Josh said, but Brendon glared at him with white-hot fire in his eyes, and not flames of passion, but the burn-in-hell kind. "Isn't it?"

"The bastard approved the resources three weeks ago, but didn't bother to tell me. So today when I passed the dean in the hallway, he asked me why I hadn't already set up my lab and gotten to work—the implication being that I've been sitting around wasting time for three weeks, which was exactly what Nungesser told him—that he'd approved it and he didn't know why I was procrastinating." Brendon groaned and picked up his keyboard. He looked about ready to throw it across the room. "So now I have to somehow make up for three lost weeks of lab preparation and get this Halloween display done that Nungesser pestered me into doing. I know why he's doing this, but it makes me mad."

"Hey, it's all right. I've seen the plans for the display, and I think it's going to be really cool." Josh grinned and tried to be as positive as possible.

"It would be if I actually had enough time to set up. But Nungesser's got the room I'm supposed to use tied up with a symposium until the day before the event, so there isn't much time to get things set up, and I can't do it all on my own. I could have had everything staged ahead of time, but now I have to spend that time getting my lab set up so the next time I see the dean I can talk about progress instead of making excuses and looking like a largemouth bass." Brendon began shaking. "I don't know what to do."

"Work on your research. Get your lab set up. There's nothing you can do about your display until the room is available, right?"

Brendon nodded slowly. "You've got everything in place that you can at this point?"

"My garage is full of all the things I was able to gather. I already got the modified Geiger counters to go off based on motion instead of radiation, so when everyone leaves the lab, they'll be 'contaminated' and need to go through a simulated radiation cleansing. It should be really cool. I even managed to rig up a holographic Marie Curie who'll look ghostly, like she's bent over her notebooks, from a certain angle. But everything has to be set up precisely, and then there are all the other things to complete the room." Brendon closed his eyes, and Josh hurried behind the desk and gently massaged Brendon's shoulders.

"Okay," Josh whispered. "Tomorrow is Saturday, and I have a light practice in the morning and a game in the evening. But I can help you on Sunday if you want. I don't know what you need to do to get things set up, but I can follow instructions."

Brendon leaned back, resting his head against Josh's belly. "I don't think there's anything you can do to help in the lab. I just need the time to get it done."

"Okay," Josh said, continuing to work his fingers into the muscles of Brendon's shoulders.

"I hate him," Brendon spat, and Josh felt the muscles beneath his hands tighten. "I never did anything to him, and he acts like such a butthead."

"Could you publish your paper without the lab work?" Josh asked, and Brendon stilled.

"I could, but then it would be just theoretical, and the work wouldn't have as much impact. But if I can prove it in the lab, then it would carry much more weight," Brendon explained.

"It would, but if it were published, or at least accepted for publication, then Nungesser would have to get off your back. You'd have results to show. You said yourself the lab work could take a while, and people love to see progress."

Brendon sighed. "I know. I…." He shifted until he looked up at Josh. "I just want to do good science without all the politics. I do good work, and I can make valuable contributions if my time isn't taken up with Halloween displays and Nungesser's games."

"I know it isn't fair, but we all deal with politics. Universities are hotbeds of stupid political games. They talk things to death and change very little, because too many people have a stake in things staying the same." Josh kept kneading the tension out of Brendon's shoulders. "When exactly will you get access to the room?"

"Wednesday, and the display has to be ready for review by the committee first thing Friday morning. I have classes and labs for most of the day on Thursday," Brendon explained. "I could have one of the TAs conduct the labs, but I never thought that was fair to the students. They deserve and pay for my instruction, not someone who took the same class two years ago."

"I know, and that's why the students love you. You care." Josh continued kneading and finally felt the tension in Brendon's muscles slip away. "Now, I want you to try to let go of all this for a little while." Josh leaned close, sucking on Brendon's ear. "You can't do anything about it now, and Nungesser, the old fart, isn't going to ruin our evening, is he?"

Brendon shivered, and then he carded his hand through Josh's hair. "No." Brendon didn't sound convinced.

"There's nothing you can do tonight, you know that, and worrying about it isn't going to do any good." Josh moved away, tugging Brendon to his feet. "Why don't you get a jacket and we'll go for a walk? The fresh air will help clear your head, and then when we get back, I'll help you forget about everything for a while."

"Can't we just get to the forgetting part now?" Brendon asked as he stood up, and Josh chuckled, drawing him into his arms. Josh cupped Brendon's butt and squeezed gently.

"We won't be out long, and the fresh air will do you good," Josh whispered in Brendon's ear. "Think about how much fun it will be when we get back and I warm you up." Brendon agreed but didn't move away, and Josh held the man who was quickly coming to represent the other half of his heart. "Let's get your jacket," Josh said, and Brendon slowly moved away. To Josh's surprise, he left his computer the way it was and left the room, headed for the stairs. Josh followed him, knowing now just how upset Brendon was—he was always fastidious about saving his work. Josh heard the closet door close, and when he got downstairs, he found Brendon waiting for him by the front door. Josh caught up, and they stepped outside into the crisp fall evening air.

"Where do you want to walk?" Brendon asked as he closed the door and then locked it.

"Let's go this way," Josh said, and he began walking slowly, so Brendon could catch up. "We're not going anywhere in particular, but I figured if you wanted, we could walk out this way and stop for frozen custard. They'll be closing for the season in the next few days."

"I'm not really hungry."

"When was the last time you ate?" Josh asked, and Brendon didn't answer right away. "I thought so. You probably got upset and then worked right through lunch and on past dinner." Brendon didn't dispute his assertion, and Josh guided them toward the main part of town. Once they reached High Street, he ushered Brendon into a small café he'd been to once or twice. Their service was good, and Josh was most concerned with getting Brendon to eat. "One of these days you're going to keel over in the street." They took one of the tables, and a college-age server brought them glasses of water. "Could you bring us each a hot chocolate?" Josh asked, and Brendon licked his lips. Josh wanted to suck on that pretty pink tongue, but that would come later. He still leered a little, but it was completely lost on Brendon.

Brendon shuffled out of his jacket, and the server brought their hot chocolate and took their orders before hurrying away. "Hey, Coach," Josh heard boom through the small restaurant. Two of Josh's defensive players, Stevens and Carter, wove their way between the tables, barely able to keep from knocking them over as they passed. Josh stood and shook hands with both of them before introducing Brendon.

"You're the science prof?" Stevens asked.

"Yes," Brendon answered, and Josh saw Brendon's body stiffen with tension.

"What brings you out the night before a game?" Josh asked the two men, looking at his watch.

"We weren't breaking curfew. We needed sustenance, so we're getting sandwiches to go," Carter said, but both of the players looked a bit uncomfortable.

"Is something wrong?" Josh asked with a warning both players clearly understood.

"No," Carter said. "Just different to see a guy out with a guy, I guess."

"Be careful where you're going with this," Josh warned, puffing up his chest.

"It's cool, just different," Stevens clarified. "I mean, we knew you were gay, but seeing you out with another guy brings it home. Like I said, it's cool." Stevens shifted his attention to Brendon. "Word around campus is that your classes are way cool. So I have your class scheduled for next term."

"You'll work hard," Brendon told him. "But you'll learn a lot."

Carter bumped Stevens on the shoulder. "He's the brainiac on the team. Don't know how he studies and practices like he does." A take-out number was called, and the guys excused themselves and went to get their food. They said good-bye before leaving the café.

"See what I meant about helping make better men?" Brendon asked once Josh sat back down.

"Maybe," Josh said with a smile as he watched the players pass in front of the windows.

"They didn't call me Poindexter," Brendon said. "That's progress."

Josh shook his head. "Those two would never have said that. They're huge guys, but they were also raised to be respectful. Not everyone is like Rogers, any more than everyone in the chemistry department is like you." Josh leaned over the table. "Thank goodness, because there's only so much cuteness mixed with deep blue eyes that any department can take." Brendon laughed and blushed slightly. The server brought their orders, and Brendon must have found his appetite because he tucked in right away.

"I guess I didn't realize how hungry I was," he said before taking a second bite of his sandwich.

"Don't eat the plate too," Josh teased, and Brendon paused. Josh waited for a few seconds, and then Brendon seemed to realize he was kidding and went back to eating. Their sandwiches were followed by carrot cake, and then they lingered over a second cup of hot chocolate. Then Josh paid the check, and they left and walked down the main street toward campus. Various students who recognized either of them called out their greetings. As they got farther from the center of campus, the walkways became more and more secluded. Josh took Brendon's hand, and they continued walking.

"I feel better," Brendon admitted. "I'm not any closer to being able to get everything done, but I feel better." Brendon stopped in the path. "Is that weird? I mean, I haven't made any progress, and yet I don't feel as upset about it." Brendon put the back of his hand to his forehead. "I don't think I'm running a fever."

"Sweetheart, just because you aren't as worried about something as you were before doesn't make you weird. Wondering if you have a temperature because you aren't worried—that's weird." Josh couldn't help himself. He had to tease Brendon sometimes. It was just too good to pass up.

"You're joking," Brendon said neutrally.

"Of course I'm joking," Josh said, tugging Brendon into a hug. "I don't think you're weird."

"But you just said…."

"I was joking. Now just let yourself relax, and let's go home. We'll figure things out. I promise."

"I don't understand how we'll do that unless we can slow time for the rest of the world. But that isn't likely, so I'll just have to work harder to get everything done. The kids are always drinking those energy drinks. Maybe I should buy a case the next time I go to the store. If I don't sleep for a week, I should be able to do everything I need to get done." Now it was Josh's turn to gape and wonder if Brendon was serious. Then he smiled, and Josh sighed.

"You're funny," Josh said.

"Yeah, but I had you going," Brendon said in a sort of singsongy way as he grinned from ear to ear. "I still don't know what I'm going to do."

"Come on," Josh said, taking Brendon's arm. He sped up their pace back toward Brendon's house.

"Why are we walking so fast?" Brendon asked as he struggled to keep up, and Josh slowed down a little.

"Because the faster we walk, the sooner I can get you home, and the quicker we'll get upstairs and I can make you forget all about what you need to do." *And then I won't have the urge to get mad at you for obsessing about things you can't change or affect right now anyway.* Josh pushed away the snarky comment.

"Why didn't you say so?" Brendon called as he zoomed around Josh and hurried up the street.

"So that's how it is, huh," Josh said and took off after him. Brendon began to laugh as he too broke into a run. They weren't very far from Brendon's, and Josh caught him in front of the house. Brendon laughed as Josh held him close. Josh loved the way he felt in his arms. "I never want to let you go." Josh buried his face in Brendon's neck, nibbling a little before releasing him. Brendon unlocked the house with shaky hands and stepped inside. He seemed a little wobbly, and Josh smiled. He liked that he could get Brendon off-balance. Once he closed the door, Josh pressed Brendon against the wall, kissing him hard, Brendon's whimpery noises starting immediately. "Close your eyes," Josh said, and Brendon hesitated before complying. "Take off your jacket."

Brendon shrugged his light coat off his shoulders, and Josh draped it over one of the chair backs just around the corner in the living room. "What did I say I was going to do?"

"Make me forget," Brendon answered. Josh lightly pressed him back against the wall.

"Exactly. But you have to keep your eyes closed for me and not move. Okay?" Josh asked, and Brendon hummed his agreement. Josh sank to his knees and pulled open Brendon's belt before opening his pants and tugging them and his shorts to the floor. Brendon's long cock, sleek like the rest of him, bounced toward the ceiling, and Josh smiled before licking the head.

Brendon hissed and jumped slightly. "I'm keeping my eyes closed," he whispered. "But it's hard."

Josh didn't answer, instead nuzzling Brendon's balls with his lips and nose, inhaling his lover's unique scent as he sucked and licked at his skin. Brendon was shaking and filling the hall with whimpers, and when Josh sucked both of Brendon's balls into his mouth, he gave a long, deep groan.

"That's it," Josh said after he'd let Brendon's balls pop from his mouth. Brendon was shaking, standing with his hands splayed against the wall, like he was holding on, but there was nothing to hold onto. "What do you want?" Brendon groaned and swallowed hard. Josh saw his throat working as he stroked up and down Brendon's length. He knew he was teasing him terribly, but he wanted Brendon to get used to vocalizing what he wanted, what he needed. Quite often Josh had to try to figure things out on his own, and with Brendon, that could be quite a challenge sometimes. "You need to tell me."

"I want...." Brendon threw his head back and hit the wall, but he didn't seem to feel it. "I want you to suck me," he whined, like he could hardly get the words to cross his lips. "Please, use your lips on me." Brendon's legs shook with what Josh thought must be excitement.

Josh grinned. He loved seeing Brendon this excited. It meant all the thoughts that wound through Brendon's amazing mind were shutting down and he'd focused all his attention on Josh and what he was doing to Brendon's body. Very few things in Josh's life up until then had been as amazing or as great a turn-on as that idea.

Josh leaned forward and took the head of Brendon's cock between his lips, then ran the skin back and forth over his lips. He knew he wasn't giving Brendon everything he wanted, but his high-pitched groan of anticipation was enough to spur him on. Josh sucked Brendon deeper, sliding his cock along his tongue, Brendon's flavor filling his mouth. Josh closed his eyes and took Brendon as deep as he could, bobbing his head as he did his best to drive Brendon wild. It seemed to work, because Brendon thrust his hips in time to Josh's sucking and continued his steady chorus of small moans that seemed to build on one another.

Josh's own cock throbbed in his pants, and the temptation was huge to take care of himself, but this was for Brendon, and if his plans came to fruition, there would be plenty of time for him. Right now, Josh needed to get Brendon out of his head, and this was the best way he knew.

"Josh!" Brendon cried. "I'm gonna come!"

"Not yet," Josh said after letting Brendon slip from his lips.

"Why?" Brendon asked, barely above a whine.

"Because I want you to wait just a few more minutes," Josh explained, watching as Brendon's cock bobbed and jumped in anticipation. Josh stroked him very slowly, and Brendon moaned. He tried to take himself in hand, but Josh stopped him. "I want you to forget everything but me," Josh said as he rubbed the spot on the underside of Brendon's cock, just below the head. Brendon whimpered and thunked his head on the wall again. "I don't want you to hurt yourself," Josh said, then he sucked Brendon deep into his mouth. He bobbed his head hard, teasing Brendon's skin with his tongue. He knew his lover wasn't going to last much longer, and if what he was hearing was any indication, Josh figured Brendon was approaching the edge very quickly. He pulled off again. "Is this what you want?"

"Yes," Brendon answered shakily, then he swallowed hard. "Please, Josh, no more teasing."

"No. No more teasing," Josh agreed, and then he sucked Brendon back into his mouth. He was determined now to give Brendon the release he craved. When he lifted his gaze, he saw Brendon rolling his head back and forth against the wall, filling the room with nonsense sounds. His legs shook, and Josh hoped Brendon remained upright.

"Josh," Brendon whispered, and then his entire body shook. Within fractions of a second, Brendon came, shooting down Josh's throat with the force of a geyser. Josh swallowed again and again, taking whatever Brendon had to give.

Brendon stilled, breathing like he'd just run a race. Josh let him slip from his lips and stood up, then tugged Brendon into his arms. Brendon seemed almost deadweight, and Josh held him up, cradling him as he kissed and loved on him. "Are you okay?" Josh asked, rubbing Brendon's back under his shirt.

"Yes. My legs don't work, but I'm okay," Brendon told him and then met his gaze with a grin.

"Do you think you can make it upstairs?"

Brendon nodded and then groaned softly when Josh released him. He waited for Brendon to get his balance and pull up his pants before following him up the stairs. Josh grinned, seeing Brendon's butt hanging out of his pants as they reached the top of the stairs. In his bedroom, Brendon kicked off his shoes, then dropped his pants and pulled off his shirt. Josh got his shoes and shirt off as well before taking off his pants. Brendon climbed on the bed, and Josh pounced beside him, setting them both to bouncing. Brendon laughed, and Josh did too as he pulled Brendon into his arms. He loved to hear Brendon happy and, for the moment, worry-free.

Josh pulled Brendon close, sliding against his warm skin, and held him tight, breathing in Brendon's scent as his dick pressed against Brendon's butt. They hadn't discussed anal sex at all, but Brendon seemed to have gotten the idea, because he pressed back against him, moving his butt up and down along Josh's shaft. "I'm not a child, Josh," Brendon whispered. "I know what gay men do, and I know what I want."

"I never said you were, but I didn't want to pressure you," Josh whispered into Brendon's ear before sucking on it. He loved the rich taste of Brendon's skin.

"But I want you," Brendon whispered. "I want to feel you inside me. I want us to be together."

Josh swallowed hard. "I want that too, but I don't have anything with me."

"You mean like condoms?" Brendon asked, and he pulled open the drawer near the bed. "I wasn't sure what kind to get."

Josh lifted his head and stared into the drawer, which held what looked like every kind of condom known to man. "Goodness. If we're together for the next thirty years, we're going to have to work to use all those."

Brendon smacked him lightly on the leg. "Don't exaggerate."

"Okay, I promise," Josh said and rolled Brendon until he was on his back looking up at him. "I love this. You're an incredible man," Josh whispered before kissing Brendon with all the love in his heart. He knew without a doubt he'd fallen hard for Brendon. He'd known that for a while now, but Brendon wasn't particularly forthcoming with his own feelings. Josh figured Brendon showed them in his own way, but he rarely talked about them, and that left Josh wondering.

Pushing his curiosity aside, Josh reached into the drawer and grabbed a condom. He wanted Brendon's first time to be special. "How do you want me?" Josh asked, and Brendon looked a bit bewildered. "It'll be easiest for you if you're on your belly, but then you won't be able to see me."

"Oh," Brendon said. "What do you like?"

"Honey, I want this to be special for you," Josh said, nuzzling Brendon's neck. "This needs to be about what you're comfortable with."

"Then I want to see you," Brendon said. Josh looked in the drawer and found that Brendon had bought all kinds of lubricants too.

"Okay, but roll on your belly for me for now," Josh whispered, and Brendon turned slowly. Josh set the condom and lubricant on the bedside table and closed the drawer. Then he positioned himself between Brendon's legs and leaned forward, running his tongue between Brendon's shoulder blades. "Your skin tastes really good," Josh said as he ran his hands down Brendon's sides. He kissed and licked his way down Brendon's spine to the small of his back. Brendon shivered and ground against the bedding beneath him, thrusting his butt up and down. Josh stroked Brendon's butt, and he moaned. Josh kissed his lower back, licking and sucking, listening to Brendon's moans.

Josh parted Brendon's cheeks and ran his finger lightly down his crack. Brendon gasped, and Josh wetted his finger before lightly teasing the skin around his opening. "Josh," Brendon whined.

"Is this okay?" Josh asked, but all he got for a response was a whimper. Josh teased the skin again and then trailed his tongue down behind it. Brendon cried out something unintelligible and threw his head back when Josh ran his tongue over his opening and then worked the puckered flesh.

"How... what...." Brendon sputtered as Josh probed his opening. Brendon gasped for breath and pressed backward. "Josh," he whined.

"I know," Josh said, and continued licking and sucking until all he heard were low groans that went on and on. Josh loved those sounds and continued eating Brendon out until all he got were whimpers. Brendon held the edge of the mattress in his hands and turned his head to the side, moaning softly. Josh reached to the bedside table and grabbed the lube, then slicked a finger. He teased Brendon's opening and then slowly worked the tip of his finger into Brendon's body. Brendon tensed, gripping Josh's finger with his muscles, and Josh waited until he relaxed before sliding deeper.

Brendon felt like fire around his finger, and once he adjusted, Josh slowly began to move, tilting his finger slightly. "Holy Christ!" Brendon cried, and Josh smiled.

"Found it," he said, gently working his finger over the spot a few more times. Brendon quivered beneath him. Josh added a second finger, trying to relax and stretch Brendon's muscles. The last thing he wanted to do was hurt him in any way, and Josh knew the best way to avoid that was slow, sensual, and careful preparation.

Once he thought Brendon was ready, Josh removed his fingers and slowly rolled Brendon onto his back. He reached for the condom and opened the package, then rolled the condom down his length. "Okay, sweetheart," Josh said, "lift your legs and place your feet on my shoulders. I'll go slowly, and you have to promise you'll tell me if you want me to stop."

"Okay," Brendon agreed, and Josh stroked Brendon's legs as he got into position and pressed to Brendon's opening. At first, he met resistance, and he didn't want to force entry, so he took his time, and then Brendon's body opened to him. Brendon gasped, and Josh stopped.

"Do you want me to stop?" Josh asked. His mind was racing, but he wouldn't hurt Brendon; he cared for him way too much.

"I'm okay, just surprised," Brendon gritted out between his teeth, and Josh slowly pushed forward. His head throbbed as Brendon's body gripped him, surrounding him with heat. It took a long time, but eventually Josh was seated deep in Brendon's body. His cock jumped, and he closed his eyes, reveling in the intimacy of his connection with Brendon. Josh leaned forward, kissing Brendon as deeply and passionately as he could.

"I love you," Josh whispered and slowly began to move. Brendon gasped as Josh withdrew and then moaned as Josh pressed back into his body.

"Jesus," Brendon swore softly.

"I know. It's hard to tell which is better, in or out," Josh told Brendon, and he nodded. "Hopefully they both feel good." He continued thrusting as slowly and as gently as he could. He needed to give Brendon a chance to get used to the movement. Josh wasn't sure how long he could keep up this slow pace—his mind screamed for him to take Brendon and make him his.

"They do," Brendon said, wrapping his arms around Josh's neck. "Yes," he added as Josh snapped his hips. Then he pulled himself closer and brought Josh into a sloppy kiss. "Don't stop. Please don't ever stop."

Josh adjusted the angle of his movements, and Brendon gasped, inhaling sharply. "Okay?" Josh asked.

"Don't you dare fucking stop," Brendon cried and began to shake beneath him. Josh had never heard Brendon talk like that. "Yes, God yes! Right there!" Brendon gripped Josh's shoulders so tightly he knew he was going to have bruises, but he didn't stop or care. "Oh Jesus!" Brendon's cry morphed into a long moan, and then he pressed up against Josh, moving with him as Josh picked up his pace. They rocked together on the bed, bodies entwined, gazes locked. Josh stared deeply into Brendon's deep blue eyes, now clouded with lust and passion.

"You're so beautiful like this," Josh said, watching as Brendon dropped his mouth open. Josh began moving faster, his body driving him. Instinct took over and he gave in to it, letting his heart guide his head.

"Yes, please, just like that," Brendon gasped, holding him tight, like if he released Josh all this might end. Josh had no intention of stopping, not for anything. Brendon was amazing, and soon the room filled with their moans and the soft sound of skin on skin. Josh stroked Brendon's side and then trailed his hands down his belly, gripped his cock, and began stroking Brendon as he continued thrusting deep and hard. Sweat beaded on Josh's chest and then dripped down his stomach as he saw beads of moisture rising on Brendon's skin. Josh wasn't sure how much longer he could keep up this pace or keep his release at bay. It had been building for a while.

"Brendon, I'm…," Josh gasped, trying to keep himself together.

"Me too," Brendon cried. His cock jumped in Josh's hand and then Brendon started coming, shooting over Josh's hand and onto his chest. Brendon's cries and the tightening of his muscles pushed Josh over the edge and he came in a blinding flash, filling the condom before collapsing on top of Brendon.

It took him a few minutes to realize he was probably crushing Brendon. Their bodies separated, and Josh rolled onto the mattress. "Did I hurt you?"

"No," Brendon whispered.

"I didn't mean to squish you," Josh said as he pulled off the condom, tied it, and then dropped it in the trash. "I'll be right back," Josh said as he climbed off the bed and hurried to the bathroom. He wetted a cloth and grabbed a towel before returning to the bed. Brendon hadn't moved. His eyes were closed and he almost looked like he'd gone to sleep, but Josh knew he hadn't. Brendon's thoughts and concerns were starting up again—Josh could see it in the small lines near his mouth. "Come on, sweetheart, don't worry about things now." Josh washed Brendon's skin and then gently dried him off before returning the supplies to the bathroom.

When he came back to bed, Brendon was still staring at the ceiling. Josh got between the covers and tugged Brendon into a tight hug, refusing to let him go. "Try to get some rest. There's nothing you can do tonight, and everything will seem better after a good night's sleep. At least that's what my grandmother used to say when I was a kid." He loved holding Brendon more than anything else in the world, even more than the sex, which Brendon made so amazing with his wide-eyed innocence and energy. But it was the quiet afterward, with Brendon in his arms, that he loved more than anything else. "Do you know how incredible you are?" Josh asked, and Brendon slowly turned his head until their gazes met.

"I'm nothing special, at least not outside the classroom," Brendon countered.

"Hey. You're very special, and I don't mean because of what you can do up here." Josh lightly tapped the side of Brendon's head. "You have a gentle heart, one without guile or deception. You don't play games and you don't lie."

"But people take advantage of that," Brendon said, "and it makes me feel weak and stupid."

"You aren't stupid, and as for those who try to take advantage, they'll get theirs in the end." Josh squeezed Brendon a little tighter. "I hate hearing someone would treat you like that."

"I can take care of myself," Brendon said. "I'm not a child."

Josh waited for Brendon to roll over. "I know that," Josh whispered, but it was the tension he felt building in Brendon's body that really concerned him. Nungesser had put that tension there, and Josh hated it. He held Brendon until he fell asleep and then lay awake for hours, wondering how he could help.

Chapter Five

BRENDON TOOK a deep breath, inhaling the familiar, clean, slightly chemical scent of his new lab. He'd ordered in all the equipment and supplies he couldn't requisition from what the department already had. Of course Nungesser had been the world's biggest pain in the ass, and Brendon had had to do the paperwork over twice because of some picky item Nungesser wanted. Brendon now knew for sure that the man was being petty and throwing up as many ridiculous roadblocks as possible. It had taken time for everything to arrive, and he was still waiting for a few things, but he wouldn't need them until later in his research. For now, he had everything he thought he needed to equip his small lab, and he could finally get to work. Brendon was anxious to start. All his notes were prepared. His methodologies and protocols were set, written, and ready to be published along with his results.

He checked the clock and sighed softly. He really wanted to get to work right now, but he had a class to teach and he didn't want to be late. So, reluctantly, he gathered his things and took a last glance at his pristine lab before closing and locking the door. Then he hurried to his office, grabbed his materials, and headed for class.

"Hey, Prof," Connie, one of his students, said as she took her place. Brendon stopped in the aisle next to her seat. "Are you excited about the charity display? I hear engineering has theirs done already."

"We'll be ready in time," Brendon assured her. He would get access to the room right after class, and while he only had two days to set up, he had a plan to get everything done before the display had to be open.

"I was just in the room, and it's empty," she said, and Brendon wondered what was going on. "According to the campus website, the judging is tomorrow morning." Brendon's mouth went dry. She had to be wrong. "If you need help, please let me know."

"Thank you," Brendon said, his mind running in a million directions as his heart pounded. Nungesser had given him all the dates… that bastard. Brendon looked around the room to make sure he hadn't actually sworn out loud. That would just get him into more trouble. "I'll need to get everything from storage after class." Brendon tried to keep his racing thoughts together as he searched through his memory for what he might have missed. He had to get started as soon as he could....

"Are you okay, Professor?" she asked, and Brendon snapped out of his worries, forcing his attention back to the present. He told himself not to panic.

"It seems I was given some incorrect information." *On a number of fronts.* "I'll need all the help I can get." He didn't know what he was going to do, except work all night if he had to in order to get the display to the point where he didn't embarrass himself or the department.

"Then I'll see you later," she said happily, and Brendon continued to the front of the room. After a bit of uncharacteristic fumbling, he got his materials for class up and running.

The lecture had none of his usual energy. Brendon's mind was running in too many directions, but he got through the material and did his best to keep his concentration on his students and away from the daunting task of setting up a complicated display in a matter of hours. He had planned on getting the most sensitive pieces of the display set up today, with volunteers set to come in tomorrow to help with the rest. He'd had a lot of people interested in helping, but he'd told them to come in tomorrow. At the end of his lecture, Brendon put out a call for anyone willing to help to meet in the display room in an hour. He figured it would take that much time for him to get the basic design laid out in the room.

Brendon hurried back to his office and found Nungesser waiting for him. He should have known.

"Cutting it close, aren't you?" Nungesser said in the hallway without waiting for Brendon to open his office. Brendon unlocked the door and stepped inside. He didn't have time for him right now. "I knew you were all talk and no action," Nungesser said as soon as Brendon closed the door.

Brendon whipped around as intense anger built inside. "You bullied and badgered me to do this, and then you didn't give me the correct information. I never did anything to you, and you've done your best to undermine my work. Yes, I think this whole Halloween Charity display contest is a waste of energy, but it's for charity and I agreed to do it. But you have lied and withheld information on purpose. For what? What could be so important that you want the entire department to look bad?" Brendon saw something in Nungesser's expression, but he didn't understand what it was. "I've been here not quite two years, and you've gone out of your way to make me feel unwelcome and unwanted. Why? What did I ever do to you?" Brendon set his materials on his desk. "All I ever wanted was to teach and do good science. I don't want to be department head. I don't want anyone's job." Brendon knew he was almost pleading, but he needed an answer. He didn't understand Nungesser at all. He waited for some sort of answer, but it became apparent he wasn't going to get one.

"You should have verified all information to make sure you knew when everything was happening," Nungesser finally said. "I may have been mistaken about some of the details, but you should have verified them." He reached for the doorknob. "I see you got your lab set up…. Maybe you'll actually get a chance to use it, if you're lucky." Nungesser pulled open the door and left the office as Brendon sank into his chair. Maybe he should start looking for another position. He'd thought Dickinson would be perfect. It was located in his hometown and he could live in his house, but maybe it wasn't worth it. Maybe he could find someplace where he'd fit in better.

His phone rang, pulling Brendon out of his pity party. "Hello," he said after snatching it off his desk.

"Brendon, what's wrong?" Josh asked.

He told Josh what had happened. "He told me the wrong information on purpose," Brendon said. He heard Josh swear. "I'm going to have to work until they kick me out of the building in order to get something together. I need to cancel our dinner for tonight." Brendon checked the clock and then stood up, gathering his keys so he could start assembling the things for the room that he'd already gotten together. "I better go so I can at least try to not make a fool of myself." Brendon hung up and left his office. He unlocked the small storage room where he'd put the supplies he'd gathered for his display and then retrieved one of the service carts. He began loading the supplies and wheeled them through the hall to the old science lab. The room designated for the display was in the old section of the building, which was scheduled for renovation next year. It was perfect for what he had in mind.

Brendon unloaded the supplies and then made two more trips. He hoped some of his students showed up to help. Regardless, Brendon got to work—he had a lot to do.

His NERVOUSNESS kept his energy up for a while. A few students showed up from his class, and they managed to get a ladder from building services and switch out the light bulbs in the room. Brendon had realized very quickly that the key to his display was managing light. Marie Curie discovered radium, which glowed in the dark. So he needed to control the lighting closely if his effect was going to work. Next he put the students to work blacking out all the windows with dark curtains over the existing shades. Unfortunately, once that was done, the kids had to leave for class and Brendon was on his own. There was so much to do he wasn't quite sure where to start. A few of the other professors stopped by to "help," but all they did was offer suggestions and talk over options with one another rather than actually doing anything useful. Dr. Hanlon actually spent two hours arranging the laboratory glassware in one of the cabinets before stepping back and deciding he didn't like it. Thankfully, he had to teach a class, so Brendon was spared another two hours of his ruminations that led nowhere.

By the end of the afternoon, Brendon had gotten the holographic projector in place, but that was about all. The room was filled with half-completed projects, and there were still a number of things that hadn't been started, including the luminous arrows that needed to be painted on the floor to direct people through the room, and the replicas of the infamous notebooks, which in real life were still too radioactive to touch, which had to glow as well. He figured the arrows could be painted last, just before leaving the room, but he couldn't find the template he'd made for them.

"Hey, sweetheart, how's it coming?" Josh said as he entered the room. Brendon stopped what he was doing and rushed to him.

"It sucks. There's no way I'm going to get this done without help, and it doesn't look like I'm going to get much of that." Brendon held onto Josh, resting his head on his chest. He wanted to cry, but he was too angry and pissed off at Nungesser for that. He'd probably cry like a baby once he'd actually failed, but until then, fear and disgust were keeping him going. To his surprise Josh didn't return his hug and actually moved away. Brendon was crushed. "Not you too," he whispered.

"Hey, Coach, what do you want us to do?" a huge man asked as he entered the room, followed by others.

"I brought you some help," Josh told him with a grin. "You need to tell them what to work on." Brendon gaped as eight huge guys, most in sweats and T-shirts, filed into the room. "They have a few hours they can give you before curfew, so let's get going."

"Okay," Brendon said, a bit stunned. Then he shook it off. "Start with those boxes," Brendon said, pointing to large lead-lined cases.

"They weigh a ton. They're some medical products that were made with radium. They mixed radium into the ceramic glaze, and drinking out of them was supposed to have healing properties. They aren't really dangerous, but use gloves anyway. Put the jars in the cabinets with the glassware. They should make everything glow."

"Is anything in here really radioactive?" one of the men asked.

"Other than those jars and the dials on your watches, no. The jars are very weak, but there are regulations about prolonged exposure. Overreaction, but we'll play nice."

"Okay," the man said, and then they all got to work wheeling the heavy boxes to where they were going to be setting up.

Brendon put some of the guys to work building the "decontamination area," and he gave a couple of others phosphorescent paint to start making some of the everyday objects glow. Once he had everyone busy, he and Josh worked to set up the fake Geiger counters that everyone would pass through when they went to leave.

"I can finish this," Josh said with a smile once Brendon had explained how the equipment worked.

"Thanks," Brendon said and wandered around the room.

"What else do you need?" one of the men asked in an amazingly rich voice as he stood in front of the large cabinet of glassware. That portion of the room was already dark enough that Brendon could see the glow emanating from the objects.

"You can put up the radiation signs, but I have some gel to coat them with so they'll glow." Brendon fished around in a box until he found the gel and then handed it to a football player.

"What about me?" Mr. Deep Voice asked.

"I need a narrator, and you'll be perfect," Brendon said. "What's your name?"

"Ethan," the big guy rumbled.

Brendon sorted through his notes until he found the script. He had planned to record the script himself, but hearing this guy's deep voice set his mind racing. Brendon led him into a quiet room. "All you need to do is read this. Don't rush, and you can have as many tries as you want." Brendon set up a microphone on top of his computer. "This starts it, and this stops," he said, pointing to the corresponding controls. "Just read it through a few times out loud and then record yourself. When you're happy with it, let me know and we'll listen together. Okay?"

"Sure, Prof, I can do that," he said. Brendon expected him to be nervous, because Brendon knew he himself hadn't been looking forward to doing the narration, but Ethan seemed comfortable with it, and as Brendon left, he heard him reading through the script with comparative ease.

"Ethan's a ham, he'll do just fine," Josh told him when he returned to the room. Work was going on everywhere. "In ten minutes we're going to douse the lights so the professor can see what else needs to be done," Josh called through the room, and everyone seemed to pick up the pace. Brendon continued working on the "radioactive" lab books. He wanted the holographic Marie to lean over her glowing notebooks like she was working on them. He got them in place just as the others finished up their tasks. Brendon turned on the projector and stepped back.

"Turn out the lights, Josh," he said, and everyone stilled. The lights went out, and then Josh turned on the black lights they'd installed in some of the fixtures. The cabinets and signs glowed, as did the notebooks. Everyone moved slowly toward the entrance as the holographic figure leaned silently, spectrally, over the lab table.

"God, that's creepy," one of the guys whispered, and Brendon smiled. That was exactly the effect he'd hoped for. After a few seconds, the figure turned and disappeared. Thirty seconds later she was back, leaning over the notebooks. Brendon had placed them in almost the right spot. He walked over, adjusted the notebooks just a bit, and then stepped back. "She really looks like she's writing," one of the guys whispered. It was perfect. No one talked out loud—everything was in a whisper, like they didn't want to disturb her work.

"Turn on the lights," Brendon whispered. Even he was speaking in hushed tones, and it was all his illusion. The lights came on, and Brendon blinked.

"The guys don't have much time," Josh said. "They need to get back to their rooms in half an hour."

"We're almost done with the decontamination chamber. We just need to hang the lights," one of the men said as they went back to work. Ethan returned and handed Brendon the laptop and microphone.

"Okay," Brendon said, running through the list of things in his head. "Let's paint the arrows on the floor, but just the outlines. That way we won't overuse the effect." The men got to work. They'd been able to make three templates, and the painting went rather quickly. Brendon knew most of the glow paint would wear off as people walked through, and what didn't wouldn't really matter—the room was being remodeled anyway.

By the time the half hour was up, the painting was done and the room was almost ready. There were still a few things that had to be finished, but Brendon needed to set those up. "Thank you all so much," Brendon said to each of the men, shaking their hands as they left. "You were all an amazing help." They fist-bumped with him and smiled as they left the room. Brendon heard them talking and laughing as they left.

"What else do you need to do?" Josh asked with a yawn.

Brendon opened one of the lab drawers and pulled out a Bunsen burner. "Get one of the large flasks from the cart," he told Josh as he worked to set up a stand. He placed the flask on it and filled it with the solution he'd set aside. Then he added the stopper and a coil of tubing that wound its way around spectacularly. "When I start the burner, the liquid will boil slowly and the steam will rise into the tubing. Then the liquid will cool and condense, and after winding through all the tubing, end up back in the flask. Those are small check valves to make sure the liquid only goes the way I want. It'll make a show, but not go anywhere, and the solution should glow, so it'll look good." He lit the burner, and they waited a bit for it to start boiling. While they did, Brendon checked out the Geiger counters as well as the recording. It was perfect. Brendon transferred it to a flash drive and loaded it into the sound system he'd set up. Like the hologram, it would play and then pause thirty seconds before playing again.

"Are you up for the entire effect?" Josh asked, and Brendon nodded. He set up everything and made sure it was all on before turning out the lights. Then they wandered along the path.

The recording sounded in Ethan's deep voice: "Dr. Curie was a pioneer who discovered radium and developed many of the protocols we use today." The holographic Marie Curie leaned over her notebooks. "However, the effects of radiation were not known, and even today her notebooks are too radioactive to handle." As they passed the Geiger counters, the devices began to click, and they headed to the decontamination chamber, where lights flashed and fog descended around them. The effect was eerily amazing and exactly what he'd been going for.

"Are you ready to go?" Josh asked.

"Almost," Brendon said as he walked back toward the main room. The solution was bubbling away in the flask, making interesting, glowing steam as it wound its way through the tubing. "Perfect," he said and then turned off the Bunsen burner. "I'm almost afraid to leave," Brendon commented, stepping around the painted arrows. He turned off the various pieces of equipment, and the room glowed with the phosphorescent paint. "I'm afraid that Nungesser will try to sabotage me." Brendon knew he was probably being ridiculous, but he was so unnerved by the department head, he wouldn't put anything past him right now.

"It's going to be fine. Your lab is set up and the display is amazing. It's almost chilling, and the way you have the narration turned low, it adds to the ghostly effect. The whole thing is worthy of Disney." Josh hugged him, and Brendon closed his eyes. He couldn't believe he'd somehow pulled it off… they'd pulled it off.

"I never could have done this without you," Brendon said, and he tilted his face upward. Josh looked green in the ghostly glow, and Brendon smiled. In that second, in the near dark with the eerie glow of phosphorescent paint, he knew what he felt. "I haven't understood much of what I've been feeling these past few weeks." Brendon closed his eyes as Josh kissed him. "I'm not a person who deals with feelings well. I have them, but I don't understand them, so I try to keep my mind on things I do understand, things I can feel and see. But I understand something that I didn't before, something I can't see, touch, or hear, but it's real because I feel it, and now I know what it is." Brendon swallowed hard, then said, "I love you, Josh." He rested his head on Josh's shoulder. "I look forward to seeing you, and my day isn't complete without you in it. When you're not around, I wish you were." Josh held him tighter.

"Let's lock up and go home," Josh whispered, and Brendon nodded. He pulled out of the hug and followed Josh out into the darkened hallway.

"We'll need to be here early in the morning so the paint can sort of recharge in the light," Brendon said as he pulled the door closed, then checked it was locked and that he had a key.

"Don't worry. I'll make sure you get here in plenty of time for the judging, and I want to see the look on Nungesser's face when he sees what you did. It's amazing," Josh said, putting his arm around Brendon's waist as they walked toward the exit.

Brendon had walked to work that morning, and Josh had driven, so they walked to Josh's car, the cool fall breeze whipping the dry leaves around. The campus was bathed in the light from dozens of decorative fixtures shining on the trees and paths. In the quiet of the late evening, it made for a romantic sight, especially with Josh holding him close.

This was what he wanted. He hadn't even known what was missing from his life until he'd found it, and now his greatest fear wasn't Nungesser, the charity display, or even his research—it was not having Josh in his life.

"So will you be able to start your research now that this charity thing is over?"

"Yes. But I'm going to take my time. The research will still be there next week and next month." Brendon leaned his head on Josh's shoulder.

"Why the change?" Josh asked.

Maybe Brendon was becoming more attuned to Josh, but he could have sworn he heard trepidation in his voice. He could have been wrong, though.

"Life is about priorities. When I was young, my priorities were school, homework, studying, and any research I was doing. If I got caught up, I could do fun things like read the various journals I got. I was in college when most kids were out playing and having fun. Then I got a master's and a doctorate."

Josh stopped walking. "What are you saying?"

"That, maybe, my research won't be the most important thing. That you're the most important—we're more important." Brendon hoped that he was saying what he meant to. "Yes, I enjoy my work, and I'm not going to stop, but I want to have some time to go on a picnic or maybe ride a horse."

Josh chuckled. "You certainly picked the wrong time of year, but I understand what you mean. You need a chance to live a little."

"Yeah," Brendon said softly. "I want to see and do things, and I want to do them with you."

"Me too."

They reached Josh's car, and Brendon got in the passenger seat for the short ride to his house. Josh drove to Brendon's house, parked around the back because there were no empty places in front, and they walked through the garden to the back door. Once inside, Josh began going through his refrigerator. "We both need something to eat," he said. "But your cupboard is bare, Mr. Hubbard." Brendon wondered what Josh was talking about and was about to ask him to explain when Josh said, "Never mind. Tomorrow night we'll go to the grocery store."

Brendon had vegetables, and Josh began pulling them out, probably to make a salad. "I've been thinking about getting a dog," Brendon said.

"Where did that come from?" Josh asked as he pulled out the cutting board. "I think it's a great idea, but you've never mentioned it before."

"I always wanted one as a kid, but I was too busy. I want to get a dog. Do you think I could get one from a shelter or something? A nice dog that needs a home." Brendon left the kitchen. "I want to change out the furniture too." Everything had been his parents' and it seemed to Brendon like he was seeing his own house for the first time. He desperately needed to do something with the house to make it feel more his and less like his parents'.

"How about you come and eat first, before you fall down," Josh told him, and Brendon returned to the kitchen.

"Are you mad?"

"No," Josh said. "I was scolding you, but I meant it as good-natured scolding. You probably haven't eaten since breakfast this morning, and it's almost ten o'clock. You need to eat and take care of yourself, because I worry about you." Josh handed him a huge bowl of greens with all kinds of vegetables and lunch meats cut up in it. "It's the best chef's salad I could come up with."

Brendon followed Josh into the living room, and they ate quietly, sitting on the sofa. As soon as he'd eaten the last bite, exhaustion caught up with him, and Brendon could hardly keep his eyes open. Josh carried away the dishes. When he returned, he turned out the lights and then nudged Brendon up the stairs. Brendon cleaned up and got undressed, then fell into bed. He remembered Josh getting in next to him, holding him close, his warmth surrounding him, and that was all.

"BRENDON." JOSH'S voice invaded his dream, making it better. "We need to get up." Brendon opened his eyes and yawned. The last thing he wanted to do was get out of bed. He was still so tired, and his legs didn't want to move, but he got up anyway and shuffled to the bathroom. After cleaning up and a hot shower, he dressed and found Josh downstairs with a small breakfast ready. They ate fast and then headed out through the garden to Josh's car.

On the drive over, Brendon was a nervous wreck. He kept envisioning that someone had gotten into the room and messed up all their hard work, but when he and Josh arrived outside, nothing had been disturbed. Brendon unlocked the door and turned on the lights that hadn't been blacked out. Then he turned them off again and swore. "What is it?"

"I forgot about the light through the doorway. Granted, people aren't going to be coming in this way, but we need the room as dark as possible."

"I'll get something to darken the window. You make sure everything is set up and working. How much time do we have?" Josh was already moving.

"Less than an hour," Brendon said as he walked through the room, making sure the blackout curtains were all set and in place. He adjusted them until the last bits of light were gone. Then he got all the equipment turned on. The Geiger counters were working, as was the hologram. Brendon then left the lights on so the glowing elements could charge. Everything was almost perfect.

"It doesn't look like much," Nungesser said from the doorway, and Brendon gritted his teeth, watching as Nungesser wandered through the room.

"Please don't touch things," Brendon said when Nungesser reached for the notebooks on the table. "Everything is exactly where it needs to be."

"This is going to be a complete failure," Nungesser said. "The room looks like any lab in any old building in the country. Other than the radiation signs and the clicking fake Geiger counters, you could be anywhere." Nungesser stepped closer. "And you painted on the floor? What a mess. This is going to be a complete failure." Brendon could hear the pleasure in Nungesser's voice. "I see you got your lab set up. That's good," Nungesser said. "Maybe your replacement can use it," he whispered. Brendon swallowed hard.

"You haven't even seen the whole thing yet," Brendon said levelly.

"What's to see?" Nungesser countered loudly. "There's nothing here. The committee, including the dean and board members, will be through to judge this monstrosity, and they'll see you can't do anything!" Nungesser turned and then stopped. Brendon followed Nungesser's gaze and saw the dean of the School of Sciences standing in the doorway.

"What's all this about?" the dean asked as he stepped into the room to look around, with Josh not far behind him. Josh began putting black paper on the windows as the dean approached Brendon. "I have to agree with Dr. Nungesser. This doesn't look like much," he said quietly. "I came by to see the chemistry department's entry, and I must say…."

Brendon swallowed. "Then let me show you everything," he said softly, barely able to speak. Brendon directed the two men to the next classroom. "Everyone will enter through the adjoining room," he explained.

"Give me just a minute," he added, and then he hurried to complete the final details. He made sure everything was turned on. Josh had finished with the door, and he closed it. They turned out the lights and the room glowed eerily. The arrows showed the way, the radiation signs glowed their silent yellow warning, the chemicals bubbled and smoked through the glass tubing, and the cabinets glowed an eerie green, as did the notebooks. Brendon turned on the sound and then carefully opened the door to the other room.

He said nothing and let the whispered narration guide them. Brendon saw both Nungesser and the dean jump when the holographic figure bent over the notebooks and then disappeared. The two men passed the Geiger counters, which began to click since they'd passed the "radioactive notebooks." The sign next to them pointed to "Decontamination" in the same eerie green glow as the books. They entered the decontamination chamber and the lights flashed and Brendon heard the mist hiss as they went by. Brendon turned on the lights, and instantly all the magic disappeared, turning the room into a seemingly normal lab.

Brendon waited, expecting them to come back in, but nothing happened. Then a soft knock sounded on the door. Brendon opened it to see the dean, alone.

"I apologize, Brendon. You did an amazing job—fun, scary, and educational at the same time."

"Where's Dr. Nungesser?" Brendon asked.

"He went back to his office," the dean said, and Brendon nodded. "There isn't much that escapes my notice," the dean added. "Keep up the good work, and I'm very interested to hear about this research of yours." He turned to leave but then stopped. "And remember, I was the one who hired you, not Nungesser, and I'm very interested in your work and believe you'll do great things for yourself and this institution. I wouldn't have hired you if I didn't." Then he turned and left the room, leaving Brendon to stare after him.

"What did that mean?" Brendon asked as he turned to Josh, who was grinning at him. "You look like you just ate the canary."

"The cat that ate the canary," Josh corrected with a smile that touched Brendon's heart. "And to answer your question, I believe he just said Nungesser won't be bothering you any longer and he wants you to get to work and not worry about the butthead." Josh looked toward the door and then back to him. "He has faith in you and knows you'll do good work, so go ahead and do it. I wouldn't be surprised if the chemistry department has a new department head fairly soon."

Brendon couldn't help smiling. He liked the sound of that. "I think you need to get to the athletic center, and I need to get this set up for the committee and then the paying guests."

"You do realize it's Thursday," Josh said, and Brendon looked around. "I do have a practice in a few hours, but until then I'm all yours, so let's get this ready for judging and to make some money to stop breast cancer." Josh grinned and then tugged him into a quick hug. Then they separated and got to work. Brendon put the sound and the hologram on a regular timed loop and then made a final check of everything. Some students showed up to help man the room, and he explained how everything worked and stationed them at the entrance and exit. When Brendon heard footsteps in the hallway, he peeked out the door and saw people who he thought must be the judges, so he flipped off the lights and set everything in motion.

"Isn't it funny how the room comes alive when you turn off the lights?" Josh whispered in his ear, as Brendon sat on a stool partially blocked by one of the cabinets and waited. "I'll see you after practice," Josh told him, and Brendon watched as he left. Seconds later, he heard people talking, but they immediately hushed as they entered. The quiet narration began, and the visitors followed the glowing arrows around the room, starting in surprise when the hologram moved silently to the notebooks. "Marie Curie's notebooks are still too dangerously radioactive to be handled, even after almost a century." The judges whispered to each other, and Brendon could hear the chill in their voices. The Geiger counters went off as they should, and then the guests left for decontamination. It was perfect, and Brendon smiled as he realized he'd truly done what he'd set out to do.

The judges were followed by people who had paid to see each of the departmental displays as a fundraiser. Brendon stayed in the room for a while to make sure everything was going okay and then slipped out between groups. He had one of the students take his place to watch over things and then headed to his office for a few minutes. He'd really done it. Well, actually he and Josh had really done it, because the room wouldn't have come together if it weren't for Josh and his team. After a few minutes of quiet, Brendon wandered back to where a line had formed to tour the room. It seemed word had gotten around.

BRENDON SPENT the rest of the morning and part of the afternoon watching over the room and checking on things to make sure everything was still running smoothly. During a lull, he had the students turn on the lights for a bit to make sure everything retained its glow. By the end of the day, he was exhausted and very satisfied. After the last group left, Brendon began removing the important equipment from the room and then turned everything else off. The rest of the display could be taken down later.

"Is it over?" Josh asked as he came up behind him.

"Yes. It was a huge success," Brendon said as he placed the holographic projector in its case. Then he gathered the important pieces from the room and placed them on a cart before locking everything up. "I think once this is put away, I'm ready to go home." They walked down the now quiet halls together and then outside into the bright, crisp fall afternoon. Instead of going straight to Josh's car, they wandered the paths through campus. Leaves fell from the trees and littered the path. The distinctive red Adirondack chairs that were the campus icons had been gathered into groups and were filled with students enjoying some of the last nice days before winter.

"I love you, Brendon," Josh told him as they walked.

"I love you too, and I'm sorry it took me so long to realize it." Brendon moved closer. "Things wouldn't have worked out like they did if it weren't for you, and I'd still have Nungesser on my butt." Brendon held Josh's arm. "Do you think we can go home now, so I can thank you properly?" Brendon smiled in what he hoped was a suggestive way, and they slowly walked back toward the car.

When Josh pulled up in front of the house, Brendon didn't move to get out.

"Are you waiting for something?" Josh asked.

"No. I was just thinking. I've lived more in the past few weeks than I ever have in my life, and I don't want that to end. I know you said you were my boyfriend, but I want you to be my forever boyfriend." He hoped he was saying it right.

Josh leaned across the seat. "I am your forever boyfriend, and you're mine. I knew that after our first date."

"Then how come I didn't know?" Brendon asked, and Josh enfolded him into his arms.

"Because sometimes you aren't the smartest man in the room, or even the car," Josh whispered in his ear, and Brendon moaned softly. He could definitely live with that.

ANDREW GREY

BIOCHEMISTRY

To Alix B.
Because she's as much fun as this story.

Chapter 1

"Isn't it a little early to be leaving for class?" Peter said, yawning as he padded through the dorm room wearing nothing but a towel on his skinny hips.

Peter looked a bit like a bean pole in a skirt, but Kurt didn't say anything like that. He'd only met Peter a few days earlier, when they'd moved in to the junior dorm. Kurt had managed a transfer to Dickinson College in Carlisle, PA, from Shippensburg after the end of his sophomore year, and he was both excited and terrified by his new school. Academically, Dickinson was a definite step up for him, and Kurt hoped he had what it took to make the cut. He'd never failed before, though, and he didn't intend to begin now.

"I need to find my way around, so I thought I'd wander before class." Kurt packed his books and laptop in his new Swiss Gear backpack, a gift from his dad, and got ready to leave.

"I forget you're new here," Peter said as he stood in the corner facing the wall and began to dress. Kurt looked away to give Peter some privacy, but he could still see his skinny white butt in the mirror that hung behind the door. "Head north through the quad and keep going. When you cross the street, you can't miss the science building. Just look for the iridescent blue and purple tiles on the building." Peter pulled on a pair of jeans and then rummaged for a shirt. "You have nothing to worry about."

Peter had told him that he and his roommate from the year before had planned to room together this year too, but Peter's former roommate had had to transfer away because his family could no longer afford the tuition. Kurt's situation was just the opposite. He'd originally been accepted to Dickinson as a freshman, but his folks hadn't been able to afford it and he hadn't thought the student-loan debt was worth it. He'd instead gone to Shippensburg, worked really hard, and gotten top grades. He'd then applied as a junior, and not only had he gotten in, but he'd been awarded a scholarship on top of some financial aid. But his scholarship came with GPA strings attached, though he intended to blow past every single one of them. He and Peter seemed to get along okay so far. Kurt had been nervous initially, afraid he'd get some fundamental 'phobe for a roommate. He'd been lucky. He'd already met some of Peter's friends, two of whom were gay, so his own coming out had been cool and no big deal.

"Text me when you're done with class, and we can meet up for lunch," Peter said.

"Cool, I'll do that," Kurt said and then pulled open the door and left the room. He hurried down the stairs, pushed the outside door open, and stepped into the early fall sunshine. He smiled as he walked across the campus, passing groups of students hurrying to class or gathering in groups and sitting in the big red Adirondack chairs spread throughout the campus lawns.

Two guys in football jerseys walking side by side approached from the opposite direction. Kurt moved to one side of the walk and continued on. As they approached, they seemed oblivious to him, and the one closest to Kurt bumped him with his shoulder as he passed. Kurt's feet nearly went out from under him in the dewy grass. He managed to stop himself, but not before he twisted his ankle slightly.

"Watch where you're walking, Short Stuff," the guy called back. He then turned to his friend, and they laughed as they continued on.

"Are you okay?" a girl asked as she hurried up to him. "I saw the whole thing and I'll be a witness if you need one," she added seriously. "I'm Cathy. Prelaw."

"I guessed that. The prelaw part, not the Cathy. And I'm all right, thanks." His ankle hurt a little, but he'd be fine. His mother had sent him with a first-aid kit that would have every doctor's office in four counties green with envy. She was a hypochondriac and liked to project her tendencies onto her only child. "Thank you." He made sure he still had all his stuff.

"Where are you headed?" Cathy asked with a huge smile.

"I have a biochemistry class in the science building. This is my first term here, so I'm still learning my way around." He brushed off his pants. "Where are you going?"

"Calculus class," she answered and pointed to one of the older buildings. "I'll see you around," she said with a smile and then headed off, and Kurt made his way, definitely a bit more slowly, toward the science building. He found it easily enough and climbed the stairs to the room indicated on his schedule. He'd been expecting a lecture hall, but his room turned out to be a normal-sized classroom with rows of long, curving tables and chairs. He took a seat and began pulling out his things for class.

Other students began to arrive, and the room filled quickly. Of course, he didn't know anyone, but he smiled at the girl who sat on one side of him. She smiled back and began getting ready for class. The students quieted when the door opened at the front of the room and a teaching assistant approached the podium.

"Good morning. I'm Professor Brendon Marcus." Kurt looked around to see if this was a joke, but the other students didn't react. "This is Introduction to Biochemistry, and we're going to be exploring the chemistry of life." He passed a stack of papers to one of the girls in the first row. "The syllabus is coming around. It includes the reading lists as well as required experiments, field work, and term-paper requirements." The professor turned toward Kurt as he talked, and Kurt's heart missed a beat. He was adorably beautiful, with incredible blue eyes. Kurt looked away and admonished himself.

The syllabus had just reached him when the back door opened and someone came in. The guy came down the row and took the seat next to Kurt, so Kurt grabbed an extra copy of the syllabus and handed it to him. It was the guy who'd knocked him off the sidewalk.

"Hey, Short Stuff," the huge guy whispered as he took the stapled pages. Kurt looked around exaggeratedly. "What's going on?"

"Nothing," Kurt said, turning toward the football player. "Just making sure this isn't *Planet of the Apes*." Then he turned and faced forward with a slight smile as the professor continued with his introduction and then went into his first lecture.

Kurt took notes and did his best to ignore the guy next to him. As soon as class was over, Kurt gathered his things and made for the exit well ahead of the lumbering ape with no manners. He zipped down the hall to the lab. There were two lab periods for the class, and the one directly after class fit his schedule. He got out his workbook and a notebook. Then he pulled his lab coat out of his bag and put it on.

Dr. Marcus came in a few minutes later. "Many professors have assistants who conduct their labs. I don't." The door opened at the back of the room. "It's good of you to join us, Mr. Samuelson," the professor said. "Now let's get started." Kurt turned and groaned inwardly as the ape stood at the station next to his. "Pair off into teams quickly." No one moved, and Kurt groaned.

"Looks like it's you and me, Short Stuff," the ape said with a smile that Kurt wanted to smack off his face.

"Fine," Kurt said and turned away to pay attention to the professor. He couldn't do anything about his lab partner, but he'd make sure his work was correct and complete no matter what.

The lab was almost a disaster not once, but three times. They had to work together, but Ape Boy seemed more interested in everything around him than the lab work, and when Kurt needed an extra set of hands, Ape Boy almost poured the solution in too quickly. Only Kurt turning the stopper in the nick of time prevented them from having to start all over. By the end of the period, Kurt had his results and had taken all the notes he needed for the write-up. He cleaned up their station. "You didn't take any notes," Kurt said to his partner. "How will you be able to do your write-up?"

"I'll use your notes, Short Stuff."

"I don't think so, Ape Boy," Kurt said. He finished putting the last of his papers in his bag and headed out of the room. If he was lucky, maybe the guy would drop the class. Kurt would be better off doing everything alone. The bell rang, and Kurt hurried to his next class. It had to be better than the one he'd just left.

After two more classes, he texted Peter and got a response to meet him in the student union. Kurt walked over slowly. His ankle had started to ache a little by the time he arrived at the union dining hall. He found Peter and sat down to check his ankle. It didn't appear swollen, and he figured after lunch he could probably go back to the room to wrap it before his next class.

"What happened?" Jamie, Peter's cute blond friend, asked and then turned when his boyfriend Luka sat down next to him. They scooched close to one another, and then Jamie looked across the table. "You were limping."

"Some ape guy refused to move over on the walk, and I ended up on the wet grass and twisted my ankle a little. It's no big deal." Kurt set his bag near his feet. "The thing is, the ape's in my biochemistry class and I ended up with him as my lab partner." The others all began to laugh. "It's not funny. He didn't bother to take notes, and when I asked him about it, he said he'd just use mine. Like that's going to happen. He's some dumb football player, and if he thinks he's coasting on my work, he's crazy." Kurt noticed that both of them were no longer looking at him, and Kurt followed their gaze. "That's the ape himself, the one getting in line."

Luka laughed. "When you said ape, I thought it was some fat guy. That's Freddie Samuelson. He's a football player, but more important." Luka stared at him, his laughter fading. "What dorm do you live in?"

"Samuelson Hall… no way!" Kurt exclaimed and then slapped his hand over his mouth. "You've got to be shitting me."

"Nope—Daddy," Jamie said.

"So the term 'more money than brains' refers to him," Kurt said cattily, and the others laughed. "Not that I care. I'm not doing his work for him," he pronounced. "You guys go get food. I'll hold the table until you all get back." The cafeteria was beginning to fill, and he was willing to sit for a while and keep his weight off his ankle. Kurt let his gaze wander around the large room and it settled on Ape Boy… er, Freddie. He smiled at the thought. He couldn't take his eyes off him. From a distance he wasn't so menacing, and Kurt got a chance to take in the dark curly hair, broad shoulders, and small waist, and when he turned around, buns of steel stuffed into tight jeans.

"What are you staring at?" Luka asked as he put down his tray.

"Nothing," Kurt answered quickly. "Just waiting and watching people." He stood up and walked to the line. Thankfully, it moved quickly and he got a tray. He made a salad and got a deli sandwich, staying away from the fried food. His skin had finally cleared up, and he wanted it to stay that way. Kurt got two glasses of diet soda, since they were small, and then headed back toward the table.

"What happened to you, Short Stuff?" Freddie asked as he nearly barreled into him… again.

"You, Ape Boy," Kurt snapped. "You pushed me off the walk and I twisted my ankle. I got stuck with you as a lab partner, and now you try to bowl me down at lunch." Kurt seethed and stepped closer. "I don't give a crap how big you are or who your daddy is. Do your own work and stay away from me." Kurt did his best to stride over to the table and plunked down the tray before taking his seat.

"Who pissed in your Cheerios?" Peter said when he joined them.

"He and Freddie had words, and from the look of things, our boy here got the last word. Freddie walked away looking completely confused and maybe a bit shell-shocked," Luka explained with a grin. "It's about time someone put that guy in his place. I had a class with him last year. He spent the entire class conning another student into doing his homework for him or looking at the paper of the guy next to him. All he seems good at is playing football." Jamie joined them, and they all ate and talked. Thankfully, the conversation stayed away from Freddie What's-his-face and on more interesting subjects.

"You guys should come over tonight after class," Luka offered. "Jamie just got a super cool game for Xbox, and we could play for a little while."

Kurt shook his head. "Sounds like fun, but I have to study. I already have hours of reading to finish and a lab I need to write up. And that's just from this morning's class. I still have the ones this afternoon."

"Bring your stuff over. We all have to work, but it gives us a chance to chill for a while. We play Xbox for an hour after dinner and then spend the rest of the evening studying." Luka leaned in closer to Jamie. "You can't work all the time."

"Okay, you convinced me, but not too long," Kurt agreed. They finished up lunch, and Kurt headed back to the dorm. He got an Ace bandage out of the first-aid kit he kept hidden under the bed, took off his shoe and sock, and wrapped his ankle. It immediately felt better. Once he got his sock and shoe back on, he headed out to class.

Thankfully, his afternoon classes were ape-free, and after the last one, which ended at four, he headed back to the dorm. "Short Stuff," he heard float over the quad, followed by laughter, and Kurt looked up to where Freddie stood with a bunch of his buddies.

"Ape Boy," Kurt called back and continued on without looking back. That guy was a real ass, and Kurt gripped the strap of his backpack tighter in his hand. At his dorm, he banged open the door and marched inside, muttering under his breath through the lobby, up the stairs, and into his room.

Peter looked up from the desk as Kurt came in. He raised his eyebrows, but didn't say anything and went back to work. Kurt placed his bag next to his desk and began pulling out his books and papers. He organized his assignments by due date and then moved to the more comfortable chair to read. He had six chapters to read and two outlines to prepare for the next day's classes. He figured he'd get the reading out of the way before dinner and then he could start on the other work afterward.

"So what's got you all worked up, as if I didn't know?" Peter asked. "It isn't a big campus, so you're going to run into him." Peter continued working, and Kurt cracked open his biochemistry book and then placed it on his lap.

"My biochem professor looks like a student," he observed, and Peter chuckled.

"You must have Dr. Marcus," Peter told him. "I had him for basic chemistry last year. He's a good teacher and very fair. He got his doctorate at, like, twenty-two or something, and if the rumors are true, he bats for your team. Apparently he and one of the assistant football coaches are together." Peter went back to his work, and Kurt figured the conversation was over, so he picked up his book once again.

By the time the guys knocked on the door for dinner, Kurt had finished his biochemistry chapter as well as his lab write-up. He'd also completed his reading for one of his other classes, so he was doing pretty well. He didn't have one of his classes the following day, so he placed that reading assignment on the bottom of the list.

"Are you two ready to go?" Luka asked, and Kurt marked his place and stood up, stretching his back and neck. They left the room and walked as a group down the stairs and out across the lawn to the dining hall.

The overlapping conversations were almost too much as hundreds of kids packed the place, all of them talking. Because he was on scholarship, he had to be careful with his meal plan. He got fifteen meals a week, but thankfully, he didn't often eat breakfast, so he figured he could stretch them over the weekends as well. His meal card was swiped by one of the student workers at the door, and that reminded him that he needed to stop by the library the following day to see about his on-campus job. He made a quick note on a scrap of paper, which he then placed in his wallet, along with his meal card, and got in line.

It moved fairly quickly, and he talked to the guys as they passed tables and caught snippets of conversation.

"Short Stuff."

Kurt groaned and slowly turned around.

"Did you finish the lab write-up?"

"Yes," he answered and then turned around, ignoring whatever else was said. The line moved away from Ape Boy's table, and Kurt refused to turn around to look at him. "That guy is an ass," Kurt said, and Luka snickered. "What?"

"He keeps looking at you. He doesn't want anyone to know he's looking at you, but he is," Luka told him.

"Come on," Kurt scoffed lightly.

"He's got his head forward, but I can see him glancing at you."

"He's probably trying to figure out how he can get a copy of my work." Kurt grabbed a tray and began moving through the various food stations. He wasn't sure what he wanted and ended up with another salad as well as some ham and potatoes. He could go back for more if he wanted, so he headed out and found a table.

They ate and talked. Once they were done, he and Peter stopped by their room to drop their stuff and then headed to Luka and Jamie's. They played Xbox for an hour and then all got down to work. Mostly they all had chapters to read and outline, so there wasn't much conversation. By early evening, they were largely done, and Jamie turned on the television. They sprawled out on the padded carpet and laughed through reruns of *Big Bang Theory* for an hour. Kurt began to wind down, yawning, and the others yawned as well. He and Peter said good night and walked down to their room. Kurt went down the hall to the bathroom, then came back and climbed into his loft bed. Peter flicked off the lights and then climbed into bed, and that was all Kurt remembered until he heard Peter moving around in the morning.

KURT CHECKED the clock and jumped out of bed, then ran to the bathroom. If he didn't hurry, he would be late for his appointment at the library, and he wanted to make a good impression on his employer. After shaving and showering, he dressed in a rush, grateful he'd packed his backpack the night before. He raced out of the room and down the stairs before hurrying across campus. He was forced to veer off the walkway into the grass by a group of slow students and tried to come to a stop at a muddy patch near a broken sprinkler head. He stopped, but his feet kept going. Kurt managed to twist to keep from falling on his backpack, but came down hard on his side.

"Crap!" he swore and began picking himself up. Before he knew what was happening, he was lifted onto his feet. His pants were wet, among other things.

"You need to be more careful, Short Stuff."

Kurt groaned and turned around. Freddie Samuelson stared at him with a small smile on his face.

"Thank you," Kurt said, pulling off his soaked windbreaker. Luckily, it had taken the worst of it, so he wasn't a complete mess.

"No problem," Freddie said, and Kurt glanced around to make sure he had everything and then headed off toward the library again. "So where are you going in such a hurry, Short Stuff?"

Kurt stopped walking and turned around. "Would you stop calling me that? My name is Kurt. Kurt Maxwell. I'll make a deal with you: I'll stop calling you Ape Boy if you quit with the Short Stuff crap." Kurt continued walking toward the library, and damned if Freddie didn't fall into step with him. "What do you want? I have an appointment I'm almost late for."

"I need your notes and stuff for the lab," Freddie said.

"Okay." Kurt paused. "I'll give you the notes, but you have to do your own work from there, and I won't do it again." Kurt sighed. He didn't want to be a complete dick. "You're my lab partner, so if we work together, things will go better. But I'm not doing your work for you."

"What if I need help?" Freddie asked, biting his lower lip.

"We'll cross that bridge when we come to it," Kurt said. "Now, I've got to go." Kurt turned and rushed toward the library, arriving just in time for his interview. It didn't last long, and he left with a job and an appointment to come back for training. Kurt left happy and headed to biochemistry class.

Since he arrived early, he took a different seat, hoping different people would sit next to him. The rest of the students came in, and Kurt relaxed as the seats began to fill. His hope didn't last, though—Freddie sat next to him anyway.

"Hey, Short St—I mean, Kurt," he began. Kurt turned away and growled. "Come on, I don't mean anything by it."

Kurt shook his head, and thankfully Dr. Marcus entered the room and began his lecture. Kurt listened carefully and took notes, writing down formulas and the processes that acted on them. He glanced over at Freddie. He had a notebook out, but halfway through class he'd barely taken any notes, and he seemed to be peering blankly at the front of the class. "Can you remember all this?" Kurt whispered, and Freddie shrugged. "You need to take notes." The lecture continued, and Freddie wrote some things down. Kurt paid him less attention and continued working through the class.

Once the bell sounded, he left the science building and walked across the quad. They only had lab twice a week, so today he had a break, and he decided to use it to his advantage. He found one of the red chairs on the lawn and settled into it. He pulled out his biochemistry book and notebook and decided to finish up the assignment before his next class. It would mean less work that evening.

"Do you study all the time?"

Kurt knew that voice without looking up. "I don't have rich parents," he said. "I'm here on scholarship, and if I want to stay, I have to work hard and keep my grades up." Kurt glanced over the top of his book as Freddie pulled up one of the other chairs. "What are you doing?"

"Joining you," Freddie said.

"Why? You obviously don't care about the classes you're taking. You spent the entire class staring into space. How will you pass?"

Freddie laughed. "Coach Josh and the prof are tight, if you know what I mean. He'll make sure I get a passing grade."

"Is that what he told you?" Kurt asked, but Freddie didn't answer. "Because I don't see Dr. Marcus like that at all. He worked hard to get his degree and become a professor. He's only a few years older than us, but he's not a slouch, and he isn't going to let anyone slide, boyfriend or not." Kurt lifted his book and returned to his reading. "I don't know where you got that information, but I doubt it's right."

"A bunch of the other guys took Marcus's class and they said it was good, so I assumed... crap!" Freddie tugged Kurt's book out of his hands. "What am I gonna do?"

Kurt yanked the book back. "I suggest studying and doing the work. You're already behind if you haven't done the reading and aren't up to date on the problems and exercises, so I suggest you get started."

"I don't know how to do this," Freddie began. "I play football—it's what I do."

"Don't you have to keep up a GPA to play?" Kurt asked.

"Yeah. So I take easy classes and do enough work to get by and still have time to practice. You gotta help me, man. If I fail this class and get kicked off the team, my dad will kill me and cut me off."

Kurt so wanted to be a dick. But damn it, it wasn't in him. "Okay. I have to work in the library this evening. Come by at eight and I'll help you."

"The library?" Freddie asked.

"Yeah. It's the building over there," Kurt said, pointing. "The one with all the books." He shook his head. "I'm not going to do your work for you. I know that's what people have done in the past, but I won't. So either meet me there at eight, having read the chapters assigned so far, or you're on your own." Kurt checked the time and then went back to his reading. When he looked up again, Freddie had left.

"You what?" Peter asked and then broke into peals of laughter. "You let Ape Boy talk you into helping him. Good God, I've got swampland in Florida to sell you."

"The guy's already lost, and I'll be working at the library anyway," Kurt said. "He might not show up." He was half hoping he didn't. "What's the worst that could happen? I end up with a useless lab partner. Wait… I already have that," Kurt quipped as Peter closed the closet door. "What are you all dressed up for?"

"I have a dinner and study date," Peter said with a smile. "She's an art history major." He looked in the mirror and made sure his collar was straight. "Don't wait up."

"Peter," Kurt called before he closed the door. "Don't you need your books?" Peter hurried back in and grabbed his bag before leaving again.

Kurt chuckled and went over to the cafeteria for dinner. He took his books and read at the table. No one bothered him, and when he was done, he packed up and headed right over to the library.

Elaine, one of the librarians, explained his job. Basically, he sat behind the counter and checked out books and materials using the computer. He also directed students to the various areas of the library and acted as the information desk. "Don't be nervous. If you get stuck, I'll be in my office, right over there. Just call or come get me."

"I will," Kurt said.

"Don't worry, honey," she said with a smile. "It's early in the semester. There will be very few students in here tonight. Most of them will be back in their rooms or having a good time. So relax, and if that backpack is any indication, you brought some of your work with you. As long as you pay attention, go ahead and read." She walked away, and Kurt settled behind the counter.

She was right—there were so few people in the library it was ridiculous. In the first hour, he only had two people approach the desk, and one of them wanted directions to the bathroom. It took fifteen minutes before he actually went through the book-checkout process. At nearly eight, he looked around, but saw no sign of Freddie. Kurt huffed and returned to studying. Since it was slow, he might as well get some of his classwork done. Every few minutes, he checked the clock, and at ten after, he gave up and continued his work.

Chapter 2

FREDDIE'S GYM workout with the team ran late. He cleaned up fast and grabbed his gym bag. He'd shoved his books in the bottom of it and he needed to get going.

"We're going out for a brew," Hopkins said with a smile as he pulled a T-shirt over his sculpted chest.

"Can't tonight. I got a work session," Freddie said and headed toward the locker room door. He didn't want anyone asking a lot of questions. Within a few seconds he was outside, hurrying down the sidewalk and then across the quad toward the library. As he approached, Freddie checked the Rolex his father had given him for his last birthday and then headed inside. He was late, but he saw Short Stuff sitting behind the checkout counter on a stool. Yeah, he knew his name was Kurt, but he still thought of him as Short Stuff. Well—short, fiery, and kinda cute. Although he kept the cute part to himself. Thinking guys were cute was a surefire way for the guys who blocked for him to decide they didn't care so much. It didn't matter if Coach Josh was gay. He wasn't the one on the field or the one everyone counted on to bring home a win. That was him, and he was good at it. "Kurt," he said softly.

Kurt lowered his book and stared across the counter before slapping it closed. "You're late."

"I know. The team workout went longer than it was supposed to, and I figured you wouldn't want me to rush over here all grungy, so I cleaned up and got here as soon as I could," Freddie explained, and he could have sworn he saw Kurt swallow hard and his eyes widen for just a second.

"Okay," Kurt said. "Did you read the chapter?"

"Yeah," Freddie said honestly. It had taken him almost two hours, but he'd gotten through it. He dropped his bag and fished out his book, wrinkling his nose at his sweaty clothes.

"Sit at the table over there and get a notebook. Now that you've read the chapter, you need to outline it," Kurt said.

"Why? That isn't the assignment," Freddie protested. "I thought you were going to explain stuff to me."

"I'll help answer questions as best I can," Kurt said.

"Then why the outlining?"

"Because you retain more of what you read *and* write. It's the process of writing that helps you retain information. So when you study, write down what's important, even if you don't go back to it. The process helps you learn." Kurt stepped away to help another student, and Freddie saw the guy stare at him. He stared back and growled softly under his breath.

"Go on and get to work. Outline the first two or three pages and be sure to include the important points, definitions of terms, formulas, and any procedures or processes you think you'll need later," Kurt instructed. Freddie picked up his bag and walked to the table, where he dropped the bag on a chair. He pulled out a notebook and looked through his bag for a pencil.

"Freddie," Kurt whispered, and when Freddie looked up, Kurt tossed him a pencil. He caught it and sat down, then opened the book and got to work.

Most of what he read made no sense, but he forced himself to work. He wrote down what caught his eye and copied down definitions to terms he could barely understand. But he kept going. Two pages, then three—he continued until he was most of the way through the chapter. Then he looked up and saw Kurt staring at him. Kurt looked away fast and returned to his textbook.

"How are you doing?" Kurt asked.

Freddie shrugged and stood up, then walked over to the desk. He handed Kurt the notebook and watched as he read it. Kurt looked at him and then back at the notebook. "What the hell do you know anyway?" Freddie snapped. He snatched the notebook out of Kurt's hand and threw it and his textbook in his bag and headed for the exit.

"Stop," Kurt said.

"I know I'm stupid. You don't have to tell me," Freddie said.

"I don't think you're stupid," Kurt said and stared at him. Freddie didn't need any more of this and took off out the library door.

His first instinct was to head back to the rec center and pound some weights. He checked his watch and groaned. It was late and they would be closing. Instead, he headed toward his place off campus. As he approached the house, he could hear the beat of the music from three houses away. By the time he reached the front door, he could tell the place was rocking, and that was fine with him. Freddie pushed open the door, expecting a party, but he only saw his two housemates sprawled on the sofa with beer cans in their hands. Freddie threw his bag in the corner, went into the kitchen, and pulled open the refrigerator door. He grabbed a can, opened it, and chugged the beer without closing the door. Then he grabbed two more before heading toward the living room, kicking the refrigerator door closed behind him.

"Where were you?" Johnny Cartwright slurred. He was on the football team with Freddie, a defensive end. The man was freakin' huge and could drink like a fish. From the cans piled on the table, he and Carl Melbourne, his other housemate, had been drinking for a while. The head coach had encouraged the team to avoid booze during the season, but he'd done so with a wink—he'd been a college player himself, after all. He knew the score: as long as they were legal.... "You missed the good news," Johnny shouted over the music, and Freddie walked to the iPod dock and turned it down.

"She said yes, man," Carl said as he leaped off and then around the battered sofa, where he crushed Freddie in an iron grip. "Brittany said yes." He jumped and danced around him, shaking the entire floor.

"Congrats, man," Freddie said and faked a smile and some excitement for his friend. "It took you long enough to ask her," he teased, letting some of his own problems slip away. Carl bounced back around the sofa and flopped down into his seat. "Did you set a date?"

"She wants to get married next fall after we both graduate," Carl answered, raising his beer can in celebration. Freddie opened his second beer, and they clinked cans. He drank half of it in a few gulps, burped loudly, and then finished the can. He didn't even taste the stuff, but he didn't care. All he wanted was a buzz and to forget.

"So where were you?" Johnny asked.

"At the library," Freddie said. "I gotta pass biochemistry or I'm off the team. I've only had two classes and I already don't understand shit." He tensed, wanting to throw the beer can against the wall.

"Then drop the class," Johnny suggested.

"Can't, it's Marcus. If I drop, Coach will hear about it." He didn't want to answer questions about why he was dropping the class. "And I gotta have one more science class to graduate. I thought it would be easy." Freddie plunked himself down in an old armchair, and it creaked under his onslaught.

"So get your lab partner to do the work. That's what you did last time," Carl said. "You got money—offer to pay him." Freddie nodded. "He probably needs the cash, and you need the grade, so work something out." Carl upended his beer and added the can to the stack. Then he groaned and stood up, swaying back and forth slightly. "I gotta go to bed. I promised Brittany I'd meet her in the morning." He loped off through the small house. The stairs groaned under his weight, and then Freddie heard him moving around above him as he popped open his third beer. He sipped this one and closed his eyes.

"Yeah... pay the kid," Johnny said, agreeing with Carl. "If it's going to bring you down like this, it's not worth it. Man, you gotta have your head clear for the game this weekend. It's the biggest one of the regular season."

Freddie gulped from the can. "He won't take it," he said. "I asked him for his notes in class, and he gave them to me but said that was the last time." Freddie leaned forward in the chair. "I met him at the library and he tried to help me, had me outlining the chapter and shit. He says I gotta do my own work." Freddie scoffed and drained the beer, then crushed the can in his frustration. "I don't know any of this shit, and none of it makes any sense."

"I don't know what else to tell you, man," Johnny said. "You gotta do what you gotta do. I'd give his way a try. What have you got to lose?" Johnny stood up and turned off the music before tottering toward the stairs. Freddie expected him to fall down, but he made it up the stairs, and a few minutes later, Freddie heard the bathroom door close. He thought about having another beer, but decided against it. Instead, he grabbed his bag from where he'd tossed it, turned out the lights, and went upstairs.

Since Freddie paid the most rent, he got what had once been the master bedroom. He had a bed and dresser, but not much else. There was no need. No one but him ever came in here, and he wasn't into a bunch of froufrou crap anyway. Freddie unpacked his bag and threw his dirty clothes in the laundry basket. He waited for Johnny to get done in the bathroom before taking his turn, and then returned to his room, got undressed, and climbed into bed.

In the darkness, he tossed and turned, rolling first to one side and then the other. He punched his pillow for good measure, and a few minutes later, rolled over again. He kept thinking about Short Stuff, knowing he wouldn't take money and let Freddie coast off him. What surprised Freddie was that he didn't want Kurt to. He was a nice kid who'd offered to try to help him. Few people in his life had done that without wanting something in return. Even the things from his father came with a price, or as a reward, usually for football. His car had been given to him when he'd made the varsity team his freshman year. He got his watch when he led his team to the league championship last year. Hell, he swore his dad only paid for the nonscholarship portion of college so he could play football. He certainly didn't care about Freddie's grades as long as he could stay on the team. It wasn't Kurt's fault he was as thick as they came, and twice as dumb. All he knew and seemed to understand was football. That came naturally. Everything else was a fight, and it was getting harder. The freshman and sophomore classes had been pretty easy to fake his way through, but the junior-level classes were a lot harder, and he knew he was going to fall behind. The problem was, he didn't know what to do about it.

THE FOLLOWING day in biochemistry class, Freddie gave Kurt back his notes. He'd made a copy of them, and tried to take notes and understand what the professor was saying. But like most of his other classes, he only caught part of what was happening. He wrote things down anyway, but it didn't help. Toward the end of class, Kurt leaned over and looked at his notes. Freddie saw him and pulled away his notebook. He didn't know if he was doing it right, but he was trying and didn't need Kurt to remind him how dumb he was.

At the end of class, Kurt packed up his things and walked down front to where Dr. Marcus was packing up. Freddie left the room and waited out in the hallway. When Kurt came out, Freddie fell into step with him.

"I need to get through this class," Freddie whispered as they walked down the hall. Kurt glanced at him quickly and kept walking. "If you'll help me, I can make it worth your while."

"You want me to tutor you?" Kurt asked. "I suggest you talk to the professor. He can probably point you to a TA who can help."

"I don't mean that kind of help. I can make it worth your while if you'll share your work with me," Freddie said, and Kurt stopped dead in his tracks, staring at him.

"Are you kidding?" Kurt asked frantically, looking around. "No way! What part of me being on scholarship don't you get? Not that I'd ever do that for anyone, but a few dollars won't make up for getting kicked out of school. Besides, you won't learn anything if I do your work for you."

Freddie inhaled and puffed himself up to look bigger. That always worked around campus when he wanted something. "I'm sure a few bucks would come in handy."

Kurt scoffed. Then he turned and walked away.

Freddie swore under his breath and looked toward the rec center. He had a few hours to kill before his next class, and he could do that in the weight room. He jogged the two blocks back to his house. He bounded up the stairs and hurriedly packed a gym bag. Then he grabbed both his book bag and gym bag before heading out and back toward the rec center.

The team locker room was quiet, and that was fine. It wasn't likely any of the other guys would be here this time of day. Freddie stripped down and changed before hitting the weight room. He'd just sat down on one of the benches to get to work when he heard footsteps.

"You know you shouldn't work out alone." Coach Josh's admonishing voice rang through the empty room.

"I wasn't doing anything heavy," he explained and heard the coach grunt, but he didn't stop him, so Freddie got to work. Freddie pressed, yanked, pulled, and cabled his chest for an hour. When he finished, muscles burned and throbbed, which was exactly what he wanted. This, he was good at, and his body showed it. When he flexed in the mirror, his chest bulged, and his guns popped when he flexed his arms. He was strong, and damn, it felt good. His heart pumped and the blood raced through him. He was on top of the world and no one could touch him, not here or on the field.

Freddie yanked his towel off the bar he'd draped it over and wiped down his face and neck. His workout done for the day, he walked into the locker room to clean up. He grabbed another towel before stripping off his sweaty clothes and heading for the showers. He cleaned up quickly, wrapped the towel around his waist, and headed back into the locker room to change. As he passed Coach Josh's office he stopped and glanced through the glass. He looked again and thought he saw Kurt leaving through the office's other door. He continued into the locker room. He pulled open the locker, took out his bag, and began to dress.

"Freddie, stop by my office when you're done," shouted the coach.

"Okay," Freddie said, stifling the groan that rose in his throat. He wanted to punch the back of the locker. Kurt must have ratted him out, and now there was going to be hell to pay. He finished dressing and thrust his dirty clothes into his canvas gym bag with such force, he probably tore a few stitches. Not that he cared. "You wanted to see me," he said as he entered the coach's office.

"Sit down," the coach said seriously and glared at him. "I just had a visitor, a friend of yours from one of your classes."

"He's no friend of mine," Freddie growled, and the coach glared back at him.

"I'd say that young man was a good friend, and if you aren't aware of it, then you're one sorry son of a bitch." Coach Josh shook his head and then kicked the door closed. Freddie braced for the worst. "Do you have a clue who your real friends are?" the coach asked as he pulled open the closet door. "Stand back against the wall and read the bottom line."

Freddie got up, moved across the office, and stared at the bottom of the eye chart.

"Okay," Coach Josh said, "read the lowest line you can."

"E, O, C, V, L," Freddie said, and Coach nodded, closing the door.

"What I want to know is how you can play football with sight like yours," Coach Josh said, and Freddie realized he wasn't here to be yelled at, or worse, to get kicked off the team for cheating. "I want you to see an eye doctor, and I'm suspending you from the team until you do."

"What?"

"That's right. You need to see an eye doctor. There's one the team uses. I can get you an appointment today, but you can't play until I get a clean bill of health." Coach Josh smiled. "And be prepared—you're going to need glasses."

"But our first game is Saturday," Freddie complained.

"Then you better make that appointment," Coach Josh told him. "And don't you dare take this out on that kid who talked to me. He probably did you a huge favor, and it took guts for him to come here on your behalf. He said you probably wouldn't listen to him—he hoped you'd listen to me. And you will."

"Yes, Coach," Freddie said.

"I know you will because I can't let you play if I know there's something wrong." Coach looked up a phone number and picked up the phone. After dialing, he talked for a few minutes to someone on the other end. "Three o'clock will be fine. The thing is, he's going to need glasses he can play in quickly." Coach listened, and Freddie stared at the floor, wondering what kind of dweeby geek glasses he was going to end up with. "Good. I'll make sure he's there." Coach hung up the phone, wrote down some information, and ripped the top page off the pad on his desk. "You're expected at three. It's just a few blocks from campus. The doctor will examine your eyes, and he said he'll do his best to fit you for glasses in a few days. You can practice and play with the team as long as you do this."

"Okay," Freddie agreed. He didn't really have a choice. "I'll be there, but I really don't think this is necessary."

"It is. You're half blind and you don't even know it. You've spent years compensating for the fact that you can't see well. I'm just upset none of us caught it sooner. As bad as your vision is, you shouldn't be able to play football, but you certainly do well enough on the field. Just think how much better you'll play once you can actually see the ball." Coach glanced at the clock. "You need to get to class, but I expect you to stop by after you see the doctor. If you don't, I'll be forced to have a conversation with Coach Norris, and he won't be as lenient." Coach Josh loomed over him. Freddie was big, but Coach Josh was bigger and could be threatening as hell. "Go on, and I'll expect an update later."

Freddie stood up and left the office. He grabbed his bag in the locker room, along with his books and headed out. He didn't have enough time to go back to the house, so he ended up carrying his gym bag with him for the rest of the morning. He ran home and dumped his stuff just before lunch and then headed over to the union to meet the guys.

When he walked in, the first person he saw was Kurt, sitting at a table with six other guys. He marched over. "Can I talk to you?" he asked. Everyone at the table turned to him, and a few of the guys tensed, like they were ready to come to Kurt's defense. Kurt stood up and stepped away from the table, but he didn't go very far. "How could you go behind my back like that?" Freddie asked.

Kurt laughed at him. "Please. I noticed you having a difficult time seeing in the library. You kept moving closer to the page, and your writing was huge, like you couldn't see what you were doing. And for the record, you had just offered to pay me to do your work for you. I didn't know what to think. So I asked your coach to help you. I figured you'd listen to him. From the way you're reacting, I guess I was right." Kurt backed away. "I did what I did because it was right—you need some help. If you want to be angry with me, then so be it. I told you at the library that I didn't think you were stupid, and I don't. I thought you couldn't see very well." Kurt turned and walked back toward the table.

"How did you know?" Freddie asked.

Kurt stopped and looked at him. "My mom is legally blind," Kurt said, and Freddie took a step back in surprise. "She can see forms, sharp contrast and bright light, but she can't read, drive, or anything like that." Kurt looked down, and the noise from hundreds of students talking and chattering faded into the background. "I remember as a kid when she used to read to me, and then the books got closer and closer to her face until she couldn't read anymore. Then she couldn't drive and had to relearn how to do everything. So when I saw you, I had to say something." Kurt sat back down and began talking to his friends.

Freddie had no idea what to say. Yes, he wanted to be angry, but how in the hell could he be mad at someone like that? Freddie turned and walked rather blankly until he found Carl and sat down. "You two fight like an old married couple," Carl told him.

"Shut up," Freddie snapped.

"What's wrong with you?" Carl snapped back.

"I offered to pay for his help and he turned me down flat. So I went to the gym to work out. I saw Kurt leaving the office when I was on my way back to change, and then Coach Josh called me into his office."

"Oh shit," Carl said as Johnny sat down with his tray, and Freddie brought him up to date.

"Bus-ted," Johnny said.

Freddie shook his head. "He didn't say anything about that, but Coach is sending me to an eye doctor. He thinks I have trouble seeing, and he'll suspend me from the team if I don't go."

"Is that all?" Johnny asked as he dug into his food.

"No," Freddie groused. "Coach says I'll probably need glasses."

Carl and Johnny looked at each other seriously for two seconds and then began laughing. "You're going to look geeky," Carl teased, and they continued laughing for a few seconds. Freddie stood up and left the table. He got in line and filled his tray. He was starving. When he returned to the table, Carl and Johnny stared at him.

"I'll punch the first one of you who laughs," he growled and plunked down his tray.

"It's no big deal," Carl said. "They make prescription goggles that can be worn during play. We were teasing, but it really isn't a big thing. You know Jensen wears glasses."

Freddie humphed and began to eat. When he looked up from his tray, he saw Kurt. He stared at him, forcing his eyes to focus. "Fuck," he grumbled between bites. Kurt looked back, and Freddie looked away. He swore under his breath once again as he tried to figure out his fascination with the smaller man.

"It's not that bad," Johnny said, and Freddie glanced up at him. "You were mumbling under your breath."

"Sorry," Freddie said and continued eating.

Carl and Johnny got up to leave before Freddie had finished eating. Freddie said good-bye and went back to his food, paying little attention to the people around him. He kept glancing at Kurt and occasionally found him looking back. Whenever he saw him looking, warmth spread through him. A few times he actually smiled and thought Kurt might have smiled back.

People stood up and sat down around him, but Freddie barely noticed until books plunked down on the table and someone sat across from him.

"What did the coach tell you?" Kurt asked him.

"I don't see why you care," Freddie answered before downing the last of his milk.

"I'm not heartless," Kurt said.

"And I'm not stupid," Freddie countered.

"I never said you were," Kurt said.

"I saw that look at the library, and then in class when you stared at my notes and stuff," Freddie countered. Kurt smiled back at him, and fuck if his stomach didn't do a little flip.

"I never thought you were stupid. I was looking at your notes in class to make sure I wasn't wrong. I didn't think I was, so I talked to the professor, and he pointed me to your coach."

"Why do you care?" Freddie asked. Kurt shrugged and looked away. "I'll do my best in lab, I promise you that."

"It isn't that."

"Then what is it?" Freddie challenged. Kurt leaned slightly across the table. He even parted his pink lips to say something, but then stood up instead.

"I only wanted to help," Kurt said softly, and then he turned and walked briskly toward the exit. Freddie sighed and stood up, grabbing his tray. He dropped it on the dish belt and headed out. He had a class that afternoon, and thankfully it was a phys ed class—he always aced those. And then he had to see the eye doctor.

TWO DAYS later, Freddie left the house and walked across campus to his first class. The world felt funny and seemed to move in different ways than it had his entire life. At times the sidewalk seemed to rise up to meet him, and he stumbled. The doctor who'd examined his eyes had been appalled and had berated him for much of the exam. But he'd also spent extra time with the lab. He'd put an emergency rush on Freddie's lenses and had stayed late to make his glasses. Turned out he was a huge football fan.

Freddie stopped walking and took off the glasses. Everything returned to what he thought of as normal, except the world now seemed fuzzy around the edges. He'd never noticed it before. Freddie put the glasses back on and continued down the sidewalk. The eye doctor had said it would take a few days for him to get used to them and suggested he wear them as much as possible. He also promised a set of prescription playing goggles in time for the game. Freddie was just happy he hadn't gotten stuck with frames that looked like something from out of the sixties.

When he got to class, Freddie kept his head down and sat in his usual spot. To his surprise, Kurt wasn't there. He looked around to see if he'd moved, because Kurt was always there early. "Jesus," someone swore and pointed out the window. Freddie took one look and bolted out of the classroom. He ran down the hall and took the stairs two at a time to the ground floor before bursting out the door so fast it banged like a shot against the stops.

"What the fuck do you think you're doing?" Freddie bellowed as he marched up to where two freshman football players had Kurt pinned to the ground. One of them hit Kurt, and Freddie saw red.

"He's a fag and he was looking at us," one of them said. Freddie pulled him off Kurt and tossed the kid aside. Then Freddie grabbed the second one and tossed him like he was nothing. People came running, teachers and students spilling out of the surrounding buildings.

"Are you okay?" Freddie asked Kurt as calmly and gently as he could given the adrenaline pounding through his body. Kurt groaned softly. "Don't try to move if you're hurt."

"I… I'm okay," Kurt said softly and began to move.

Campus police officers arrived, and Freddie told them what he'd seen and done.

"Ratting out fellow players," one of the guys called.

"You won't be playing for long," Freddie growled. "This is not how we behave here at Dickinson," he said loudly, and to his surprise, the other students applauded. "Let me help you up," he said to Kurt, and Kurt slowly took Freddie's hand and got to his feet. Someone brought over Kurt's backpack, and he looked through it, his face falling as he pulled out his laptop, or what was left of it. A huge crack ran through the top of it. "Don't worry about it," Freddie said. "Maybe it can get fixed. Or if not, you could get a new one."

Kurt nodded and headed into the building. The campus police stopped them, and Kurt agreed to speak with them after class. "I'm already late," he said.

"You're limping," Freddie said as he watched Kurt climb the stairs.

"They reinjured my ankle," Kurt told him. He was also covered in bits of grass, and dirt stained his clothes. At first Freddie wondered if he should touch him, but he went ahead and brushed the grass off the back of Kurt's T-shirt. The warmth of Kurt's skin reached his hand and he finished quickly.

Class hadn't started, but the professor stood in the front of the room. "Are you all right?" he asked Kurt.

"Yes, thank you," Kurt answered and pulled his notebook out of the now stained and torn backpack. The professor nodded and began his lecture. Freddie took out his notebook and watched the front of the class. He realized now he could see the board and everything the professor wrote.

"Nice glasses," Kurt whispered after a few minutes.

Freddie humphed and then smiled back. He returned his attention to the class, which seemed to fly by. Once they were dismissed. Freddie looked at his notebook and found he'd taken pages of notes and that he understood what the professor had said. Well, at least some of what he'd said.

"You aren't missing stuff now," Kurt told him as he packed up his things. "You'll probably need to spend some time catching up, but now you won't miss part of what's on the board or spend time trying to compensate for what you can't see."

"Yeah, I guess," Freddie said, touching his glasses for, like, the millionth time. They still felt strange on his nose, and he wanted to scratch around them all the time. "Do you think you could help me? Maybe we could meet at the library sometime?"

"Sure. I work there Tuesday and Thursday nights and on Sunday afternoons." Freddie pulled a face. "I know, but I'm the new guy so I get the crap hours. It's spending money, though, so I'm good." Kurt stepped gingerly on his injured foot. "I can meet you there Sunday at one if you want," he offered, and Freddie agreed. He needed help or he was in trouble. "Okay, I'll see you then."

For some reason Kurt's excited smile sent a ripple of happiness through him. He knew he had feelings for other guys. He'd known since he was a kid, but he'd ignored them as best he could. He was a football player, after all. But something about this slight, small person, with his big heart and eyes that shone when he smiled, got under his skin. And seeing Kurt happy made him happy. He wasn't sure he should allow himself to dwell on it. Maybe it would be best if he found someone else to help him.

Chapter 3

FREDDIE WAS still basking in the glow of a win as he banged open the locker room door and headed out in the fall evening air. He took a deep breath and then released it, savoring the sweet scent of victory. His phone vibrated in his pocket, and Freddie pulled it out.

"Hey, I heard you played a great game," his father said happily. "Apparently it was one of your best."

"Yeah?" Freddie asked. He hadn't been aware of that, but his dad loved the smell of victory, his own in the boardroom or Freddie's on the gridiron. "I was afraid playing would be difficult with the new glasses, but everything was really sharp."

"Good, good," his father told him.

"Where are you?" Freddie asked, wondering if his dad had come into town to see the game and surprise him. He'd done that a few times, and he certainly seemed to have up-to-the-second information.

"At the penthouse in the city," his father answered, and Freddie heard what he thought was his father sipping from a glass, probably very expensive Scotch. "Some friends were at the game." He sipped once again. "Anyway, what I really want to hear about is what happened earlier in the week. Apparently you were some sort of hero, stopping an attack on campus." His father paused. "I know you have a good heart, but just because you're the quarterback of the football team doesn't mean you should get involved in these kinds of altercations."

"What the hell, Dad?" Freddie asked. "I should have let them beat him up?"

"They were football players. You should be loyal to the team," his father said. "In business, some people are lions and others are sheep. And you're a lion."

Freddie shivered. He'd known his father could be ruthless when it came to business, but up till now, he'd never really seen it firsthand. Sure, he'd heard stories, but his dad was actually telling him not to help people, or worse, to only help the right kinds of people.

"Image can take you a long way, because that's all most people see or know," his father said. "So you have to protect it. Don't get me wrong; helping someone is good, and it's got the right people watching you, but be careful, because helping... people like that boy too much can get powerful people talking in ways that aren't helpful." Freddie had stopped walking, and he stared blankly across the quad, unable to believe what he was hearing. "Do you understand what I'm saying?"

Freddie swallowed hard. "Yeah, Dad. I read you loud and clear."

"Good," his father said brightly. "Now go on and celebrate a great game. I'll talk to you soon." His father disconnected, and Freddie gripped the phone, the urge to chuck the damned thing against a tree almost overwhelming. How could his dad be so stupid? *People like that...,* Freddie thought as he began walking toward town. He needed to eat, and some of the guys were meeting at Alibis to celebrate. He really didn't feel like it now, but he'd already promised he'd be there.

"Freddie, great game," a guy called as he rushed past. Another followed and high-fived him before continuing on.

People like that... kept playing in his mind. What if his dad discovered *he* was "people like that"? He was so screwed. There was nothing he could do about it except make sure his dad didn't find out, and the easiest way for that to happen was to do what he'd done all his life—concentrate on football and forget about the rest. It wasn't like he could tell people. His father's attitude had certainly communicated that loud and clear. He continued his walk to the bar just off High Street. As soon as he pushed inside, some of the guys tugged him to a table, and one of the waitresses sauntered over. He ordered a beer and food before grabbing the seat at the head of the table to preside over their celebration. Even though the celebratory mood had pretty much been sucked out of him, he put on a smile and pretended to have a good time, which got easier and easier as the night went on and the liquor and beer continued to flow.

After eating his fill and then drinking a few beers, doing a few shots, and then sharing something really sweet with one of the girls because... well, it was expected, he got up to leave. Thankfully he'd had plenty to eat or he'd be smashed off his ass. Instead, he managed to walk to the house. He drank a lot of water, took a couple aspirin, and collapsed into bed. The last thing he remembered was a fleeting thought about... *people like that.* But he was too drunk to care. Mission accomplished.

By Sunday afternoon, Kurt had finished his homework for the week. He was caught up, the sun was shining, and he'd even gotten a really nice new laptop courtesy of the college, who had apparently expelled the students who'd attacked him and refused them any sort of refund. He walked toward the library through the warm September afternoon. There was a slight nip in the air, and it wouldn't be long before the leaves changed color and temperatures dropped, but right now it was gorgeous, and the students still on campus were making the best of it. A football passed overhead as Kurt walked across the lawn.

Things had most definitely changed for him. He watched everyone and made sure there were always other people around when he walked across campus. He didn't feel as safe, and over the past few days, he hadn't left his dorm after dark. As he approached the library, he checked for movement in the bushes or anyone lingering around before hastily climbing the stairs and then rushing inside, his heart pounding until he was punched in and stationed behind the front desk. These attacks of momentary panic had happened a few times.

"Are you okay?" Janet, the girl he was relieving, asked sympathetically. "I heard what happened."

"Yes, I'm fine," Kurt said with a smile to cover up the jitteriness. He hated feeling this way. The men who'd jumped him were in custody. They were being charged with assault, and since their families lived out of state, they were cooling their heels in jail. "I guess things are still really vivid for me right now. I'll be okay."

"If you're sure," she said and hurried to punch out and enjoy the day.

The building was a morgue. A few students sat at the worktables, but mostly the place was empty. It was still too early in the semester and way too nice outside. Kurt knew he wouldn't be here if he hadn't had to work. Rather than waste time, Kurt settled on his stool and pulled out his philosophy textbook and settled down to read ahead. He'd signed up for a class on nineteenth-century philosophy and had been assigned a text on Kierkegaard that was kicking his butt. The professor had arranged for a visiting lecturer from Drexel, in Philadelphia, to come to class. She was one of the foremost Kierkegaard scholars in the country, and Kurt wanted to be able to ask intelligent questions. The hardest part wasn't the text or what he was reading, but the fact that he kept looking up to see if Freddie had come like he'd said he would.

Kurt tamped down his excitement. He knew he might as well forget whatever feelings he was developing for the big lug, because they weren't going to be returned. Freddie had been nice to him, but Kurt was pretty sure it was because Freddie wanted something. Kurt was even more sure he knew what that was, and it had nothing to do with his short, skinny body and everything to do with passing biochemistry with as little fuss and work as possible.

Yet there were times when Freddie looked at him in a way that sent heat rippling through him. His eyes would blaze in an unguarded moment, and then the fire disappeared. And Kurt couldn't forget the gentle, caring tone Freddie had used when he'd been lying on the ground, afraid to move in case he was hit again by his attackers. He still heard that voice in his dreams at night. He was such a mess. Freddie was a football player, a huge, strong, straight-as-an-arrow football player, and Kurt was only seeing what he wanted to see… or more accurately wished and hoped was there for him to see. It wasn't real, and he needed to remember that.

Kurt marked his place and closed his book before helping a student check out some reference materials. "It's all due Monday before noon," he reminded the girl and then finished the checkout. He should have returned to his reading, but he couldn't concentrate. He knew Freddie had said he wanted help, but Freddie had had years of skating by and covering up. It had become a habit, and he was good at it. Kurt figured Freddie had been passed in high school and so far in college either because of who his father was or simply because he was some sort of football god. Those habits didn't just stop overnight, and even if Freddie had discovered a major impediment to learning, it didn't mean he wanted to learn. Kurt had to admit most people would continue to skate by if they could, because it was easier.

"Can you help me?" a student asked, pulling Kurt out of his woolgathering.

"Of course," Kurt said and spent a few minutes showing the student how the reference system worked. Thankfully, most university libraries used the same system, so he knew it well from his time at Shippensburg. After explaining it to the other student, Kurt returned to the desk. Freddie stood in front of it, looking around. "I thought you weren't coming."

"I overslept and then I had to eat," Freddie explained. "I hurried over as soon as I could."

"Okay," Kurt said, suppressing a smile. He shouldn't have been so happy Freddie had shown, but he was. "Did you bring your biochem book?"

"Yeah," Freddie said without enthusiasm.

"Good. Since you largely missed the first week, we're going to go back to the beginning. You did read the first chapter already, so skim it, write down the important points, and then go on to chapter two. Did you try the exercises assigned?" Freddie cocked his head to one side, and Kurt rolled his eyes. "Okay, forget I asked. But you'll do them now, and once you've done them, we can review the answers together."

Freddie didn't say anything, but he did sit at the same table he'd used before. He pulled his book and a pad out of his bag and got to work. Kurt went back to his reading, hiding his smile behind the book.

Kurt read and worked for another hour, occasionally looking over his book to where Freddie sat, head down, working on his assignment. Kurt was happy about one thing—working the desk gave him the chance to study Freddie, almost at will, without him knowing.

Danged if Freddie wasn't hot as hell. Kurt kept watching his legs as they bounced nervously, encased in tight jeans that left little to the imagination. And neither did the skintight T-shirt, stretched at the arms and across Freddie's chest. He wondered if Freddie was smooth or if those muscles straining the cotton fabric were dusted with hair as dark as what he had on his head. Kurt shifted on the stool and rearranged things for comfort. Freddie lifted his head, and Kurt immediately looked back at his book, hoping Freddie hadn't seen him staring.

Freddie's shoulders bounced up and down, and Kurt knew he'd seen and that he was laughing. "What's so funny?" Kurt asked.

"You," he said, chuckling, "me." He continued laughing, shaking his head. "I think I got the first questions done," he said after a while. Since no one was around and the library was dead, Kurt went over to the table.

"Let's see what you have," Kurt said and sat next to Freddie. "Numbers one and two are correct. Three isn't, four… five… and six are right, but"—Kurt looked at the rest—"seven and eight are wrong, nine is part wrong, ten is correct."

"Shit," Freddie swore softly.

"It's okay. Look up the sections for each question you got wrong in the chapter and find the correct answers. It shouldn't take long. Then you can finish your lab write-up and all you'll need to do is read half of chapter two by Monday." Freddie groaned, and Kurt chuckled. "This is what students do. We study hard so we can learn."

"You mean get good grades," Freddie countered.

"No, I mean *learn*. The more you learn, the better grades you get. They go hand in hand." Kurt stood up and went back to the desk. He checked the clock—he only had half an hour more to work. It took Freddie another fifteen minutes to get all his answers right. Then Kurt took pity on him and helped him outline the lab report so all he had to do was fill in the detailed information. He didn't figure it was cheating because he wasn't supplying the answers, just the overall form. "You have to get this done by Monday morning," Kurt told him as he stood up and packed his things. The library was closing in a few minutes, so he got to leave.

"Do you want to get a pizza or something?' Freddie asked sheepishly. "You know," he added nervously, "to thank you for helping me."

Regardless of the jolt of excitement that raced through him, Kurt nearly said no. He didn't have other plans, but he was on the verge of lying and saying he did. This crush he had on Freddie wouldn't do him any good, and neither would spending time with him if he didn't have to. It would probably be best for him to wish Freddie a good weekend and say he'd see him Monday. "Okay, that would be nice," he answered instead, because he was a glutton for punishment and frustration. "I need to stop at my dorm to put my books away and stuff."

"Yeah, me too. How about if I meet you at Mediterranean Pizza in an hour?" Freddie asked.

"Umm," Kurt began, "I don't know where that is. I haven't been here long enough to know where most things are yet."

Freddie smiled and chuckled. "I should have known that. It's just a few blocks up the main road that runs through campus. Head toward town and look on the left. You can't miss it." Freddie pointed, and Kurt nodded. He figured he could find it.

They left the library together and quickly went in different directions. Kurt headed toward his dorm, and he saw Freddie going toward the student-housing section of Carlisle. Once Freddie was out of sight, Kurt picked up his pace, thankful he'd wrapped his ankle.

In the dorm room, he found Peter watching television. "We're going to head down to dinner soon. Are you coming?"

"Not tonight. I'm going out for pizza," Kurt said. He opened his bag and began unpacking.

"Is this a date?" Peter seemed inordinately pleased.

"No, it's just having pizza. Freddie asked me because I helped him with his biochemistry." Kurt snickered. "Believe me, it's anything but a date. The guy is so straight it's sickening."

"But he keeps looking at you," Peter said.

"So do you, but that doesn't mean you're hot for my bod," Kurt countered. "He's just being nice." Kurt went down the hall to the bathroom and made sure he didn't look bad. He decided to change his shirt, so he went back to his dorm room and opened his closet, then stared at the selection.

"If this isn't a date, why are you fussing like a girl?" Peter teased.

"Just because I want to…," Kurt began and then trailed off into a sigh. "I know, I'm totally being stupid." Kurt took off his T-shirt and pulled a light-blue button-down from his closet. He really wished Luka or Jamie were there to answer his questions, but they'd left for the weekend. Peter was a good guy, but he couldn't ask him… gay questions. There were limits to what he felt he could subject Peter to, and confessing a crush on the star of the football team was probably over the line, as was asking him for dating advice. He pulled on the shirt and then checked himself in the closet mirror one more time before grabbing a light jacket.

"I'll see you tomorrow," Peter said as Kurt got ready to leave. At first, he thought Peter was teasing him.

"I take it you have a date?" Kurt asked, and Peter grinned.

"She asked me to a party at her place," Peter said with a wickedly playful gleam in his eye. "It should be a blast, and if I'm lucky…."

"Have fun," Kurt said and headed out.

The lights around campus were coming on as he walked to High Street and then toward town. It was a nice night with a slight breeze. He was glad he'd brought a jacket. It was comfortable now, but the hint of chill told him the warmth wouldn't last much after sundown. As he got closer to town, he kept a look out for the pizza place. A block away from campus, he spotted the sign ahead and picked up his pace. He was still a little early, but after he pulled open the glass front door and stepped inside, he saw Freddie sitting at one of the tables toward the back. Every single table was full, and he had to weave through the busy restaurant until he reached the seat across the table and sat down.

"You found it," Freddie said.

"Your directions were good." Kurt looked around. The walls were dark and adorned with neon beer signs and commemorative trays for Coca-Cola. It was pretty basic, but smelled out of this world, and his mouth watered. He hadn't eaten in hours, and his stomach let him know with a rumble that had both of them laughing.

"What can I get you?" the college-age waitress asked. "Hey, Freddie, how you doing?" she asked once she actually looked at them. "Haven't seen you around yet this year."

"I guess not," Freddie said with a smile. "Do you like everything?" he asked Kurt, and Kurt nodded. "Then give us a jumbo pizza with everything except anchovies, an order of breadsticks, onion rings, and a couple Cokes." Freddie smiled at her one last time before she left.

"Is that an ex-girlfriend?" Kurt asked.

Freddie didn't seem to know how to answer. "You could say she's a girl who'd like to be a girlfriend," he finally said with a shrug. "There are lots of girls who'd like to go out with me." Freddie leaned over the table. "My dad has money," he said as though it was some big secret, like his family name wasn't plastered on major campus buildings. "So I get a lot of girls who'd like to sink their claws into me."

"Conceited much?" Kurt retorted with a smile, and for a split second he thought he might have gone too far because Freddie didn't smile back.

"Not really," Freddie said. "At least I don't think so. I'm just not interested." Freddie paused when the waitress brought their drinks. He smiled at her and then waited for her to leave. "I dated the head cheerleader in high school. That girl drove me crazy. All she wanted to do was hang on me and be seen with me."

Kurt paused. "Isn't that why you were dating her? To be seen dating the prettiest girl in school?" He couldn't help smiling. "At least I never had that problem."

"I take it you've been…." Freddie swallowed hard. "Out for a while?"

"Yes. I came out as a senior in high school. To most people it was no big deal, but a few people tried to make my life difficult." Kurt sucked soda through his straw. "I have a double whammy. I've always been rather slight, so I was picked on for that. When I came out, it gave the small minds more ammunition. But my friends stuck by me, and so did my folks. The rest of them could go to hell as far as I was concerned."

"Damn," Freddie whispered.

"My mother used to say I had a Napoleon complex, but just because I'm short or gay doesn't mean I should take a bunch of crap from people." He sat back and silently challenged Freddie to disagree with him.

"Hey, man, I'm sorry for the Short Stuff comments." Freddie held his hands up in mock surrender, and Kurt laughed. "I won't do it again, I promise."

"Okay." Kurt grinned. "But can I ask you something?" he said, getting serious. "Aren't you worried that other players will see you with me and start to wonder? I'm not exactly in the closet, and while I'm new here and not many people know me…." He wasn't sure where he wanted to go with this thought. A week ago he never would have expected he'd be having dinner with Freddie, and yet here he was… and he was having a good time.

Freddie took a deep breath and sighed. The server brought the bread sticks and onion rings, along with small plates. Freddie dug right in and began to eat as though he were starving. Kurt took a single breadstick and a couple of onion rings, leaving the rest for Freddie.

"Is that all you're having?" Freddie asked before swigging from his soda glass.

"I have an appetite to go with my size," Kurt answered. "I've never been a big eater, and I want to save room for pizza." He took a bite of the breadstick after dipping it into the container of red sauce. It was tangy with a hint of sweet behind the spice. "Where does your family live?" Kurt asked once he'd swallowed.

"It depends on the time of year. In the summer we have a place in the Hamptons, and in the winter my folks have a house in Florida. My dad spends a lot of his time in New York, so we have a penthouse there too." Freddie spoke of all that as though it was normal, and Kurt tried not to stare at him openmouthed. "Where do your folks live?"

"Bethlehem. My grandfather was a steelworker, and my dad repairs cars. He has his own shop. My mom used to manage the office for him, but she can't do that anymore. She still helps out where she can, but it's a lot harder for her." Kurt finished his breadstick and nibbled on one of the thick-cut onion rings. "For the first two years of college, I went to Shipp because I could afford it. I'd applied here, but didn't get enough scholarship money. I reapplied last winter, and they awarded me a scholarship."

"I have an athletic scholarship for part of my school, and Dad pays the rest. As long as I'm playing well, he's happy."

That didn't sound right to Kurt. "Can I ask you something? Why does your dad only care about you playing? You'd think he'd want you to be successful."

Freddie sighed and shoved a whole onion ring into his mouth. He chewed and then swallowed while Kurt continued nibbling. "My dad wanted to play football, but he broke his leg when he was fourteen and couldn't play. Once he found out I was good, he encouraged me, and it became what I am to him. I'm his son who plays football, and that's what he's proud of. My younger sister, Helen, is musically gifted and is attending Julliard. My older brother, Gerard, is taking after my dad and is actually working with him. He'll take over the family manufacturing business. It's my job to win football games." Freddie lowered his gaze to the table and went on eating.

The server brought the pizza. Kurt took a single slice of pizza and slowly ate while Freddie continued attacking his food like it was his opponent on the gridiron. "You know it isn't going anywhere," Kurt said gently, and Freddie slowed down.

"People think money solves everything, but it doesn't," Freddie said. "My mother spends her time with her leagues and charities because she's lonely as hell. Since Helen started music school, Mom has no one to mother, so she does charity. Dad works all the time. Not that we need any more money. There's more than any of us could ever spend." Freddie stopped eating and stared at him. "The only way I can get his attention at all is to win games or act out."

"But you aren't a teenager any longer…," Kurt prodded.

"Right. And acting out now comes with lots of consequences. Besides, being an ass doesn't get you very far."

"You could have fooled me that first day," Kurt said seriously.

"I know, and I'm sorry. I treated you like crap, and you still tried to help me," Freddie said softly. "No one has ever done that before. I have lots of friends as long as I have money, but they have a tendency to evaporate when my allowance is running low."

"So kick them to the curb. Your friends should like you for you, not for what you can buy," Kurt said. "I've never had money, but I know people like me or hate me, as the case may be. But at least they aren't fake."

"I suppose," Freddie admitted, and they let the subject drop. Kurt continued eating slowly. He was already getting full, but Freddie was still going strong. He'd finished off the breadsticks and the onion rings and eaten half the pizza before he started to slow down. Kurt took a small second slice, and Freddie ate the rest. "Sorry, I had a busy morning. Guess I was hungrier than I thought."

"It's okay. I had all I wanted. Thank you," Kurt said.

"No problem," Freddie said, wiping his mouth with a napkin before leaning back in his chair.

"Where are your friends?" Kurt asked.

"They went home for the weekend. My folks are in New York. They had some big charity benefit. Last night was a cocktail party, and today was some big golf tournament on Long Island. Dad was golfing with some other CEOs, and then tonight they're going to a big charity auction. The last time they went, Mom came home with a painting by some artist no one had ever heard of, or probably will ever hear of. The thing was ugly, and I think it's now hanging in one of the guest bedrooms."

"The one for the people you don't like?" Kurt joked.

Freddie smiled. "Something like that. Mom likes the thing and she swears he's going to be famous. She'll come home this time with some other piece of crap, and Dad will pay for it to make her happy."

"So if your dad is only interested in football, what about your mom?"

Freddie genuinely smiled. "She's actually pretty cool. She has her charity things, but she loves to bake too. She doesn't do it very much anymore, because none of us are at home, but she used to make bread and cookies and stuff. My dad's folks had money, but Mom was raised poor. For a while I wondered how they got together, but Mom told me she saw Dad and that was it. She didn't care if he was rich or poor—she loved him, and she still does. They're happy. Most of their friends have divorced at least once, but they've stayed together for thirty years. My mom and I talk on a regular basis, but the only time I hear from my dad is on football nights after the games."

The waitress stopped by the table, flirted with Freddie a little, and then took the dishes. She returned with the check, and Freddie pulled out a black credit card and handed it to her. She then left the table again. "It used to bug me that he couldn't be bothered much, but it doesn't anymore," Freddie told him, but Kurt knew it was a lie. The sadness and dejection that flashed across Freddie's expression for a second told him a lot more than Freddie's words.

"Then screw him," Kurt said, and Freddie's eyes widened. "If your dad only cares about football, screw him. You're more than that. You have things you're good at and you care about people."

"How do you know?" Freddie asked with a skeptical tone in his voice.

"You raced all the way out of class to help me. Nobody else did that—just you." He wanted to say something about the way Freddie had spoken to him, but he left that part out. "You're willing to stand up for what's right. Lots of guys won't do that. Do you think your friends, the ones you sit with at lunch, would do that?"

Freddie shrugged.

"I doubt it, but you did," Kurt said. The waitress returned with the receipt, and Freddie signed it and took his card. Then they stood up, and Kurt followed him out and onto the sidewalk. They walked back toward campus, their way illuminated by streetlights and the headlights of passing cars. As they got closer to campus, the lighting became more regular and less harsh. "My dorm's over there," Kurt said as they approached the quad. Freddie paused and leaned against one of the stone posts the made up the decorative gate to the main quad. "I really should get going," Kurt added after a few seconds of Freddie staring at him.

"How did you know you liked boys?" Freddie asked, and Kurt took a step back, wondering where in the hell that had come from.

"Why?" Kurt asked, instantly alert and wondering what was going on. Had all this been some elaborate ruse to get him alone? "What's going on?"

"Nothing," Freddie said breathily. "I just need to know."

"I can't answer that. It's something I just knew. It's part of me, part of who I am. But if you want to know how I figured it out, that's pretty easy. I never looked at girls with any real interest." He didn't want to go into any details that would freak Freddie out. "I really need to go."

Freddie nodded, and Kurt turned, pushed open the wrought-iron gate, and began walking across the lighted quad in the direction of his dorm. After a few seconds, he heard someone behind him and suppressed the urge to run. Instead he turned to look and saw Freddie hurrying toward him. "What's wrong?"

Freddie took his hand and pulled him across the yard and between two of the buildings. Kurt fought him for a few seconds, but Freddie was too strong. In the shadows, Freddie pressed him against the stone building, stepped close, and kissed him.

At first, Kurt was so surprised he didn't react. His shock lasted all of two seconds, and then he returned Freddie's kiss, wrapped his arms around his neck, and sucked hard on Freddie's mouth. Damn it, if the star quarterback was going to kiss him, then Kurt was damned well going to kiss back. Hell, if given the chance, he would give him a kiss Freddie would compare every other kiss to for the rest of his life. Kurt slipped his tongue between Freddie's parted lips, tasting him for the first time. The rich, slightly salty, heady masculine flavor went straight to his head. Without thinking, Kurt moaned softly and thrust his tongue deep, and Freddie sucked on it. His entire body was on fire, and he was so hard it hurt. Kurt paused the kiss for a brief second as he tilted his head the other way and then pulled Freddie's head forward. He held him tight and threw everything he had into the kiss, cradling Freddie's cranium in his hands as he ran his fingers through Freddie's short, soft hair. Kurt had no illusions that this was going to last. This kiss was a product of the darkness, and in the light of day, everything would change. Freddie would be the football star, and he'd just be another student, but in the darkness, here... now... Kurt had Freddie and he wouldn't let him go.

Freddie pulled away, and Kurt heard a slow, ragged breath. Then Freddie kissed him again, intensely, passionately, maybe even desperately.

Voices from outside penetrated the edges of Kurt's hearing. Freddie must have heard them as well, because he stilled and then backed away. Kurt could still feel Freddie's breath against his skin as he heaved air into his lungs. The female-pitched voices came closer and got louder. Freddie backed away, and Kurt pressed back against the side of the building. He wanted to pull Freddie into another kiss and let the girls get an eyeful if they came this way. But that wasn't going to happen. In the dim light, he could see Freddie's eyes. They were wide and filled with fear. Freddie pulled back, and their gazes met just before Freddie took another step away and then began to walk away from the voices. After a few seconds, Freddie passed outside the shadow of the building, and Kurt saw him striding quickly away under one of the lamps. He waited to see if Freddie would pause or turn back to look, but he didn't. Kurt took another soft breath and stood still as a group of girls passed in front of him. He didn't move or make a sound, and they went by without noticing him.

It took Kurt a few seconds to compose himself and make sure no one else was around before he stepped out of the shadows. He didn't want to startle anyone. When he heard no more voices, Kurt stepped away from the building and slowly walked toward his dorm, looking around him constantly. He hid behind the notion that he wanted to ensure he was safe, but really, he was hoping to see Freddie waiting for him somewhere. He wasn't, and Kurt arrived at his dorm without encountering anyone or seeing Freddie again. He went inside and climbed the stairs, unlocked the door, and stepping into the room. In the darkness once again, he sat on the edge of his bed, wondering what the kiss meant. All that stuck in his mind was how Freddie couldn't get away fast enough.

Chapter 4

FREDDIE COULD barely think. He'd kissed Kurt. Not just kissed him—pressed him against a building and damned near had his way with him. Even back in his room at the house he shared with the guys, he still trembled with excitement. Football, with its rush of excitement, had always been a high, but this…. His mouth was dry, his heart raced, and he breathed in short, excited gasps. Even now, his blood still raced, and he could hardly sit still. He wanted to burst back out of the house, race down the street, and yell at the top of his lungs about what had happened, what he'd discovered. But that same thought paralyzed him with fear, a feeling very new to him.

On the gridiron, huge men intent on stopping him raced at him, ready to knock him over, or worse. It was part of the game, part of what he loved—being a modern-day warrior. Sure, he knew fear, but when he was playing, he could shift that fear into action. But this, the fear someone would find out and learn about him was different, almost debilitating, and he didn't know what to do with it.

"Freddie," Johnny called up the stairs. "Is that you?"

Freddie stood and walked to the open doorway. "Yeah, I just got in." Johnny didn't answer further, but Freddie heard music start. Freddie left his room and descended the stairs to the first floor. Johnny and Carl sat in the living room. A girl Freddie didn't know sat with Johnny, and Brittany sat next to Carl. She was all smiles. They were all drinking and still celebrating the win from the day before. Johnny tossed him a can. Freddie caught it and flopped in one of the chairs before opening the can. He downed most the beer in a few gulps before burping.

"You're a pig," Brittany teased, and then Carl did the same thing, burping even louder. Johnny, of course, couldn't be outdone, and he added his own entry in their burp fest. The two girls seemed appalled for a second before giggling. The one next to Johnny even gave it a try, but she didn't make much noise. It didn't matter, though—they were laughing and happy. Freddie finished his beer and grabbed another from the twelve-pack on the table. He opened it and began drinking, figuring he might as well try to forget the doubt and fear.

"Slow down," the girl next to Johnny said. "I'm Cindy." She walked over and, to Freddie's surprise, sat on his lap. He looked at Johnny, who seemed shocked as well, but he didn't say anything. Then she leaned close. "I'm up for both you and Johnny. I've always wanted two sexy football players at the same time." She sucked on his ear, and Freddie knew he should have been excited, but nothing was happening. Freddie wondered how he was going to put her off, because he wasn't about to do what she wanted.

"Baby," Johnny growled as he got up and tugged her off Freddie's lap, "I'm more than enough man for you." Johnny tugged her gently until he was back in his chair and then pulled her down onto his lap. She giggled and wriggled her hips against him. "I got plenty for you all alone." Johnny pulled her close. He whispered something to her, and she giggled and did another hip wriggle. Obviously she was happy with what Johnny had. Freddie finished his beer and reached for another. Brittany and Carl were talking, and the music blared over everything else.

He continued drinking while Johnny and Cindy began making out. Soon Carl and Brittany did the same. Freddie grabbed another beer and stood up to leave the room. He wasn't interested in watching his friends make out with girls. It only reminded him of the kiss he'd shared earlier with Kurt, but he didn't want to think about that either. All he wanted was for all of it to go away. So he opened the beer as he wandered into the kitchen. He drank it, then threw away the can. Then he pulled open the refrigerator door and grabbed two more cans. He kicked the door closed and slowly wound his way up the stairs to his room. He set the cans on the dresser and then went down the hall to the bathroom. He relieved himself, because beer was never owned, only rented. After flushing the toilet, he lumbered back to the bedroom, grabbed and popped open a beer, and sat on the edge of the bed. He could still hear the music from downstairs and he felt like shit. His stomach roiled, and he set the beer back on the dresser.

He was alone, and nothing was going to change that. His friends were having fun, enjoying themselves, and he was on the outside. He didn't want what they did, and damn it, if they found out what he wanted, they probably wouldn't be his friends any longer. He knew Coach Josh was gay and that the guys seemed to accept him, but Coach Josh wasn't showering with them every day.

Freddie stared at the beer cans on the dresser and left them where they were. He'd had enough to drink, and he still had the work he'd promised Kurt he'd finish for class in the morning. He went to the bathroom and got a drink of water, then settled himself on his bed, pulled open his lab book, and got to work.

He regretted those beers after an hour of trying to work. He was tired and needed to sleep, but had to finish this before his class first thing in the morning. At least some of what he was doing made sense after Kurt's help, and…. "Damn," he swore softly. Everything seemed to pull his thoughts back to Kurt.

Laughter in the hallway outside the door pulled his attention— giggles coupled with Johnny's deep laughter. He knew what they would be doing in a few minutes. Sure enough, the door to the room next to his closed, and a few minutes later, the rhythmic squeaking of the bed and the cries to various deities left little doubt as to Cindy's thoughts about Johnny's prowess.

"A screamer," Freddie said, holding his head. "She had to be a screamer."

Freddie wondered what it would be like if Kurt made those sounds. Though listening to Cindy and Johnny go at it was pretty hot, Freddie had the feeling Kurt would be more intense. He forced his clouded mind back to the task at hand and consulted Kurt's notes to answer the questions and complete the report. Then he closed his books and shuffled off to the bathroom. In the hallway, he heard moaning in stereo, and he rolled his eyes before going into the bathroom. He used the facilities again, then took an aspirin and downed another glass of water before returning to his room. Thankfully, most of the evening's entertainment seemed to have concluded by the time he got back.

He undressed, took off his glasses, and got into bed, hoping the beer would ease his way to sleep. It didn't. Now that he was alone with his thoughts, the beer didn't do a damned thing. Freddie ended up replaying the kiss in the darkness with Kurt, and despite the alcohol, he got hard enough to pound nails, just like he had during the kiss. For a few seconds, he debated taking care of things. The clincher was Johnny and Cindy picking that moment to start going at it again, so Freddie closed his eyes, imagined he was with Kurt, and took matters into his own hand.

HE SLEPT like shit even after the rabbits in the next room ran out of steam. He barely made it to class in time, and his head throbbed like hell. That was what he got for drinking the evening before he had classes. He sat down in his seat and plunked his book bag on the table just before Dr. Marcus began his lecture on the lab they were going to be doing that week. He dug out his homework and passed it to the front. He glanced at the seat next to him and Kurt glared back, clenching his jaw. He said nothing, and Freddie forced his attention to the front of the class. At least he was only dragging and the headache had subsided. Granted, he hadn't drunk that much. He opened his notebook and began writing down what he hoped were the important points as the professor explained the lab work. "All right," Dr. Marcus said when they were done, "let's get back to chapter two." Thankfully, Freddie had read it, and for the first time in a long time, what the professor spoke about began to make sense.

Freddie turned to Kurt with a smile on his face because he knew that was due to him, but his smile was met with a brief scowl and then a turn back to the professor and the lecture. Freddie did as well, giving up trying to talk to Kurt during class.

"I finished the write-up for the lab," Freddie said later, as he stood at the lab station next to Kurt, waiting for the lab to begin.

"That's good," Kurt said. "I'm glad for you."

"Your help yesterday was amazing. I understood stuff today." Freddie bumped Kurt's shoulder, and Kurt took a step away, glaring back at him. "Sorry, I didn't mean to hurt you."

"No, I'm sure you didn't. But it's easy to do things you don't mean," Kurt said, and Freddie wondered what he was talking about. "I suppose you didn't mean last night to happen either," Kurt whispered, and Freddie paled. "I thought so. That was obvious by you running across the quad like a scared rabbit." Kurt turned away, and Freddie groaned as fear once again bloomed in his gut. Other students came into the room, and the lab period began. There was no time to talk, and after the class time ended, Kurt gathered his books and left the room without saying anything. Freddie went to his other classes, figuring he might get a chance to speak to him at lunch.

No such luck. He couldn't find him at all, so Freddie sat quietly at his table, eating and ignoring the blow-by-blow that was going on around him regarding Johnny's exploits with the multitalented Cindy. "Yeah, I heard, all of it, over and over again," Freddie said at one point, to cover his near complete lack of interest.

Once he was done eating, he took his tray to the dish belt after telling the guys he had things to do. He somehow had to talk to Kurt. He kept swinging from remembering how amazing the kiss had been to near petrifying fear about what would happen if Kurt began telling people. However, Kurt seemed to have pulled a disappearing act, and Freddie needed someone to talk with. Since he could think of only one person that fit that bill, Freddie hurried home to get his bag for practice, walked over to the rec center, and knocked on Coach Josh's door.

"How are the glasses working out?" Coach Josh asked, motioning Freddie inside.

"Good, I guess. I'm still getting used to them, but I think they're good," he answered nervously.

"You played well with them during the game on Saturday. Coach Norris and I were a little worried they might change things enough that you'd have trouble, but you did great," Coach Josh said. "So what can I do for you?" Coach Josh sat down and swiveled his chair around. "I doubt this has to do with football or your glasses." Coach Josh was the defensive coach, and Freddie, being the quarterback, played offense. "So what gives?"

Freddie looked around and felt his cheeks heat. He reached over and pushed on the door. It swung and softly clicked closed. "I don't know how to ask this."

"My experience is to just say what's on your mind," Coach Josh said evenly. "What you have to say won't go any farther than this office. I've heard just about everything, from girl troubles to helping with appointments at the local clinic, so you don't need to be embarrassed."

"That's just it. For stuff like that I'd go to Coach Harper." He worked with the offense and was the coach Freddie worked with most often. "This requires that I talk specifically to you."

The coach nodded slowly. "All right. The college supports and encourages diversity, and sometimes that makes others uncomfortable. But we're all better off knowing people who are different from ourselves. If anyone does something to make you uncomfortable, I want to know, but the reverse is also true. If you do something to make someone else uncomfortable, or act on your discomfort, we need to make it right."

Freddie shook his head and blinked behind his glasses. "I don't think I'm following," Freddie said.

"Sorry. I end up having the diversity conversation with most of the players at some point because I'm gay, and I guess I figured that was what this was about." Coach Josh grew quiet. "The floor is yours."

Freddie squirmed slightly in his chair. "Last night I kissed a guy for the first time, and I really liked it," he blurted out and then took a deep breath. "He's the guy who came to see you."

Coach Josh smiled. "You mean Kurt?"

Freddie nodded his agreement. "He's in biochemistry with me, and he was helping me at the library. We went out for pizza afterwards and then walked back through campus, and when we were in a dark place, I kissed him. And he kissed my socks off back."

"I take it nothing like this has happened before?" Freddie shook his head. "Are these feelings a real surprise or…." Freddie stared at his feet. "I see. You've had them for a long time but either ignored them or hoped they would go away, but they haven't."

"Yeah. I had them in high school," Freddie admitted.

"You know, it's okay. You're gay, so what?" Coach Josh said.

"It's not that easy," Freddie countered.

"I know that." Coach Josh paused for a few seconds. "What do you want to do about it?"

"I don't have much choice. I want all of it to go away," Freddie told him.

"Do you want Kurt to go away? Do you want to never see him again? Because the desperate expression on your face right now tells me that's not true. You care for Kurt. But that isn't what I'm asking you. Do you want to stay in the closet, or are you asking me how to come out?"

"I don't know." Freddie looked out through the glass walls toward the locker room. "Everything will be different."

"The coaching staff will support you. Have no doubt about that. Most of the students on campus will support you. This is a very diverse and accepting campus. The administration has worked hard to see to that. There are gay professors, as you probably know." Coach Josh smiled just a little.

"That's why I came to you. I knew you would understand."

"So would a lot of people. This isn't the seventies or eighties, when coming out was a huge deal. Some kids come out in junior high school, at thirteen or fourteen, nowadays. Sure, some guys might give you grief, but most will support you."

"I guess," Freddie said without energy.

"Okay, then why don't you tell me what's worrying you?"

"Everything," Freddie said and waved his arms dramatically. Then he realized how he looked, pulled his arms down, and folded his hands on his lap.

"You can't deal with everything all at once. So break it down and think about what's truly bothering you," Coach Josh said calmly. "You aren't the first person to go through this, and you won't be the last. I went through it; Kurt went through it; Brendon—Dr. Marcus—went through it. So take a deep breath and tell me what's at the heart of the trouble."

"All I have is football—it's what I'm good at. I've never been really smart like Kurt or my brother and sister. I was the jock, the one good at sports." He tried to get his mind around the real issue.

"You can be gay and be good at sports. The two are not mutually exclusive. But I will tell you what I tell a lot of the guys: this is Dickinson College, a small, but highly regarded liberal arts college. We have a reputation for many things, but football is not among them. It's not likely you'll make it to the NFL. This isn't Penn State, Ohio State, Auburn, Michigan, or USC. This is Dickinson. Here you're a big fish because you're the star of the team, but once you graduate, that's it. You need to have something to fall back on, and that's your education... period. I know you said you've been getting some help in biochemistry. What about your other subjects?"

"But...."

"But nothing." Coach Josh looked around. "Screw your brother and sister and whatever talent they have. To me they aren't important—you are. And what's truly important is your education. My family is just like yours. My parents are professors, and my sister's a doctor. I could go on. I'm a good coach and I love doing it. But I couldn't if I hadn't worked hard for my education." He took a deep breath. "As for the gay part, that's really immaterial. If you come out, you'll have a lot of supporters on campus, I can guarantee that."

"It's off campus I'm worried about," Freddie confessed.

Coach Josh sighed. "I can't help you there. I don't know your family. But I can tell you that in this day and age, most people already know other gay people. Your family is from New York, right?"

"Yes," Freddie said.

"Then your family probably knows many gay people. I know you may think there's a difference between having gay friends and a gay son, and I wish I had answers for you, but I don't." Coach Josh moved slightly closer.

"I do know that this is your decision. You have to decide what you want, and no one, not your mom or dad or anyone else can make that decision for you."

"I guess," Freddie said and then stood up. "Thanks for listening."

"I'm here if you want to talk again," Coach Josh said.

Freddie nodded before he grabbed his bag and opened the office door. "Thanks," he added before striding out to the locker room to get ready for practice.

He spent the next two hours running plays, drilling, and sweating his ass off. After Coach Norris dismissed them, he hit the showers and left the rec center, avoiding the other guys. He needed time to think and ended up wandering around campus. His thoughts kept going back to his talk with the coach. However, he still got nowhere.

Freddie had no idea what he wanted to do now. He was just as nervous and scared as he'd been before he'd talked to Coach Josh, but maybe a little less confused. Without knowing what else to do, he wandered over to the library. Not that he intended to work, but he was hoping he might find Kurt there. Unfortunately for Freddie, Kurt didn't work on Mondays, so he wasn't behind the desk, and Freddie walked through the work areas, but didn't find Kurt in any of those, either. He really didn't know any other place Kurt hung out, so he began walking home.

He passed Samuelson Hall and shook his head at the letters engraved in stone over the lintel. Then he remembered something Kurt had said when he'd been chewing him out in the cafeteria that first day. Freddie couldn't stop a smile as he remembered the fire in Kurt's eyes. He might be small, but Short Stuff was a real firecracker.

Freddie pulled open the door, still chuckling at the memory, and nearly slammed into one of the guys who sat with Kurt at lunch. "Hey," Freddie said. "I'm looking for Kurt."

"I'm not going to help you," the bean pole said.

"I just want to talk to him," Freddie said softly. "Honest."

The guy paused briefly. "Fine. I'll call and ask if he wants to see you. But if he doesn't, you leave, or quarterback or not, I'll hurt you in ways you can't imagine."

Freddie stepped back and raised his hands. "I only want to talk to him." He watched as the guy walked to one of the house phones and dialed a number. Freddie shifted his weight from one foot to the other while he waited. "Okay, I'll tell him." The guy hung up.

"He said he'll be down." The guy crossed his arms over his chest and stared at him. Freddie did the same and stared back. Two could play that little game, and Freddie was bigger and had a hell of a lot of intimidation experience. But it didn't seem to be working.

Freddie saw Kurt walking toward them over the other guy's shoulder and smiled, ignoring the other man all together. He walked around him and right up to Kurt.

"Do you want me to stay?" the other guy asked.

"I'm fine, Luka, thanks," Kurt said and then turned to Freddie. "What do you want?"

"Can we talk somewhere?" Freddie asked.

Kurt looked around. "I was going to get something to eat." He looked suspicious and cautious.

Freddie nodded and motioned toward the door. It wasn't what he'd had in mind, but he'd take the opportunity. Mainly because he figured it was the only one he was going to get. He followed Kurt outside and down the sidewalk to the dining hall. Kurt showed his card and had it swiped. Freddie did the same.

"I thought you had to live in the dorms to get a meal plan," Kurt said.

"Not really. You just have to be willing to pay for it. It's one of the things my mother insists on. She figures that way I'll be more likely to eat something other than pizza and takeout. I get the ten-meal-a-week plan and it's enough to get me through." They walked through the line, and Freddie filled a tray with beef, noodles, salad, vegetables, french fries, and cheesecake for dessert.

"Good God," Kurt said when he met him at a table. "Are you really going to eat all that?" Freddie laughed when he saw the meager portions on Kurt's tray.

"I'd starve if I only ate that," Freddie said. "Most days I have practice and a workout. If I don't eat a massive diet, I'll pass out." He set the cheesecake aside. "I'm not supposed to have that, but it looked good. I love key lime. Do you want to split it?"

"No, thanks. I have to watch the amount of dairy I eat. The pizza on Sunday was about my limit, and if it had been drowning in cheese, I would have had to pull a lot of it off." Kurt began to eat.

Freddie tucked in. He was starving, and as soon as he tasted the first bite, his appetite took over. He ate his salad, then the beef and noodles, followed by the vegetables. Finally, he slowed down.

"You wanted to talk to me," Kurt reminded him.

"I did," Freddie said, looking around. "I went to see Coach today." He shifted in the chair. "I needed some time to think about stuff, and I needed to ask him some questions about being…." God, he couldn't say the word. "You know."

"Yeah, I know," Kurt said snarkily. "I live it every day, remember? I was the one who got attacked. And I was the one you couldn't get away from fast enough once you thought someone might see you. I know. I've been there before and I won't do that again. I've had people who were my friend after dark, but in the light wouldn't even speak to me."

"I'm sorry." Freddie set down his fork.

"This must be bad if it stopped you from eating," Kurt said and then smiled slightly.

"I'm confused," Freddie whispered, "and scared."

"Were you confused about what happened last night? Is that what has you worked up? Because if you're worried I might tell someone, you can relax. I don't kiss and tell. Not even to my friends." Kurt returned to his dinner, eating slowly. "Is that what you wanted to hear?"

Freddie sighed uncomfortably. For part of him, that was exactly what he wanted to hear. "Yes and no," Freddie answered honestly, and then he quickly scanned the room. "Your friends are all staring at us."

"No. They're staring at you, I'm sure," Kurt told him. "I haven't mentioned anything to them about what happened, but they've figured out something occurred and it involved you, so they're closing ranks and probably making sure you don't try to hurt me."

"I'd never do that," Freddie said, shocked.

"Well, yeah, I get that, I guess," Kurt said. "But you know you hurt me already. I guess you didn't mean to, but you did." Kurt leaned over the table. "You used me to satisfy whatever curiosity you were feeling and then ran off like a scared rabbit."

"It wasn't like that. I panicked when I heard the other voices," Freddie said and looked around. "Can we finish eating and go for a walk where we can talk more privately?" Sweat began to bead on his neck and forehead. Freddie knew he owed Kurt an explanation, but he needed to do it privately, not in the middle of a crowded cafeteria.

"All right," Kurt said after what appeared to be a few seconds' deliberation. "We can talk." Kurt swallowed hard and Freddie stared at him, watching his delicate throat work. He blinked a few times to pull him out of those thoughts. Then he returned to his dinner and finished up his food. Kurt was done as well, so Freddie took both trays to the dish belt and then returned. The table was empty, and he saw Kurt standing near his friends. He weaved between the tables toward the door and waited for Kurt. His stomach jumped and churned, and Freddie wished he hadn't eaten so much.

Kurt left his friends and headed over toward him. Once he caught up with Freddie, they left the dining hall. Freddie led them toward one of the sidewalks that wound through a lightly wooded area of campus.

"What did you want to talk about?" Kurt asked.

"I talked to Coach. Coach Josh, Dr. Marcus's boyfriend," he clarified. "After what happened last night, I was confused. I know I shouldn't have run away and left you. That wasn't right, and neither was letting you think that kiss was some experiment. It wasn't. It was a real kiss, and my first one with a guy." Freddie swallowed around the lump in his throat. "I'm gay," he whispered.

"Okay," Kurt said with a shrug. "You're gay."

Freddie stopped under one of the huge trees. He hadn't known the reaction he'd been expecting, but it certainly hadn't been that.

"I'm glad you're able to admit that to me." Kurt turned to face him. "Do you want a medal?"

"No. But I guess I expected you to be happy," Freddie said.

"Why?" Kurt whispered. "Look, I know what this is. You're figuring out you're gay and I'm the closest person you can talk to. It's not like you'll take me seriously as a boyfriend or anything." Kurt looked away. "I'm just the first guy available. I'm not in your league at all." He turned back to Freddie. "I'll listen if you want to talk, and I'm happy you're beginning to deal with who you really are. That's always a huge step." Kurt stepped backward. "I have to go." He turned and strode off quickly down the sidewalk.

It took Freddie about two seconds to make up his mind and take off after him. He'd always been fast and he quickly caught up to a startled Kurt. "Come with me," he said and grabbed Kurt's hand.

"What are you doing?" Kurt asked.

"Trust me," Freddie said and hurried toward the rec center. He went around the building to a courtyard. It had probably been open green space when the building had been built, but now the plants were overgrown, and from inside, only a wall of green was visible. Freddie lifted a branch and then motioned Kurt through. Inside, they were in a world of their own. An old concrete bench stood to one side, pine branches growing toward it but not quite reaching.

"What is it, Freddie?" Kurt whispered.

"This is hard for me to talk about, but I like you. I really do," Freddie admitted. "We don't talk about feelings in my family, ever. It's a sign of weakness." He brushed off the bench and shivered.

"What?"

"I hate spiders," Freddie admitted without thinking, and Kurt chuckled. "We're all afraid of something, and I hate the things. Always have." Kurt pushed the spider off the seat, and Freddie sat down on one edge. "I know I'm not the smartest guy around, but I really like you. I think I have since that first time you told me off."

"That has to be the weirdest thing I've ever heard." Kurt laughed under his breath as he sat down.

"It's not weird. Your eyes blazed and you had a ten-foot presence." Freddie turned so he could see Kurt. "You're a very handsome man."

"I'm short and small. Just the right size to fit in a locker," Kurt mumbled. "I found out firsthand once."

"I guess what I mean is that you have a big personality. You're interesting and kind," Freddie said, struggling with the words. "I've known you for a little over a week, but it seems like I've known you forever, like if I hadn't known you, I'd have missed out on something really important and special."

"I'm just me," Kurt whispered. Freddie leaned in, and when Kurt didn't pull away, Freddie closed the gap between them. Freddie wasn't sure at first who kissed who, but within a split second, Kurt had taken control of the kiss, deepening it. Freddie moaned softly and parted his lips. Kurt slipped his tongue between them, cupping Freddie's head as he pressed their mouths together harder.

Freddie was on fire and instantly hard as nails. He'd kissed girls before, and he'd had sex with them too, but it had never felt right. This, on the other hand, felt perfect, right, and like coming home. When the kiss broke, Kurt didn't move, and Freddie gathered him into his arms and hugged him close.

"What are you going to do?" Kurt asked.

"I don't know," Freddie whispered.

"Most people on campus are going to be supportive," Kurt said.

Freddie swallowed hard. "It's not on campus I'm worried about. Well, I am, kind of, but I guess most of the guys will get used to it. They accept Coach, so…." He shrugged. He really didn't want to talk about this right now. Kurt's warmth soaked through his shirt, and Freddie closed his eyes. He gasped softly and tensed when Kurt pulled his shirt out of his pants and slipped his hand under and along his skin. Kurt paused, and Freddie held him tighter.

"You feel really good," Kurt whispered, and Freddie's belly muscles fluttered when Kurt ran his hand over his abs and then up to his chest. Noise from outside seeped into their green cocoon, and Kurt paused. "I wondered what you were like under your shirt." Kurt slowly ran his hand across Freddie's chest, flicking his nipples lightly and sending a shiver down his spine. Other voices joined the first, and Kurt pulled his hand away. Freddie listened to a screaming fight between two girls, and neither of them moved. Finally, the voices faded away, and Kurt stood up. "I should go."

Freddie nodded. "Can I talk to you again?"

"Yes," Kurt said with a smile. "I'll see you tomorrow in class, and we can study together, if you want. The library should be pretty quiet, and we can review the last exercises."

"That would be great, although since we're discussing biochemistry, I was hoping we might go someplace where we could make a little of our own," Freddie said.

"Maybe," Kurt said softly, but with banked fire in his eyes. "Are you sure you want to do this? With me? I can tell you there are lots of guys, ones more in your league, if you know what I mean." Kurt stared at the ground.

"If anyone's out of anyone's league, it's me," Freddie admitted. "You're the brain, and I'm just the dumb jock."

"How about we see what happens?" Kurt offered, and Freddie nodded. His entire body quivered with the kind of excitement he usually only felt after a game. Freddie stood up and tugged Kurt to him. Then he wrapped him in an embrace and kissed him. He took a page from Kurt and took charge, the way Kurt had earlier. He cupped Kurt's cheeks and kissed him as though the world were ending, because for Freddie, the world as he knew it was coming to an end. From now on, everything would be different. He saw that now, and in that moment of passionate enlightenment, he realized nothing would be the same, no matter how much he might wish it. Freddie had gotten a taste of the true joy life had in store, and he couldn't go back, not now, not ever.

THEY LEFT the grove and walked across the lamplit campus. "I'll see you tomorrow in class," Kurt told him with a small smile.

"Okay," Freddie agreed, and they parted company. Freddie watched Kurt until he was near his building and then walked briskly off the campus and down the side street. As he approached the front door, the house seemed quiet, which he was grateful for. He tried the front door. It was locked, which was strange because the guys were obviously home. Both their cars were parked on the street. He unlocked the door and went inside. Both Carl and Johnny were in the living room watching television. "Hey, what's going on?"

Johnny mumbled something, and Carl elbowed him in the side. "Nothing," Carl answered.

"It's not nothing," Johnny groused and shifted away from Carl. Johnny had a textbook on his lap, which was a surefire way to make him grumpy. He hated to study and lived for football, beer, and fucking, not necessarily in that order. Classes were a necessary evil so he could keep doing the other three.

"Yes, it is," Carl countered. "And it's none of your business." Carl got up and left the room. He returned with a can of Coke and pulled a book off the coffee table.

Johnny got up and left the room, shooting a scalding look at Freddie before climbing the stairs. Freddie jumped when a door slammed sharply. "What's with him?"

Carl shook his head slowly and opened the can. "He was waiting for some chick outside one of the dorms and saw you walking with that guy from your biochemistry class. The kid you rescued last week."

"Kurt," Freddie supplied, flopping into one of the chairs.

"Yeah, him. And rumor has it you were talking to Coach Josh in his office this afternoon, so naturally, he put two and two together in his pea brain, came up with eleven, and decided you're gay."

Freddie went still and couldn't breathe. He opened his mouth to deny it, but nothing came out. "Carl, I…."

"Holy shit, you are," Carl said surprisingly calmly. "Well, I'll be damned."

"I told you," Johnny called down the stairs and then slammed the door again. A few seconds later, the door opened. "I'm moving out of here. Ain't living with a fag," he added and then slammed the door for the third time. Freddie winced, the insult cutting deeper than he would have expected.

"Then go, pea-brain," Carl called as he leaned back on the sofa so his voice carried well up the stairs. "Brittany's brother is gay, and he's a good kid."

Freddie's head spun. "Good God, who else knows?"

"Doesn't matter, by the time gossipy Gerty up there gets done, everyone on campus will know." Carl drank from his can. "It doesn't matter to me at all. In fact, I've sort of wondered. You never seemed comfortable around girls. You liked them well enough, but never chased them like the rest of us. Makes sense now." Carl gulped once more from his can, and Freddie desperately wanted a drink, preferably vodka. Maybe a bottle. "So, are you and Kurt…," Carl asked.

"I don't know. Shit, we—"

"Okay," Carl cut in. "Ground rules. I don't care what you do or who you do it with, but don't you dare start talking any details, or so help me I'll punch you into the ground. There are limits. Just so we're clear."

"We kissed a few times. That's all," Freddie said, but Carl already had his hands over his ears making "la la la" sounds. Freddie rolled his eyes and waited for him to finish. "Ya done?" he asked. "I don't know anything about what me and Kurt are."

Thudding footsteps sounded on the stairs, and then Johnny appeared, carrying a big-ass suitcase and a black garbage bag. "I'm out of here," he announced. "I'll get the rest of my shit tomorrow." He glared at Freddie. "When he ain't here."

Freddie opened his mouth to protest, but Carl beat him to it. "Fine, but if you've taken anything that isn't yours, I'll take it out of your hide, and don't expect to get your rent back for this month, because that ain't happening. And don't think about taking any of the food or nothing, either. You're leaving without notice and you forfeit everything." Carl came to his feet. "You hear me, pea-brain?"

Freddie sat in stunned silence as one of the guys he'd thought was his friend prepared to storm out. But what really shocked him was Carl's defense.

"How can you stay here with him?" Johnny asked.

"Who, Freddie? The guy who saved your ass with Coach last year after you got drunk and mouthed off to half the team? The guy you've known since we all got assigned to the same suite in the freshman dorm? Seems to me there's nothing wrong with him and everything wrong with you. So go, but don't expect to get a lot of support. Not on campus. You're in the minority here, and no one will condone that crap." For a second, Freddie thought Johnny would change his mind, but he pulled open the front door and muscled his stuff outside before slamming the door closed.

Carl went out the door right behind him. Freddie thought he was trying to talk him into coming back, but he returned alone. "I got the bastard's key. Figured he'd clean us out later otherwise." He set the key on the table and put his feet up. Carl's phone rang a few minutes later, and he was smiling before he answered it. "Hi, honey. ... Yeah, come on over." Carl listened again. "We could use your help."

"I take it Brittany's on her way over," Freddie observed after Carl hung up. Before Carl could confirm what he already knew, he heard shouting on the street. Freddie jumped up and raced to the door. He pulled it open and saw Kurt standing on the sidewalk.

"Get out of here! Fag! You already screwed with him enough!" Johnny yelled at him and then dropped his bags and raced at Kurt in full tackle mode. Freddie raced forward as Johnny got ready to plow into Kurt, who stepped aside and watched as Johnny went flying and ended up face planting on the sidewalk.

"Ouch," Freddie said as he reached Kurt. "Are you okay?" he asked before turning to Johnny, who was picking himself off the darkened sidewalk. His face was scraped deeply in places, and he had blood running out of his nose. "Do you need help?"

"Don't touch me," Johnny cried and moved away.

"Fine," Freddie said as blood ran down Johnny's face. Carl came out and then rushed back inside, returning a few minutes later with a cloth. "You better call an ambulance. He's bleeding badly."

"I'm fine," Johnny said and moved away. Thankfully, Brittany arrived, took one look at Johnny, and made him sit down on the step while she looked at his face.

"You're going to be fine. But you should have someone look at your nose. It's pretty bad and might be broken," she told Johnny, who seemed determined to get the last of his stuff in his car. Then, without another word, he took off, and the rest of them went inside.

"What happened?" Brittany asked as soon as the door closed, and everyone spoke at once. She held up her hand and looked at Kurt.

"I have no idea, other than he started calling me names when I came by to return Freddie's wallet. He wasn't really paying attention, and I stepped aside and tripped him as he went by." Kurt looked at him. "Is he really on the team? Because he can't be that good…."

Carl laughed, and they all sat down, with Freddie sitting next to Kurt on the sofa. "He left because he figured some things out about Freddie."

"I gathered that," Kurt said. He reached into his jacket pocket, pulled out Freddie's wallet, and handed it to him. Freddie hadn't even realized his wallet had been missing. "I realized I'd lost my keys and went back to the bench. I found them and your wallet on the ground behind it."

"Okay, so what's going on?"

Freddie put his arm around Kurt, moving him a little closer. He saw Brittany's eyes widen and her mouth fall open. She was a great girl, but was rarely quiet. However, it looked like Freddie had rendered her speechless. "To make a long story short, Johnny has decided he doesn't want to live here any longer," he said.

"I'm sorry," Kurt whispered.

"It's okay."

"So you two are together?" Brittany asked, shaking her head. "I never would have guessed. You're so not each other's type." She slapped her hand over her mouth. "God, I didn't mean it that way. I guess I never—"

"Quit while you're behind," Carl said.

Brittany nodded. "Sorry."

"It's okay," Freddie said softly. He had bigger things to worry about, like the fact that his entire world had changed in a matter of hours. He'd come clean with Kurt and Carl, and he had no doubt that the news of his orientation would be spread around school as fast as Johnny could run his mouth.

"We'll help however we can," Brittany said, and Carl nodded.

Freddie smiled and turned to Kurt. "I'm not going anywhere." Kurt leaned against him. Freddie got the idea there was more Kurt wanted to say, but he didn't. "What do we do now?" Freddie asked. He'd lost one of his friends, and he wondered what else he would lose because of this.

"Don't worry about Johnny. If it's okay with you, I'll start making a few calls to people I know will be supportive," Brittany offered. "It's going to be the talk of campus for a while—there's nothing anyone can do about that—but it will pass." Brittany's phone chirped, and she checked it and frantically began texting for a few seconds. "It's not like it's that big a deal. You're gay; so are lots of cool people. No one really cares. It'll be something for people to talk about for a few hours and then they'll move on to something else."

Freddie wished he could believe that. But for him, this was about more than gossip and what other people thought. This was his life, and he wasn't prepared, not at all. But he had to be, and fast, because all hell was about to break loose. He just wished he knew which quarter it was going to come from.

Chapter 5

KURT WAS worried. Freddie looked miserable. Kurt alternately looked at Carl and then Brittany, wishing he had some answers. "For most people, accepting who they are is a gradual process. But for you, everything is happening all at once. Are you going to be okay with all this?" Kurt asked Freddie softly. "Most people come out quietly, telling their family and friends. They don't have to tell an entire campus."

"Oh God," Freddie said and rubbed his nose, skewing his glasses. "My father. He's going to kill me."

Kurt lightly rubbed Freddie's arm. "He's your dad. He'll understand. Maybe not at first, but he will."

Freddie shook his head violently. "No, he won't. After those guys attacked you, he told me to be careful who I hang around with. Saving someone was okay. 'Just make sure it's the right kind of person.' I almost got sick."

"He actually said that?" Brittany asked in horror.

"Not in those words, but that's what he meant. And to make it worse, he knew about what I'd done after the game on Saturday. It's like he has a spy or something on campus. Why he'd do that, or care, I don't know. He's so busy and he never had time for me growing up, so why he's obsessed with what I'm doing now is…." Freddie shook his head again.

Brittany nudged Carl and whispered into his ear. He nodded and they both stood up. "We're heading upstairs." Carl bumped Freddie's shoulder, and Brittany squeezed his arm as she passed.

"I should go too," Kurt said as he stood up.

"Don't," Freddie asked softly and then lifted his gaze.

Kurt swallowed hard and his mouth went dry when Freddie held out his hand. Kurt took it, and then Freddie stood up. Neither of them said a word as Freddie turned out the lights and locked the front door. Then he led the way up the stairs.

Kurt was both nervous and excited. Freddie was leading him to his bedroom. He wanted this, there was no doubt about it, but Kurt had never had an easy time separating sex from emotion. For him they were linked, not like many of the other guys he'd been with, who seemed to be able to screw a knothole. Being with Freddie was taking a chance, and he hoped he was ready for the possibility of heartache, because Freddie had just opened the door, and with a gentle hand on the base of his back, guided him inside.

The room was sparse, with almost no reflection of the person who lived there. The rest of the house had been rather generic, with a few pictures on the walls and old furniture, but nothing that really reflected the people, and this room had the same feel. It could be because school had just started, he didn't know, and before he could give it any more thought, Freddie had tugged him close.

Kurt tilted his face upward, and Freddie kissed him greedily. Kurt could feel barely contained energy coursing through Freddie's body as they moved toward and then tumbled onto the bed.

"I've wanted this for so very long," Freddie said.

"Yeah, but do you want me or just any guy?" Kurt asked.

Freddie was still for a second and then kissed him hard and deep, holding Kurt with almost breath-stealing tightness. Kurt repeated the question in his mind, but the whole idea flew from his head when Freddie slid his hands under Kurt's shirt, then broke the kiss just long enough to tug it off.

Kurt gasped when Freddie slid strong hands over his bare skin. He'd been touched before, but it had never been accompanied by the zing of a million tiny electric shocks. He arched his back and wrapped his arms around Freddie's neck, deepening the kiss still further.

"Did that answer your question?" Freddie asked breathily.

Kurt hummed softly and locked his gaze on Freddie's. Breathing shallowly, he waited to see what Freddie would do next. But nothing happened. He seemed at a loss. Kurt took control. He shifted and used small, gentle touches to position Freddie on the bed. Then he opened Freddie's shirt, button by button, kissing the exposed skin as he went. As he moved lower, Freddie panted softly and his stomach muscles quivered beneath Kurt's lips.

He undid the last button and pulled Freddie's shirt from his pants. The fabric lay open, and Kurt stifled a gasp. He ran his hands along the deep valleys of Freddie's stomach and then over the muscular mountains that formed his chest. A quiver rippled beneath Kurt's hands, and he stroked the skin covered with soft, dark hair. "Whenever I used to dream about men when I was young, I always pictured them with a hairy chest and belly that looked just like this," Kurt admitted, running his hand down Freddie's belly before teasing the skin just above his pants.

Freddie sat up, and Kurt pressed him back. "Stay where you are," Kurt said, shifting until he straddled Freddie's hips. He leaned forward and licked over Freddie's chest before swirling his tongue around one of Freddie's protruding nipples. Freddie hissed softly, and Kurt sucked the tiny bud, using his teeth to lightly scrape the skin.

"Jesus," Freddie whispered.

"You just wait," Kurt whispered. He licked up Freddie's chest, nibbled the base of his throat, and then slid up his neck, giving one of Freddie's ears a nibble before kissing him hard. Freddie wrapped his strong arms around Kurt and pressed them together. Kurt reveled in the gentle scratch of Freddie's chest against his. He felt Freddie slowly slide his hands up and down his back before pressing beneath his jeans. Now it was Kurt's turn to moan softly. He shifted slightly, and Freddie opened his belt and pants before he slid his hands down the back of Kurt's jeans and cupped his butt.

"Is that okay?" Freddie asked.

Kurt squeezed his eyes closed, arched his back, and ground his pelvis into Freddie's. He desperately wanted these pants out of the way, but he didn't want to stop touching or kissing Freddie long enough to do it.

His pants slid down his hips, as Freddie pressed them farther and farther down. Kurt shimmied until they slipped down his legs. He then kicked them off and went to work on Freddie's, opening his belt and then pushing them down. Freddie lifted his ass, Kurt got the jeans past his hips and then ground his cock next to Freddie's. They both moaned softly. Freddie's shoes thunked to the floor, and then he kicked off the last of his clothing. Kurt pressed to Freddie's warmth and luxuriated in the skin-to-skin sensation.

"Damn, you feel good," Freddie whispered.

"Not half as good as you," Kurt countered, running a hand over Freddie's chest. He lightly tweaked a nipple, and Freddie growled softly. Then Kurt added his tongue, swirling and sucking on Freddie's exposed skin before slowly shimmying down his body.

Freddie vibrated as Kurt licked and kissed searing-hot skin. He kissed and sucked his way down his belly, following the dark trail to the hefty treasure that jutted from a nest of dark curls. Kurt wrapped his fingers around Freddie's thick length and lightly stroked a few times just to see Freddie's reaction, which was as beautiful as it was erotic.

Freddie's mouth hung open and his eyes rolled as Kurt grasped firmly and stroked slowly up and down Freddie's throbbing shaft.

"God…," Freddie muttered.

Kurt grinned and then tilted his head, parted his lips, and slid them over the head of Freddie's shaft. Freddie gasped, and Kurt sucked him deeper, hollowing his cheeks as he took more and more of him. Freddie thrust slightly, and Kurt stilled him with a light touch on his hip. Then he sucked him deeper and slowly bobbed his head while sliding his tongue around the crown.

"Jesus," Freddie hissed softly.

Kurt pulled his head away. "Hasn't anyone ever done this?" Freddie shook his head, and Kurt smiled before sucking Freddie deep and hard. To say the whimpering sounds that came from the huge, strong man were gratifying was the understatement of Kurt's life. They made his heart soar. Kurt loved the feel of a thick cock sliding over his tongue. Freddie's was the largest he'd had, and damned if he wasn't going to make the most of it. He stretched his lips and relaxed his throat to take Freddie as deep as he could. When he did, the little whimpers became cries, and the entire bed shook with Freddie's excitement.

They hadn't talked about protection of any kind, and Kurt had the presence of mind not to bring it up now. So to be cautious, he let Freddie slip from between his lips, wrapped his fingers firmly around his shaft, and stroked quickly. Freddie's cock jumped in his hand. "That's it. Show me how much you like this," Kurt whispered. He wet a finger and slipped it down between Freddie's legs, then pressed it lightly to his opening. "Let go and give me what I want. Show me how hot and sexy you are."

"Fuck…," Freddie whined.

"Oh yeah, let go and come for me." Kurt teased the skin behind Freddie's heavy balls and slipped a finger just inside Freddie's body. Freddie's cock jumped and throbbed in his hand, and Kurt tightened his grip, adding just a bit more sensation. He knew Freddie had to be right on the edge. He pressed his finger deeper, located the spot inside him, and rubbed it slightly. Freddie came unglued, whimpering as his entire body tensed and then his cock throbbed as he came. "God, that's beautiful," Kurt whispered as he stared at Freddie, watching the utterly blissful expression—his mouth hanging open, eyes wide.

Kurt stilled and waited to see how Freddie would react. Now that he'd gotten what he needed, Freddie's behavior would tell Kurt a great deal. Would he be caring? Gently dismissive? Aloof? Kurt waited to find out.

What he didn't expect was aggression, and Kurt squeaked when Freddie hugged him close and guided their lips together. The kiss was gentler, the need gone, but no less intense. Kurt shook with deep need, and Freddie stroked down Kurt's back, cupped his butt cheeks in his hand, and pressed their bodies together.

Kurt held Freddie in return and flexed his hips, moving against him. He really hadn't expected Freddie to return the favor—being next to him was enough—so when Freddie rolled them on the bed, he was surprised. When he licked and kissed his skin, Kurt moaned softly. But when Freddie carefully took him into his mouth, Kurt nearly lost it right then and there. He'd expected Freddie to be reticent, but instead he was a tiger. He wasn't practiced or smooth. There were definitely fits and starts, but Kurt didn't care.

"Fuck, not all of you is short or small," Freddie commented after a few seconds and then stroked him a few times to accentuate his point before sucking Kurt once again.

Kurt wanted to say something about good things in small packages, but gave it up as soon as Freddie's lips settled around his shaft. Everything else flew from his head. He gripped the bedding, doing his best to keep from thrusting. Within moments, his mind floated and he was seconds away from coming. Kurt had the presence of mind to signal as best he could and then tumbled into the abyss as Freddie stroked him. Kurt clamped his eyes closed as his release washed over him. Then he lay still and let his mind float until the bed shook briefly and Freddie's warmth disappeared.

He didn't open his eyes when he heard Freddie leave, but he did when the door opened again. Freddie had wrapped a towel around his waist, but he let it drop and walked naked to the bed. He gently cleaned Kurt's skin and then climbed on the bed, tugged down the covers, and made Kurt comfortable before joining him. "Go to sleep," Freddie said, and Kurt nodded.

"I should be telling you that," Kurt said. "Rest. We'll sort it all out in the morning." He only wished he knew how, for Freddie's sake.

"SO, WHAT kept you out all night?" Peter asked as soon as Kurt opened the door to their dorm room. "And wearing the same clothes as last night, only really rumpled." He chuckled. "Looks like somebody got lucky."

Kurt humphed and closed the door. "Let's just say it was quite the evening, and I need to shower and get ready for class."

"So who did you get lucky with?" Peter asked. Kurt glared at him for a few seconds, and Peter's eyes widened. "No way! He's actually gay!"

"God," Kurt retorted. "Why do you find this so fascinating? You're straight, remember? I can see Luka and Jamie acting like this, but you're starting to scare me." Kurt opened his side of the closet and pulled out the clothes he was going to change into. Then he stepped into the hall, headed for the bathroom.

"Come on," Peter said before Kurt closed the door. "You bagged the quarterback of the football team. That's the equivalent of us straight guys doing the head cheerleader. Of course that's news."

"Come on. I didn't bag him," Kurt said, rolling his eyes. Then he shut the door to cut off the rest of the conversation and went into the bathroom. He stood at the sink, shaved, and brushed his teeth, then stripped off his clothes and started the water for a shower. A few seconds later, he stepped under the water and pulled the curtain closed. Kurt could have sworn he hadn't slept more than twenty minutes the entire night before. He hadn't been able to believe he was with Freddie and that they were in bed together. At some point during the night, Freddie had rolled over and tugged him close. He'd been near dozing off, but then, as soon as Freddie was so close and the warmth of his body melded with Kurt's, he found himself wide awake, hoping morning would never come.

Kurt moved under the spray and let the hot water revive him. Then he washed and showered a little longer before turning off the water and stepping out of the shower. He dried his skin and pulled on his clothes. He stepped out of the bathroom, went back to his room, and checked the clock. He had to hurry or he'd be late. He wrapped his ankle and then yanked on his socks and stepped into his shoes, taking two seconds to tie them before checking that he had his books in his bag. Then he said a quick good-bye to Peter and rushed out the door.

He made it across campus and to the science building with a few minutes to spare and took his seat in class. The other students talked quietly, but that changed as soon as Freddie entered the room. Almost every head turned, and then people began talking in earnest whispers. Kurt knew exactly what it was all about, and by the look on his face, so did Freddie.

"It'll pass quickly enough," Kurt whispered.

Freddie nodded and sat down. "Let's begin," Dr. Marcus said from the front of the room, and the class quieted and they got to work.

"Is it true?" the girl next to Freddie whispered, and Kurt rolled his eyes.

"Excuse me," Dr. Marcus said from the front of the room. "Do you have something to share?" The girl shook her head, and the professor returned to his lecture.

The tension flowed off Freddie like rainwater from a roof. Kurt could feel it. "Just ignore them and pay attention to the class. That's what you're going to be tested on. Not their gossipy prattle." Kurt glared at one of the girls who kept turning around, and she eventually stopped.

At the end of class, Kurt gathered his books, and a few of the other students hung around. Freddie shoved his books into his bag and didn't growl at them. Once he was packed up, Kurt walked with him out of class.

"Was it like this for you?" Freddie asked.

"No, but I wasn't the star of the football team," Kurt said. "Don't let it bother you."

Freddie nodded, but looked sort of lost. "I…," he began.

"I didn't mean to sound all stupid in there," said the girl who had sat next to Freddie. "I think it took guts for you to come out like that." She smiled up at Freddie for a few seconds and then hurried away.

"See? It's going to be okay," Kurt said, trying to be encouraging, even though Freddie looked like a deer caught in headlights. Freddie turned away from the other students and stared at Kurt. A chill went up Kurt's spine as Freddie's expression turned cold. Kurt turned to see if the expression was directed at someone else, but there was no one behind him. He felt as though Freddie had punched him in the stomach, and every name he'd ever been called echoed in Freddie's expression. Suddenly it was four years earlier and his bully in high school was once again shoving him into a locker.

"I gotta go," Freddie said and hurried away.

Kurt stared after him, hoping Freddie would turn around. But he didn't, and Kurt watched him rabbit away just like he'd done the night of their first kiss. Once Freddie had disappeared into the crowd of students heading for their classes, Kurt joined the flow and walked out of the building.

He had extra time before his next class and decided to use the hour to try to get some work done. He headed back to the dorm, figuring he'd be better off there, where it would be quiet, than sitting someplace more public.

It didn't quite work out that way. He sat at his desk to complete his biochemistry assignment, but he kept reading the same section of text over and over again. "Damn it," Kurt swore softly and then sighed for acting like a fool. He'd thought Freddie had liked him, and he'd deluded himself into thinking Freddie would rely on him and allow Kurt to help through this crisis. Hell, he'd actually thought working with Freddie to get through this would draw them closer together. Kurt shook his head. He'd gotten so caught up in what had happened the night before he'd actually let himself think he and Freddie could be boyfriends.

The room door opened and Peter came in. He closed the door and set down his books. Kurt looked up. "What happened?" Peter asked. "You look like hell."

"What I should have known would happen. Freddie freaked and took off after class," Kurt said and turned back to his books. "He looked at me like I was the world's biggest freak." Kurt shook his head. "I was so stupid. I actually thought he liked me. But once the heat was on, he couldn't get away fast enough."

"I'll be right back," Peter said, and he left the room, leaving the door open. He returned a minute later with Jamie right behind him.

"What happened?" Jamie asked, and Peter shut the door.

"I was stupid," Kurt said. Then he told Jamie about the night before and what had happened after class. "I thought he liked me. But the way he looked at me, it was like he was blaming me for everything." Kurt turned away. "I should have known, and I should have just left instead of staying last night."

"You stayed because you cared," Jamie said. "And that's a good thing. You cared about him. If he wants to be a dick, that's on him, but what's happened isn't your fault."

Kurt sighed. "I told myself that more than once. When he showed up yesterday and said he wanted to talk, I knew I should have run away, but I didn't. He ran before, and I should have known he'd run now."

"You haven't known him that long, and other than the one class, you don't have to have anything more to do with him," Jamie said. "If you wanted, you could talk to Dr. Marcus and ask if you could get a different lab partner. Then you wouldn't have to deal with him at all."

Kurt nodded, but he wasn't really listening. "The thing is, I really like him. He's fun to be around and has so much energy. I think so many people like him because he's the quarterback or because he has money, but I'd like to think I like him for him. Maybe he was only showing me what he wanted me to see."

"I don't know. And maybe you were seeing what you wanted to see. He's obviously good at getting what he wants," Jamie said.

Kurt nodded. "You can say that again. I'd already told myself I wasn't going there after the first time he ran away, but I let him do it again anyway. There won't be a third time."

"Good for you," Jamie told him and then tugged Kurt to his feet and into a deep hug. "You're going to be fine. We all endure heartache and pain. It's what makes us stronger."

"Thanks," Kurt said. "I ought to be Hercules by now."

"You have a good heart and want to help people, and you thought you could help him. But that guy's beyond help," Jamie said. "He's so used to getting what he wants and being the center of attention that he can't handle anything that threatens that. And it's much easier for him to turn on you and blame you for it than it is to man up and deal with it himself."

"That requires him to actually be a man," Peter scoffed. "I doubt he's capable of that. It sounds to me like he's still a little boy. He had the choice to stand up and accept who he was, but it looks like he can't." Peter lightly patted his shoulder. "I hate to say this, but don't be surprised if he has a girl on his arm soon to try to dispel all this talk."

"The thing is, his friends… well, most of them… accepted him."

"I have to go," Peter said, and Kurt nodded. Then Peter left, closing the door behind him.

Jamie pulled Peter's desk chair over and sat across from Kurt. "Some people build their self-worth and image from what everyone thinks about them. Freddie has probably been top dog for most of his life. In junior high, he played football, and in high school he was probably placed on a pedestal like a god. Even here, a college where football isn't the center of the universe, everyone knows who he is. Freddie is the star of the football team. That's his role; it's what he does."

"But…," Kurt began and then gave up. "There's more to him than that. I've seen it."

"But he probably doesn't see it that way. And if he's the football star, he most certainly can't be gay." Kurt opened his mouth to protest, but Jamie stopped him with a gentle touch. "Whether he's gay or not doesn't matter. He'll date girls, and the heat will die down. He'll probably say he was just experimenting...." Jamie paused. "He might say things that will hurt you."

"Like what?" Kurt asked. He didn't think Freddie could hurt him any worse.

"He might try to blame everything on you. He could say you talked him into it, or agreed to help him with his homework if you could get in his pants."

Kurt cringed and propped his forehead in his hand. "You think he'd do that?"

"I don't know what he'd do. I'm only trying to help prepare you for what could be coming. It doesn't matter what really happened, only what people think might have happened, and in the court of public opinion, he has a lot more weight and credibility."

Kurt glanced at the clock and sighed again. "I need to get ready for my next class." He didn't want to go anywhere. Maybe if he stayed in his room for a few days, this whole thing would blow over.

"Don't let any of this get you down. You're here to study and learn. All of us are behind you, and we know what really happened," Jamie said. Kurt lifted his gaze until their eyes met. "We've got your back; never forget that." Jamie stood up and hugged him once again. "Get ready for class and do your best to forget all about this. You need to keep focused on what's important."

"Yeah," Kurt said. He began gathering his things. "I always liked to think of myself as being a pretty good judge of character."

Jamie chuckled loudly. "Everyone likes to think that, and regardless of what anyone wants to tell you, we all suck at it. We can't see how people really are, only what they choose to let us see. Some people are better at that than others, and I'd say Freddie Samuelson is a master." Jamie opened the door to leave. "Be thankful you found out now, rather than later." Kurt nodded, knowing Jamie was right.

"I'll see you at lunch," Kurt told Jamie, and he nodded before pulling the door closed. Kurt finished gathering his things and left for his next class.

THE NEXT three weeks were surprisingly uneventful. No one seemed to be paying any more attention to him than before the kerfuffle with Freddie. The rumor mill had quieted, and as far as Kurt could tell, no one seemed to care any longer, other than the fact that the football team had lost their last two games.

Kurt had seen Freddie around campus a number of times, but he'd kept his distance, even going out of his way to avoid him. In biochemistry class, Freddie had switched seats and now sat on the end of one of the rows. One of the girls sat next to him, and Kurt paid attention to class, not caring where Freddie sat. As far as he was concerned, Freddie could sit in the hall and watch the lectures by hidden camera.

When Kurt turned toward the door, Nadine, the girl who'd asked Freddie if "it" was true, said, "You still watch for him, don't you?" He turned around quickly once again.

"I'd like to think I don't really care," Kurt told her, and she sighed.

"Well, if it's any consolation, he's a total putz. If I thought you'd be interested, I'd latch on to you and never let go." Nadine bumped his shoulder, and they shared a smile. "I have no idea how you can work with him as your lab partner," she whispered.

Kurt shrugged. "I concentrate on the work and try my best not to kick him in the nuts." He flashed her a grin, and she giggled behind her hand. Kurt laughed and waited for the prof to come in. Out of the corner of his eye, he saw Freddie come into class. Kurt thought he saw Freddie look at him, but then he sat on the other side of the room. The professor came into the room, and Kurt turned his attention to the front.

Once the lecture was over, Kurt headed to the most difficult hour of the week. He pulled out his lab coat and stood at his station while everyone else came in. He'd thought multiple times about asking Dr. Marcus to change his lab partner, but he didn't think it was fair to the other students or the professor to bring them into the mess with Freddie, so he stuck it out. It was only an hour twice a week.

Freddie came in and joined him at the lab station. Kurt took out his lab exercise book to get ready. He refused to look at Freddie, and for the past couple weeks he'd ignored him except when he needed him to do something. Other than that, he did most of the work, took his notes, and left the lab as soon as he could.

"Are you ever going to speak to me again?" Freddie asked once the lab had started and Kurt was busy setting up the equipment according to the instructions.

"Not if I can help it," Kurt said without looking away from what he was doing. "You made your feelings crystal clear a few weeks ago."

He continued working. "Get the Erlenmeyer flask," Kurt instructed, switching topics without thinking. "And if your little speech about your image and reputation the day after you ran away from me wasn't enough, the bimbo hanging on your arm was more than enough."

"I have a reputation and an image. That doesn't mean we can't be friends...."

Kurt stopped. "If you say on the side or something stupid like that, I'll pour hydrochloric acid down your pants. Maybe that can whittle your ego down to size," he whispered forcefully. "Now get your attention on this experiment and off anything else." Kurt turned back to the lab table and got to work.

He heard Freddie sigh, but forced his attention on the experiment and away from everything else. Like the last two labs, it was a battle. He registered every move Freddie made, and a few times when Freddie got close to him, he could smell his deeply rich scent. Kurt refused to look at him, because every time he did, he remembered tanned skin, rippling muscles, and the way the hair on Freddie's chest had erotically scratched his skin. Kurt knew he was being dumb and that he needed to forget all of it. He was trying his best, and for most of the week, he was successful. But with Freddie so close to him, like he was now, it was as hard as he was under his lab coat. "I have to be some sort of masochist," Kurt mumbled.

"What did you say?" Freddie asked.

"Nothing," he said quickly and finished the setup. "Let's get started. The sooner we're done, the sooner I can get out of here." Kurt listened as the professor explained some of the pitfalls to watch out for, and then they got to work, with Kurt's attention focused exclusively on the task at hand. He refused to allow Freddie's proximity to influence his thinking and what he needed to do. It was, he knew that, and every time Freddie leaned closer to him, Kurt got distracted, but no way would he let Freddie know he was getting to him. Kurt closed his eyes for a second and reminded himself that he'd been willing to help, that it had been Freddie who'd run away from him and who he was. Freddie had been the one to lead him on, and it wasn't happening again. Kurt opened his eyes and got back to work.

The lab period seemed to drag on. More than once, while they had a few minutes, Freddie had tried to start a non-class-related conversation, and Kurt had either ignored him or shut him down outright. At the end of class, they cleaned up, and Kurt made sure he had all his notes and data before getting ready to leave.

"Kurt, can we please talk?"

Kurt sighed, but figured he might as well get this over with. "Okay. We can talk outside." Kurt left the lab and walked down the hall. He didn't look back and waited until he was outside. He walked away from the building and stepped off the sidewalk. "Talk."

Freddie sighed. "I was hoping we could be friends and that you'd try to understand why this is for the best."

"I think I really do understand that now. What happened really is for the best. See, I really like you. But you aren't ready to accept who you are, and I refuse to have someone in my life who isn't willing to be open and honest. And you're not. You're still hiding. This time behind some girl's skirts."

"Kurt," Freddie said softly. "I like you too. We just need to be careful."

Kurt shook his head. "No, Freddie. I know what you're asking, and the answer is no. I won't be anyone's dirty little secret, especially not yours. I want someone who will allow me to be part of his life." Kurt could see the conflict in Freddie's eyes. This was a man used to getting what he wanted, and Freddie seemed to want to have his cake and eat it too. "Freddie, do you see us walking into your parents' summer place in the Hamptons for a party where I'd be welcome?"

Freddie paled. He opened his mouth, but nothing came out.

"That's what I want. Someone who's willing to let me be part of his life. You'd never bring me home to meet your family, regardless of whether they'd accept me or not—you'd never try."

"You don't understand," Freddie told him.

"Actually, I think I understand really well." Kurt took a step away. "I hope that someday you'll be able to stand up for yourself and be yourself. But I won't help you hide or be a part of your lie." Kurt cleared his throat to keep his voice from cracking. "I've worked too hard and fought too long to be my own person to hide it now."

"But I...."

"A friend of mine told me something a while ago. I've thought about it a lot, and I think he's right. You're the quarterback and that's what you do," Kurt said, and Freddie nodded slowly. "But I think you need to realize you're more than that. You showed me you were when you helped me, and the one night we had together was magical. I know you showed me part of who you were then, something few people get to see. But…." Kurt turned away slightly. He couldn't look into Freddie's eyes any longer. "When you're willing to realize you're more than just a football player and willing to accept that your self-worth doesn't come from how others see you, but how you see yourself, then maybe you'll be ready." Kurt took a deep breath and released it. "Maybe then you'll be ready to stop living for everyone else." There was nothing else for him to say, so Kurt turned and walked away.

Chapter 6

FREDDIE DIDN'T turn when Carl came in. He simply tipped the beer can to his lips and stared at the television. Carl came in, stood between him and the television, and stared for a few seconds. Then he shook his head and left the room. Freddie heard him go upstairs and then the muffled sound of the bedroom door closing, but he barely noticed anything else, not even the television show he was watching. They hadn't talked much in the past few weeks, and Freddie really didn't give a damn. He didn't care about much of anything anymore.

His phone vibrated on the coffee table. Freddie glanced at the display and groaned before answering it. Ever since the phone call that rocked his world, he'd been dreading his father's calls. "Hi, Dad."

"I'm glad I didn't come last weekend to watch that slaughter," his father said about the game the previous Saturday. Actually, Freddie was surprised his dad hadn't called earlier. "I hear you've seen the error of your ways and done what I told you to do. Your image will take you places, and it's all you've got."

"Why do you care? And what's with the spying all of a sudden? Do you have detectives following me and people hiding in the bushes?" Freddie was ready to chuck the damned phone out the window.

"Don't be smart," his father snapped. "You know I went to school with one of the deans and several members of the faculty. Besides, I give enough money to that school, and the least they can do is make sure my son doesn't end up as the poster child for faggot football." Freddie squeezed the phone so hard he was surprised it didn't explode in his hand. "I understand you're dating a girl," his father said, his tone lightening.

"Her name's Courtney. She's really nice and a friend of Carl's fiancée, Brittany." Actually, she was arm candy, just like he was for her. Courtney wasn't interested in him as a person any more than Freddie was interested in her endless prattle about shoes and the colors people were wearing. She made his father happy, and that was what mattered.

"So I can assume you took our last little talk seriously," his father said.

"Yes, Dad. I always take you seriously," Freddie said.

"Good, because my firm will be looking for someone in client relations in the next year or so, and you would be perfect for the job. It would get you in front of powerful people, and all you need to do is speak their language. Part of that is being a real man and the other part is being able to share interesting stories. Every single one of those clients wishes they could have what you have now. So don't mess it up, and we can put you on track for a decent career. Lord knows your brains and grades aren't going to get you anywhere."

"So you've said on more than one occasion," Freddie mumbled and then tipped the beer can up, draining what was left. "I need to go. Courtney is coming over to study this evening."

"Why don't you see if she'd like to come home with you for a weekend? You could bring her to New York so we can meet her." He sounded almost giddy at the prospect.

"I'll have to see, with practices and games," Freddie answered noncommittally.

"Okay," his father agreed. "But you remember our deal."

"I know, Dad. You made that very clear a few weeks ago. I've done exactly what you wanted." He heard Carl on the stairs. "I need to go."

"All right, but you see you keep doing that," his father said before disconnecting.

Freddie dropped the phone like it was on fire.

"What's been with you these past few weeks?" Carl flopped into one of the chairs. "You've been a bear, so we've all just left you alone. But you're becoming impossible to live with. The guys on the team are avoiding you except for practices and when we're playing. But that's just turning everything to shit, like the last two games."

"So everything is my fault," Freddie erupted. "The entire world is on my shoulders."

"No, it's not!" Carl yelled back. "But we can't help if you aren't willing to talk."

Freddie stood up to leave the room. "Trust me, dude, you don't want to be involved in this one. It's so fucked up, it'll screw with anyone and anything that touches it." Freddie walked into the kitchen for another beer, but stared into the refrigerator. Then he stepped back and closed the door. Drinking wasn't the answer any more than ignoring the team was the answer. "Damn! Shit! Fuck!"

"You don't have to talk if you don't want to, but, dude, you need to be happy, and anyone can see you aren't happy with Courtney. Hell, you barely look at her, and when you do, you scowl unless she's looking at you." Carl walked to the sink and ran water, presumably to wash the mountain of dishes piled in the sink.

"It's so fucked up," Freddie muttered.

"Maybe, and you're the only one who can unfuck it," Carl told him. "But you don't have to unfuck it alone."

The angry energy that had propelled him into the kitchen fell away, replaced by exhaustion, both mental and physical. "I tried to talk to Kurt today after biochem class."

"And he wouldn't give you the time of day," Carl said levelly.

"Nope. Not that I can blame him. We never had a fight, but I...."

"You ran away," Carl supplied.

"Yeah," Freddie said. "I was dumb, but then I thought I'd done the right thing after...." Freddie stopped. "I can't drag you into this mess of crap. None of us needs that."

"Dude, we're buds and teammates. Getting dragged into messes of crap is part of the deal." Carl threw a dish towel and Freddie caught it. "Now, dry the dishes and tell me everything."

Freddie picked up a plate. "Okay, but remember you asked for it."

THE FOLLOWING morning, Freddie woke with a splitting headache. All night long he kept reliving Carl's shocked and then angry reaction to what he'd told him. "You have to be fucking kidding me?" he'd said so many times that Freddie's brain had played it over and over again. What had been really bad was that Freddie hadn't been kidding, and as he told Carl the unvarnished truth, he had to agree with Carl. The story sounded like something out of the fifties rather than the twenty-first century. But, unbelievable or not, Freddie couldn't do anything about it.

He got out of bed and shuffled into the bathroom, where he cleaned up, brushed his teeth, and took some aspirin. Then he showered, which left him feeling moderately better. After dressing, he slowly descended the stairs and heard soft voices in the kitchen. He found Carl, Brittany, and Courtney sitting at the table, each with a mug of coffee in front of them. "Don't you have class?" he mumbled, pouring himself a mug. Then he took the last seat and stared at the tabletop.

"Yeah, we do," Courtney said and then she lightly kissed his cheek. "We'll talk later. Maybe I'll see you tonight?" She sounded too chipper for words, and Freddie stifled a groan, wondering what she could want to talk about. He nodded anyway and sipped from his mug. He had to get ready for class as well, but didn't have the energy to get up at the moment.

Courtney left the kitchen, and Freddie took another sip of coffee before lifting his gaze. Brittany and Carl were sharing a kiss, and he watched them for longer than he should. They truly cared about each other, and when she was in the room, Carl had a difficult time keeping his eyes off her. That was what Freddie wanted—someone who would look at him that way. He'd never have that with Courtney. There was only one person he wanted to have that with, but he was lost to him. Kurt had made that very clear the day before. Freddie pushed back the chair and got up, taking his cup with him when he left the room to give them some privacy. He carried the mug with him as he got his crap together for class and practice before returning to the living room with his stuff.

"Snap out of it," Brittany told him as she pulled open the front door.

"Thanks, Cher," Freddie said. "I should be thankful you didn't slap me."

Brittany broke into a fit of giggles. "God, you are gay. No straight man knows *Moonstruck*." She stepped away from the door. "It's going to be okay."

"He told you what happened?" Freddie said, glaring at Carl.

"No, he didn't. He said you needed our help and you'd tell us all about it tonight." Brittany said, and Freddie groaned. "Don't give me that. We're your friends and we're here to help. So quit acting so testosterony and let us help you." She grinned and left the house.

"There's nothing anyone can do," Freddie called back to Carl. "It is what it is. Besides, like I told you, it's best for him too." He grabbed his bag to leave.

"You really care for him, don't you?" Carl asked with one foot on the lowest step.

"I don't know what I feel," Freddie said. "Everything is turning to shit, and I don't know fuck about crap." Freddie pulled open the door and left the house. Then he went back inside and grabbed a jacket before leaving once again and heading to class.

It started to drizzle as he walked across campus, the weather mirroring his mood. People ahead of him seemed to feel him coming and got out of the way. Inside the science building, he stormed up the stairs, and at the top, he barreled into a kid who was bent over, picking up dropped papers. "Watch where you're going," Freddie bellowed as the kid scrambled not to end up sprawled out on the floor. Kurt turned and looked up at him. In that instant, Freddie's anger melted. "I'm sorry," he said quietly and extended his hand to help Kurt to his feet.

"Who pissed in your Cheerios?" Kurt challenged.

"My father," Freddie answered without thinking.

Kurt nodded once and stared at him. "I doubt he's going to care if you're angry with the world."

"If he were here, I could be angry with him, but he's not, so...." Freddie took a deep breath. "Like I said, I'm sorry."

And holy fuck if Kurt didn't smile, and it was like the sun came out from behind the clouds for just a brief second on a stormy day. "I need to get to class," Kurt said after clearing his throat. Then he turned and hurried down the hallway.

Freddie couldn't take his eyes off him. He simply stood there and watched his little butt swing in those jeans. It wasn't until he disappeared from sight that Freddie realized he'd been gawking like an idiot and headed to biochemistry class.

Kurt was surrounded by girls, like he had been for the past few classes. Freddie sat at the opposite end of the room, one row back, and pulled out his notebook.

"I have your exam results," Dr. Marcus said moments after entering the room. "Overall I'm very pleased." He set a box on the edge of the desk, and everyone filed down and located their exams. Freddie found his and stared at the C- on the page. At least he hadn't disgraced himself completely. He went back to his seat and shoved the paper in back of his notebook, then peered down the row to where Kurt was all smiles and others were leaning over to see his paper. He sighed and smiled to himself. When it came to Kurt, Freddie knew he'd been a fool in many ways, but at least he'd done one thing right. Even if it had cost him his heart.

WHEN HE was done with class, Freddie hit the rec center. He opened his locker and began changing clothes for a workout. They were scheduled for a rigorous practice after the last two losses, so he figured he wouldn't do anything too strenuous. He undressed and pulled on his shorts.

"Samuelson, Coach Norris wants to see you," one of the freshmen said from behind him. Then he added in a whisper. "You better hurry— he sounded mad." The kid took off like a frightened bird, and Freddie finished getting dressed before striding out of the locker room and down the hall. The football coach had the office of honor in the rec center, just off the lobby. It probably should have been the center director's office, but Coach had more clout. Freddy pushed open the door and stepped inside the outer area before knocking on the coach's closed door.

"Freddie," the head coach, Coach Norris, said as Freddie stepped inside the shut the door. Both Coach Harper—the offensive coach—and Coach Josh were there. "Son, we're worried about you." Coach Norris was an institution at Dickinson. "You seem distracted, and quite frankly you've been playing like your head's in your ass rather than on the field. Your teammates are avoiding you because you've been pricklier than a bear with a splinter. So what's the problem?"

Freddie glanced at Coach Josh and then back at Coach Norris. "It's a personal issue. I know it's been affecting my play, but that won't happen any longer," Freddie said and sat up straight in the chair, looking Coach Norris in the eye.

"Don't blow smoke up my ass and try to tell me what you think I want to hear. If something's bothering you, I want to hear it. I've heard it all," Coach said, staring daggers at Freddie. "Is it girl trouble? We heard all that rumor business about you a few weeks ago. Is that what's bothering you? Because I can put an end to that kind of talk mighty quick."

Once again Freddie glanced at Coach Josh. He knew Coach Josh knew at least part of the truth, but to his credit, he hadn't told the others about their conversation. Freddie sighed. "No, it isn't girl trouble. This has to do with my father." The statement wasn't exactly a lie, but it got the conversation off the subject of girls, rumors, and stuff like that. And he hoped it stayed that way. "He's putting a lot of pressure on me lately."

Coach Norris nodded slowly. Freddie wouldn't say that Coach and his father were friends, but they were acquaintances, and they had similar goals. "Your father doesn't matter on the field. This is about the team and the school. We need your heart and soul in the game, not sitting on the sidelines whether you're in the game or not. There are other players who will give us 100 percent if you aren't willing. It's obvious to all of us you haven't been doing that. Other players have been making mistakes, but you're the leader, and on the field we've been rudderless for the past two games and it shows. We have a game this Saturday and then a week off. I want your best between now and then. Otherwise I'll be forced to look at someone else for your position."

Freddie had no idea what to say. His stomach roiled at the thought of losing his position on the team. Football was what he did. It would be easier for him to cut off an arm than to willingly give up the position he'd worked hard for. "I know what I have to do," he said confidently. "And I won't let you down." He met the coach's eyes with a steely gaze and waited for his response.

"See that you don't." Coach checked his watch. "Go finish your workout and meet Harper on the field a half hour before practice. He has some new plays he needs to go over with you." The coach looked down at his desk, and Freddie stood up and left the office. The two other coaches followed him, and Freddie walked back to the locker room with Coach Josh.

Inside, he opened his locker and got his workout gloves and gear before walking toward the weight room. What he had intended to start as a light workout turned into an exercise in working out frustration.

"Don't overdo it," Coach Josh said after Freddie clanged the weights in the stops. He handed Freddie a towel, and Freddie wiped his face and arms. "I didn't say anything in Norris's office, but I think I have an idea what all this is about."

Freddie didn't meet his eyes. He didn't want to talk.

"Get cleaned up and come to my office. We need to talk," Coach Josh said. "Whatever you're trying to bury and forget is showing up all over the place." Coach Josh motioned around the weight room. "Notice anything?" Coach Josh asked. "It's deserted. It wasn't that way when you came in here, but it is now. They left because they don't know when you're going to go off, and it's easier to avoid you than being the ones stuck cleaning up the mess, whatever it may be." Coach Josh stood up. "You've got ten minutes."

Freddie breathed deeply and watched Coach Josh leave the room. He wiped up the sweaty bench and left the weight room.

Freddie got cleaned up, dressed, and knocked on Coach Josh's office door exactly ten minutes later. Then he went inside and sat down. "I don't want to talk about it."

Coach Josh turned from where he'd been working at his computer. "You don't have a choice. This is eating you alive, and you either talk about it or you're going to fail and lose your spot on the team. You know that as well as I do, so the time for you to act like an ass is over." Coach Josh crossed his arms over his chest. "You can either tell me about it, or I'll challenge you to a wrestling match. I'll kick your ass from here to kingdom come, and then you'll tell me anyway, so I think it's time you spill your guts."

Freddie groaned before beginning. "I want things to be the way they were before all this gay stuff."

"You mean alone and miserable? Or just you in denial?" Coach Josh asked. "Freddie, you are who you are."

"I guess," Freddie agreed reluctantly. "But that doesn't mean I have to like it."

"Why not? Being gay has nothing to do with the way you play football. It just describes the gender of the person you'll fall in love with." Coach Josh paused. "Is that the issue? Have you fallen in love with someone?" He sounded a bit like Brittany, when she got all mushy talking about Carl.

"I-I…," Freddie stuttered. "Is this appropriate?"

Coach Josh became serious. "Freddie, I'm trying to help. You're playing like shit, your concentration is completely shot, and you can't remember a play for crap. That tells me you have other things on your mind, and given our last conversation, I can assume it has something to do with you being gay. I've seen the girl hanging all over you and the look of complete disinterest on your face. Hiding isn't going to help. You need to face who you are and accept it. It's the only way."

Freddie groaned again and ran his fingers nervously through his hair. "It isn't what I think that counts."

"Sure it is. This is about you, not anyone else. What you think of yourself is immaterial from what anyone else feels," Coach Josh told him, but when Freddie met his gaze, he saw confusion. "There's something else going on, isn't there?"

"There's enough crap going on to fill a sewer," Freddie sighed.

"Well, why don't you start with how you feel?"

"Is this high school and you're one of the girls? Because that's how this sounds," Freddie challenged.

Coach Josh leaned forward, puffing himself up before Freddie's eyes. "Do I look like a girl to you? I'm trying to help, and you're being a jackass."

Freddie squirmed under the coach's glare. "Okay. I really like Kurt. He's the guy who told you I was having trouble seeing. My roommate, Carl, and his girlfriend, Brittany, found out, and they were cool with it. I actually thought I could deal with the whole gay thing. Then, in class, everyone was talking about me and looking at me funny. I didn't feel like me anymore. It was weird and I guess I freaked."

"Okay. Freaking out when you're figuring out you're gay is kind of normal."

"Yeah, but I blamed the whole thing on Kurt and then avoided him. He knew it, too, because he's refused to talk to me much except when we're in lab together. I really messed things up with him and I feel bad."

"You know if you talk to him and tell him how you feel, he'll probably forgive you if you're sincere," Coach Josh told him.

"I know. I thought about that right after all this shit went down. I wanted to say I was sorry, because I really do like him. He's kind and caring, but he's strong too." Freddie smiled. "And he doesn't put up with my crap." Freddie couldn't help smiling when he thought about Kurt. Thoughts of him made Freddie happy.

"So why didn't you? It sounds like your friends were supportive and you had a boyfriend, or potential boyfriend, who cared. Why would you give a rat's ass what people you don't know thought about you?"

Freddie shifted uncomfortably in the chair. "I figured that out too. But…." He sighed. "I got a phone call from my dad the day after Kurt and I… you know… for the first time. He knew and he was mad as hell."

"Your father lives in New York," Coach Josh said.

"Yeah," Freddie agreed, nodding slowly.

"So how did he find out so fast?" Coach Josh asked, and Freddie stared at him openmouthed. He hadn't given that a thought, and he nearly smacked himself on the forehead.

"Fuck. It had to have been Johnny Cartwright. He was my roommate, along with Carl, and he freaked when he found out. He actually moved out of the house the same night he found out." Freddie jumped to his feet, ready to beat the shit out of him.

"Calm down," Coach Josh told him quietly. "You can't change anyone's mind by beating the crap out of them. And right now, how your dad found out isn't as important as what he said to you." Coach Josh motioned to the chair, and Freddie sat down.

"He wasn't happy. My ears hurt after he got done yelling, and the things he said…." Freddie swallowed. "He called me things I never… no father should call his kid stuff like that." Freddie swallowed again and put his hands over his face. He didn't want anyone to see him. "And he was right. I am all the things he called me. They're all true. I've used those same words to describe other guys, but that's what I am."

"They're not true," Coach Josh said. "And no father *should* ever call his son stuff like that." The coach stood up and walked back and forth across the office. Freddie jumped and nearly ended up on the floor when Coach Josh punched the old locker he kept. The sound was so sharp it rang in Freddie's ears for a few seconds. "What kind of man does that to his own kid?" Coach Josh asked. Freddie didn't answer. He sat in his chair and waited for Coach Josh's anger to subside. Eventually, Coach Josh sat back down. "So was that all he did?"

Freddie shook his head. "My dad is used to getting what he wants. Eventually he hung up, after calling me every name in the book. Then he called back to yell at me some more and to tell me no son of his was going to be gay. If I didn't straighten myself out, he'd take away my car, the apartment, and stop paying for my tuition." Freddie's voice cracked. "He told me I could sell my ass on the street for all he cared." Freddie took a deep breath to stay in control. "He really doesn't give a damn."

"Freddie," Coach Josh whispered.

"All he's ever cared about in my life was football. As long as I was playing, he was happy. I should have known he didn't really care." Freddie banged the arm of the chair with his hand. "This is my eldest son, the wunderkind who'll take over for me one day," he said, mimicking his father's voice. "This is my daughter, the musical prodigy, and this… well… Freddie is a football star." He took a deep breath. "The asshole!" He wanted to cry, but he'd be damned before he let anyone see that happen.

"Okay, so he threatened you. You know you have a football scholarship. He can't pull you out of school, and you could get student loans for the rest. It would be harder, but you could stay in school and complete your education." Freddie stared at Coach Josh. "I take it that wasn't all," Coach Josh said in a very measured tone.

"No, because I told my father to go to hell. He could take a long walk off a short pier for all I cared. Like you said, I'd figure out a way to stay, if I could. But I wasn't sure how the college would react if dear old Dad decided not to make his next donation."

"The college does not make or change policy based upon a donor. They all know that," Coach Josh explained.

"Yeah, well, like I said, my father is used to getting what he wants. After I told him to go to hell and hung up, he called back an hour later and… he made an offer I couldn't refuse. He said I had to give up this gay business, date a girl, and clean up my act. He said my reputation was all I had and that he could work with that to keep me from having to dig ditches after I graduated."

"What sort of deal? What was the offer?"

Freddie stared at Coach Josh. "He said that as long as I played ball, everything would be fine, but if I didn't, he'd see to it that Kurt's scholarship was rejected for next year. It turns out that Kurt's scholarship money comes from the Samuelson Foundation, and my father is the one who directs those funds. He said he'd make sure Kurt had to leave school."

Coach Josh's mouth dropped open.

"That was my reaction exactly, but I agreed. I didn't have a choice," Freddie said, certain Coach Josh would understand.

"You always have a choice," Coach Josh told him. "You may have thought you were doing the right thing, but keeping quiet was only hurting yourself and Kurt. And if I'm a betting man, I'd be willing to place money that your father is counting on you keeping quiet. See, most scholarships are awarded through the college. There are private ones, but the full scholarships, like you're describing for Kurt, are administered through the college itself, and the reason for that is to insulate the student from the donor. Basically, to prevent what your father said he was going to do. Because Dickinson feels very strongly about creating an environment conducive for learning, and those kinds of games definitely do not fit the bill."

Freddie was shocked. "So you're saying I did all this for nothing?"

"No, I'm saying you should look at why you did it in the first place. You need to figure out why you did what you did and how you can make it right. Living a lie isn't good for anyone."

"So you're saying… what?"

"I'm saying you're back where you were after our last conversation. You need to do what's right for you. I know your father isn't happy with having a gay son, but that's what you are, regardless of how he feels. And you're going to be happier if you accept who you are and fill your life with people who care about you for you." Coach Josh grinned. "You're also going to win more football games. Because, really, do you think that act with the girl on your arm was fooling anyone? I hear what the guys are talking about, and what they want is to win football games. And most of them don't give a crap if you're gay or straight. They want to win, just like you do."

"But what about everyone else?"

"People will talk. They did about me when I first got here. It passes, and it will for you too." Coach Josh placed a hand on his shoulder. "People will ultimately respect you for taking the harder road and being honest rather than hiding. In the end, your father might do the same thing."

Freddie thought for a few seconds and nodded. "I can't live my life for my father."

"Nope. I wish I could tell you your father will come around in time. I certainly hope he does. But if you want my advice, start with your mother. Mothers are usually more understanding, and once she's on your side, your father will be a lot easier to deal with."

"I'll give it a try," Freddie agreed. "And I'm going to throw all this into the game and take it out on the opposing team." Freddie's energy spiked upward. He'd been going about this all wrong. Like on the gridiron, he needed to fight rather than back off, and that was exactly what he was going to do.

FREDDIE FINISHED his classes for the day, and the team had a grueling practice that seemed to get all the losing mojo out of everyone's head, including his own. Johnny tried to cause trouble, but the other guys shut him down fast and the rest of practice was all business. The guys all ran back to the locker room, yelling the entire way. Freddie showered quickly and then walked back into the locker room.

"Don't want no fags showering with me," Johnny said loud enough for everyone to hear. He looked like he was all ready to leave and hadn't bothered to change.

"You're full of crap," one of the other guys yelled over the top of the lockers.

"Not that you have anything worth seeing," another of the guys said.

"We're a team," Carl said, and he loudly closed the locker next to Freddie's. "It doesn't matter if Freddie's gay, or if I am. We're still a team, and if we want to win, then we need to act like it." Carl glared at Johnny until he turned and left the locker room without saying another word. Then Carl went back to his locker. "Hopefully that's the last of that crap," Carl said loudly and looked around at the other guys.

Most of them simply went back to getting dressed. No one balked, and Freddie took that as a win. "Thanks, guys," Freddie said, and most of the players he could see nodded and went about their business.

"I've got a brother who's gay," Smithy, Freddie's wide receiver, told him. "He tried to kill himself before he finally told us what was wrong. Hiding ain't worth it and will eat you alive." Smithy clapped him on the shoulder. "Johnny's been spreading it around for the last few weeks; it didn't matter to most of us then, and it doesn't now." Then Smithy pulled him into a hug and clapped him loudly on the back. "As long as we win," he added, and the other guys whooped and laughed as the last of the tension in the room faded away. Freddie dodged as one of the guys tried to snap him with a towel. He threatened him and opened his locker, then pulled on his clothes quickly, freeing up his towel for retaliation.

They laughed and snapped towels at each other for a few minutes, and then they finished getting dressed. Freddie got his things together, and he and Carl got ready to leave.

"Hey," Smithy said. "I heard you had room at your place."

Freddie nodded. "Yeah. There's Johnny's room, and another small bedroom over the garage. Why?"

"I need a place. Things aren't working out where I'm at," Smithy said. "My brother came to visit for the game and things got a little rough. I figured things would be better at your place."

"Take care of what you need to and move your stuff in when you can," Freddie said, and Smithy grinned. "Coach had said he thought the team would be supportive, but I didn't believe it."

"Dude, we're a team and that's all there is to it," Smithy said. "We play football, but we're not animals." He smiled, and Freddie grinned.

"Thanks, man," Freddie said. He'd been worried about the team's support, but that didn't seem to be an issue. He knew his father was going to be a major dick, but Freddie no longer cared.

The three of them left together, and then Smithy turned toward his own place. Freddie and Carl walked home. Freddie's heart pounded with relieved excitement. He could hardly believe it.

"I told you weeks ago it would be okay. But you totally freaked out."

"I know." Freddie knew he'd panicked, and that move had cost him so much. He'd let his father back him into a corner, and he'd fallen for his father's crap hook, line, and sinker. "Now I need to figure out how to make it right." Carl didn't respond, and Freddie grew quiet, hoping like hell that Kurt would give him a few minutes to explain. He didn't have hope that Kurt would give him another chance, but at least he could explain why he'd done what he did.

They approached the house and saw that the lights were on. Freddie tried the door and it opened. He heard Brittany's voice on the phone and then she hung up. "Hi, honey," she said happily, and then she wrapped herself around Carl before he could drop his bag on the floor. After they'd kissed and Freddie made his way around them, he stopped, dropping his bag on the floor when Kurt stood up from where he'd been sitting in one of the chairs in the living room.

Chapter 7

KURT STOOD nervously when he heard Freddie's voice. The surprised expression on his face when he saw him was encouraging. It had taken some convincing by Carl's fiancée, Brittany, to get him here. He hadn't wanted to come at all. He'd already expended so much mental energy on Freddie, and he'd been hurt twice before. But she'd been persuasive, so after he got done with work at the library, he'd come over. Now he wasn't sure if it had been a good idea or not.

"What are you doing here?" Freddie asked, and Kurt glanced at Brittany, hoping she'd come to his rescue.

"I asked him here. You've been such a butthead, and I was hoping you would talk to him," Brittany said. "He deserves to know the truth, and then you can let him decide what he wants to do."

"The truth about what?" Kurt asked, shifting his gaze to Freddie.

"Come on," Brittany whispered to Carl. "Let's go upstairs and leave these two alone." Brittany took Carl's hand and pulled him toward the stairs. "Call if you need anything," Brittany said with a wicked grin, and then Kurt heard them climb to the second floor.

"What is it you want to tell me?" Kurt crossed his arms over his chest and waited.

Freddie shifted his weight from side to side. Kurt could tell this was hard for him, but there were things he had to say. He could see confusion in Freddie's eyes as his emotions seemed to tumble on top of each other, and he knew none of them was exactly pleasant for Freddie. But he didn't intend to make this easy.

"If you aren't going to say anything, then I'm going to go," Kurt said. "I have a lot of work I need to get done." He took a few steps toward the front door. He was leaving, and this was going to be Freddie's very last chance. If Freddie wanted any hope of any sort of... anything... with Kurt, then now was the time to say so.

"I... it's just that...," Freddie stammered.

Kurt looked toward the stairs. "Brittany said you had something to tell me. Have you changed your mind?" Freddie shook his head. "Am I going to have to play twenty questions to figure it out? Because I hate that game. I hate most games. So just say what you want to say."

Freddie's mouth opened and closed, but he couldn't seem to make his voice work. Kurt walked to the front door and reached out to pull it open.

"I'm gay," Freddie blurted.

Kurt paused and turned back toward him. "I already knew that."

Freddie nodded. "There's nothing going on between Courtney and me. She's a friend of Brittany's."

"Okay," Kurt said questioningly, releasing the doorknob.

Freddie took a deep breath. "I was wrong, okay? I was wrong to blame my confusion and difficulty accepting all this on you. I should have been upfront with you and told you what was going on." Now that the dam had been breached, the words came freely. "I get it now."

"Get what?" Kurt asked.

"Everything. I think I really get it. My dad has only ever seen me as his son who plays football. It was my job, what I did. But I always wanted him to see me as more than that. I want to be more than that."

"That's good," Kurt told him.

"Yeah, but see… I pushed away the one person who actually saw me that way. You told me I was more than that and you tried to show me. You were willing to help me with my studies and cared enough to help me get these." Freddie pulled off his glasses. "I was in college before anyone realized I needed these. No one gave a damn that I couldn't see shit as long as I could play football. But you did." Freddie shifted from foot to foot. "I was so stupid not to see it before."

"You weren't looking for it," Kurt said softly.

"No, I wasn't. And I'm sorry. I'm sorry I didn't come to you weeks ago. I should have. But…." Freddie stammered once again. "But my dad read me the riot act after he found out. I think Johnny told him, but I'm not sure."

"I understand," Kurt said. "You panicked under his pressure."

Freddie shook his head. "It's not that, and I don't want this to sound wrong. See, I told my dad to go to hell, and I think that shocked him." Freddie smiled. "And it felt good too. But he called back and told me he'd make sure your scholarship for next year wouldn't be available unless I did what he wanted." Freddie swallowed hard.

Anger burst out of him. "That fucker did what?" Kurt snapped and pounded the door. "The son of a bitch. I'll rip his nuts off." Kurt shook with rage. "What kind of person is he? The heartless piece of shit! Wait a second—my scholarship came through Dickinson. Does he have that much influence?"

"He doesn't, but I didn't know that. He made it sound like the scholarship came directly from the Samuelson Foundation," Freddie explained. "And I couldn't let him do that to you." He turned away from Kurt.

"You did that for me?" Kurt asked, and Freddie nodded. "That has to be the stupidest, dumbest… sweetest, most caring thing anyone has ever done for me. You didn't have to, though."

"I didn't know that. My dad threatened me up one side and down the other, and I didn't care. But as soon as he threatened you, he'd found my soft spot."

Kurt lightly tapped him on the back, and Freddie turned to face him. "I'm your soft spot?" Kurt asked.

"Yeah. I was mad at you. Blaming you for all this, and as soon as my dad threatened you, I caved like a wuss. And I knew I was right when I saw your smile and the way the girls around you were grinning after Dr. Marcus handed back the biochem tests. You deserve to be here because you're going to go places, and I figured if I had to pretend to be with Courtney to make that happen, then it was worth it."

Kurt rolled his eyes. "Was it worth losing those two games?"

Freddie shrugged. "Maybe, maybe not. I spent my free time with the coaches and they read me the riot act. But then I talked to Coach Josh." Freddie shuddered slightly. Kurt was starting to understand that all this talk about feelings was enough to make Freddie's balls shrivel and his testosterone levels drop through the floor. "He told me about the scholarship stuff. And most of the team seems to be okay with me being gay. Some of the guys aren't going to accept it, but I can live with that."

"See, you're already happier," Kurt told him with a smile.

"I'm getting more comfortable in my own skin, I guess," Freddie said.

"And it's a great skin," Kurt said with a leer that really didn't come off with his dancing eyes.

"Does this mean I'm forgiven?" Freddie asked tentatively.

"I'm not sure yet," Kurt began. "Do you promise not to do anything like this again? And… you'll talk to me when you feel freaked as opposed to rabbiting again? You've done that twice. If you do it again, I'll do my best impression of Elmer Fudd and fill your butt so full of buckshot, you'll rattle on the gridiron."

Freddie raised his right hand. "I'll try. I tend to act before I figure out how I feel."

"All you have to do is talk. That really isn't so hard," Kurt told him.

"And to answer your next question, my father invited Courtney home for Thanksgiving. But I'm not going to take her. And yes, I intend to tell my parents. I'm going to start with my mother, and I'll make it clear that I intend to bring my boyfriend home for visits. And if they don't like it, then I won't come at all." Freddie stepped closer to Kurt. "I want a relationship. I haven't had any real ones. The few I've had haven't been built on honesty. So I'm going to make mistakes."

"We all make mistakes." Kurt met Freddie's gaze with a hard look. "But I want you to clearly understand. I will not be denied or hide in a corner. If you want to be in my life, then you do so openly and proudly. I will do the same with you. Yes, there will be times when we need to be careful, but this crap of hiding me off to the side is the quickest way to good-bye I can think of. So if that's what you want, say so now."

Freddie swallowed. "All I can say is that I'll try."

"You don't have to wear a sign that says you're gay, and I promise I won't drag you to a gay pride parade unless you want to go, but I suspect you'll find, like most people do, that it's liberating and safe to be in a crowd of people who think the way you do. And where us holding hands," Kurt said as he took Freddie's, "won't be frowned on."

"How can you be so comfortable with this?" Freddie asked.

"I've had more time to get used to it, and I didn't have as much to lose. I'm just some nerdy kid. No one looks up to me as a role model. I'm not the one out on the field every Saturday with half the student body chanting my name, hoping I'll make the play that scores a win." Kurt swallowed hard. "What I don't understand is why you're even interested in me. You're not the only gay player on the football team. There are others and there will be others. Plenty of guys look a lot better than me." Now it was Kurt's turn to look at the floor.

"Hey. Maybe being around you has broadened my horizons. But you're plenty cute enough for me." Freddie moved closer, and Kurt thought about stepping back. They still had more to talk about, and if Freddie pulled him into an embrace, Kurt would probably fold like a house of cards. "Short Stuff."

Kurt growled. "Ape Boy," he retorted, and then Freddie moved even closer, so close Kurt felt the heat from his body. Freddie seemed to move in slow motion, wrapping his arms around him, pulling Kurt close, and then Freddie kissed him. Kurt closed his eyes and deepened the kiss, sucking lightly on Freddie's lower lip. Freddie slid his hands down Kurt's back until he cupped his butt. He then lifted Kurt off his feet, cradling his butt in his hands, and Kurt wrapped his legs around Freddie's hips. "Don't get any ideas," Kurt said.

"About what?" Freddie asked, stilling. Kurt gently tilted Freddie's head and sucked on his ear.

"I hope you have condoms upstairs in that room of yours, because I'm going to blow the top of your head off when I fuck you." Kurt knew exactly what Freddie had been thinking, and he intended to fully disabuse him of that notion once and for all. Freddie stilled, and Kurt went for broke. "Think about how good you're going to feel when I have your butt in the air, my tongue buried inside you. You're going to scream loud enough for the neighbors to hear you when I finally let you come."

Freddie shivered and Kurt knew he had him. "When you…?"

"Oh, yeah. I'm going to make you scream to high heaven, and then, when you come, your head is going to feel like it's ready to explode." He sucked on Freddie's ear. "I may be smaller than you, but I know what I'm doing, big boy." Kurt wriggled against Freddie's body, grinding his throbbing cock against his stomach. Freddie shivered again, and Kurt knew he felt it.

"But…," Freddie began.

"Hey," Kurt whispered. "A real man does what's going to make him happy." He stroked the back of Freddie's neck and behind his ears. "What we do in the bedroom stays between us. It's private, and it has nothing to do with ego or anything else." Kurt kissed Freddie hard. "We don't have to do anything you aren't ready for."

"You just surprised me," Freddie said.

"And, sweetheart, I have so many more surprises planned for you." Kurt kissed Freddie again as the big man vibrated. Kurt held on as Freddie began to move. He slowly climbed the stairs, holding Kurt tight until they reached the bedroom. Freddie carried him inside and then kicked the door closed before walking them to the bed. Freddie laid him down on the mattress and kissed him hard and deep.

When Freddie broke the kiss, Kurt shifted and tugged off Freddie's shirt and then his own before attacking Freddie's belt and jeans. Freddie groaned softly, and Kurt deftly opened them, parted the fabric, and shoved them down his hips.

Freddie arched his back when Kurt licked his chest and then swirled his tongue around Freddie's nipple. Freddie whimpered softly and held still above him. Kurt loved that he could make the big guy whimper and moan. It helped even the playing field. Freddie could have easily overpowered him and taken charge, but he didn't. Instead, Kurt took control, and Freddie made whimpery, moaning sounds that filled the room with energy. God, he loved that. Freddie kicked off his pants, and Kurt slid his briefs down his legs. Freddie's cock bounced out and pointed straight at him. "Are you going to do what you did last time?" Freddie whispered.

"Lie on your back on the bed," Kurt said, and Freddie shifted his weight. He watched as Kurt kicked off his shoes and then stripped off his pants. Then he climbed on the bed, running his hands up Freddie's legs from ankle to thigh. "You are one sexy man. You know that?"

"People have told me that once or twice," Freddie retorted.

"They have, huh?" Kurt said, before kissing the inside of Freddie's right thigh. "I bet they used words, didn't they?"

"Uh-huh," Freddie whimpered.

"But I don't have to use any to tell you what I think of you." Kurt kissed the skin right next to Freddie's balls, and Freddie held his breath. Kurt smiled and then licked up Freddie's cock. Freddie groaned deeply, the sound reverberating through the room. "I bet you no one has ever told you anything like that before."

"No," Freddie whined.

Kurt licked up him again and then sucked Freddie into his mouth. Freddie tensed, his breathing coming in short pants as Kurt sucked him deeper. Freddie whimpered, and without releasing his cock from between his lips, Kurt shifted on the bed until his knees rested on either side of Freddie's head. Then he slowly lowered his hips over Freddie's face. He sighed around Freddie's cock as he felt his own slip between Freddie's lips.

God, the heat was amazing as Freddie sucked him deeper. They moved together, sucking and licking each other to near oblivion. Kurt could hardly think, but he wasn't ready for this to end, so he kept his body under control and resisted the instinct to thrust hard and fast. He needed Freddie hot and begging for it. So he released Freddie's cock and pulled his legs forward. Kurt stroked over Freddie's butt, teasing his skin lightly with the tips of his fingers. Freddie gasped and sucked harder when Kurt lightly teased the fluttery skin around his opening.

Kurt pushed himself upward, slipping his cock from between Freddie's lips. "Roll over," Kurt whispered, and Freddie paused for a few seconds before complying. "Trust me. I'd never do anything to hurt you," Kurt said, stroking up Freddie's wide back and then down and over his firm, muscular butt. Damn, the man was hard all over, and Kurt kissed and licked his hot skin. Freddie shivered and moaned when Kurt massaged his tight, muscular ass. Then he parted Freddie's cheeks and teased his puckered skin. Freddie hissed softly and stilled. "Are you okay?"

"Yes." Freddie whispered. "I just never saw myself as the guy who had things done to him. I always saw myself as the one who did stuff." Kurt smiled and slowly stretched out over Freddie's body, resting his throbbing cock against Freddie's crack.

"Believe me. You'll get a chance to do stuff. I'm not a selfish lover, and I really want to know what you feel like inside me. But right now, I need you so bad." Kurt sucked on one of Freddie's ears.

Freddie wriggled back at him, and Kurt's cock throbbed as he slowly thrust his hips. Kurt slithered slowly down Freddie's back, kissing and licking his skin as he went. When he got to Freddie's butt, he parted his cheeks and ran his tongue along his crack before teasing the small, puckered opening.

Freddie came unglued. "Jesus Christ!" He gasped for air, and Kurt licked him again and then probed the tight opening. Freddie writhed beneath him, moaning constantly. "What are you doing to me?"

"Making you feel good," Kurt said. "I want you to know exactly how good you can feel." Kurt shifted and turned Freddie's head to bring their lips together. "I also want you to always equate me with the most pleasure you've ever had in your life, and I want you to know just what I feel for you." They exchanged sloppy kisses, and then Freddie rolled onto his back, pulling Kurt to him. They kissed deeply, holding one another.

"You do make me feel good, just by being here," Freddie whispered between deep kisses.

"We don't have to do anything tonight," Kurt said, holding Freddie tight and closing his eyes. The sensation of being held tight, his body sliding against Freddie's, was almost enough for him to lose it.

"I want to feel you," Freddie whispered into his ear. "I want to be connected to you. The past few weeks have been hell. I missed you all the time, and whenever I saw you, all I could think about was what a mess I'd made of things. I should have talked to you. And not been such a yutz."

"Is that why you said that stuff about being friends the other day?" Kurt asked, stilling and gazing into Freddie's eyes.

"Yeah. I only wanted to be close to you. But I shouldn't have asked you what I did. You deserve more than that—we both do."

"Yes, we do. I'm glad we both realize that now."

Freddie stroked over Kurt's cheek and then around to the back of his head, drawing him forward until their lips met once again. Kurt loved the way Freddie tasted—like musk and man, with a hint of honey and spring.

"I want you," Freddie said, breaking the kiss.

"Are you sure?" Kurt asked. A little dirty talk was fun and all, but he wouldn't hurt or push Freddie into something he wasn't ready for.

"Yeah, I'm sure," Freddie whispered.

"Okay. How will you be comfortable? On your belly will be easier for you, but on your back means we can kiss and I can see you." Kurt lightly stroked Freddie's cheek, and then Freddie settled on his back with his knees raised.

"I got stuff in the nightstand," Freddie said. Kurt pulled open the drawer and retrieved a condom and a packet of lube. He recognized them from one of the safe-sex program packets that had been handed out earlier in the year. Kurt put everything close at hand and then settled between Freddie's legs. He wanted to take things slow, but his excitement pushed him forward. Kurt opened the packet and slicked two fingers before gently teasing Freddie's opening. He watched Freddie's expression and then slipped the tip of his finger inside him. Freddie's breath hitched, and Kurt slowly pushed his finger in further.

Freddie's eyes widened as Kurt bent his finger slightly. "Is that okay?" Freddie moved slowly and gasped, his mouth falling open. Not all guys had a pleasure spot, but Kurt was thrilled that Freddie did and that he'd found it. He rubbed the tiny bundle of nerves, and Freddie about came unglued.

"What is that?" Freddie gasped between panting breaths, his cock throbbing against his belly. Kurt did it again, his own cock jumping with excitement.

Kurt grinned. "That's heaven," he answered and slowly added a second finger. "You need to relax for me." Kurt twisted his fingers and reveled in Freddie's rolling eyes, small panting breaths, and moans that would have done the most wanton man on the planet proud. Freddie groaned when Kurt pulled his fingers away.

Kurt opened the condom package and stretched the latex over his aching cock. He lubed himself and Freddie before getting into position. Kurt pressed to Freddie and held still, their gazes meeting. Kurt lightly stroked Freddie's hairy chest, petting the stunning man.

"Don't wait, Kurt," Freddie whispered, and he pressed forward.

Freddie's body opened to him, and Kurt slid into white-hot heat that clamped around him. He moved as slowly as he could, but instinct propelled him forward, and it took all his willpower to stop it. This was Freddie's first time, and he needed to make it special. Kurt paused and gently stroked Freddie's sides. "You feel amazing," Kurt whispered. He continued moving as slowly as he possibly could. When his hips touched Freddie's butt, they breathed together, blowing out deep breaths. Kurt closed his eyes, his cock jumping and throbbing uncontrollably deep inside Freddie's body.

"We're connected," Freddie observed.

"Yes, we are," Kurt agreed and began to pull out a little before Freddie pulled him back in.

Kurt slowly began to move. But whenever he pulled out, Freddie pulled him back, like he didn't want them to separate. And Kurt didn't either. Nothing in his life had prepared him for the sheer, heart-deep joy of being with Freddie like this. He slowly picked up speed, and Freddie moved with him, groaning softly.

"How does that feel?" Kurt asked.

"Fucking fantastic," Freddie said and pressed into the movement.

Kurt held Freddie's ankles, spreading his legs further apart. "Damn," Kurt gritted. He wasn't going to last long at all. Kurt's entire body shook and his balls threatened to crawl inside, he was wound so tight. Kurt transferred Freddie's ankles to his shoulders and leaned forward slightly to balance his weight. Then he stroked Freddie hard and fast, snapping his hips and listening to Freddie's cries, which got sharper and louder with each passing second.

Freddie's cock jumped in his hand and his cries grew in intensity. His body stiffened and Freddie's muscles tightened around Kurt. Within seconds, Freddie went to pieces, moaning and shaking as he came. Kurt had never seen anything so erotic in his life, and the last of his control broke. Kurt came within seconds in a blinding rush that shook him from head to toe.

Kurt didn't move. He was afraid to break the spell that had settled around them. Kurt knew a lot of things happened before and during sex, but once it was over, things could change. He waited to see if that would happen and braced himself for it.

Freddie gently stroked his chest, and Kurt slid his eyes open. Their bodies separated, and they both moaned softly. Then Freddie tugged him forward, encircled him in his huge arms and hugged him close. "Kurt, I think I—"

He placed a finger over Freddie's lips to cut him off. "Don't say that now. Things are too muddled in our minds. After sex, people will say anything with an endorphinal soup running through them. If you have something to say to me, tell me when you're not all sexed out." Kurt lifted his gaze to meet Freddie's. "I've wanted someone to say those words to me for a long time. So don't say them lightly or at the spur of the moment. Say them when the time is right and when you know deep down it comes from the heart."

"Okay, but…."

"Freddie, we've just gotten together, and feelings like that need time to develop and grow. I hope they will, I really do. But give yourself time—give us time."

Freddie nodded. "I missed you these past few weeks and I've made some decisions. I've decided that school is going to come first. I want an education and I don't want to be a washed-up football player with no skills or hopes after I graduate."

"Good for you," Kurt said, resting his head on Freddie's shoulder. "I know you can do it."

Freddie chuckled, but the sound quickly morphed to one of pain. "You always did. Too bad my father never showed that faith in me."

"Speaking of your dad…, what are you going to do?"

Freddie took a deep breath, and Kurt smiled as he lifted with Freddie's huge chest. "I don't know. I guess tomorrow I'm going to call my mother and explain things to her. Hopefully she'll understand. Then I might have a chance with my father." Freddie sighed and then took another deep breath. "I suppose I should call my brother and sister."

"Do you think they'll understand?"

"Probably," Freddie said and nuzzled Kurt's neck. "But I can't live my life for them."

"No, you can't," Kurt agreed. "But take it one step at a time and only make the steps you're comfortable with. The rest will take care of itself."

"I guess," Freddie said, holding Kurt tighter.

"Hey," Kurt whispered, lifting his head and meeting Freddie's gaze. "You don't have to do it alone. I'll help you with your studies where I can, and I'll certainly be there when you want to yell about your dad. It won't be perfect; coming out never is. But you'll find out who your real friends are and the people who love you for you." Kurt stroked Freddie's stubbly cheek. "I lost friends. There were a few people I'd known for years who will no longer speak to me. There's nothing I can do about that." Kurt kissed Freddie lightly. "It's happened to you too."

"Yeah, but he's not much of a loss," Freddie said. "Just a guy who I thought was my friend, but hung around because of what I could do for him." Freddie chuckled, and for a second Kurt felt like he was on top of a bouncy castle. "You were never like that. You gave me crap from the first day I met you."

"That's why you like me," Kurt retorted with a smile, and then he rested his head once again on Freddie's shoulder.

"Yeah, Short Stuff," Freddie agreed, "that's why I like you."

Kurt grinned and blew a short raspberry on Freddie's shoulder, but the usual protest died on his lips and he closed his eyes, letting the warmth and scent from Freddie's skin surround him.

Epilogue

"ARE YOU really sure about this?" Kurt asked skeptically as they hurried through New York's Penn Station from the Amtrak terminal to the Long Island Railroad stations.

"You've asked me that eight times," Freddie answered calmly. "And yes, I'm sure. Mom specifically invited you for Thanksgiving. She desperately wants to meet you." Freddie led Kurt to the platform. Their train was still ten minutes away, so they stood in line. The Amtrak train they'd taken from Harrisburg had been late, but they'd made it and were about to take the final stage of their journey. Kurt had fretted most of the four-hour trip to New York. "We're only staying until Saturday morning, so it's just a few days."

"I thought we were leaving on Sunday?" Kurt asked, confused.

"Mom and Dad are leaving for Florida on Saturday, so I got us a hotel in New York. I thought I could show you the city." Kurt had told him once that he'd never been to New York, so Freddie had decided to surprise him. "I'll even let you drag me to the Public Library." Freddie nudged Kurt and he nudged back.

Freddie had spent more hours in the library this term than he had in the first two years he'd been in college. When Kurt was working, Freddie came in to study, and his grades so far showed the extra effort. He'd even gotten As and Bs on a few of his exams, mostly thanks to Kurt's patience, but he was absorbing the material and the work was getting easier. When the conductor called their train, they showed their tickets and headed down the escalators to the platform and got on the train. They found seats so they were sitting in the direction the train would be moving and stowed their bags on the shelf above.

"Are you sure your father isn't going to try to carve me up for dinner?" Kurt asked as the train started to move.

"Things with Dad are still… complicated." His father hadn't exactly been thrilled at having a gay son. To say the least, especially after Freddie called his bluff. It turned out his father hadn't been paying as much of Freddie's college tuition as he'd let on. His mother had been seeing to all that, and she had been supportive beyond belief; so had his brother and sister. So it turned out Dad had left himself out in the cold on this issue. "I think he'll come around." Freddie grinned. "If I'm honest, I'm hoping you'll work some of your magic on him."

"Me?" Kurt said.

"Just be yourself. The whole family will be there, and everyone is anxious to meet you. The last time I talked to my dad and told him you were coming, he didn't actually say anything negative, so I figure Mom is wearing the old grump down." He'd visited Kurt's family a few weeks earlier and their support of his and Kurt's relationship had gone a long way in helping Freddie deal with his own family issues. In short, he wanted his family to be like Kurt's.

"Okay," Kurt agreed skeptically.

"Don't worry. The Hamptons will be fun, and there will be enough for us to do that we won't have to sit around and stare at each other. The season is coming to the very end, and a lot of people have left, but places will be open for the holiday and you'll love it." Freddie placed an arm around Kurt's shoulder. "There's nothing to worry about."

They rode farther and farther out on Long Island. The train made a number of stops, and after each one, the cars got emptier and emptier. One station out, Freddie called the house to let them know where they were, and by the time the train stopped and they got off, a car was waiting for them. "Is this for us?" Kurt stared as Freddie's father's chauffeur opened the passenger door of the limousine.

"Yup," Freddie answered. Freddie hadn't expected them to send this, but Kurt stretched out in the back and seemed to enjoy the ride to the house, or at least he seemed less nervous. They pulled into the drive, and Kurt peered out the window, whistling softly.

"How rich are you?" Kurt asked. "I mean, I knew your folks had money, but I didn't know they were, like, Vanderbilts or something." They waited for the gate to slide open, and then the limousine pulled down the drive and up to the house. Freddie had never really given the place much thought. It had been his grandfather's house. Built in the thirties, it was a Hamptons Tudor landmark.

"Don't worry about it, okay? It's just a house."

"Yeah, sure it is," Kurt said and got out of the car, staring up at the building. Maybe bringing him here hadn't been such a good idea.

"Come on, let's go inside." Freddie took Kurt's hand and led him up the front steps. "There's nothing to be worried about." *Other than possibly his father.* Freddie opened the door, and they stepped inside.

"Honey," his mother said and walked into the hall. She hugged him and then turned to Kurt. "I'm so pleased to meet you." They shook hands.

"It's nice of you to have me, Mrs. Samuelson."

"Call me Norma, and come on through. We're in the sitting room."

"What about the bags?" Kurt whispered, looking all around him. They took off their coats, and Kurt handed his to Freddie, who placed them with the bags.

"They'll be taken up to the room. Don't worry," Freddie said and winked at Kurt as they followed his mother.

The rest of the family was in the sitting room enjoying cocktails. Everyone greeted Kurt warmly. Even Freddie's father was cordial, and they sat down. Freddie stayed close to Kurt, who was edgy and nervous.

"So how's the team?" Freddie's father asked.

"The season's almost done and we have a respectable record," Freddie answered.

"Barely," his father said, and Freddie ground his teeth. "You could have done better if you hadn't been distracted."

Freddie didn't know what to say.

"Excuse me, sir," Kurt began. "But Freddie is very focused. He's worked hard for the past few months. He played well, and he's getting better grades than he's ever gotten. So if you'll excuse me for saying so, he's focused on the right things. Sure, Freddie loves football, and he always will. But he's working hard so he can have a life after football." The smile Kurt flashed at him warmed Freddie's heart and almost made him forget where he was, because he was already leaning in to kiss him. He caught himself and glanced at his mother, who was smiling.

"I agree," she said, and Freddie shifted his gaze to his father.

"Well, I'll be damned," his father said. "Could I speak with you?" Freddie's father stood up, and Freddie did the same. He glanced at Kurt, gave him a quick smile, and then followed his father out of the room and down the hall to his lushly appointed office.

"Look, son," his father said once he'd closed the door. "I won't claim to understand this gay thing. But I will admit I was wrong to pressure you the way I did. And your mother is working on helping me accept… the rest of it." Freddie tried to say something, but his father stopped him. "Let me say this: if you being gay is the trigger that forced you to grow up and take responsibility, then you can be as gay as you want."

"Thanks, Dad. I guess," Freddie said, not quite sure how to take his father's comment.

"Are you really knuckling down to study?" his father asked.

"Yes. I'm getting better grades. Kurt is very smart and he's helped me develop better study habits. He's amazing, Dad; he really is." Freddie paused. "I know this will be hard for you, but I care about him a great deal."

His father did indeed look uncomfortable, but he nodded and stepped back toward the office door. "We should get back to the rest of the family." He opened the door and stepped out. Freddie waited a few seconds and followed. It wasn't a glowing commendation, but it was a step and he'd take that.

When he reentered the sitting room, Freddie stood in the doorway and listened as Kurt animatedly discussed music with his sister, brother, and mother. "Freddie, why didn't you tell us he was such a dear?" his mother asked.

"Do you mind if I steal him away for a few minutes?" Freddie asked, and Kurt stood up. Freddie guided him to one of the sliding doors. He opened it, and they stepped out on the patio, then closed the door behind them.

Breaking waves crashed at the base of the bluff, and Freddie led the way to the stone wall. "Is everything okay?" Kurt asked. "How did it go with your dad?"

"Not bad, I guess," Freddie said. "I think he likes you." He turned and pulled Kurt to him, blocking the brisk wind off the ocean. He realized he should have thought this through and gotten jackets for them before stepping out here.

"Then what is it?" Kurt asked.

"I used to come out here when I wanted to think." Freddie looked out over the water. The night was clear, and the moon shone on the cold water. "You told me once to wait until I was sure." Freddie cupped Kurt's now chilled cheeks in his hands. "Kurt, I'm sure I love you. So many good things have happened in the past few months, and they're all because of you." Freddie kissed him. "You make me happy."

Kurt snuggled close—Freddie hoped not just to get out of the wind and keep warm. "I love you too." They kissed again, long and slow.

Warmth spread through Freddie, and the wind didn't register at all. Then Kurt rested his head against Freddie's chest and wound his arms around Freddie's waist.

"Are you getting cold?" Freddie whispered.

"No," Kurt answered, burrowing closer to him. "Well, maybe a little, but I don't want to move. You just told me you loved me, and I want to hold on to the moment."

Freddie gently tilted Kurt's face so their gazes met. "We can go inside, and later I'll tell you all over again, as many times as you want."

ANDREW GREY

ELECTROCHEMISTRY

To Dominic, Elizabeth, Jane, Lynn, Julianne, Tammy, Hayley, Shannon, Ariel, and everyone in my Dreamspinner family.
I could not do this without all of you. I love each of you.

Chapter 1

I KNEW I would always remember the first time I saw him. The only job I could get was at the Giant, and on weekends I had the graveyard shift. I got paid extra for it, and there weren't a lot of customers, so mostly I stocked the shelves or manned the service desk. I got a lot of studying done because there really wasn't that much work to do. Anyway, I was standing outside the front doors, taking a break, when he pulled into the parking lot in a green VW Beetle convertible. He zipped past the front of the store, "I Will Survive" blaring from the car speakers and him singing along at the top of his lungs… off-key. I couldn't help smiling as sheer joy radiated in every direction.

The song ended, and then everyone within hearing distance was treated to an encore of Cher's "Turn Back Time." The exuberance continued, spreading like sunshine just breaking through thick clouds. When the song was over, I listened for another, but the parking lot grew quiet. After a few seconds, I realized I was holding my breath, waiting for more, but none came. The night returned to normal, the mundane returning after a moment of excitement. But I wasn't ready to go back inside. Instead, I checked my watch and waited, looking at where the car had tucked in between two others. Then I saw him: a small, slight guy walking toward the store, swinging his hips like the music was still playing. I looked for an iPod or smartphone, but saw nothing. The music must have been in his head, and he was just loving it. Hell, so was I.

There hadn't been many times in my life when I'd encountered a presence that exuded unapologetic and uncontained joy, but this was one of them, and it pulled me in its wake. Before I could think, he'd passed through the sliding doors, and I followed after him, because what choice did I have?

In the fluorescent light, he was stunning: slight, but well proportioned, wearing flip-flops on perfect feet. My gaze traveled upward past nice calves to a tight little butt that swung back and forth as he walked. He had a tiny waist, then his back expanded upward, widening at his shoulders, and his head was topped with a mop of unruly frosted hair.

"Brad," Helen whispered, pulling me out of my daze. I blinked a few times and then hurried over to my station behind the service desk. The night manager, Rick—short for Richard, but we called him Dick behind his back because that described him to a tee—was heading our way. Most of the time we could do what we wanted as long as there weren't customers, but we had to stay at our duty station, like this wasn't a grocery store but the Starship Enterprise. There was one thing I knew: Rick was not, nor would he ever be, anything like Patrick Stewart.

Behind the desk, I watched as best I could. The guy bebopped down the fresh fruits and vegetables aisle, grabbing a bag of apples before moving on.

"You know Rick the Dick will throw a hissy fit of epic proportions if he catches you checking out one of the customers," Helen whispered exaggeratedly from the first register. I already knew that, but I couldn't take my eyes off him. He was just my type: cute as a button, attractive in a "not trying to look like he was trying too hard" kind of way. Of course I knew everything he wore was part of the persona, but he was definitely trying to look like he'd just thrown on the outfit. He certainly knew what looked good on him, because not everyone could wear a shirt with pink, purple, green, and white stripes, but he sure as hell could.

"I know," I mouthed back. I pulled my thoughts to the old lady in front of me and helped her with the ad price on twelve cans of store-brand cat food. I smiled and made sure she was happy before thanking her and watching her leave. All I could think was how sorry I felt for the cats that were going to eat that.

Helen looked around and scooted over to the desk. "He's coming up the dairy aisle. I'm going to have a problem with my register tape, so you can ring up Mr. Cuteness." She winked at me and then skittered back to her register just as Rick came around the corner. She looked innocent and smiled at him as he passed.

Rick wasn't much older than I was, and for the millionth time, I wondered what he'd done to get this position. He must have been sleeping with someone, because he certainly hadn't gotten the position on his ability, people skills, or math acumen. I swear, Rick could barely count to twenty with his shoes on. "There's a cart of canned goods in the back," he told me as he approached. "When it's slow, go ahead and stock them."

"Is it the one to the left as you enter the stock area?" I asked, and Rick nodded. "I tried last night. It's overstock that was sent by mistake.

We don't need it, and Larry said to leave it for now when I told him about it this morning." Larry was the general manager.

Rick looked at me like I had two heads. He always did that when I knew something he didn't, which wasn't difficult. He was about to argue, I could see the gears grinding behind his eyes, but the cutie approached, and Rick would never say anything in front of a customer. The cutie headed toward Helen, but she had her receipt tape printer cover open, so he looked around.

"I can help you," I said cheerfully, and the guy headed over.

Dang if he didn't have the deepest blue eyes on the face of the earth, and a perfect smile with lips that gave me wicked thoughts that I had to push away. Thankfully I was behind a counter. He set his items in front of me, and I began to ring him up. I had this guy right in front of me, he was adorable, obviously gay, and I didn't know the first thing to say to him. I'd been watching him for fifteen minutes. "The apples are on sale if you buy two," I said, and then I cringed on the inside. *That was all I could come up with?* Like my shopping acumen was going to impress him.

"Thanks," he said and made no effort to leave. "One's fine."

I continued ringing him up, hoping like hell some spirited and interesting banter would pop into my head, but I had nothing. By the time I finished and had bagged his stuff, he was already pulling out his wallet. I told him the amount, and he paid before grabbing his bag and leaving the store.

"That was pathetic," Helen said. "You mooned over him the entire time he was in here, and that's all you've got? 'They're on sale if you buy two....'" She snorted with laughter. "No wonder you haven't had a date. What's your best pickup line? 'Wanna polish my apples?'"

She hooted again, and I rolled my eyes. I knew she had a point. I'd never been good at talking to guys I was interested in. Mostly I'd watch them and stay away, so they never knew I was there and found boyfriends who weren't me.

"Come on, you're a great guy. You're cute in a nerdy sort of way, and you're smart. What you gotta do is engage people in conversation. You know all kinds of stuff, and if you'd actually talk to them, they might find you interesting."

Now I really rolled my eyes. "Please," I said, looking around and stepping from behind the counter when I saw that Rick wasn't within earshot. "Have you taken a look at me? I'm skinny as a rail." I turned around. "And I have no butt," I added in a stage whisper. "My jeans go from waist to legs with nothing in between."

"You do too," Helen said. "It's just hidden." She lasted about two seconds before laughing. "You are kind of buttless in those pants. But it's the pants. You need to get better clothes."

"Yeah," I said. "My folks have money. I don't." Mom and Dad had agreed to pay my tuition and room and board, but nothing else. Dad wanted me to earn part of my education, hence the job at the grocery store. If I wanted money for extras, I had to earn it. Not that I was really complaining. I was getting a great education at Dickinson, and I was earning part of my way. Dad had made his money himself. He was an ophthalmologist and had started his own practice that had grown to include multiple optometrists and a large office on Long Island. He'd built the business from nothing, and he wanted me to learn the same skills.

"You don't have to have a lot of money to dress well. You just need someone who has the eye." She smiled sweetly, and I returned it.

"That's good, because I have something to ask you. My folks are going on a cruise over Thanksgiving…."

"And you want to go," she finished. "Sure, I'll help cover your shifts."

"No," I told her. "Actually I was wondering if you wanted to go. They got me a stateroom and said I could bring a guest. You'd have to cover your own expenses on the ship and get a ticket to Fort Lauderdale, but they're only a couple hundred bucks."

Helen's eyes bugged and she squealed like a madwoman. Then she covered her mouth and did a little dance behind the counter.

"But you gotta help me look better," I said.

"That's such a deal," Helen said with a grin.

"What has both of you so happy?" Rick asked, walking up the aisle.

"Brad and I are going on a cruise," Helen said.

Rick paused. "You two?" He chuckled and then turned back to Helen. "You know he's too light in the loafers for you." Rick stepped closer to Helen. She was a pretty girl, thin, with long, raven hair that shimmered in the light. "Now, that's not to say I wouldn't be interested."

"Please," Helen retorted. "I'm not dating you."

"Well, I can't let you both have time off at the same time." He sounded so smug I wanted to punch him. Helen simply smiled and leaned over the counter.

"I think you will, because otherwise your little proposition will be construed as sexual harassment. And I have a witness." Helen straightened and stood tall. "So, Brad and I will both be gone the week of Thanksgiving, and you're going to arrange it." She smiled deviously, and I actually saw Rick shrink slightly. "We'd both be so grateful."

Rick turned and I saw abject hatred in his expression. "You're still never going to get anything from him."

"Please. We're friends, and he's going to get farther with me than you ever would." Helen flipped her hair back. "I can help you," she said as a customer approached her register. Rick stepped away, and Helen ignored him. I decided now was a good time to arrange the bags and supplies under the counter and hoped like hell that Rick went back to the office or wherever he spent most of the night. I didn't really care as long as he wasn't bothering either of us.

Once he was gone, Helen let out another squeal and then grinned. "Now all we've got to do is live with him until Thanksgiving. He's going to be a pain in the ass, but I can keep him in line. It's only three months away, and we can survive until then." She looked around. "So tell me about this ship—is it one of those big ones?"

"Yeah. We're on a big Royal Caribbean ship. It has everything—zip line, surf machines, all of it. We'll be having fun for seven days straight." I couldn't help smiling. It was going to be so much fun. Yeah, I was bringing a girl, and my mother would take that as some sort of sign that I was over the gay thing. My parents loved me, but there were times when they were so oblivious. Like the time we went up to Maine when I was twelve, and Mom and Dad wanted to dig clams. Now, why anyone would want to do that was beyond me, but we went. We got a bucket, and Dad got these scoopy-shaped shovels. It was fun and I had a good time, until they actually expected me to pick up the clams. The shells were okay, but the other parts were slippery and slimy. In the end, I dug them up, but my dad had to put them in the bucket.

That should definitely have been a clue. Nope, Mom was ever hopeful she'd have a daughter-in-law someday and that she'd get to help plan a huge wedding. I tried telling her that she could still plan a wedding—there would just be two grooms—but she wasn't interested. To her, weddings had brides, and it was all about the dress. I loved my mom dearly, but there was no way in hell I'd wear a wedding dress for anyone.

A customer came up and we had ourselves a minirush, then things quieted down and I left the desk to see what needed to be stocked in the back. The night shifts were quiet and could drag on forever, so the trick was to keep busy. I found a cart of things that actually needed stocking and wheeled it out to the canned goods aisle and got to work. I was just getting into the groove when I was paged to the front.

I lifted the section of counter and approached the customer service area to find the cutie looking over the counter at me. "I got the wrong thing," he said and pushed a box of macaroni and cheese over the counter. The energy he'd exuded earlier was markedly absent, and he seemed incredibly subdued. "Apparently, there is some sort of difference."

"What is it you need?"

"It has to be Kraft," he said.

"Give me a minute," I told him and hurried away. I knew what he wanted and went right to the aisle. I grabbed the blue-and-gold box and walked back to the desk. I saw him shuffling from foot to foot nervously. "Is this what you need?" I asked and handed him the box.

"Yes," he breathed. "Who can tell them apart? I don't eat this stuff, but I'm supposed to know that there's a difference?" I rang up the exchange, and he paid me the twenty cents' difference. "Thanks for your help," he said and then turned and left.

Damned if I didn't watch him the entire time until the sliding glass doors closed behind him. When I looked up, I saw Helen looking back at me, shaking her head. "Real memorable," she said.

"What was I supposed to do?"

"I don't know, offer to show him, maybe ask him what classes he's taking. He was wearing a Dickinson polo, and it looked really nice on him. Chat him up, what could it hurt?"

It was too late now, so I shrugged and went back to work. But I kept thinking of him the rest of the night, and even in the morning, when I finally got some time all to myself.

Chapter 2

I SAW him a few times on campus. He was always surrounded by a huge group of friends. What surprised me was that one of those friends was the quarterback of the football team. Something there didn't add up. The world seemed to have tilted on its ear. Most of the guys he hung out with seemed normal and a little nerdy like me, but then there were the football players, who also seemed to be part of the circle.

"They're all friends," Helen said one day in mid-November when she saw me watching. She sat in the red Adirondack chair next to mine, bundled against the chill on the sunny afternoon. "God, you still haven't gotten up the guts to talk to him, have you?"

"No," I said, holding my books in front of me like a shield.

"You see the guy standing next to Freddie? That's his boyfriend."

"No way!" I said way too loudly and turned away when people turned to look. "You have to be kidding me."

"Nope. They've been dating for almost a year. Apparently there was some brouhaha about it last year, but nobody cares now. He's still a good quarterback, and the team has accepted them." Helen grinned. "I think it's great. It means everyone on campus got a wake-up call, so for anyone coming out, it's no big deal."

"That's cool," I said, still glancing at them… as I watched a guy walk up to the guy I was afraid I was becoming obsessed with.

"By the way, his name's Jordy, and you waited too long. He's dating someone."

Helen tilted her head as another guy joined the group. "I told you, you should have talked to him." The guy slipped an arm around Jordy's waist and pulled him close. Jordy went to him, but there was something about the way they stood together….

"Stop staring. It's a little pathetic and needy."

"Thanks," I said. "Is that why you came over here, to berate me?"

"No, I wanted to ask about the stuff I should pack. We're going in less than a week. I can't believe we're leaving this cold behind for sun and fun."

"Pack pool stuff, shirts, T-shirts, sundresses and stuff like that. It will feel like summer. Also, there are two formal nights at dinner, and Mom loves to make a big deal out of it." I leaned close. "Mom has already gotten me a tux to wear, so you'll need a couple of really nice dresses." I felt bad because Helen was here on scholarship and I'd completely forgotten about that part of the deal.

"I've got that covered. I saw that part online and found a couple nice things at the secondhand store in town." I had to hand it to Helen; she really had a knack for making the best of things.

"Bring good walking shoes and stuff like that, 'cause there will be shopping and things to do at the ports. Mom said she'd book a snorkeling excursion on St. Thomas if we wanted to go. We can find fun stuff to do on Sint Maarten. Maybe we can rent wave runners." I smiled, and Helen practically shook with excitement. "This is going to be a blast." We talked for a while longer and then got up and hurried off to our next class.

The rest of the week went okay, though the weekend crawled along with work. The following week seemed to slow interminably. I was busy with classes and that was fine, but it was the chemistry exam just before the Thanksgiving break that was really kicking my rear end. The professor always seemed brilliantly absentminded. He seemed to know everything about chemistry, though, and one of the other students told me that he was up for some big award for some research he'd done. But I found it hard to get over the fact that he was just a few years older than me—he'd already done so much, and I hadn't done anything.

Finally, the last class ended. I packed and managed to get a ride to the train station in Harrisburg for Helen and me from a friend, who agreed to drop us off on his way out of town. Four hours later, we were at Penn Station in New York City, where my folks met us. They'd gotten a hotel in the city for the night because our flight out of Newark to Fort Lauderdale was really early the following morning.

My mother and Helen hit it off right away, which was both scary and wonderful. I could see the hopeful look in my mother's eyes.

"Let her have whatever hope she wants," my father said as he and I waited for Mom and Helen to come down to the lobby.

"I'm gay, Dad. That isn't going to change." I could not believe I'd just said that in the middle of the Marriott hotel lobby. "I don't know why Mom insists on hiding her head in the sand. It just makes things harder for me." I turned away to watch the glass-enclosed elevators as they slid up and down the column in the center of the building, like some perpetually moving sculpture. "It makes me feel like I'm not good enough and that I need to be something I'm not to make her happy." There, I'd finally said it to one of my parents.

"I'll talk to your mother," Dad said.

I understood that most guys came out to their mothers first, but I'd told my dad. He wasn't just my dad; he was also a really good friend and a great listener. I'd always thought that was part of what made him such a successful doctor. Of course, Dad had been thrilled when I'd told him I was majoring in science. He'd figured it was the gateway for me to follow in his footsteps and go to medical school. Not that I was opposed to medicine, but I wanted to go into experimental chemistry and do research. "Thanks, Dad," I said as I saw Mom and Helen get off one of the elevators and walk over toward us.

"Doesn't she look nice," Mom said to me, glancing at Helen.

"That's quite enough, Margaret," Dad chided, taking her arm. Mom glanced up at him innocently, and Dad guided her away. I could hear them talking softly and knew the topic.

"Your mom's really nice."

"Yeah, she is. I should have warned you, though. She's in the market for a daughter-in-law." I waited, and Helen was quiet for two seconds before laughing loudly. That was one of the things I loved about her—she saw the absurdity in life better than anyone I'd ever known.

"She isn't getting one in me," Helen said between bouts of laughter. "Although, can you think of a better addition to your family than me?"

Now it was my turn to laugh. "Maybe if you had different parts." Helen's laughter had begun to die, but it picked right up again.

"What are you two laughing about back there?" my mother asked.

"Plumbers," Helen answered without missing a beat. My mother looked at us like we'd both lost our minds, but didn't press it further, and we left the hotel to go to dinner. The restaurant was really nice, and once we were done eating, we returned to the hotel for the night.

We had to get up at the buttcrack of dawn to catch our flight, so both Helen and I were still half asleep when we boarded the plane the following morning. It wasn't until we were getting ready to land in Fort Lauderdale that both of us woke up and fought to look out the window for a glimpse at the largest cruise ship afloat.

"Have you been on a cruise before?" Helen asked as we walked down the jetway.

"Yeah, a few years ago. It was a lot of fun, but there was a bunch of stuff I couldn't do because I wasn't old enough." I nudged her. "Dad said he added some money to our onboard accounts and that was our limit for the week. When it's gone, we're on our own." She seemed surprised. "That's my dad. He never mentions stuff like that. He just does it."

The airport was a zoo, with everyone trying to get to and from ships. Various people held signs for different cruise ships, but Dad got a cab, and soon we were on our way to the port. Helen looked out the window the entire time.

"I signed both of us up for mani-pedis tomorrow," my mother told Helen as we rode. "It's going to be so wonderful to have a girl to pamper and do things with."

Helen looked at me, and I shrugged. She was on her own as far as my mother was concerned. Mom could be a force of nature, and as long as she and Helen seemed to get along, I wasn't about to get in the way. "That's really nice," Helen said and leaned toward the window as the ships came in sight. "Is that one ours?"

"No," I said. "Ours is the big one over there." I pointed across the way, and Helen's eyes boggled as we pulled into the lot near a ship towering two hundred feet above us. The cab drove up to the port building, and we all piled out. Dad paid the bill, and the driver piled our luggage at the curb. I helped Mom with her bag, and we headed toward the terminal.

Inside, we waited in line to check our luggage. Then we headed into the terminal, where we were photographed and got our SeaPass cards. Then we took the escalators to the upper level and sat in the lounge until it was time to board.

"This is so cool, but why are we in the private lounge when everyone else is out there?" Helen asked.

"Dad booked a family suite, so we get to sit with the suite guests," I explained. It seemed Dad had gone all out for this vacation. We sat back, and Helen and I talked about all the stuff we wanted to do as soon as we got on board.

"The first order of the day is lunch, and then we can tour the ship to get to know where everything is. Then you can lie out in the sun or whatever you want to do," my mother said.

"Margaret, leave the kids alone. They're old enough to take care of themselves," my dad said. Mom was about to argue when Dad leaned close and whispered something in her ear. Mom smiled, and I looked away, because Mom and Dad getting mushy was not the way I wanted to start my vacation.

I was about to turn to Helen when she jabbed me in the side. "Look over there, third seat from the left." I glanced where she indicated. "Do you see him?"

"Who?" I asked, and then I saw him. "Jordy?"

"Yup." Helen grinned. "Think about it." I did for a few seconds and then wondered what I'd say. Besides, he supposedly had a boyfriend. "I don't see the guy he was hanging around with at school. Maybe they broke up."

"Not that it matters," I told her. "I wouldn't know what to say to him."

"Oh, for Pete's sake," Helen said whispered. "Just say hi or ask him to coffee or something."

"Yeah, sure. I could do that." *Not that it would matter in the least.* Jordy was cute and had this presence when he walked into a room. I was just me, and there was nothing I could do to get his interest. At least there were more than five thousand other people on the ship, and it wasn't like I would be running into him all the time. Heck, maybe if I was lucky I wouldn't see him much, and I could go on with my fantasy that I was actually interesting.

"They're boarding us," my dad said, and everyone in our area stood and filed to the machines that checked you onto the ship. We each inserted our cards, and they checked us against the pictures they'd taken earlier. Then we followed the sign to the ship and climbed the boarding ramp. At the top, we stepped onto the ship and were hit with a barrage of crew members offering hand sanitizer. I took a little of the stuff, rubbed my hands, and then proceeded onto the promenade of the ship.

"We can't get into the room for a few hours, so let's head up to the buffet," my dad said. "Then your mother and I will go relax, and you two can hit the pool deck or whatever else you want to do."

"I want to ride the FlowRider," I said to Helen. "Are you up for that?" I'd been looking forward to the onboard surfing experience.

She laughed. "You better believe it." That was what I loved about her—Helen was up for anything and nothing intimidated her. We made our way to the elevators, talking about all the things we were going to do. On our ride all the way up to the sixteenth deck, we talked excitedly.

In the buffet, we found a table and sat near one of the windows. It wasn't the greatest view of the port, but I didn't care. I was on vacation with my best friend, and we were going to have the time of our lives. No work, school, or classes for a whole week.

"Hey," Helen said, turning to the table next to us. "I didn't know you were going to be here. How cool is that?"

I turned and found Helen talking to Jordy. "Mr. and Mrs. Jergens, this is Jordy. He goes to Dickinson with us." Jordy got up and shook hands with my parents and then turned to me. "The silent one is Brad." Helen nudged me in the ribs, and I remembered to smile and try not to look like the doofus I felt I was.

"Hi," I managed, and shook his hand. "I've seen you around a few times."

"Yeah, me too. You work at the Giant sometimes." Jordy smiled, and I was thrilled he remembered me. "I'm here with my folks and sister. They wanted to take a last family vacation before we all got too old." Jordy returned to his seat at the next table, and after a few minutes the rest of his family joined him. They all introduced themselves and talked the way people did on cruise ships. Jordy's family lived outside Philadelphia on the Main Line. His mom and my mom talked, and I wished I could think of something to ask Jordy.

"After lunch we're going to get into our suits and try out the FlowRider. Do you want to join us?" Helen asked Jordy.

"That would be cool. I tried the one at Hershey Park once, but it wasn't very good," Jordy said, and then he looked at me. "Have you ever been on one?"

"They had one on the last cruise we went on, so I got a chance to learn. I'm not very good either, really," I said before I got too tongue-tied to talk any longer. Jordy, the guy I'd crushed on since that summer night at the grocery store, was sitting one table over from me and we were talking.

"Let's go up to the buffet," Helen said, and I stood up. Jordy did as well, and the three of us got plates.

"So, what's your major?" Jordy asked.

"Chemistry," I answered. "Right now I still have a lot of general ed, and, of course, math classes out the wazoo. How about you?"

"American Studies," Jordy said and then laughed. "I know. My mom and dad think I'm crazy. How am I going to get a job with a degree in American Studies? That's what they say all the time. But I love it. Why not study our own culture and what it is about us that makes us unique? American literature and culture. Sorry, I guess I'm a little sensitive about it. I plan to get my masters and eventually a PhD, so I can teach and do research." He stopped at the salad area and began loading up his plate. I did the same, not because I was particularly interested in having salad for lunch, but because he was talking to me and I didn't want it to end. "What do you like about chemistry?"

I smiled. "The way you can put two things together under the right circumstances and come up with something completely new," I answered. "My dad's a doctor, and he hopes I'll follow in his footsteps or go into medical research, but I want to go into energy research. I firmly believe that there is a way to create fusion without adding more energy than we get out of it. The sun does it, and I believe there has to be a way for us to do it too." I looked up from my plate and realized I'd filled it with tomatoes. Good thing I liked them. "Sorry, I can bore people to death about this stuff."

"It's not boring. I'm taking a chemistry class next semester. At least now I'll know who to call if I need help." Jordy grinned at me and returned his attention to the buffet. I finished making my salad and added dressing before following Jordy back to our tables, where I was greeted by a smiling Helen. I knew what she was grinning at, and I sat down next to her. Jordy sat across the table from me, and our folks sat at the next table, talking like old friends. It was so cool, and I couldn't believe I was sitting here on a cruise ship, more than a thousand miles away from campus, with the guy I had wanted to meet for months. I really must have done something karmically good lately.

"What are you studying?" Jordy asked Helen.

She had her mouth full.

"Helen's a physics major," I said for her. "She's super smart and will most likely change the world." I smiled, and for the first time I could remember, Helen was silent.

A girl, age fourteen or so, came and sat in the chair next to Jordy's. "This is my sister Angie," Jordy said.

We all said hello, and it was like someone flipped Angie's switch to on. She told us about all the things she was going to do and how she had the entire week planned out. "This afternoon I'm going to lay out by the pool, and tomorrow there's a craft session in the morning and a FlowRider lesson in the afternoon. Mom made a reservation for all of us to see the show tomorrow night." She went on, and I figured she must have memorized the activity schedule for the week.

"If she reads something, she remembers it forever," Jordy said.

"Yeah. Sometimes it's pretty cool, and other times it kind of sucks," Angie said. "If something is good, I can remember it forever, and if it's bad, I can't get rid of it." She grinned and then began to eat. "Like the time last year, when Jordy told Mom and Dad he was gay. Like that was a big shock to anyone. After years of listening to show tunes...." She rolled her eyes. I wasn't sure what to make of it, so I said nothing, but Helen and Angie struck up a conversation.

"The part that really sucks is when she doesn't seem to know when she shouldn't say the first thing that comes into her head." Jordy didn't seem too put out by what she'd said.

"I don't have the part of the brain that censors speech," Angie said.

"Personally, I think she uses that part to her best advantage," Jordy told the group, and then he put his arm around his sister and gave her a little hug. I got the feeling he might pick on her, but Jordy would protect his sister with the fierceness of a tiger.

We ate, and after we were done, we grabbed our carry-on bags. "We're going to change and go to the sports deck," I told my mom. "We'll meet you and Dad at the room later." Angie stayed with her parents, and the three of us headed toward the back of the ship.

The sports deck had FlowRiders, climbing walls, a sports court, a zip line, miniature golf course, and games of all kinds. I wasn't sure where to start. I flung my backpack over one shoulder and followed the signs to the aft of the ship. It was like young adult nirvana, every toy imaginable just waiting for me. "I'm going to change."

Helen peeled off to find a ladies room, and Jordy followed me. We pulled open the door to the men's room and went inside, where we each took a stall. I changed quickly, stuffing my street clothes into my backpack and pulling on my board shorts and an old T-shirt. I used the facilities while they were available and then left, waiting for the others outside. Jordy stepped out a few seconds after me, and I had to admit I openly stared at him. His lime green square-cut suit left little to the imagination, and when he turned around, well, damn. He wasn't wearing a T-shirt, so his lightly tanned skin and slim physique were a feast for the eyes. "Let's go on back and meet Helen," he said. I nodded like a dork and followed him, gaze peeled to the way his butt bobbed, encased in thin Lycra. I was so screwed, and thankful my suit was loose and would hide what I didn't want seen.

"You really don't talk much, do you?" Jordy asked.

"I do…." I stumbled. "Just…." *God, what do I say to him?* Helen hadn't joined us yet, and I had Jordy all to myself, with the chance to impress him—or at the very least, not come off like a dork.

Helen hurried across in a body-hugging, dark blue, two-piece suit guaranteed to have everyone at the pool deck looking at her. The color looked extraordinary on her, and given that she had all the right curves in all the right places, I figured everyone who liked girls would be looking at her, and everyone who liked boys would be watching Jordy, so I could effectively disappear. At least that was my plan.

"We need towels," Helen said, and I led the way to one of the stations, where we gave them our SeaPasses and they added towels to our accounts. Then we were ready. "FlowRider first?" Helen asked, and we all agreed.

"Boogie board or stand up?" I asked as we approached. Helen wanted to boogie board, so we got in line for that side.

"You go first," Helen said and then stepped back so Jordy could be next. We watched the others, and when it was my turn, I took the board and jumped on. As soon as I hit the rush of water, I jumped on the board and skittered on top. It was a great feeling. I climbed to my knees and zoomed from top to bottom and side to side, spraying water at the people in line. This, I'd done many times before. Then I went back down on the board, slid off, and pushed the board away, body surfing on the water. Then I caught the board and did a quick roll. The surf caught my suit and I felt it go. Instantly I bailed and pulled up the board shorts before everyone got a glimpse of what the good Lord gave me.

I managed to get them back on and handed the boogie board to the attendant, then stood off to the side and watched as Jordy took his turn. The attendant showed him how to start, and Jordy gave it a try. He spent some time learning how to control the board and then tumbled off. I waited, and Jordy stood next to me while Helen got ready to go.

"You had a little trouble," Jordy said as the instructor spent some time with Helen.

"Yeah." I tightened the tie on my suit so it would stay on next time. "It was embarrassing."

Jordy bumped my arm. "You've got nothing to be embarrassed about." I saw Jordy glance at me, and my skin went all tingly in just a few seconds. Helen started her run, and one of the guys helped her until she got the feel of the board. Then he had her try to get to her knees, but she wiped out. Helen came up with a grin, and we all got back in line.

"You really know what you're doing," Helen told me. "Too bad you flashed everyone in line."

"Wait till your top ends up around your waist," I told her. She glared at me. "Or up around your neck." Helen smacked me on the arm and then began adjusting her suit. We spent quite a while boogie boarding. Both Helen and Jordy really got the hang of it. Then we moved to the other side and got in line for stand-up surfing.

I always felt for the guys who manned this station, because they spent their days trying to show people how to surf. It wasn't easy, but once you got the hang of it, surfing could be way fun. I went first and took the board, held it over the stream, and leapt on.

This was a rush. The water flowed under me as I stood, surfing the waves, weaving back and forth, having the time of my life. This was the one athletic thing I was good at, and only because, on previous cruises with my folks, I'd signed up twice for FlowRider lessons. With most other sports-type things I had two left feet, and balls were my nemesis. But this I'd learned I could do. After a few minutes, I slid to the front and out of the stream.

"That was so cool," Jordy said and took his turn. The attendant helped him onto the board and then out into the stream, holding his hand. Damn, I wished I could be the one holding Jordy's hand and get to talk to him like that. Jordy lasted a few seconds once the attendant released his hand, but he'd done it. Jordy came out of the flow of water with a grin. He rushed over to where I stood, and we high-fived. "What a rush...."

"It is, isn't it?" I said, returning Jordy's grin.

"I'm going to boogie board," Helen said. "I like that better." I was about to go over with her, but paused when I saw Jordy's smile. "Stay with him and talk to him. He's really cute, and I think he likes you," Helen whispered quickly.

"We'll meet in an hour for zip-lining," I told her, and she hurried away. Then I got in line with Jordy. "The trick is to keep your weight distributed. If you put too much weight forward, you're going to stop the flow and the water will take the board away. Same if you put too much weight back. You want to stay upright so the board can glide over the water." We watched other riders as they took their turn. "One of the tricks is to not look at your feet. As soon as you do, you're going down, because you lean forward, and that's the kiss of death. See, like him. Look forward and stay upright. You move the board with your body, not your feet."

"Okay," Jordy said, and when it was his turn, he stayed on a lot longer, and the instructors were able to talk him through moving along the flow. It was so cool.

I remembered the first time I'd been able to stay on, and it had been a rush. The line was getting longer and the sun hotter. I got my bag and pulled out the tube of sunscreen to put some on.

"Can I borrow some?" Jordy asked.

"Sure." I handed him the tube after getting enough to coat my shoulders and arms. I was about to ask him if he wanted me to do his back when he tossed me the tube. I finished applying and stuck the tube back in my bag.

We took another run at the FlowRider and then headed over to find Helen, who was taking her turn boogie-boarding. She was doing really well, and all the guys in line were watching her with rapt attention. Helen was going to be popular. When she wiped out, one of the guys from the line helped her out and smiled at her. We waited while they talked for a few minutes, and then she joined us. "He gave me his cabin number and asked me to stop by sometime."

"Do you know him well enough?" Jordy asked. I was about to ask the same thing.

"Of course not," Helen retorted. "But it's nice to be asked." She turned over her shoulder. "But I wouldn't mind seeing more of him."

Jordy giggled and placed his hand in front of his mouth. "There isn't much else to see. He's pretty much showing off everything he has right now." Helen looked him over rakishly. "I'm just saying, it ain't bad, but you could do better. He looks like the kind of guy who's interested in one thing, especially if he's already giving out his room number."

"You sound like this one," Helen said, bumping my hip with hers. "I didn't come on this trip to get busy. But a little attention in that department isn't a bad thing, either."

"I doubt you'll have to worry about that," I said, noticing the guys as they looked her way. "Let's change and try out the zip line, or we can just go down to the pool deck and do the zip line later." We chose the pool deck and walked in that direction, stopping in at the Wipeout Café for a quick snack as we went. We used our bags to save a table, and got burgers and salad before sitting down.

"My mother would wonder how I could possibly be hungry already," Jordy said as he tore into his burger with gusto.

"So would mine. But I am hungry," I echoed and began to eat.

Helen picked at some salad while the two of us ate. "You're going to work off whatever you eat. On ships like this, you walk everywhere, and we'll go to the gym and use the spa area, so you don't need to worry about food."

"Please, when have you ever seen me turn down food? I'm just not really hungry right now." She sipped her diet soda, and we finished our food and then moved on to the pool deck with its swimming pools, hot tubs, and lounge chairs for taking in the sun. It was also the place where everyone seemed to wear way too little, like the retired guy in the thong.

"Sort of makes you want to gouge your eyes out, doesn't it?" Jordy whispered to me, and I nodded. Helen gasped and then nudged my arm. She didn't point, but I saw where she was looking. It was terrible, and yet I could not stop looking.

"Yes, they do make things that big," I whispered and had to turn away. "We need to get used to it, because while none of these people would be caught dead dressing like this for the local pool or beach, on the ship, anything goes." We headed for the water and swam a while. Helen got out pretty quickly and lay in the sun. Jordy and I swam and then got in one of the whirlpools to bubble for a while. When we got out, I checked the time and went to get Helen. "We should be able to get into the rooms now, so we can drop our stuff."

Helen tied up her top. Jordy was already gathering his stuff. "I'll see you guys around," he said. We exchanged cabin numbers, and then Jordy hurried off. I watched him go while I waited for Helen.

"Don't worry. He wasn't blowing you off. Not given the way he was checking you out when you weren't looking." Helen grabbed her stuff. "Let's drop this off, Romeo." She lifted her bag, and I nodded. Dumping this stuff in the room was definitely a good idea.

We headed for the elevators, but ended up taking the stairs. Everyone seemed to have the same idea, and the elevator lobby was jammed. Our cabin was on the ninth deck. I slid my key into the lock, and we went on through. The cabin was small, the usual size, but when I opened the connecting door, we joined to my parents' much larger cabin. Theirs had a separate living and sleeping area with a sectional sofa and a huge television that spun so it could be seen from either room.

"Go ahead and unpack your things," Mom instructed. Our main luggage probably wouldn't be delivered for a few hours, but we went back into our cabin, divided up the space, and began putting away what we had.

"Where are we going to put the suitcases?" Helen asked, and I lifted the edge of the spread on her bed.

"Just slide it under here when it's empty. I use mine for dirty clothes." I dropped the bedspread and opened the closet. "Everything is really efficient. There's more storage in the bathroom, and in the back of the closet, there's a safe. Do you want to go back to the pool deck or change out of our suits?"

Helen didn't answer and peered into the bathroom instead. "Is that the shower?" She sounded horrified, and I looked where she was pointing. "If I bend over in that thing I'll lose what's left of my virtue."

"That's the shower, but Mom already got the thermal suite package for all of us, so we can go down there and use the showers. They're the size of real showers, so don't worry. I've done this before and I've got the place wired. Like when we go to the spa, be sure to take your bag and put one of the towels in it. That way we won't have to worry about the pool towels anymore." I lowered my voice. "The last time I didn't return one, and Dad got charged twenty-five bucks. He was pissed beyond belief, so I try to avoid them if I can."

"I'll remember that," Helen said. "Let's go back up to the pool. I want to work on my tan while the sun's bright."

"Okay, I'll tell Mom," I said. The connecting door was closed, so I knocked softly. My dad opened the door slightly and peered around. I told him we were going, and he nodded and closed the door again. "Let's go."

"Okay," Helen agreed, and we left the room with our pool towels flung over our shoulders. "What was that about?"

"I don't want to think about it," I answered.

"Thank you," she said, and we continued down the passageway and then up the stairs. On the pool deck we found loungers, and I slathered on more sunscreen while Helen got comfortable. She was one of those people who never burned, and while I wasn't too bad in the sun, I'd learned that a sunburn on a cruise was not fun in the least, so I followed Dad's advice and used the sunscreen.

"Is this one taken?"

I turned around and saw Jordy smiling at me. He sat down, and I couldn't help grinning. "Did you get settled?"

"Yeah, sort of. The steward didn't have the beds set up correctly, so they need to change them. Mom didn't know why it was such a big deal, but I wasn't going to sleep with Angie. The kid's a bed hog, and she kicks in the middle of the night. The last time I had to sleep with her, I woke up with bruises. How about you two?"

"It was cool. We didn't decide which bed was whose, but Helen can have the one she wants. It doesn't matter to me."

"I want the one nearer the balcony," Helen said. "You can have the one near the bathroom."

"I laughed. "Not that it matters in the middle of the night. The flush will wake the dead, I swear." I chuckled, and Helen turned and gaped at me like I was kidding. "Like I said, it doesn't matter as long as the first one up is quiet."

"You better believe it," Helen said, placing her head on her pillow. "I don't want to have to kill you."

"Helen's a night owl, so she'll sleep in. I usually get up and get going. So we'll both have to be quiet."

"Angie goes to bed early, so I always have to be quiet," Jordy said with a shrug. "Not that it matters. I'm more of a morning person than a night person."

"Someone needs to take me dancing after dinner," Helen said without looking up.

"How about Mr. Here's My Room Number?" I asked. I moved away, but not quickly enough—Helen smacked my leg. "I'm a terrible dancer," I admitted. But I'd bet Jordy was a great dancer, and I was more than willing to go dancing just to see that. I'd become very adept at being the wallflower.

"There's music tonight all over the ship. We can find something," Jordy offered and settled on his lounge. He pulled sunglasses out of his bag, stuck them on, and then got some sunscreen and slathered it on. When he started rubbing it into his chest and stomach, I had to stifle a groan. Damn, how I wanted to ask if he'd let me do that. I watched for way too long and then turned and settled on my lounger. Thankfully there was an umbrella next to mine, so I put it up and made sure it didn't shade Helen before putting on my sunglasses and lying back to soak up the warmth.

It was heavenly—up to a point. Jordy lay on one side of me, largely in the shade, and I adjusted the umbrella so it covered both of us. Every time he moved, I glanced over to watch him, thankful I was wearing sunglasses so he couldn't see where I was looking. This was almost too good to be true. Jordy was not only on the cruise, but was hanging out with us. I wished I knew what to say to him.

"Are you going to go back to the FlowRider this afternoon?" Jordy asked.

"Sure. Helen will probably be here for a while, but we can go back if you want. The lines get longer as more people board."

"You two have fun," Helen said without moving. "I'll know where to find you. Just don't go off somewhere fun without telling me."

I sat up and grabbed my towel. "Let's go." I put on the T-shirt I'd brought along, and we walked toward the back of the ship.

"Helen seems really nice."

"She's a great friend. We met last year in freshman English and became instant friends. When I needed to find a job, she helped me get one at the grocery store. We work mostly the same shifts, so it helps having someone else with my weird schedule. Working nights can be hard, but I've been blessed with the ability to sleep at weird times, so it works for me. It's harder for Helen, but she needs the money, so she works the graveyard shift for the extra pay." We reached the sports deck, and Jordy stopped to let a group of girls pass. They giggled and looked him over before continuing on.

"If you don't mind my asking, you don't look like you need to work like that. The suit you're wearing is expensive, and your dad said he was an ophthalmologist, so…."

"Mom and Dad pay the tuition and room and board, but I need to work for anything else I want. When they told me that, I was pissed, but it's more than fair. I had no idea about money when I first went to college. In a month, I burned through the money in my account that was supposed to last the entire semester. That's when Dad said I had to get a job."

"That's cool," Jordy said with a nod. "The line doesn't seem to be too bad. I'd like to try surfing again." Jordy headed toward that side of the ship, and I followed.

We spent the rest of the afternoon surfing, or in Jordy's case, learning to surf. It took time and patience, but Jordy was getting the hang of it. I had a ball surfing and watching Jordy. Eventually Helen joined us, so we moved to the boogie-boarding side. It was an amazing afternoon, and I couldn't believe how much fun I was having. I hated for it to end, but as the sun set, Jordy had to get ready for dinner. He said good-bye, and I watched him go with a small sigh.

"You really like him, don't you?" Helen whispered as we stood in line for one last ride.

"Yeah," I said.

"So I gave you the dancing opening—you should have asked him," Helen told me.

"You know I can't dance."

"So? He definitely can, with the way he moves. You have to not worry so much and just go with things. There isn't anyone on the ship that you're going to see again, besides me, and I don't count. I've already seen you dance." She took her turn before I could retort, and then I took mine. The guys were closing the FlowRider, so we gathered our stuff and went back to the cabin.

I let Helen have the bathroom first and quickly changed out of my wet stuff. When she was done, I took my turn, and then knocked on the connecting door. Mom opened it, all smiles, and we settled on the sofa in their cabin. "Did you two have a good time?" My mom was still pouring it on thick.

"It was great," Helen began. "We rode the FlowRider, and I worked on my tan. We met up with Jordy and spent a lot of the time with him."

"Tonight and tomorrow we don't have to dress up for dinner, but the day after tomorrow is the first formal night. I thought we could have our picture taken then." I had little doubt that there would be pictures taken of Helen and me together, at my mother's direction. "I brought some extra jewelry pieces," my mother said to Helen. "I thought that we could see how some of them look with your dress, if you like."

"That would be nice," Helen said and shifted on the sofa. I knew Mom wasn't trying to be mean and meant well, but it hadn't quite come out that way. It took my mother a few seconds before she realized how she sounded.

"I didn't mean…." My mother gasped and turned away. Mom had a good heart, just sometimes she stuck her foot in her mouth.

"I know," Helen said graciously. "I don't have much along that line, so your help would be appreciated." I smiled at her.

"What time is dinner tonight?" I asked to change the subject.

"We have the first seating, at six thirty," my dad said. "And we need to head down to our muster station for the lifeboat drill. Then we can get ready for dinner." We left the stateroom as announcements were being made. Everyone started filing down, and we joined the flow of traffic. On the promenade, we found our station, checked in, and waited with everyone else. I looked around, but didn't see Jordy; not that I'd really expected to.

"You sure can pick them cute," Helen mumbled and pointed across the way. There was Jordy, standing with his family in one of the other groups. He looked adorable. He smiled when he saw me looking, but then a group of people stepped in front of him, blocking my view. I turned back around and listened to the instructions, announcements, and watched the video. Then the captain made his announcement, and we were dismissed.

I glanced around and saw Jordy making his way over. My mother sighed softly. "If you want to eat at the buffet with your friends, that's fine. But I expect you to go to dinner with us on the formal nights."

"Thanks," I told her, knowing it was quite a concession. She loved things like family dinners and parties. They were what she enjoyed most. Entertaining to her was almost a blood sport. She lived to play hostess. I turned and smiled as Jordy walked over, my heart doing a little flip. I tried to settle it and keep my expectations in check. He was being nice and needed people to hang out with. He had a boyfriend back at school—I'd seen him with my own eyes. Granted, the guy had looked like the world's biggest jerk, but that was probably the green-eyed monster rearing its ugly head.

"That was interesting," Jordy commented as he approached.

"It's required, and now the fun can really start. We can go to dinner, and all the venues will be open soon." I walked over to the nearest monitor and began touching the buttons to bring up the schedule. "There's a comedy show tonight," I said. Helen didn't seem interested, and I continued looking. "It should be really funny."

"Okay. It says we need a reservation," Helen observed.

"Mom took care of it. She always plans in advance." I turned to Jordy. "We can go to guest services and make your reservation if there's space—if you want." We headed off, and I felt on top of the world. I knew how things worked and was able to help the others navigate. I knew it was dumb, but it made me feel important and useful. Once we had that done, we wandered the ship, learning where everything was located, and then went up for dinner.

We had to stand in line for the buffet—it seemed everyone had the same idea. Thankfully, it didn't take long, and we got a table and went to fill our plates.

"So, Jordy, is there someone waiting for you?" Helen asked, and I wanted to slide under the table.

"You mean do I have a boyfriend?" Jordy asked and made a face. "It's complicated. I've been seeing this guy, Mark, for about a year. He's brought balance to my life. See, I can be impulsive, and he's thoughtful and steady. Mark plans things out, while I tend to go by the seat of my pants." Jordy took a bite of his stir-fry, and I wanted to die. I'd already gotten my hopes up, and I knew I shouldn't have. "He's practical, and I'm a little wild. So we bring balance to each other."

"He didn't want to come with you?" I asked, and then I coughed to cover up a slight crack in my voice.

"It wasn't in his plans for the break. He hadn't budgeted the money, so I came with my folks." There wasn't any excitement in Jordy's voice. It sounded like he was talking about his Aunt Harriet rather than someone who was supposed to make his heart soar.

"But...," Helen prompted. "You said it was complicated." Jordy shrugged and didn't say anything more. God bless Helen; she didn't let things go easily. "I take it things are *very* complicated."

"He didn't want me to go. Mark said I could come stay with his family for the holiday. I like his family, they're pretty cool, but he actually expected me to give up a cruise to spend the week sitting around his family's house playing Scrabble and Pictionary. He told me that was the practical thing to do."

"It sounds to me as though he uses 'practical' to mean what he wants to do," Helen said, and I half expected Jordy to get upset, but he shrugged instead.

"Like I said, it's complicated," Jordy reiterated, and the conversation moved on to happier topics, even though I had a million questions. Were things really serious with this guy Mark, or did I have a chance? I ran the questions through my mind and realized they all sounded either dumb or really needy. Not exactly the way I wanted to sound, so, as usual, I simply kept quiet. Besides, just because Jordy was here and we were hanging out, that sure as hell didn't mean he was interested in me. I took a glance down and suppressed a sigh. I was nothing to look at; I never had been. A few years ago, before I left for school, my mom had gotten my senior pictures, and I'd heard her describe them as ordinary. Of course she hadn't known I could hear her, but that word stuck in my head. I was ordinary and I knew it; nothing special, just average, at least in the looks department. That was why I worked so hard in school and in the rest of my life. I knew people who skated by on their looks; I'd seen it at school in the way some people were treated. That would never be me, and somehow, even if someone as extraordinary as Jordy was available, he wasn't likely to be interested in anyone as ordinary as me.

By the time we finished eating, it was dark. The sports deck lights were on, but a lot of the attractions there had shut down. We debated getting our suits on again, but decided to wander the promenade and see if the shops were open. They were, and there was live music as well. It was rather sedate, and some of the older passengers were dancing. Helen hurried ahead of us, and as soon as she approached where the dancers were, she grabbed me and pulled me into the group.

"You know I can't dance," I whispered, trying my best to move along with her.

"You're doing pretty well," she said with a smile. We were moving on the dance floor, and I wasn't stepping on toes or bumping into people, so I guessed that was okay. After a few minutes, I felt a tap on my shoulder. When I turned around, Jordy stepped in and swept Helen out of my arms. I left the area and stood where others were watching while Jordy twirled and whirled Helen around. The other dancers stepped aside as Jordy put on a show with Helen, showing her off and putting a smile on her face. When the song ended, he thanked her and walked over to where I stood, holding out his hand.

"Come on, let's show these people what's what," Jordy said. The next song started, and Jordy tugged me onto the floor.

"This is crazy," I whispered, and Jordy began propelling me around the makeshift dance floor.

"No, it's not. Are you having fun?"

Surprisingly, I was, and I told him so. Once I went with it, I really *did* have fun. Jordy had his hand in mine and one on my hip, and he guided me around the dance floor until I felt like Fred Astaire—or was I Ginger Rogers? Didn't matter. I noticed people watching, but big deal. Jordy was paying attention to me and looking into my eyes. His gaze was intense, and

I got swept up in his deep eyes and fluid movement. When the song ended, he stopped, and I blinked a few times before I remembered where I was, and then I walked to the edge of the circle.

"You looked good," Helen said. "And you should have seen some of the old folks. I swear more than one pair of dentures hit the deck."

I wasn't sure how I felt about that. I didn't like making a spectacle of myself.

"Don't be so... you... for a while. None of these people know or care. You'll never see any of them again, so just let go and have fun." Helen grinned slyly. "I could tell you were having fun, so go for the gusto. Besides, I saw how he was looking at you."

"He has a boyfriend," I said, turning around to watch Jordy, now dancing with an older lady.

"Please... *it's complicated.* That's code for 'it's not working and I can't figure out how to tell him.' There's no spark there. I heard that, and so did you. So you have an entire week to sweep him off his feet or let him sweep you off yours. Like I said, go for it. What's the worst that could happen?"

"He could dump my ass," I whispered.

"Or you could have him for a boyfriend," Helen said, shifting her gaze to where Jordy flowed around the floor like liquid sex. Every gaze was glued to him. The women wanted to take their turn, and the men wished they were him. When the music ended and then changed to something with more of a beat, Jordy spun his partner and began to move. Jesus, I could not take my eyes off him. He spun and whirled, kicking and moving with the beat. My throat went dry, and I felt Helen touch my arm. "Go on out there with him."

"Are you kidding? I'll put someone's eye out," I retorted.

"Just do what he does," she said and pushed me forward. I took a step to keep from falling and ended up standing in front of Jordy, who lifted his arms and gyrated his entire body like a cross between a snake and a belly dancer. I couldn't do that, but I did start to move and hoped like hell I wasn't making a fool out of myself. Jordy smiled at me and took my hand, helping me move along with him.

"That's it, loosen up a little and let your body go," he said.

There was only so much I could do, but I did my best and somehow managed not to cause injury to anyone around us. Others joined in and I felt less conspicuous, and soon that entire portion of the promenade was rocking like crazy. The band kept playing as the exuberance continued to build. Still others joined in until the ship was rocking out. When the music did end, I was sweaty, winded, and more alive that I could remember feeling in a long time. Jordy grinned at me and took my hand, leading me out of the crush of people. We found Helen and made our way up on deck as the ship's whistle blew to indicate that we were about to leave.

We hurried up to the pool deck and crowded by the rail. "It's too bad we can't throw confetti like they used to do on television," Jordy said. "I used to watch *Love Boat* reruns, and I wanted to throw streamers and confetti and stuff as the ship pulled away. I suppose it made a mess and was terrible for the environment, but still." He could barely stand still and bumped into me more than once. I got to hoping he was doing it on purpose and figured it didn't matter. I liked him touching me, even if it was accidental. We waved and cheered as the ship moved away from the dock. One of the other ships began blowing its horn, and then yet another joined in, this one actually playing the *Love Boat* theme. A cheer went up when it was done, and all three of us laughed. Jordy began to sing the theme from the *Love Boat* at the top of his lungs in that off-key way he had, and Helen joined in. Soon half the people on deck were singing the theme, and the ship chimed in once again. It was a real party, and damned if I couldn't get the idea out of my mind that Jordy had started it all.

Once we were away from the dock, the lights faded and we started down the channel lined with expensive homes, heading out to sea. Only then did the party begin to die, and people drifted away.

My heart still pounded in my ears as Jordy's sister hurried up to him. She tugged on his arm and spoke to him in a rather frantic manner.

"I need to go, but I'll see you at the comedy club," Jordy said.

He flashed a smile and then hurried away. I rejoined Helen, and we wandered the promenade, glancing in all of the shops. We didn't buy anything, mainly because we had agreed to hold the money my dad had put on our account for later in the week. It had seemed like a lot of money when he told me, but gratuities would be taken out, so it really wasn't as much as it originally seemed. "Your dad and mom are so cool," Helen remarked when we saw them up ahead, stepping out of the Guess store. The ship had a Coach store as well, and I was pretty confident my mother would be sporting a new bag at some point in the cruise. "They didn't have to give us money for stuff on board."

"They are," I agreed. I knew I had it pretty easy, especially compared to Helen.

She stopped. "I mean it. My folks do what they can, but that isn't much."

"I'm glad you were able to come," I said. I knew it was a hardship for her. She was giving up a week's pay at work plus the cost of the plane ticket. Granted, we'd been able to find her a good fare, but it was still a hardship.

"Me too," she said softly. "This is the first real vacation I've ever taken."

"You're kidding," I said, but her expression told me she was telling the truth.

"My folks don't have money for stuff like this. When I told them where I was going, they thought I was crazy." She stopped for a second and then pulled me into the Champagne Bar and looked around before leading us to a table in the corner. "I'm on scholarship."

"Yeah, and you said you live in LA." Helen never talked much about her life back there. She always seemed to avoid it.

"We live in East LA. It's an area that's pretty rough and not the most pleasant place. Nothing like Carlisle or the life your family has. I guess I'm lucky, though. I was smart, and my parents encouraged me. My mom has said that the only way I was going to get out was to work my way out. She and Dad did extra shifts and stuff so I could have what I needed for school. I had to work, but school came first, Mom made sure of that. And when it came time for college, we applied to every school and for every scholarship there was, including the program at Dickinson."

"I know. They take groups of kids from LA and New York and bring them to campus. But I didn't know you were part of that." Helen nodded slowly. "There's nothing to be ashamed of, if that's what you're thinking."

Helen shrugged. "I really want to fit in. Back home I never did."

"You fit in," I told her. "A lot more than I do." It wasn't like I was Mr. Popular, and Helen had plenty of friends.

"Well, when I told her I was going with you, she said I should stay back at campus and study." Helen paused again, and I saw her look around and then at herself. "I feel out of place. I bet no one else is wearing clothes they got at a secondhand store."

I leaned back in the chair. "I thought that was your look," I whispered.

"It's what I can afford."

I sighed. "So what? You always look nice, and if that's what people see, then they aren't worth your time." I swallowed. "Knowing you has changed me. I never had a sister, and now I always think of you as the cool, funky sister I never had before. So don't change a thing, not for me or anyone else."

"You mean that," she said softly.

"Of course I mean that. You're my best friend." I hugged her tight. "You're the best friend I've ever had." I released her and sat back in my chair. A waiter asked if we wanted a drink, but we both declined. I checked the clock over the bar and stood up. "We need to get down to the fourth deck so we can get a good seat."

She and I headed down a deck and realized we were at the wrong end of the ship, so we went back up and walked the length of the promenade before descending again and approaching the club. There was still ten minutes before the show, but people were already lining up for the seats that hadn't been reserved, so we had our cards scanned and went inside to find seats.

We looked for Jordy, but didn't see him, so we took two seats with a third next to us and waited. He came in a few minutes later and sat next to me. "My sister locked her card in the room, so I had to let her in."

"I'm glad you made it in time," I said with a smile and caught Jordy's gaze.

The lights went down and the show began. We laughed our butts off for the next hour. The comedians were raunchy, silly, and spot-on with jokes about the tiny showers and the captain. The coolest part was when the second guy asked if there were honeymooners in the audience, and a pair of guys in front stood up. I glanced at Jordy, and we shared a grin. The performer on stage didn't miss a beat, but he did have to tailor the joke for two men. People cheered, and when asked their wedding date, the one man said they'd been together for almost twenty years and then thanked the good people of Maryland for the chance to make it official. They didn't kiss or anything, but it was really nice.

The show ended a little while later, and we all got up to leave. I was tired, and Helen reached the exit before yawning. "Are you going dancing?" I asked her.

"Can we do it tomorrow?" Helen asked with another yawn, and Jordy smiled.

"Sure."

We said our good-nights and parted, then Helen and I headed for the cabin. Inside, I let her use the bathroom first, and when she was done,

I cleaned up and dressed for bed. Helen was already under the covers, and I turned out the light and knocked on the adjoining door. I didn't get an answer, so I got in bed.

"I think he really likes you," Helen said.

"It doesn't matter," I countered. "He has a boyfriend and probably just wants someone to hang out with for a few days."

"Somehow I doubt that's all there is to it," she said. "The boyfriend is most likely history, and I saw the way he looked at you when you were dancing."

I snuggled under the soft bedding in the cool room and left it there. Helen was good at reading people, and I hoped she was right.

IT DIDN'T look like it. We didn't see Jordy the following day except for a passing wave as he headed into the buffet with his sister and we were on our way out. The next day we docked in Nassau. Mom, Dad, Helen, and I went into town. We had talked of going to Atlantis, but we only had half a day in port, so it wasn't really worth it. I would have loved to go, especially after I had seen the resort from the stateroom balcony that morning, but we all figured there wasn't enough time.

It didn't really matter, and we wandered through town and the straw market. We didn't find anything we wanted to buy, but my mother made notes of things she saw and wanted to look at on the other islands.

"You can stop looking around every few seconds," Helen whispered to me. I shrugged, trying to be cool, but I knew she saw right through me. "Please, you've been looking for him for almost two days. Give it a rest."

"But you said...."

"You said what?" my mother asked from behind me.

"Nothing," I said quickly, and we began to walk a little faster to put some distance between us and my mother with her doglike hearing.

"Give it time. The times I've seen him he's been with his sister, so I suspect he's had kid-sister-watching duties. I know I would if I was with my family... at least part of the time." Helen's attention was drawn by a display of T-shirts, and I got her one in her size. It was purple and looked good on her. "You don't need to buy it for me," she protested, but I was already paying. I got a blue shirt for me that I added to the total, and we left with our souvenirs.

There really wasn't much else to see, so we walked back to the ship after taking a stroll through downtown. Mom and Dad suggested having lunch in the main dining room, so after having our bags scanned and checking back on to the ship, we dropped our stuff in the stateroom and went to lunch.

The main dining room was elegant without being too opulent. A huge chandelier hung from the top deck all the way through the open center of the three decks. Helen didn't seem comfortable, and I leaned over to her to find out what was wrong.

"There are so many forks and stuff," she whispered. "Which one do I use?"

"When in doubt, use the outermost one and work your way in," I whispered. Not that it mattered to any of us, but I understood how Helen felt. Tonight was one of the formal nights and there would be an extensive place setting at dinner. I made a note to give her some pointers before then. At least she'd be more comfortable, and the point of the trip was to have a good time.

"Are you enjoying yourself?" my father asked Helen.

"Very much. I want to thank you again for letting me come with you." Helen sounded so formal, and I knew that was a sign of her discomfort. Her plate was set in front of her, and she seemed a little lost, tentatively picking up her fork and knife.

I wasn't sure if helping her was best and decided to leave her alone so she wouldn't feel self-conscious. "So, are there any plans for the rest of the day?"

"Just dinner," my mother said, "and we thought we'd have our picture taken." I stifled the groan that welled up. Every time we were together and dressed up, my mother wanted a picture. "It'll just be once, and I won't ask again this trip, I promise."

"Okay," I agreed and turned to Helen, who nodded timidly. The rest of our food came, and the conversation fell off as we all ate. "Do you want to head up to the pool deck after lunch?"

Helen swallowed. "Let's do the sports deck, so you can do some surfing, and then we can go to the pool deck," she suggested. "I want to do the zip line again."

"Cool." We finished eating and said good-bye to my parents, who lingered over their coffee.

"Have fun, and don't get sunburned," my father said as we were about to leave. I rolled my eyes and agreed before we took off out of the dining room and hurried up the stairs to our deck. There was a wait for the elevators, as always, and Helen seemed as impatient as I was to get going. The ship had left port by the time we got back to the room, and we watched it pull away from Nassau from the balcony before changing into our suits. Then we grabbed the stuff we needed and headed out.

The FlowRider was hopping, with a lot of people waiting in line. We set our things where we could watch them and got in line. I let Helen go ahead of me, and when her turn came, I waited and watched while the attendant helped her.

"Hi!" Jordy said as he hurried up to get in line.

"Hey." I couldn't help smiling. "You been busy?"

"Yeah. I made a deal with my folks and agreed to watch my sister yesterday so they could have a day alone. If I did that, they said I could have the rest of the cruise to myself, so I jumped at the chance." No one had gotten in line behind me yet, so Jordy took the spot, and we waited our turn. Helen did really well, and once she was done, I took my turn. It was a blast standing on top of the rushing water. I moved and swooshed from one side to the other, sometimes spraying water on the crowd. When I'd been on long enough, I stepped off and watched Jordy as he got ready for his turn.

Dang, he looked good in his red flame suit, which left little to the imagination, and I was having a major amount of fun imagining what was hidden. I took a seat at the base of the machine and watched as Jordy got in place. The man could move; I'd seen that.

"Imagine you're dancing," I called to him.

Jordy stuck his tongue out at me and then got on the board. He got out into the flow with help and was doing fine, but as soon as the attendant let go, Jordy fell and went tumbling in the surf, which jetted him up to the top. I waited for him to come up and join me as Helen told me she was going to the boogie-boarding side.

"You need to use those dance moves when you're trying to ride," I told Jordy once he sat down. "It's all about fluidity and balance, and that's what you have when you dance."

"Yeah...."

"I'm serious. I sort of figured it out as I was watching you. I was using the balance I use when I'm riding the flow while we were dancing.

I imagined I was on the water and I didn't embarrass myself, so try thinking you're dancing. You don't watch your feet when you dance, you look at your partner and where you want to go."

"Okay," Jordy said, holding up his hands. "I'll give it a try." He stood up and got back in line, with me following like a puppy dog. Jordy was fun, and he had a way about him that made me want to stand in his shadow. The energy, the brightness of his smile, the way he moved, all caught my interest and held it. My practical side kept trying to tell me not to pay attention to that, but I pushed it away. Boyfriend or not, I was going to enjoy what time we had.

Jordy did well on his next try, managing to stay upright and even move a little back and forth. It was a start, and when he fell, this time he came up grinning. After I took my turn, we headed over to where Helen was riding the surf, boogie-boarding like a pro. Of course she was getting extra attention from the attractive attendant with an Aussie accent. We got in line, and I couldn't help grinning.

"You really like her," Jordy said.

"Helen? She's my best friend, like the sister I always wished I had." I moved up in the line. "She hasn't had it easy, by any means, and yet she always smiles and is ready to help anyone else. Why?"

"Nothing. It's just that the two of you are always together, and I was hoping that maybe I… er… we could go somewhere and talk or something."

I wasn't sure what Jordy was getting at, but I nodded. "That shouldn't be a problem." Once Helen's ride was over, she came up with a huge grin, handed over the board, and got back in line. "Jordy and I are going to have a snack," I told her.

"Cool, I'll see you later," she said with a smile and turned back to the others. She began talking to the people around her, and I stepped back and rejoined Jordy. We walked over to the Wipeout Café and got snacks before taking seats at one of the tables just outside.

"So what did you want to talk about?" I asked.

"I don't know, really. I was just wondering about you, I guess."

"Me? There isn't much to wonder about. I'm a chemistry major and spend more time than I should on my school work. After class and on weekends, I work at the Giant for spending money and stuff. I like to think I'm a good student. What about you?" I asked, trying to get the subject off me. I didn't want to bore him to death, and I was afraid that was a distinct possibility.

"There isn't much to tell," Jordy said.

"Okay, where did you learn to dance like that?" I asked.

"Ballet," Jordy answered. "I started when I was six. The other boys wanted to play sports, but I asked my mom to take me to dance class. I quickly found that I was pretty good at it. The music spoke to me and came out through my body and feet. In a few years I was at the top of the class, and my mom started taking me to special classes. That was the first time I came to Carlisle—because of the Central Pennsylvania Youth Ballet. They have a great program and they taught me a lot. But after a while I wanted to do other things."

That certainly explained a lot about the way Jordy moved and the source of his smooth grace. "Did you want to dance professionally?"

"At one time, but I got hurt and couldn't do it anymore. My ankle got messed up, and I couldn't dance at that level any longer without risking permanent damage. The doctors said if I did, I could end up not being able to walk anymore or having to use a cane for the rest of my life. So I gave it up for the most part and decided to take my life in a different direction." Jordy seemed matter-of-fact about it, but I could tell there was loss beneath. His eyes gave it away.

My mouth hung open for a few seconds, then I said, "That must have been awful. How can you give up something you love?"

Jordy shrugged and set down his fork—not that he'd eaten much. "I did what I had to. It wasn't easy, and I still miss it a lot. Every year I used to dance the *Nutcracker,* and the last time I was the Nutcracker Prince. Since I stopped dancing, I haven't been able to go. It's just too hard. I thought of teaching, but the world doesn't need another ballet teacher who couldn't or didn't make it in the professional world."

"Did someone hurt you, or…?"

Jordy chuckled. "I wasn't Showgirled. No one dropped marbles on the stage or anything like that. I landed wrong after a particularly high jump, and my ankle couldn't take the stress. The doctor said it had most likely been building up for a while and that was the last it could take. Like I said, I was planning to dance professionally, but threw my energies into school after that. Think about it—I was a ballet wash-up at nineteen."

"Nineteen?" I whispered to overcompensate, so I didn't yell. "All that happened by the time you were nineteen? Jesus, that's a lot to take."

"It is. But I still dance, just not as athletically as I used to. My ankle has healed, and it's strong now, but it's too late for me to go back. Too much has happened, and I'm getting too old. The dance world has moved on, and I have other dreams now. I want to finish school, get a master's, and then my PhD so I can teach at the university level. I want to do research into American culture, learn what makes it tick and try to explain it."

"Just like me. I want to unlock the secrets of energy. I'm thinking nuclear chemistry or something like that. See, nuclear power has had such a bad rap for a long time, but it doesn't emit greenhouse gases, and if we can figure out the cold fusion problem, the possibilities are endless." I smiled. "That's what everyone says, but if we can figure that out, then maybe if people look far enough ahead, we can foresee other problems too. We didn't do that last time, and we need to this time." My excitement was getting the better of me, and I began talking faster, but I couldn't seem to help myself. "Think about it: a power plant that mimics what the sun does and the byproduct is other elements that we can use."

Jordy squinted at me. "I don't understand."

"See, stars are where everything comes from, and they make elements by fusing atoms together. To make it simple, a star gets its energy by fusing hydrogen into helium. But as it gets older, it runs out of hydrogen, so it starts fusing helium into heavier and heavier elements—silicon, carbon, oxygen, and so on. Sometimes, if the conditions are right, it fuses gold, silver, aluminum, and so on. But when a star creates iron, it's written its death, and within seconds, it builds up a core and explodes." I used my arms to imitate a huge burst. "A supernova, and that sends all those elements out into space. The elements that make up this chair and table, even you and me, we're all stardust, the products of explosions and stars that exploded billions of years ago and created the elements that make up our sun, the planets, the moon, you and me, and everything. So if stars can create elements through fusion, then if we can harness it, we could create new elements in the process. We just need to make sure they aren't wonky or create more of a mess than the problem we're trying to solve."

"You mean, like, blowing up the planet or something?" Jordy asked.

"Exactly," I agreed. "Sorry if it was too much."

"No. It's good that you feel passionately about things." Jordy turned and looked out over the water. "I like that you get excited about something other than money and plans for the rest of your life," Jordy added in a mutter, and I wasn't sure if he meant for me to hear it or not. "Sorry," he said a few seconds later and turned back to me.

I suspected he'd been talking about Mark, but I returned my attention to the few pieces of apple salad that remained on my plate. I wasn't sure how to ask him about his boyfriend, so I kept quiet. To me, it would make sense that if they were happy, Jordy would talk about him all the time, but he'd said very little and only when asked. I didn't want to get my hopes up and had pretty much decided it would be nice to have a friend.

An announcement interrupted my thoughts: "The dodgeball tournament will begin in fifteen minutes. If you're interested, sign up for a team at the sports desk."

"Are you game?" Jordy asked.

"Sure. We should change out of these wet things first, though," I said. Jordy agreed, and we were just getting up when I saw Helen walking across the deck in our direction. "We're joining the dodgeball tournament, are you game?" I asked her.

"Sure," she answered, and we all went to change. I was mostly dry by now, so I just put on a T-shirt and good shoes and left the restroom. Jordy changed out of his bathing suit into a pair of board shorts and a blue "Ballet Dancers Do It with Grace" T-shirt. I couldn't help smiling, and that turned to laughter as he pirouetted over to me.

"You're such a goof." *And an incredibly hot one at that.*

Helen came out, having changed completely into jean shorts and a white T-shirt. This was going to be some game of dodgeball.

"I figured I could flash the other team to distract them," Helen quipped.

"Oh God. If I'd have known I was going to actually see girl parts, I would have invited someone else." That quip earned me a slap on the shoulder. "Hey, I'm just saying."

"You can survive the girls." Helen shook her chest slightly, and both Jordy and I broke into laughter as one of the guys walking nearby stumbled and nearly fell flat on the deck. "Time to kick some dodgeball butt!"

The other team had no idea what hit them. Helen was a madwoman. She threw like a bullet and picked off the opposing players one by one. The rest of us did our part, but Helen was the star. I swore once or twice, when the team was in a little trouble, that she'd make good on her threat to flash the girls as a distraction, but she simply played like a maniac. By the time the tournament was over, our team had won and the others were left slightly dazed. It was a blast, and we even got medals for our victory.

We celebrated with soft drinks and then changed and headed to the main pool deck. It was time to cool off, then bubble, and finally—for me, anyway—to lie in the shade and relax in the warm glow of victory. I was having fun and enjoying this trip more than I had enjoyed one in a long time. I turned my head and half closed my eyes, watching as Jordy took the lounger next to mine. I didn't want to seem like a stalker, but I couldn't take my eyes off him: lean, trim, with strength of body and a personality as strong as an electromagnet.

"After dinner, I thought maybe we could go for a walk or something," Jordy said.

"That would be nice," I agreed and rolled over to hide what I didn't want the entire world to see.

Helen walked by and smiled at me. She must have heard and was letting me know it was fine. I didn't want to leave her all alone if she'd wanted to do something. I closed my eyes and let the warmth surround me. Things seemed to be working out. This was the second time Jordy had proposed that we be alone, so maybe there was hope.

THE FORMAL dinner went fine. Before we went into the dining room, we got our picture taken, and my mother seemed pleased. The ship was cool enough that wearing all the dressy clothes wasn't uncomfortable, and Jordy even complimented me on my tuxedo. He wasn't wearing one, but he looked incredible in his coat and tie that had been cut to move with his body. No one should look that good in clothes. It just wasn't fair.

Helen and my mother got involved in a conversation after dinner that had them engrossed. I didn't try to figure out what they were talking about and simply excused myself and told Helen I'd meet her in the room later. They barely noticed I was leaving, which was fine, as Jordy and I took off our jackets, went up the elevator to the eighth deck, and stepped out into a garden at sea.

Central Park was just that, a park in the middle of a huge cruise ship. The skylights from the promenade ceiling created lighted sculptures down the center of the garden, with its paths, plants, trees, sculptures, restaurants, shops, and even cricket sounds. If not for the slight rocking, we'd never have known we were at sea.

"This is one of my favorite parts of the ship so far," Jordy said. "It's really peaceful, and I'm told that sometimes they have music out here." Jordy glided down the path.

"I heard that too." We walked through the plants, light spilling out of the bright shops. There weren't many people around, which made the path seem rather intimate, almost like we had the space to ourselves. We reached the other side, and Jordy made the turn to start back, taking a different path.

"I don't know what to do," Jordy began. "I never seem to know when to leave anything behind. My mother always said I was a pack rat, and maybe she's right. I can never throw anything out."

"Okay." I wasn't sure where Jordy was heading with this, but if he wanted to talk, I was willing to listen.

"I think that goes for emotional things too. I never seem to know when to let go."

Was he trying to tell me what I thought he was trying to say?

"I hang on because I'm never really sure if things are going to get better. Then they don't, and I'm shocked. It's been a pattern for a while, and one I think I need to try to break." Jordy stopped and turned toward me. It got very quiet, and even the breeze that had blown steadily through the garden stopped, as though the air was holding its breath the same way I was. Jordy stepped closer, and I remained still, heart pounding with excitement in my ears.

"Jordy," Angie said breathlessly as she hurried up. "I locked my key thing in the stateroom again." I closed my eyes, and Jordy backed away. I wanted to scream. I'd been so sure he was going to kiss me, and I wanted to know what his lips felt like, how he tasted. Would he kiss me gently or pull me to him? I blinked and pushed the notion out of my head.

"Okay," Jordy said indulgently. "I'll go let you in, but you need to be more careful."

"I asked Mom, and she told me to try to find you. I figured you'd be up here." Angie had his hand and was already pulling Jordy away.

"Okay. I'll be right back," Jordy told me, and I nodded. He went with his sister, and I found a chair that was surprisingly comfortable and settled down to wait. I didn't know how long Jordy would be, and after a few minutes, I began watching people as they passed. After checking my watch, I settled my jacket over my legs and watched as the lighted sculpture that spanned over the park changed colors. After half an hour, I figured Jordy wasn't coming back. I stood up and was about to leave when he stepped up to me and sat down.

"Sorry it took so long," he said. "I let Angie in the room and then she couldn't find her SeaPass. We had to look for it and eventually found it in the pocket of the clothes she'd been wearing before dinner. Sometimes little sisters are a real pain."

"I never had one, so I wouldn't know."

"You're an only child?"

"Sort of. Mom had two other children. One lived just a few weeks. He was born way too early and couldn't make it. The other had a heart condition and lived less than a year. I was the one in the middle."

"Oh, man," Jordy said.

"Yeah. Dad said it was hell on my mom, and after they had me, he said they should stop, but Mom wanted to try again. They didn't press their luck any further after that, though. Dad told me once that, at the time, he didn't think Mom could have taken another round of heartache."

"That's tough," Jordy whispered.

"Yeah. In one of the cemeteries near where we live there are two small graves. Mom never talks about it, but I know she still goes there sometimes. I've been there, but it doesn't have a connection for me. I was too young to remember any of it, but it's still very real for Mom."

"Even after all this time," Jordy said.

"They're still her babies. She held them and nurtured them, especially the last one. I think the first one she lost was easier, but they had Doreen for nearly a year. I was about two when she died. I've tried to remember her, but really can't." I tried to think of a way to change the subject. "Are your folks going to the show tonight?"

"Mom wasn't interested. We did make reservations for the ice show later in the week. I still can't believe there's an ice rink on the ship in the tropics. It's just too cool."

"I think they have open skating a few times. We could go down and take pictures of us skating and then swimming an hour later. That would test the strength of your ankles. I was never very good at it, but I've been skating a few times."

"I think I'd rather not. The ankle is strong, but I don't want to take that kind of chance," Jordy said. I turned to look at him, hoping things would pick up where they left off, but it seemed the moment had passed, and Jordy sat back in the chair and grew quiet. "It's really nice out here. Comfortable too."

"Sure beats classes," I said, and Jordy made an affirmative sound. I settled back as well and figured I'd go with what he wanted. I wasn't really sure how to ask him about what might have happened earlier, and the more I thought about it, the more I figured I'd probably read the wrong things into Jordy's posture.

"I should head back and find my family and rescue Helen." I stood up and slipped on my coat. "I'll see you tomorrow." I wasn't sure what else to say, and when Jordy didn't offer anything else, I said good night and left. I did turn around just before I passed the first bend in the path. Jordy hadn't moved and simply stared ahead. I turned back and continued on my way.

Chapter 3

"I'M NOT quite sure what to make of him," I confessed to Helen the following evening. We'd hung out with Jordy for a good portion of the afternoon. "I keep getting the idea he wants to talk to me about something, but then he doesn't say anything. The few times we've been alone, he's said things that don't make a lot of sense." I sat on the side of my bed as Helen fished through one of her drawers. "Yesterday he talked about being a pack rat and didn't know when to let things go, and today he was talking about commitments and wanting to keep them."

"Okay…."

"I thought yesterday he was getting at that it was time to end things with his boyfriend, but today I'm not so sure."

Helen stopped. "Maybe you're hearing what you want to hear. Jordy could just be talking and there isn't some underlying meaning. I know you like him and that's cool, but that could be coloring the way you're reacting to him." She closed the drawer.

"But what if I'm right and he was talking about ending things with his boyfriend?" I asked.

Helen walked around the bed and sat next to me. "Then he's leaving a relationship and is going to need a friend. The relationship with his boyfriend may truly be over, but that doesn't mean he's interested in jumping right into another one." She patted my leg lightly. "I still think he's interested, and he keeps watching you, but he could be a little confused and lonely." Helen thought for a few seconds. "You also don't want to be some rebound guy. So just be there and be his friend. If it's meant to be, then it will happen. Otherwise, enjoy the companionship." Helen stood up. "I'm going to get ready for bed. We're going to be in St. Thomas tomorrow, and that should be really cool."

"It isn't that late," I countered. "We could check out some music or something."

"I'm not really up for it," Helen said, and I watched her for a few seconds. She was always up for things. This was not like her at all.

"What's going on?" I'd been so wrapped up in my own musings that I figured I must have missed something.

"Nothing, really. One of the guys I met at the FlowRider asked me to go for a walk with him. We ended up outside near the fourth deck, walking along the running track, and he got a little grabby."

"I hope you put him in his place," I said and then gathered her into my arms.

"I always meet these guys that seem nice and then turn into assholes."

"They don't turn into assholes. They are ones to start with."

"So you're saying I'm a magnet for assholes, then?" Helen pressed, and I knew I'd stepped into that one. I figured it was best to be there and not say anything. I'd heard this same kind of logic used on my father when he and Mom fought about something, and it never ended well.

"Well?"

"I'm not saying anything of the kind. I'm just saying that you didn't do anything. It's his fault, and I hope he went back to where he came from walking funny."

"He did," Helen whispered.

"Good girl," I whispered and lightly rubbed her arm.

"I also punched him in the face, so he'll be looking pretty messed up tomorrow. My brothers taught me how to fight when we were kids, and I didn't hold back on the loser." Helen held me, and I smiled slightly. Helen could take care of herself, but like anyone else, she needed support. "He'll probably be telling everyone that he got hit defending my honor or some bullshit like that. Anything to boost his tiny, fragile ego."

"So what. If he knows what's good for him, he'll spend the rest of the cruise in his cabin with an ice pack on his nuts."

Helen chuckled. "He certainly isn't going to be singing karaoke, that's for sure. Not unless he wants to go falsetto. I got in a good kick, and he went down like a sack of cement. His next mistake was trying to get back to his feet. That's when I punched him and got out of there."

"But you're okay?"

"Yeah, I will be," she whispered. I could tell she was still upset, but she seemed stronger and less vulnerable now.

"If you want some help, or if he gives you a hard time, just let me know."

Helen laughed and rubbed her eyes. "What are you going to do?"

"Stand behind you while you beat the crap out of him." I wasn't much of a fighter; never had been.

"That's what I thought," Helen said and moved away. "Come on, let's go to bed."

Helen was right. I was probably projecting what I wanted to see onto Jordy. I let her use the bathroom first and changed into sleep pants and a T-shirt. Once she was done, I took my turn to clean up and then turned out the bathroom light and made my way to my bed. "It isn't fair," I said to myself.

"What isn't?"

I cringed slightly. I hadn't realized I'd spoken out loud.

"Of course things aren't fair," Helen said. I heard her roll over in her bed. "My folks work long hours, day in and day out, and get nowhere. That isn't fair." There was no heat in her voice. "Where I come from, you learn pretty quickly that fair has little to do with anything. I know you like him. Jordy seems like a great guy, but from what you described, he's also going through some stuff and may need to make some decisions. Those can't be rushed."

"I know." I was like a moth caught in the attraction of a candle, and in my case, the flame was Jordy. As I pulled the covers up, I hoped I didn't end up like the moth in the image—getting burned.

WHEN WE woke the following morning, the ship was docking in St. Thomas. Helen and I dressed quickly and then went out onto the balcony to watch as we pulled into port. Houses dotted the hills around the harbor, with hotels jutting out on rocky points of land. It looked beautiful. Helen could hardly stand still.

"Go on and get ready first," I told her. "Then when I finish, we can get off and explore."

"Are we going to a beach?" Helen asked as she opened the closet and looked through what was there.

"We can do whatever you like," I told her. "I'm going to let Mom and Dad know what our plans are." I also thought to grab my phone and shove it into my bag, in case we needed it. I knocked on the connecting door, and my mother opened it. Their cabin was still dark, so I figured Dad wasn't up yet. I told my mother what our plans were and that I'd have my phone with me.

"Okay. But be sure to call and let us know where you are." I promised and hugged her before returning to our room. Helen was already dressed and full of energy. I took my turn in the bathroom, and then we grabbed our bags and SeaPasses and got ready to leave. I had my hand on the door when the phone rang. Helen answered it and smiled. "It's for you."

I took the phone. "It's Jordy. Do you and Helen have special plans?"

"We were going to wander through town and then go to a beach. Do you want to join us?"

"That'd be great," Jordy answered, and I smiled.

"We're going to eat quickly, and we'll meet you at the aft gangway in half an hour. Is that okay?"

"Sounds good. I'll see you there," Jordy said, and we hung up. Helen and I left the cabin and got a quick breakfast in the buffet.

"He'll still be there. You don't need to choke down your food," she chastised, and I slowed down. I knew I was rushing and getting my hopes way too high. I needed to settle down and try to remember what Helen had told me. *He most likely just wants a friend.* When we were done, Helen and I grabbed our bags and took the elevator to the second deck. We followed the crush of people, and I saw Jordy leaning against one of the walls, waiting for us in tan shorts and a lavender shirt, carrying a beach bag.

"I was afraid you might have left before I called," Jordy said when he approached.

"We were just on our way out, so your timing was perfect," I said, and when Jordy smiled, my heart skipped a beat.

We got in the flow of people and scanned our cards to check off the ship, and then stepped into heat, humidity, and sunshine. It was glorious. I fished my sunglasses and a hat out of my bag, and then I was all set. I poked around to make sure I'd remembered the sunscreen, which I had, and we found an exit to the harbor.

"I figured we could walk into town, look around, and then get a cab to a nice beach if you want. The walk to town isn't far." I pointed in that direction, and we exited the harbor area. There were shops in the harbor area, but I didn't suggest that we stop.

We walked along the water's edge. As the waves lapped up near the path, Helen walked ahead, and soon it was just Jordy and me. The breeze, the water, the sun—it was nice. But it turned magical when Jordy took my hand.

I was so shocked I nearly pulled away. "What about your boyfriend?" I finally got up the guts to ask. I half expected him to let go of my hand, but Jordy smiled brightly.

"I've realized that's over," Jordy said. "Mark's a good guy, but there hasn't been any real spark between us in a while." Jordy paused, and we came to a stop. "I stayed with him because I thought I cared for him and that he was good for me. I do care about Mark, but the interest has waned in the light of someone else." We stepped off the walk and into the shade of a palm tree, its fronds waving in the ocean breeze.

"Are you sure?" I asked. "I mean, I understand that he may not be right for you, but I don't want to be some rebound guy." I swallowed, hoping what I was saying sounded right. My heart raced and I wanted to jump for joy, but things rarely worked out for me like that. "I mean, I'll understand if you think this is some shipboard thing. It happens, and I can deal with it as long as I know."

"Look, I've been thinking about this for a few days. I almost kissed you in the park, but I realized I needed my head clear, so I backed away, and then Angie interrupted us. I'm sure things are over with Mark. That's the best thing for both of us. As for what's between us, I don't know. Can we see where things go?"

I smiled and nodded. "I can live with that." Jordy squeezed my hand, and I turned to look for Helen. She was waiting for us. "We should catch up to Helen." We left the shelter of the tree and walked to where Helen waited.

"Have you two decided to play house?" she teased, and I groaned.

"Nope. We've decided to play ship's captain and the stowaway," Jordy quipped, and Helen paused for a second before bursting into laughter.

"I don't want to know," she countered and took a step back.

"Come on," I told them with a chuckle. "Let's go into town." It was super cool that they were really getting along, and the three of us talked nonstop about everything we saw as we continued.

"That's the government house there," I told them, pointing to the large white house partway up the hill above town. "The shopping street is just through here." I pointed down a wide alley, and we began walking. "Look there," I said quietly when we got halfway through. "The top of the door."

An iguana was perched on top of an open door, looking all around. Helen and Jordy reached into their bags to get their phones and snapped pictures. When they were done, I did the same, and then we got as close as we dared and a shipmate who was passing took a picture of the three of us. I took a picture of them with the iguana, and then we moved on.

Helen wandered into store after store as we made our way up the street. More than once she emerged with her eyes wide, chatting about the prices. "Are they serious?" she eventually asked.

"Yeah, they are. The jewelry is real, and those sparkles are diamonds. That's one of the ways these islands make their money. They don't charge taxes and stuff. It's worse on Sint Maarten. If you want, we can find the straw market for T-shirts and things."

"I was hoping to find something nice," Helen said.

"Then let's go back toward the waterfront. There's a shop I saw that said they had coral. That should be affordable and is something unique to this area. If they don't have it here, we can probably find it in Sint Maarten. There's also a blue Caribbean stone that they have here. I forget what it's called, but we can look for that too."

I led them down the street and to the shop I'd seen. We popped inside, and Helen bent over the cases, looking pleased. I left her alone and went back outside to sit on a bench in the shade. Jordy joined me after a few minutes. I scooted over, and he sat down and smiled at me. "Sometimes I don't understand how things work," I admitted.

"How so?"

"For the life of me I can't understand why you're here. With me, I mean. I saw your boyfriend back at school, and he's gorgeous. The kind of guy I would think you'd like." I looked down. "Not someone like me."

"I'm not that shallow," Jordy said.

I turned. "I didn't mean to imply that you were. I... maybe it's a product of my own insecurities." The word "ordinary" stuck in my mind and wouldn't go away.

"I didn't mean to snap," Jordy said. "It's a sore spot. People expect ballet dancers to act a certain way, and to an extent I do, I guess. But it surprised the hell out of Mark when I told him I loved football and we started watching the games on weekends together. Before I said anything, he'd go off with his friends and never thought of asking me to join him." Jordy huffed softly. "I think that was the beginning of the end for me."

"I never thought you were shallow, just that with as good-looking as you are, you could turn the head of any guy you were interested in. Why me?"

Jordy chuckled. "You may as well ask me for the secret of life or the mysteries of the universe, although I think you definitely have a leg up on that one. I don't know. Looks aren't as important to me. They used to be, I'll admit that. There was a guy in the ballet troupe just before I got hurt. He could leap halfway across the stage with little effort, strong and as graceful as a swan. I was so taken with him and I knew he was gay, so I asked him out. Turned out he was the biggest loser I've ever met. I swear the song 'You're So Vain' was written about him. He never passed a mirror he didn't love. Then there's Mark—big, strong, beautiful, and as rigid as possible, and not in a good way."

"So you decided to try ordinary?"

"No. I decided to try looking at the person instead of the wrapping." Jordy flashed a smile and leaned closer. I tensed, wondering what he was going to do.

"Look what I found," Helen said and sighed.

"Perfect timing," I muttered, and thankfully neither of them heard me. Jordy turned to look at her, and she showed him her treasure.

"The shop lady said it was apple coral from Curacao." Helen showed them the variegated red to off-white beaded necklace. "It wasn't too expensive, and it's really beautiful." She held it to her neck with a smile that lit her entire face.

"It goes perfectly with your coloring," Jordy said.

"It does," I agreed. "Great choice."

"Thanks. Do you want to shop some more?" Helen asked as she put her purchase away. I stood up so she had a place to set her pack and put things away.

"Let's head to the beach," Jordy suggested.

We all agreed, so I hailed a taxi and we piled in for the harrowing ride. On St. Thomas, they drove on the left side of the road, but the cars were for right-handed driving, so how anyone could see anything coming was way beyond me. It did explain why most cars had missing side mirrors, though. We climbed the hill surrounding the harbor and then descended back toward the sea, ending up at a resort. I paid the driver, and a man in a resort uniform came out to meet us.

"Are you staying with us?"

"We just wanted to use the beach," I explained.

"No worries. If you want chairs and umbrellas, let me know." He indicated a sign that explained the charges for nonresort guests. I paid for three lounges and a large umbrella, and we walked down to the beach. He set everything up and gave me a receipt before leaving once again.

We settled on our lounges, and I went through the process of applying sunscreen and then relaxed in the shade of the umbrella. Helen put on lotion and lay in the sun, while Jordy lay on the lounge next to mine in the shade. The waves crashed on the shore, and down the way, kids boogie-boarded in the surf.

"I love this," Jordy whispered. "It's quiet, peaceful, and no worries."

"Only getting back to the ship on time, and we have hours. All aboard is at four, and it's not even noon. We'll head back between two and three, so we can have fun. I have water and granola bars in my pack. We can eat at the resort restaurant if we want… or snack here and eat on the ship. Either way, it's just fun."

"Do you want to swim?" Jordy asked after a while.

"Yeah." I was getting tired of lying still. I slipped on my water shoes and ran into the surf with Jordy right behind me. Helen seemed content where she was. We splashed and Jordy ran into me, jumping on my shoulders, and we both tumbled into the water. I'd forgotten I had my sunglasses on, and when I came up, they were gone.

"I'm sorry," Jordy said as we looked around, but of course we didn't see them.

"Not your fault. I shouldn't have worn them in the water." I turned away and slapped the top of a passing wave. What was I going to do? It hadn't been his fault that I hadn't thought about them. I was pissed, because they'd been Oakleys and expensive, but not at him. "Stupid," I swore. It was hard to see. The glare of the sun off the water and sand made me squint. I tried to put it out of my mind and have a good time, but seeing was difficult, so I walked toward the beach to check if there was an old pair in my pack.

"What happened?" Helen asked.

"I lost my glasses," I grumped and grabbed my bag to fish in it.

"You mean these glasses?" Helen asked and held them up. "A man asked if someone had lost their glasses, and I recognized them. He found them in the surf."

"Sweet," I said. "Where is he?"

"He went back toward the resort."

"You got them back?" Jordy asked from behind me.

"Yeah. A guy found them in the surf." I looked in the direction Helen said the man had gone, but I didn't see anyone. "That was sure good of him."

"I thanked him for you." Helen sat up. "And you owe me twenty bucks. He was one of the locals, and I figured you'd be grateful."

"I am." I smiled at her. She always seemed to know what to do. "Thanks. I'll pay you back when we get to the ship." The glasses were a little worse for wear, but by and large they were wearable. I cleaned them up and put them in my pack. Then the three of us headed into the water, where we splashed and rode the waves. Eventually staying upright became a fight against the current, so I got out. Jordy and Helen stayed in the water.

I swore I only took my eyes away for a second. But when I turned back, I saw Helen but not Jordy. I sat up and then stood up, watching the water. Helen was waving her hands over her head, and I ran into the surf. Then I saw him, at least what I thought was him. I dove and pounded my way through the water. It was Jordy. I grabbed him and got him above the water. He gasped for air, gagged, and spat. He'd swallowed seawater, and it was going to come back up. I managed to get him to shore and thanked God he was breathing. On the sand he coughed some more, and I helped him roll over. Jordy coughed up more water.

"Please get me some water," I told Helen. "Just stay where you are for a few minutes," I said to Jordy when he tried to get up. I soothed him when he coughed again, shooting saltwater and most of the contents of his stomach onto the sand. "You swallowed saltwater, and it needed to come up." Helen brought a bottle of water, and I opened it and helped him drink. "Just take a few sips and relax. Let your system settle."

He nodded, and I looked at Helen. "What happened?"

"One minute he was there and then he was gone."

"A wave broke over me and dragged me down. It rolled me on the bottom and wouldn't let go. Then you were there, helping me up and pulling me to shore." Jordy began to shake.

"Just relax and breathe. You're okay now. You need to breathe and rest," I told him. Most of the people on the beach had gathered around. When they realized there was nothing more to see, they wandered away. I got Jordy to his feet and helped him to one of the lounges. He settled and drank some more water.

"I didn't think I was going to come up at all," Jordy said.

"You got caught in an undertow and it pulled you down. That's happened to me, and the worst part is that you can't figure out what's up or down. Just relax and breathe. You need to get air into your lungs. Is your head spinning?"

"No. I seem to be okay now," Jordy said.

"That's good. You can try to walk in a few minutes." I sat on the edge of the lounge and watched Jordy, making sure he was okay. He'd looked a little blue, but his color was quickly returning to normal. Helen fluttered nearby, and we decided to go back to the ship. We'd all had enough of the water for one day. I gathered our things and walked out front, where I was able to get a cab outside the resort. Once the cab had weaved its way to the taxi stand, I went back and got the others, and together we made our way to where the taxi waited.

Helen got in up front, and I rode in the back with Jordy. "Are you feeling better?"

He took another sip from the water bottle. "Yeah. I think it scared me more than anything else."

"That and swallowing the seawater. Your body didn't like it, but you should be fine now." I took his hand and held it tight. The thought of him rolling around on the ocean floor chilled me to the bone. I moved closer and held his hand tighter.

We rode back up the hill, through the town, and then down to the harbor. We pulled to a stop and got out. I carried Jordy's bag as we walked to harbor security, showed our SeaPasses, and then headed up the ramp to the ship.

"Is he okay?" one of the officers asked when he saw Jordy.

"I am, thanks," Jordy said. "I just got a bit too much activity in the water." They scanned our bags, and we took the escalator up a deck and then called for the elevator. We waited and then took one to Jordy's deck and helped him to his cabin. Inside, I helped him to the bed, and Helen settled in the chair.

"I think I need to rest for a while." Jordy said.

"I'm going to go back and change, unless you need me," Helen said and walked to the door. "I'll see you back in the cabin." She left the room, and for the first time I was truly alone with Jordy.

Not that I knew what to do, and this wasn't the time for amorous activity. But still, it was nice to just be alone in a relatively quiet place. "Can I get you anything?" Jordy shook his head. "I know it was frightening. I've had that happen to me, but you're okay now."

"I know." Jordy looked up from where he'd been staring at his shoes. "You saved my life."

"I just brought you to shore. You would have been okay on your own."

"No, I wouldn't. I didn't know which way was up and was trying to swim down when I started swallowing water. You pulled me up and got me back into the air. You saved my life."

I didn't know what else to do, so I hugged him, tightly.

And Jordy hugged me back. "You saved my life," he whispered.

"It's what anyone would have done, and I'm glad I was there to help," I whispered. What did you say in a situation like this? I had no idea and didn't want to sound dumb. I honestly thought Jordy was making way too big a deal out of it. But he'd been frightened. "When I looked up and saw you weren't there, I nearly panicked and just raced into the water. Helen seemed to understand that you were in trouble, and she started waving her arms, but she couldn't see you."

"How did you find me?" Jordy asked in a very quiet tone.

"Helen pointed to where you'd been, and I dove down and saw you. I guess I was just in the right place to help you. I think there were other people who'd begun to realize something was wrong, but I wasn't really looking around. My total focus was on finding you."

Jordy lifted his head away from my shoulder and locked his gaze with mine. Then he leaned closer and kissed me. I was surprised and didn't react at first.

His lips were warm and he still tasted slightly of salt. Jordy backed away, and I panicked. He'd kissed me and I'd done nothing. So I lunged forward and kissed him back, holding him tight. I wasn't sure how many chances I would get to kiss him, and now that my mind was working, I wanted to make the most of it. Jordy was a great kisser, and after some initial fumbling, he guided me gently and I tilted my head slightly. He deepened the kiss, building it until my head felt like it would explode and my entire body tingled. When he pulled away this time, I hardly noticed it. Zings raced up and down my spine, and little ripples of energy zipped through my arms and hands.

"Wow," I whispered under my breath. "Maybe I should save your life more often."

"How about we try not to make a habit of that," Jordy said with a smile and then lightly kissed me again.

A knock sounded on the cabin door. "Jordy, it's Mom."

I backed away, and he got to his feet and opened the door. She raced in and tugged Jordy to her. "Your friend Helen told me what happened. I was so scared."

"I'm fine, Mom. I got into some trouble in the waves. I got rolled and then swallowed some seawater. Brad helped me to shore." He let her hold him, and after a few seconds she released Jordy and hugged the stuffing out of me. "I'm okay, Mom, and I think you're going to crack one of his ribs if you aren't careful."

For a slight woman, she certainly was strong. She stepped back and hugged Jordy again. "Don't ever scare me like that again."

"I thought you and Dad had gone shopping?"

"We did, and as we were coming back to the cabin, we saw your friend Helen heading down the passage. She told us what happened, and I flew here." Some of her frantic tone had dissipated.

"I'm all right. Both Brad and Helen were there to help me. That's why we never swim alone." Jordy was trying to calm her, but she was having none of it. I got the idea that she was going to be plastered to Jordy for the rest of the trip. "We came back here so I could have some quiet time."

"Did you eat?"

"No, and I'm not hungry," Jordy said.

"You should get something to drink and change clothes."

I'd completely forgotten I was still in my bathing suit. We both were. Thankfully they'd dried on the way back so we hadn't made a mess of the bedding, though it was a little sandy.

"Mom, I'm okay. I'll get something to drink and probably a snack in a little while." Jordy's dad came into the cabin, along with Angie, and the hugging and expressions of worry began all over again. Not that I blamed them. I had felt the same while we were still at the beach.

"I should go change and leave you alone," I said softly. I picked up my pack from the desk and threaded my way out of the cabin. I was glad when I reached the passage and walked toward the stairs to my cabin.

I found Helen inside. She had already changed, and she jumped up when I entered. "Is he okay?"

"Other than being a little overmothered, he's fine." I grabbed some clothes and went into the bathroom. I hung up the wet stuff and pulled on dry clothes. Helen was waiting for me when I came out.

"He's really okay?"

"Yeah. He said we saved his life."

"I should have done more," Helen said. "All I knew was that I couldn't see him."

"You called attention to the fact that he was in trouble, and I was able to get to him. Without you, I might have hesitated for a few seconds and things could have been much worse. You did really good." I hugged her.

"How did you know what to do?" Helen asked after a few seconds.

"I don't know. I was never trained in lifesaving or anything like that. I just knew I had to get to him. It helped that the water wasn't deep, so swimming wasn't as important as simply getting my feet under me and getting him to shore." I released her and stepped back slightly. "He's okay, and we were able to help him. That's what's important. Jordy is okay."

"I know." She blew out a breath. "Is he going to call us after a while?"

"I don't know. I didn't get a chance to set anything up." I smiled and sat on the edge of my bed. "He kissed me when we were in his room, before his mother came in."

Helen sat down across from me. "Was it a thank-you kiss?"

"It was a 'curl your toes and make your fingers tingly' kiss," I told her. "It was really nice." I tried to keep from blushing but failed completely.

"You're so cute when you do an imitation of a tomato," Helen teased.

"He told me while we were shopping that he liked me and that he'd been thinking about things and that he realized he and Mark were history. I don't think he's told Mark, though. But Jordy seemed pretty adamant, and then he just kissed me in his cabin."

Helen smiled. "That's good, but don't go buying the wedding dress just yet."

"I know. He was excited and said I'd just saved his life. But it didn't seem like some pity kiss, or a thank-you kiss, either. It was pretty intense and hot." I felt the heat rise further in my cheeks. "He's a good kisser."

"Okay, then," Helen quipped and stood up. "I need something to eat, and then let's go out on deck so I can find me a hottie who's a good kisser. You have to approve him, though, because I seem to attract losers."

"Okay," I agreed. "Let's see if the buffet is still open and then hit the pool deck. We can stop by Jordy's on our way to see if he's there and wants to go with us." We got our stuff together and left the cabin.

As we headed toward the aft elevators, I saw my parents coming toward us. They looked happy, and my mother appeared to be sporting a new diamond necklace.

"Did you kids have fun?" she asked as we approached.

"It was an adventure. Jordy got into trouble, and Brad saved his life."

"Bigmouth," I whispered to Helen, who turned to me and stuck out her tongue. "He got tumbled and turned around a little, but he's fine. He didn't get scraped up or anything. He did swallow some seawater, but woofed it back up."

"Do you know which cabin is his?" my father asked. "I want to stop by and check on him."

My dad—always the doctor. "Yes. We were just going that way. We can wait for you if you want." Dad hurried away and returned with the small bag he always took with him. We led the way and took the stairs one deck up and then down the passage to Jordy's cabin. I knocked, and Jordy's mom opened the door.

"My dad was concerned and wants to look Jordy over, if that's okay."

"Thank God. I was about to take him to the infirmary," she said.

"Is he okay?" I asked, stepping into the cabin.

"I'm fine. Mom's just being a worrier," Jordy said. We all filed into the room when Jordy's mom motioned us inside. Jordy was lying back on the bed, resting on a pile of pillows, probably at his mother's insistence. "I'm really okay. I swallowed some saltwater and brought it back up. I'm feeling fine—no headaches, swimmy vision, nothing like that."

"Okay," my dad said. "Just humor me." He got out a light and looked in Jordy's eyes and at his head, then listened to his heart and lungs. "Please take off your shirt. I want to check for scratches. There are plenty of sharp things on the bottom of the ocean."

Jordy tugged off his T-shirt and moved to the edge of the bed. I got a good look at Jordy's back and didn't see anything. His skin looked as flawless as it always did.

"He seems fine. Are you hungry?"

"A little?" Jordy answered.

"That's a good sign. Pay attention and don't discount any soreness. It may show up over time. But it seems you were very lucky."

"Thanks to Brad," Jordy said and turned to give me a smile. He put his shirt back on and stood up. "Can I go get something to eat now?" he asked his mother, who nodded. I could tell she was still nerved up. "Then we're going to go up on deck."

"Fine, but take it easy and don't overdo it," she said. I suspected that Jordy's mother would make her way up to the pool deck just to be sure.

"Don't hesitate to call if you notice anything out of the ordinary. Seawater isn't sanitary. It's good he brought it up, but that doesn't mean he didn't ingest something that might make him a little sick." My dad packed up his things and left the cabin after Jordy's mom assured him that she would.

"Do you want to go with us, Mom?" Jordy asked.

"I just worry, you know that. I'm your mother."

"I know." Jordy hugged her. "I'm fine and you don't need to fuss over me. Go and find Dad so you can have a good time. And don't worry. There are no waves in the pools, just occasional sloshing."

She shook her head. "You're going to be the death of me yet," she said, but her posture was more relaxed, and it looked to me like her worry was abating somewhat.

"Mom, please don't worry," Jordy reassured her. "The whole thing with my ankle a few years ago was a lot more traumatic." He smiled at her, and she shook her head and stepped toward the door. "Where's Angie?"

"Up on deck with your father," his mom answered and then left the cabin.

"Your mom is only concerned about you," Helen chastised as soon as the door was closed.

Jordy looked at me. "I know," he said, and I nodded. I understood as well. Jordy was her child and she was going to hold on tight. "She means well, but she can be a little suffocating."

Helen groaned. "Nope. You haven't even begun to see suffocating until you've been in a house with two adults, five children, in LA, without air-conditioning, in the summer. Now *that's* suffocating." Helen fanned her hand in front of her face. "And it doesn't smell like a bed of roses either."

"No AC in LA?" I asked, shaking my head.

"It broke a few years ago, and Mom and Pop don't have the money to fix it, so we do without." Her answer was so matter-of-fact that I realized just how little I knew about the reality of her life outside school. She'd told me things, but the truth was harsher than I could comprehend.

"Come on," I told both of them. "We need to get some lunch, and then I promised Helen we'd find her a hottie."

"Man watching?" Jordy said, jumping off the bed. "I'm game. I have this rating system we can use. I developed it with a friend back home." Jordy moved through the cabin, grabbing things he needed as he spoke. "My guess is that you've been going for the muscle heads. They look really good, but by and large the blood stopped going to their brains a while ago." Jordy grabbed his SeaPass. "Oh, and if they juice, the important things shrink." He waggled his pinkie. "What we need to find you is a nice-looking prep school kid or maybe a cute geek like Brad, here. They're smart, can carry on a conversation, and once the fireworks are over, believe me, you want a guy you can talk to."

I wasn't sure how I felt about being referred to as a geek, but the cute part was nice to hear.

Jordy joined us by the door. "Let's go and see if we can scout you out a man. How long do you want this thing to last? Forever, or just until we come into port?"

Helen laughed. "Someone to spend time with so I don't feel like a third wheel would be nice."

"Then let's go scout out the boys!" Jordy said dramatically, and I opened the door. "And I promise I won't sing. 'Where the boys are...,'" he sang, contradicting himself, and Helen groaned.

"You can't carry a tune in a bucket," she told him. "It's a good thing you're pretty." Jordy put his hand over his heart like he'd been wounded and mimed falling against the wall before laughing and starting to sing again.

Chapter 4

THE NEXT two days were glorious. Sint Maarten was beautiful, and we were now on our way back north, with just days at sea ahead of us. Helen made friends with an Australian named Brian, and the three of us became a foursome. He was pretty cool and treated Helen nicely. He also wasn't bad to look at, which made Helen smile. She told me it was nothing serious, but he seemed to make her happy, and a little shipboard romance never hurt anyone. It seemed to make Helen glow.

"So you two blokes are together?" Brian asked at one point while Helen had gone to use the ladies room.

I didn't answer and waited to see what Jordy would say. It was funny, but I hadn't given much thought to the whole boyfriend thing after St. Thomas. Jordy and I had been spending our time together and making a party out of it.

"Yup. He and I go to the same college, but we got to know each other on the ship," Jordy said. "Crazy coincidence, isn't it?"

"Yeah." Brian said and shifted on his chair. "So what's it like when two blokes go at it? Not that I want to know the details, but my brother's a poof, and I wondered if things are all that much different. Ryan and Cowan seem happy and all, but they used to get plenty of razzing from the blokes at school."

I shrugged, and Jordy did the same. "It's different for different people, just like it isn't the same with different girls. But it's how you feel about the person that counts. At least it should be. I mean, getting your rocks off is fun and all, but it's better when you care for the other person," Jordy said.

Brian nodded. "But I thought blokes did it like rabbits. 'Cause no one can get pregnant and all. Ryan says he did before he met Cowan."

"I never did the rabbit thing," I said. Helen returned, and not a moment too soon. I'd never been so relieved in my life.

"What were you talking about? Poor Brad looks like he's about to jump overboard."

"We were just talking about things. No worries, mates," Brian said, flashing Helen a brilliant white smile that made her giggle. Dang, that was a sound I'd never heard before—Helen giggling like a schoolgirl. It was nice to see her happy and a little off-balance. She sat down next to Brian, and the two of them talked quietly. After a while, they got up and jumped in the pool.

"Do you want to swim?" I asked Jordy.

He hesitated before saying, "I think the water has lost some of its appeal. I don't want to think about what happened, but it's hard not to." I wished I knew what to tell him. "I know I shouldn't let it stop me, but…."

"The water is nice and it will cool you off. Besides, there are no waves, and you can touch the bottom because it's only four feet deep. So come in with me."

"Okay," Jordy agreed and got up off his lounge. We walked to the edge of the pool and sat on the ledge to get our feet wet. "I know this shouldn't bother me, but it does," Jordy admitted. "It sounds dumb."

"It's not dumb. But you can't let what happened stop you." I slipped into the water and turned around, waiting to see what Jordy would do. Eventually he slipped into the water and moved close to me. "I told you it was really nice."

"It is," Jordy admitted. I wished I could pull him into my arms right here, but it wouldn't be proper, not with all the other people around. Dancing together on the promenade was one thing; making out in the pool was quite another. Jordy and I hadn't had much time alone. His mother had stayed much closer since the incident on St. Thomas, and it wasn't like either of us had a cabin to ourselves. So we'd been alone long enough to kiss only a few times, and yesterday afternoon we'd had some time to lie down together for a while. I found out that Jordy had wandering hands, just like I did. Neither of us seemed to mind. Then Helen came in with the greatest timing possible. Not that either of us were really ready to take things further at the moment.

"After cooling off, are you up for something a little more active, or do you want to sit for a while?" I was getting a little stir-crazy.

Jordy chuckled. "We can go to the sports deck. I know you want to surf again, and I can see if I can do better this time."

"It just takes practice. You know they have one at Hershey Park. When I went with friends early last fall, I had a ball."

"You were showing off, more like," Jordy said with a grin. "Although I'd have liked to see the look on their faces when you swooshed back and forth, spraying the people in line." He chuckled softly.

"It was fun. But watching you is just as much fun. And the view is way better, especially when you're wearing that green, square-cut suit." It was almost scandalous how good Jordy looked. We swam for a while longer and then grabbed our things and went to the back of the ship. There was a line for the FlowRider, so we set our bags where we could see them and got in line. "Are you going to be okay when you fall?"

"I hope so," Jordy said. When his turn came, he did okay, but fell quickly. I could tell he was tentative, and when his turn came again, I stood right behind the attendant.

"Remember to use the same balance and concentration you did when you were dancing. That's what you need. That grace and poise. You always knew where your center of gravity was, and that's what you need now. The rest is geography." The attendant turned back to me like I was crazy, but I ignored him and concentrated on Jordy. I was hoping success with something on the water would help wipe away what had happened on St. Thomas.

Jordy nodded and bounced himself into the stream of water. He was unsteady at first, but then caught his balance, and I could almost see when his understanding kicked in. When the attendant released him, Jordy stood tall, using his arms to maintain his balance. Jordy shifted his weight slightly and began moving back and forth in the stream. "Lean ever so slightly in the direction you want to go and you'll move that way," the attendant told Jordy over the roar of the machine. "Don't let the side of the board clip the stream and you'll simply glide on top of it." He continued moving and a smile broke across his face. He was doing it. I remembered that moment from my last cruise when the understanding kicked in and it all made sense. He continued upright for another minute and then the board caught the stream and he went down.

This time Jordy came up with an excited smile. "I actually did it!"

"You certainly did," I told him, and he jumped into my arms. The other people in line looked at us, but I didn't give a damn. This was a triumph, and triumphs needed to be celebrated. "Now let's see if you can do it again."

Jordy did, better and better each time. After a few runs he was in control, and after a few more he asked how to get into the stream on his own. Every ride was a thing of beauty. The ship's photographer stopped by and began taking pictures. I made sure he took plenty of Jordy and then made a note to be sure to stop by the photo studio and pay whatever exorbitant price they charged for a print of Jordy on the FlowRider. And if they happened to catch his triumphant grin, that was even better.

I completely lost track of time and finally noticed that the sun was starting to get low in the sky. Glancing at the clock, I was surprised to see it was nearly four. I hadn't seen Helen all afternoon and wondered where she was and if she was okay. I mentioned it to Jordy, and we went to look for her. We found Helen at the other FlowRider with Brian. He didn't see me, but when she was taking her turn, I saw the way he looked at her, the soft smile and the way his lips parted just a little, the sparkle in his eyes. He was falling for my best friend, and I suspected the feeling might be mutual. I fully intended to ask her about it that night.

"Snack time?" Jordy asked, and I nodded. We headed to the Wipeout Café and got in line. All the other people from the FlowRider seemed to have had the same idea at the same time. The line was out the door, but we stood and waited.

"Crap, I forgot my bag." I told Jordy that I'd be right back and hurried to the FlowRider. Both our bags were still there. I grabbed them and hurried back. Jordy was just approaching the front of the line. I joined him, thankful no one complained, and we got our plates.

When we had food, we somehow managed to find a table. We'd just sat down when Helen and Brian came over, both wrapped in towels, still dripping on the deck, and all smiles. "Can we join you?"

"Of course," Jordy said, scooting around so Brian could have a place at the table. Then they dried off and got food. The line had gone down, and they returned rather quickly.

"Tonight is the second formal night," Helen said and turned to face me. "Do you think your mom will be upset if I have dinner with Brian?"

"I doubt it, but maybe you could ask in the dining room if Brian can sit at our table," I suggested. I knew my mom would be disappointed. "Mom lives for this kind of thing."

"I got that idea," Helen said and turned to Brian, who nodded.

"My folks don't really mind. They aren't the tux and suit type, so they were going to get some tucker in the buffet, so that should be aces." Brian and Helen shared a smile.

I pulled my gaze away and went back to eating. I wished Jordy could join us for dinner, but there weren't enough chairs at our table, and Jordy would need to eat with his family. "After dinner, do you want to see if we can go dancing? They're supposed to have music all over the ship."

"That would be cool," Jordy whispered. "I know it isn't your thing, but I think I'd like to dance with you. So if you're willing to give it a try, I'm willing to give you some pointers so I can spend some time in your arms."

I nodded and put down my fork. Jordy smiled at me, and I caught his gaze and got lost in his sea-deep eyes. It was almost scary how quickly I was falling for him. I knew this could very well be a shipboard romance, and once we got back to reality, things would be different. That notion tickled the back of my mind, but I deliberately pushed it away. This was too good, and I was too happy to let anything get in the way.

My mom was thrilled when she saw me in my tuxedo and Helen in her dress. She was less pleased about Brian joining us for dinner. "Mom, you know Helen and I are friends, and that's all we'll be. I'm gay and that's not just some phase I'm going through." I sat on the sofa in her and Dad's cabin just before dinner. Helen had left to get Brian and would meet us in the dining room. "It's a fact that you need to accept."

"Why do you have to take this away from me?" she asked, turning to look at herself in the mirror.

"Your delusion? Mom, you need to face reality. I am what I am, and you can't change that. Dad understands and gets it. Why can't you?" I was practically pleading with her. "It hurts me a lot that you won't accept me for who I am." I stood up because I couldn't sit still any longer. "Helen and I will never be anything but friends. I'll never be anything more than that with any woman."

Mom turned, and I saw the pain in her eyes. "I can't accept that. You're my only child. If that's true, then how will I ever have grandchildren? How can…? You're all I have."

I stepped closer and took her hand. "Mom, I'll meet someone and we'll be together and start a family of our own. We may adopt instead of having our own children like a straight couple would, but it is possible. The only difference will be that there won't be a mother, just two dads."

"But…."

"Mom, we've been over this before, and facts are facts." I sighed. "You're hurting me and making me feel like I'm not good enough for you." Mom paused, and then she gasped. "I know you don't want that, but that's how you're making me feel. I like Jordy." She swallowed and shook her head slowly. "I know it's hard for any parent to accept that their child is gay. But not being supported hurts." I took a deep breath. "I'm your only son, and I'm gay."

"I know," Mom whispered. "I was just hoping that the two of you would…." She sighed. "I should have known better." She turned toward me, and I stepped back and sat down, patting the cushion next to me. Mom glided next to me and sat down, perched on the edge of the cushion. "I always wanted you to be happy."

"I will be happy. But I have to be myself, and not what you think I should be. I can't be anything but who I am, and I'm gay. I need you to understand and try to support me." I didn't know what else to say. "I don't want to be a disappointment, but I don't know how I can be anything else."

My mother sniffed, and before I could ask her about it, she pulled me into a hug. "You've never been a disappointment." I was so surprised. "Yes, it's hard for me to accept, but that's because I want all the things for you that I had. I want you to have children and be able to lead a life like everyone else."

"I will, Mom. I'll have the same things. A great husband who loves me. And I will have a life like everyone else, just different and *mine*. It has to be one that will make me happy. I love Helen, but she's like a sister, not a lover." I had to suppress a shiver. "I don't think of her that way and I never will. I like Jordy. A lot, Mom." My voice caught in my throat.

"Then what are you afraid of?" She backed away and looked me square in the face. "You're my son, you don't need to tell me when something is wrong." I wasn't so sure of that. She'd missed the gay thing by a mile. "I can tell, all right."

"Okay, if you really want to know, I think I'm falling in love with Jordy, but I'm not sure if he really cares for me or if this is some shipboard thing and once we get back to school he'll go back to his real life and I'll be some guy he passes uncomfortably in the halls because he's ashamed of what happened… and ashamed of me."

My mother's eyes widened and her mouth hung open for a second. "Okay. First thing, with love, you need to take things one day at a time. Lord knows I had to with your father. He was as slow as molasses in January when it came to things like that. He and I had known each other for years. We were playmates as children, and then his family left town, but came back when we were in high school. He still thought of me as his playmate. We did things together, but he never saw me as anything more than his friend."

"What did you do, because obviously he changed his mind?" I'd never heard this about my parents, and wondered if I'd been paying attention all these years or if they'd just kept things to themselves.

"My friends said I should make him notice me. They suggested different clothes and stuff like that. But my mother sat me down and told me...." She paused and shook her head slowly. "I... she...." Mom paused again. "She told me that I had to be myself and that your father would come around in his own time." Mom shook her head. "My mother was a wise old bird, in so many ways. So I waited, and eventually, when we were in college, he noticed me, and once he did, he never let go."

The implication of what my grandmother had said wasn't lost on me, and I could tell my mother understood it as well. I said nothing and let it pass. "So I should do nothing?"

"I didn't mean that. You have a few days left—make them memorable. On the ship, there are lots of things to do and chances to make some fun memories and associations. That's what I did with your father. I made sure that when we were together, every moment was memorable. Then when the real world kicked in and things got tough, it was me he'd remember when he thought of happiness and fun." Mom paused for a second. "I'm saying to make the most of the time you have. That's all you can do. After that, it's up to him and whatever the world decides to throw at you."

"But what if...," I began, but then I stopped. I wasn't quite sure what I wanted to ask.

"Make the best memories you can. I can't tell you what will happen later. I wish I could. I'd love nothing more than to be able to look into the future so I can tell you what will hurt and make it stop, or point you along the path that will bring you the greatest joy. That's every mother's wish, but none of us can do that. We give our children the best we can, guide them to do what's right, and then have to sit back and watch while they find their own way and make mistakes." She dabbed at the corner of her eye. "It's the hardest thing there is, and sometimes we make mistakes along the way too." She swallowed, and I realized my mother was crying. "As a parent you only get one chance at so many things—your first steps, first words, and the first time I took you to school and had to leave you behind. That's where it all started, and now you're not my baby anymore. You're grown up and will make your own choices." She forced a smile. "Maybe that's the hardest part of being a parent—letting go."

"I understand," I whispered.

Mom shook her head. "I don't think you do. Letting go is something we all have to do. It's scary, but it's what we have to do, and what you'll have to do with Jordy once this cruise is over. He has to make his choice about what he wants, and there will be nothing you can do about it. You'll have to wait, go back to school, and see what happens."

I knew she was right, but I wanted more than that. I was starting to realize I wasn't going to get it, not from Mom, and not from Jordy, at least not now. "Okay."

Mom smiled. "But that's not a bad thing. It's also part of what makes things interesting. Life would be boring if we knew what was going to happen. The excitement and the things that make the heart race would be gone."

I sighed. "So what do I do?"

"I wish I could tell you, but I can't. That has to come from you."

"But...."

She patted my hand. "You have to decide if you're willing to take the chance that Jordy might break your heart. Because that could happen. But the other side of the coin is that if you don't take the chance, you might never know if you could have something special. That's how things work, honey."

"I guess," I said and then grew quiet. I didn't know what to say.

"Honey, I know this is hard, but you have to make the decision about what you want. Just don't sell yourself short. If Jordy is someone you care for, then make sure he cares for you back. Because you're worth it. You've always been worth it. I know you doubt yourself sometimes and don't often see what others see in you, but you are worth it. So don't sell yourself short, no matter what." She squeezed my hand. "I know I sold you short, and I'll do my best not to do that in the future, but it's even more important that you see yourself as valuable and desirable, because you are."

"You're my mother. You're supposed to say that." I smiled at her, knowing my mother rarely said things because she had to. That was one of the things I really loved about her. She was honest, and while there were times it hurt, she was also generous with praise, and it made her opinion important, because it was meaningful.

"Maybe, but it doesn't make it less true." She hugged me again as the cabin door opened and my dad and Helen came in, with Brian not far behind. My mother almost immediately shifted into hostess mode. Dad opened a bottle of wine and passed out glasses to the five of us. Dinner didn't start for half an hour, so we all sat and talked.

Helen was so excited she could hardly sit still or take her eyes off Brian. He was charming and seemed genuine to me, which was a requirement, because if he hurt Helen, Brian would have to deal with both of us.

"How long are you in the US?" my mother asked and then sipped her wine.

"A few more weeks. I booked the sail and then planned to spend time seeing the country. I flew into Fort Lauderdale a few days early and expected to be able to spend a few days at Disney World. I had no idea how far apart things were, so I had extra time. I was going to drive up the coast to Boston, but I found out that was a lot farther than I expected. And I thought Australia was big. This country is huge."

"So where are you going once we dock?"

"I was planning to spend a night in Fort Lauderdale and then fly to New York for a few days. It's lucky I work for an airline because I can get where I need to go easily. After that I was planning to go to Boston, but I think a stop in Carlisle is probably going to replace it." Brian bumped Helen's shoulder lightly, and she grinned. "After that, I have to return to Brisbane and go back to work." Brian talked a little about his schedule and the strange hours he worked. I couldn't really understand it, but his job required long hours that could get longer if flights got delayed. He really seemed to love it, and Helen was most definitely taken with him.

"When we get back, Mom and Dad are going to head home, and Helen and I will fly directly back to Harrisburg. We have classes again next week." It took me a few seconds to remember that we'd been having so much fun, Thanksgiving had passed us all right by. There had been turkey for dinner, but other than that, the fun hadn't stopped. That also meant that in a few days Helen, Jordy, and I would be back in class. Normal life would return, classes would restart, preparation for finals, term papers—all that would start and continue until the semester ended at Christmas. I was not ready for that at all.

We finished the wine, then Dad refilled glasses, and we carried them with us to the dining room.

Dinner was nice, but I was tired of sitting around in the monkey suit, so I excused myself once I was done eating and left the dining room.

The others were having a great time, but I wasn't in the mood for light and fun conversation. Helen offered to go with me, but I told her no. She should spend as much time with Brian as she could. Helen looked amazing in her little black dress decorated with a sparkly glass brooch. Brian hadn't been able to keep his eyes off her all evening.

I slipped off my jacket and then pulled off the tie, loosening my collar after shoving the tie in the inner pocket of my jacket. I stepped out on deck into the warm breeze and leaned against the railing, watching the water as the ship cut through it.

"I thought I'd find you out here," Jordy said as he approached. I smiled and turned toward him.

"Why would you think that?" It wasn't as though it was our meeting place.

"Okay, I was taking a walk and saw you out here," Jordy confessed. We stood quietly staring out at the sea for a few minutes. "Is something wrong?"

"Not really. I'm just thinking that there's only one day left and then we go back." I sighed. "Not that I don't like school, but it doesn't compare to this—warm breezes, the sound of the water… you." I turned, and Jordy did the same. We moved closer together and then kissed.

It was just like the first one. Instantly the blahs that had taken over my attitude were swept away. Energy coursed through me. Jordy pressed closer, deepening the kiss. Then he rested his hands on my shoulders, gently adding to the electricity that intensified wherever he touched me. I was almost scared to touch back, so I held on to my jacket and put all my concentration into the mint-flavored kiss.

"My parents and sister are at the show tonight. I have the cabin all to myself for the next few hours." Jordy slowly backed away without breaking his gaze from mine. Then he took my hand in his, entwining our fingers together. Like times before, I expected to be interrupted by someone, but the deck around us remained quiet and deserted. Jordy moved away from the rail, and I went along with him without thinking. The doors to inside slid open, and we passed through. My entire attention was riveted where Jordy's hand touched mine.

There weren't many people around. Jordy led us to the stairs, and we slowly ascended to his deck and then down the passage to his cabin. He unlocked the door, and we stepped inside. The door closed with a clang. I stared at the twin bed, my stomach nervously doing flips, and I wished I'd eaten a much smaller dinner. "Jordy, I…." He took my jacket and dropped it on the bed.

"Hey, it's okay," Jordy said. "We don't have to do anything." He walked through the room and sat on the banquette.

I sat next to him and wondered what in hell I was doing. I'd dreamed of this for months, ever since I'd first seen him at the grocery store. But then he'd been just a nameless pretty guy who happened to capture my imagination. Now Jordy was a real person with personality and….

"Brad, what's going on?"

"Nothing, really. I'm just nervous." As soon as the words were out of my mouth, I realized I'd assumed that Jordy had brought me here for more than conversation. What if he hadn't and I'd just made a fool out of myself? I took a deep breath to calm myself and hoped Jordy hadn't noticed.

"There's nothing to be nervous about." Jordy stroked my cheek and drew my lips to his. I moaned softly and Jordy deepened the kiss, pulling me to him. He felt so good against me. I closed my eyes and absorbed his warmth and intensity.

Jordy slowly opened the buttons of my shirt and slipped his hand inside. Warmth spread all through my body from Jordy's gentle touch. I hadn't known what to expect, but I adored his gentle, caring touch. "Just relax." Jordy kissed me and used his weight to press me back against the cushions.

I tried to take Jordy's advice, but it was impossible. The more Jordy touched me, the less possible it became to relax. Excitement on every level increased, and I had to shift a few times to keep that excitement from becoming obvious. Then Jordy pressed against me, and I felt his excitement too.

The last of my inhibitions flew out the window and I pulled Jordy to me, holding him close, kissing hard, and pressing against him. Jordy worked my shirt open and tugged it out of my pants. Jordy stroked up across my chest, and after a few seconds, I attempted to remove his shirt. Jordy shifted and I felt his balance alter. I did my best to stop him from tumbling off, but we both ended up on the floor. I laughed, and Jordy did as well.

We got to our feet, still chuckling. But that lasted only until Jordy pressed my shirt down my arms and then off. I tugged Jordy's shirt up and off and then dropped it on the bed. We stood, shirtless, and I reached out to Jordy, stroking his smooth, soft skin. He felt like heaven, and I didn't know what to do next. I didn't want to break the spell.

Jordy backed away, and my hand slipped from his skin. I wondered what I'd done wrong. Jordy picked up the desk chair and moved it to the door, placing it in front. Then he bounded back, barreling into me, propelling both of us down onto the bed. He swept the clothing onto the floor. Jordy was a live wire, sending energy in every direction. My clothes ended up on the floor with the rest, along with Jordy's, and for the first time in a while, I was naked with another man.

"You're gorgeous, you know that?" Jordy said.

I rolled my head back and forth on the pillow. I knew that was just the moment talking. I'd never been gorgeous. "You're the handsome one. I'm the geek, remember?"

Jordy stopped. "Wherever that idea came from is bullcrap. You are gorgeous." I wasn't about to argue with him at a moment like this, especially when he flexed his hips and slid his cock along mine. All rational thought flew from my head, and all I could think about was more of this.

I wrapped my arms around Jordy, stroking his back and then down to his butt. Damn, he felt amazing—all heat and smooth muscles that rippled under my hands. I cupped Jordy's buns and squeezed lightly. He moaned in my ear and arched his back slightly. "I like that," he whispered.

"I could tell." I worked his firm cheeks in my hands, pressing his hips to mine, adding additional friction to his movements. I loved how he felt, and when he flexed his hips again, I swear I saw stars. I'd had sex before, but I had never felt this kind of energy. Just from touching, I was having trouble controlling myself. I had to think unsexy thoughts for a few seconds to keep from embarrassing myself.

Jordy tasted amazing. From his lips to the base of his neck, I feasted on him, listening to what gave him pleasure, glad his parents weren't in the next cabin, because Jordy was not quiet. He filled the room with moans, whimpers, and, a few times, outright cries. Nothing in my life had ever been so sexy, not even the things conjured up by my fevered teenage libido. "Jordy," I whispered when he got really loud. He placed his hand over his mouth, but I brushed it away, replacing it with my fingers.

He sucked on them hard, and I returned the favor, sliding down his body and then slowly sucking the head of his cock into my mouth. Jordy came unglued, and I sucked harder, the head traveling back and forth along my greedy tongue. I could not get enough of him and sucked Jordy as deep as I dared. He bucked and writhed on the bed while I reveled in the excitement that I was the one making Jordy react this way. It was me driving him out of his mind. This was so much more than I'd hoped. I was crazy about this man, but it seemed he was crazy about me too. Until that moment, I'd had no idea how attractive that was.

"Brad," Jordy whispered, and he shook beneath me, sucking as hard on my fingers as I was on him. He stilled, and I let him slip from between my lips.

Jordy shifted and lunged for me, nearly sending both of us back on the floor. He kissed me wildly, vibrating against me before licking trails down my chest and then sucking at my nipples almost frantically. My legs hung off the side of the bed, but Jordy didn't give me a chance to move. He slid down me, licked trails over my belly, and then settled on the floor between my legs.

He stopped, and I raised my head, locking on his heated gaze. I shivered with uncontrolled passion as he maintained the visual—no, spiritual—connection and took me slowly into his mouth.

If I'd died at that moment, I would have known true happiness, fulfillment, and what it felt like to have someone connect with me completely. Jordy had this way of using his lips to grip me so that I felt every single movement as he slid down me. There was nothing tentative, and within seconds, he had me shaking from head to toe. "Jordy," I whispered through panting breaths, trying to control the rising pressure and excitement inside me.

"I know," he whispered back, gripping my length tight in his fist. "You did the exact same to me."

I used the brief break to catch my breath, and then I gasped when Jordy took me hard and deep in one single movement. "Jesus," I gasped again and gripped the edge of the bed in my fist. I thrust my hips forward and pressed to the back of Jordy's throat, then pulled back and settled on the bed as best I could. It took a few seconds for me to realize that Jordy had released me.

I slid back on the mattress, a fine sheen of sweat breaking out all over. My mouth hung open in an attempt to pull oxygen into my lungs. Jordy returned within seconds and dropped two packets on the bed near my hand. Then he climbed on, straddled me, and rolled his hips back and forth over my cock.

I thought I'd died and gone to heaven. The sensation nearly overwhelmed me, but the sight of Jordy's lithe body undulating back and forth, his eyes closed, back arched, head lolling back, added to the excitement. I reached out to him, needing beyond measure to increase the connection between us. Holding his hips, we moved together until he stopped and reached for the packet on the mattress.

Jordy tore open the condom and scooted forward. I figured he'd slip it on himself or hand it to me, but he reached behind him and gripped me. Jordy turned slowly, and the sensation of him rolling the condom down my shaft was almost too damned much. When Jordy stroked me, twisting his hand, I nearly came unglued. He reached for the other packet, opened it, and squirted the gel on his fingers. He reached behind him, and I groaned, knowing where those fingers were going. I wanted desperately to see Jordy pressing his fingers into his body, but knew if I thought about it too much, I would lose it completely. Jordy rested his hands on my chest and lifted his body, positioned me at his opening, and then slowly sank down. His body opened to me, and I slipped into unbelievably tight heat.

Deeper and deeper he took me, until he rested on my hips and didn't move. In those few seconds I swore I saw God. I had to close my eyes for a few seconds to avoid sensory overload. Then Jordy began to move. I shifted slightly, and Jordy growled deep in his throat. "I'm what they call a pushy bottom."

I got that loud and clear, but didn't care in the least. Jordy leaned back, gripped me tightly, and took us both to nirvana. All I could say was I thanked God the ship was moving already, because I swore if it had been in port, the entire ship would have rolled back and forth with Jordy's energy. I sweated and strained to keep up with him, finally giving up and letting him have his way. I didn't regret it for a second.

I wanted it to last forever, but it was simply too much. The pressure that had been just on the edge built with amazing speed. Jordy sped up, and I stared, openmouthed, as he stroked himself. Jordy's butt slapped my hips as his movements became more and more frenzied. In an instant, Jordy stilled, and heat splashed on my chest and belly. I could take no more and drove deep into Jordy's body, stilling as well while stars danced behind my eyes and I filled him, throbbing with each beat of my heart.

I HAD no idea how long I lay there, unable to move. Jordy collapsed on top of me, and I held him close, breathing deeply and basking in the glow of total happiness. He didn't seem to be in any hurry either. Slowly, however, the realization returned that Jordy's family would be coming back, and the last thing I wanted them to see was the two of us completely debauched, sprawled out on Jordy's bed. That would not be good.

Jordy groaned when I moved. He kissed me sweetly, and I closed my eyes for a few seconds, waking with a start when I realized I'd dozed off. Jordy stood up and went to the bathroom. He returned with a towel and washcloth. We used them to clean up and then began to hunt for our clothes. In a stroke of brilliance, Jordy opened the balcony door, and fresh, humid air flooded the cabin, erasing the scent of sex. Once we were dressed, Jordy closed the balcony door and I gathered my things. He put the trash in a plastic bag, and when we left the cabin, Jordy took it with us and we dropped it in a trash container in the first restroom we saw.

"No need for anyone to ask questions, least of all my sister," Jordy said.

We shared a laugh and took the stairs to my deck. We stopped by my cabin, and I quickly changed clothes. Then we left in search of fun. When we reached the promenade, music spilled out of the club at the end closest to us, and like a magnet, it seemed to draw Jordy in. I followed, and soon, like the rest of the place, we were moving to the beat. We danced alone, and when the music slowed, Jordy pulled me to him and we danced very, very close. It was wonderful, and when Jordy rested his head on my shoulder, I knew I was a complete goner. There was no turning back now. I had fallen for him, and I hoped from the way Jordy held me that he felt the same way.

I'd like to be able to say we talked things over, but I was too scared to bring it up. If he didn't, I figured I could bask in my bubble of delusion for a little while longer, and if he did, I'd most likely know soon enough. So I took Mom's advice and let myself be happy in the moment.

THE FOLLOWING day was both amazing and anxiety-producing at the same time. Jordy and I spent almost every minute together. But the end of the cruise approached faster and faster with each passing hour, and I knew the return to real life was approaching. Classes, school, friends—the life I'd been on vacation from, and that Jordy had been away from as well—would all be waiting for us, and I could not shake the idea that Jordy and I might only be a shipboard thing.

"I'm going to miss this," Jordy said as he sat next to me in a bubbling hot tub on the pool deck.

"Me too." I leaned back, looking up at the stars overhead. It had been the best vacation I could remember. Helen and Brian sat alone in the hot tub on the other side of the ship. I understood that they wanted some time alone as badly as we did. "Tomorrow we fly back to the cold and possibly some snow." I wasn't looking forward to that.

"Are you ready to go back to classes?"

"I guess so. It will be good to see my friends and stuff, but it's hard not to want this to last longer. There are people to bring your food and pick up after you. When you need something, all you need to do is ask." On cue, a waiter came by, and I ordered each of us a beer and handed him my card. It was simply wonderful. "What are we going to do back in the dorms at school?"

"I don't know," Jordy answered.

"My roommate is a total slob, so by the time I get back, his crap will have moved like a glacier to engulf the entire room and I'll need to fight the river of clothes and crap to put my part of the room in order." I wanted to offer to have him move in with me for the next semester. My roommate was going to move off campus and I would need a new one, but I wasn't sure if we were ready for that, and if this was just a shipboard thing, then it could get awkward.

"It doesn't sound like a good situation."

"It's not, but he's graduating at the end of the year and then he'll be someone else's problem. Carl isn't a bad guy or even hard to live with, he just doesn't understand the need to put anything away. His side of the closet has only a few things in it. Everything is set on top of his chair, the bed, you name it. How he can find anything is beyond me, but he does and even manages to look decent somehow."

The waiter returned, and I signed the sheet and took my card back. He left, and Jordy and I clinked, then swigged from the bottles. "This is the life." What could be better than a cold beer, warm bubbling water, and an even hotter guy to share it with? I so did not want to go back to reality.

"Are you all packed?"

"Yeah. The bags were tagged and left in the hallway. Helen and I each have our carry-ons for the night and morning." The luggage was most likely being picked up right now so it could be unloaded once we docked. We sat quietly for a while, drinking the beer and watching the sky.

Eventually, once the beer was gone and we ran the risk of being perpetually pruny, we got out of the water and dried off. Helen and Brian saw us and did the same. I gave them some privacy and let them say their good-nights by turning to Jordy. "I don't know if I'll see you in the morning or not. My folks have a late morning flight out, and mine leaves at just after eleven." I'd hoped we would be on the same flight home, but that wasn't to be. Jordy wasn't leaving until almost three in the afternoon, so he would be one of the last people off the ship and I would be one of the first.

"Don't worry, I'll find you on campus." Jordy kissed me, and Helen came over to join us. After another round of good nights, she and I walked back to our cabin in near silence. I unlocked the door, and we went inside. Helen immediately disappeared into the bathroom, and I used the time to change out of my wet things and into sleeping clothes.

When it was my turn, I wrung out my suit and hung it the shower to dry next to Helen's, cleaned up, and after using the facilities, I washed my hands, turned out the light, and went back into the cabin. The lights were out and Helen was already in bed. I knew she most likely wasn't in the mood for talking, but I lay awake for a while after getting into bed.

"Sometimes things aren't fair," Helen whispered after a while without turning in the bed. When we talked, she often rolled over, but I could see from the little bit of light in the room that she was staring at the ceiling the same way I had been.

"I know," I whispered. Helen got up and adjusted the curtains, cutting out the last of the light. "I set the alarm earlier, and my parents will knock on the door when they're up."

"Okay," Helen said with no energy. I could also tell she wasn't tired and would probably not be falling asleep anytime soon.

"Is Brian really going to come visit?" I asked, trying to find the silver lining for her.

"He said he would try, but that is only going to delay the inevitable. He lives on another continent, halfway around the world. It takes at least twenty-four hours of travel just to get there. So I may as well face the fact that I won't be seeing him any longer. It was nice while it lasted, but what we had here was all there was. He said I could visit him, but an airline ticket costs two thousand dollars, and that's just for the ticket. I don't have any money to spend on anything until I finish school."

I wished I had something positive to tell her, but I knew she was right. I hated that she was hurting, but there was nothing I could do for her. "You know you still have me, right?"

"I'll always have you, and you'll always have me."

"Yeah."

Chapter 5

IT FELT like only seconds before the alarm went off. I got up and silenced it. Helen barely moved in her bed. I grabbed my bag and went into the bathroom to clean up and dress. When I was done, I woke up Helen and let her get dressed while I finished packing my things. When she was ready, Helen and I made a final sweep of the cabin and then left for the last time. Mom and Dad joined us in the passage, and we walked quietly down to the theater to await our turn to disembark.

I knew it was stupid, but I kept looking for Jordy. I knew it was way too early, but I did it anyway. There were pastries and coffee in the back of the theater. I nibbled on one and sipped the strong coffee while we waited. I wasn't in the mood to talk. "Do you want some?" I asked Helen, but she zipped by me, and I followed her. She ended up in Brian's arms, and the two of them shared a few minutes. Then they called our number, and we all got our bags and followed the line of people along the promenade. I scanned my SeaPass for the last time and stepped off the ship, then walked down the ramp and back into the terminal building.

The next hour was spent finding luggage, waiting in line for customs, and then getting a taxi to the airport. Once we were all checked in, Helen and I said good-bye to my parents, and we separated to our different terminals.

"Thank you, Brad. This was the trip of a lifetime," Helen said.

"You're so welcome," I told her. "I'm glad you were with me." I reached over to hug her, and my pack slipped off my shoulder. I ignored it and hugged her anyway before hoisting it back onto my shoulder. "Let's go home." We went to our gate and sat down, instantly pulling out our phones to reconnect with the world.

The rest of the day was spent waiting, flying, waiting some more, and then finally arriving back at school. I wasn't sure how I felt about it, but in some ways it was good to be home. It was not, on the other hand, good to be cold. By the time I got to my room, I was shivering. As soon as I set down my suitcase and pack, I tugged off my T-shirt and pulled on a fluffy sweatshirt before setting to work clearing my part of the room of the inevitable mess.

"Did you have a good time?" Carl asked as he came in the room. "I bet you met a ton of guys."

"Just one, actually," I said with a smile and proceeded to tell him all about the guy from the grocery store who just happened to be on the cruise.

"So you went all that way to meet a guy you could have talked to in the cafeteria?" Carl asked. "Sounds like a wasted trip to me. You should have been on the lookout for a Caribbean beauty or one of those suave South American boys." I rolled my eyes. Carl was an average guy like me in a lot of ways, except he had a face that could stop traffic. Huge dark eyes, a patrician nose, and a jawline that could cut paper, but the thing that caught everyone's attention was his smile. I sometimes wondered if he somehow stole Mario Lopez's dimples.

"I didn't need any of that. Jordy is hot and really nice. I like him." Carl feigned falling off the edge of his chair, clothes dropping from the arms. "Okay, that isn't necessary, and you really should pick up your things. There is a closet right over there, and the clothes wouldn't get dirty."

"You sound like my mother," Carl groused, but he stood and snatched up the clothes. He looked around and sighed. "Okay, it is kind of messy."

"Kind of? The clothes are starting to take on a life of their own. They deserve better than that." It wasn't as though the things Carl had were cheap. His folks were majorly wealthy, and from what he'd told me, at home there were people to pick up after him. "Besides, what are you going to do when you get your own job and leave home? You'll have to pick up after yourself."

Carl growled. This was an old argument, but he seemed more receptive to it than he had in the past. "Now you sound exactly like my mother." He threw the clothes on the bed and began folding them. I went to the closet, grabbed a bunch of empty hangers, and handed them to him. I watched as he worked and realized he had no idea what he was doing. Shirts were inside out, sleeves the wrong way, and he was trying to force them on the hangers.

"Have you done this before?"

Carl shrugged. "How hard can it be?"

I shook my head and showed him how to hang things up. We'd only been rooming together since September. Carl could never keep a roommate and why I'd agreed to share with him was beyond me. I guess it had been a moment of weakness, but if you looked past the messiness, it hadn't turned out so bad. "See, now you can find things." He hung up his pants as well, and the room looked better than it had in months. I wasn't about to start digging into his dresser drawers, but we could see the floor and the furniture at least. He even straightened up his bed. Organizing his desk was probably too much to ask, so I stopped while I was ahead.

Carl flopped in the now clothes-free chair and stretched out his legs. "So is Jordy your boyfriend, or was this a shipboard thing?"

That was the million-dollar question. "I don't know. I guess I'll have to see what happens now."

"Is he coming over?"

"His flight was later than mine, and with the storm that's threatening, I don't know when he's going to get in." I picked up my phone and started checking flight statuses. On the news in the airport, I had seen stories about a huge storm that was expected to move in from Oklahoma, and apparently flights were already being cancelled to keep from stranding people. Mom had already texted that she and Dad had made it to New York just fine. The airline's website said that Jordy's flight to Harrisburg had landed on time a little while ago, so maybe he'd made it in as well. "There's another wrinkle. Jordy has this boyfriend he says he's going to break up with…."

Carl sucked air between his teeth. "Sounds like a shipboard thing to me. A 'what happens on ship stays on ship' sort of thing." He shook his head. "Sorry, buddy, but your hopes of a happily ever after with this guy just went up in smoke."

I probably wouldn't have believed Carl if I hadn't already been worrying over it for days. I tried to keep the disappointment off my face, but I failed.

"Hey, I'm not being mean, just realistic." Carl softened his tone. "He's got this boyfriend and now he's returning to real life."

"He said it wasn't working and that he was going to tell him when he got back." God, I sounded pathetic even to myself. Where had that come from anyway, a bad soap opera script? *The Young and the Useless,* or maybe *The Young and the Brain Dead?*

"Let me guess… you slept with him?" I didn't answer, but I didn't need to. "See, he got what he wanted, a quick roll in the hay. There's nothing wrong with that. You had fun, and so did he. Now the vacation's over."

"Jesus, you sure know how to throw a wet blanket." I had to say something. All I wanted to do was go to bed and try to forget how stupid I was.

"Don't mean to, dude. Just telling you what I think." Carl shrugged. "I could be wrong." He flashed a smile with those dimples, and I turned away. I so did not want to see hot cuteness right now. "Did he say anything about what would happen when you got back?"

"Just that he'd stop by when he got in and settled," I told Carl. Now it sounded like a brush-off, but at the time, leaning on the rail of the ship as it moved through the darkness, it had seemed sincere.

"See what happens," Carl said, and I nodded. That was all I could do. But I prepared for the worst. "Now, let's go find something to eat before my stomach eats itself."

I wasn't particularly hungry, but I pulled on a heavy coat and we left the room, heading toward the main street of town.

The Back Door Café was hopping with everyone coming back from their holiday break. Fellow students lined up at the counter to place their orders. Carl and I managed to snag a table from some people getting up to leave. I gave him my order and money, and sat down to wait. The place was quirky, but an institution, and the food was decent and reasonably priced. I pulled out my phone and called Helen to see if she wanted to join us, but I got only voice mail. After leaving a quick message, I shoved my phone back into my pocket. I said hi to people I recognized as they passed and nodded to others. The place echoed with overlapping conversations and voices.

Eventually Carl made his way back to the table and set down the sandwiches and sodas. "This place is a zoo," he commented.

"Everyone had the same idea we did," I said loudly to be heard above the din.

Carl nodded, and we gave up trying to talk much. It was no use. Everyone was talking louder to try to be heard, and it only resulted in the room getting louder and louder.

"Is that him?" Carl asked and pointed. I made out what he said and followed where he indicated. Jordy had just walked in, and I raised my hand to get his attention. He saw me and waved, taking a few steps in my direction before I saw someone tap him on the shoulder. Jordy turned around for a second and then smiled at me. Then I saw Mark step between us.

"Is that the boyfriend?" Carl asked.

I nodded.

"Doesn't look very broken up to me."

They didn't to me either. I turned away and refused to look back in that direction. But my resolve lasted about half a minute. Jordy and Mark had gotten a table, and Mark was talking urgently, holding Jordy's hand. They were deep in conversation, and I turned away again. "Let's finish up and go." I ate faster, practically shoving the sub into my mouth. All I wanted was to get out of there so I wouldn't have to watch the two of them together.

"Sure," Carl said. We finished pretty quickly and bussed the table, and we were getting ready to leave when a sharp bang split the air. Instantly the entire restaurant quieted. I checked for the source and saw Jordy's chair on the floor. He looked around, and then turned back to Mark without bothering to pick up the chair. Conversation started again, and I saw Jordy say something to Mark and then leave the restaurant in a hurry, with Mark right behind him.

Carl clapped me on the shoulder, and I nodded. It was time to go. I put my coat on and followed Carl out. Shouting and overlapping voices came from the sidewalk. We hurried in that direction. As I approached, I saw Jordy rushing toward me on a tear.

"What's going on?" I asked.

"You want to break things off with me, you twinkle-toed fruitcake?" Mark yelled down the sidewalk, where people were staring. "Go right ahead!" He turned and took two steps before pivoting back around and charging after Jordy, head lowered, shoulders forward.

I opened my mouth to say something, but was riveted to the spot. I couldn't move or say anything. Thank God Carl thought quickly enough to pull Jordy to the side. Mark clipped Carl in the shoulder, though, and he twisted and went down on the sidewalk. Mark came to a stop, took one look at the chaos he'd caused, and took off toward campus.

Jordy got to his feet, and I hurried to Carl. "Are you okay?" The sleeve of his coat was torn and covered with dirt, as were his pants.

"I'm fine, the bastard." Carl got up and rubbed his shoulder. "What a coward. Is he afraid we'll call the police?"

"No. He's afraid Coach Josh will find out," Jordy said. "He could get kicked off the football team for fighting."

"Are you okay?" I asked Jordy.

"Yeah."

The crowd had already begun to filter away. Carl looked like hell, but he professed that his clothes had gotten the worst of it. Jordy was shaken up but he, too, said he was fine.

Carl started walking back toward campus. Jordy and I went along with him. I still wasn't convinced he wasn't hurt. I'd seen how hard he fell, but Carl wouldn't accept any help. "He would have hurt Jordy pretty bad if you hadn't stepped in," I said to Carl.

"Probably. I just reacted." He winced and slowly moved his arm up and down. "What did you say to him anyway?"

"I figured a public place would be better to tell him we should just be friends. I was hoping to avoid a scene. Guess I failed, huh?"

"You could say that," Carl said as we reached the main corner of campus. He rubbed his shoulder. "He's some sort of psycho, you know that? I swear his eyes glazed over and then they shot flames or something."

"Well, Mark's a little testosterony from playing football, and he's been coming to grips with the whole gay thing. When Freddie came out last year, it made it okay to be gay on the team, but that doesn't mean all the guys were ready for it, or that all the closeted ones now have an easy time accepting who they are."

Carl stopped and turned around. "You're defending the nutcase who just tried to take you out?"

"No, I'm just explaining, I guess. He may be a nutcase, but…."

"Do you want him back?" I asked Jordy.

"God, no. He's going to have to deal with his nutcaseness and other issues on his own from now on. And I appreciate your help. If you want, I can make sure the coach knows what he did without anyone knowing where it came from."

"That's up to you," Carl told Jordy. "You're the one he really wanted to hurt. I just got in the way."

"I really don't want to hurt him," Jordy said, biting his lower lip lightly. "Things are over between us, and all I was trying to do was keep him from going ballistic." Jordy waited for the light to change, and we crossed the street, entering campus. "He'll calm down and realize that this is for the best. We weren't meant for each other."

"What did you ever see in him?" Carl asked.

"He was the opposite of me. I thought we had a yin and yang thing. But we are too different, and what I thought was him trying to help me to be a better person was him trying to control me." Jordy looked at me and smiled. "That's what I realized on the cruise. You actually help without overpowering. You helped me learn to ride the wave machine without telling me I was doing it wrong and losing your temper, not even once."

I smiled. Before I could ask my question, Carl butted in. "So does this mean you two are together? Because if you are, then we need to set some ground rules, because I'm not coming back from dinner to find a coat hanger on the door and then spending the rest of the evening trying to find some place to study while you two are doing the mattress mambo."

I rolled my eyes and would have smacked Carl on the shoulder if he wasn't already sore. "Please, we would never do that. It would be rude."

"Thank you."

"We'd put a necktie on the door, and you'd be expected to find a place to stay for the night," Jordy said, "because once this one gets going, he doesn't stop for hours."

I stared at Jordy, unable to believe my ears. Carl shivered and shook his head.

"Thanks for that. Now I'm going to have to dry-clean my brain to get that image out of my head." We continued along the walk to our dorm. "Did anyone ever tell you there is such a thing as too much information? Don't forget I've seen his pale butt more than once, and…." Carl shook exaggeratedly. "Besides, if you think I'm spending the night on someone else's couch, you're crazy."

"I was just kidding," Jordy said, and I pulled open the door for Carl.

"Do you want to come up?" I asked Jordy, who nodded and followed Carl. I closed the door and brought up the rear, watching Jordy's along the way.

Carl unlocked the door, and we went inside. Thankfully we'd picked up the place, so there were actually places to sit. Jordy and I sat on the love seat while Carl took the chair.

"Are you really okay?" Jordy asked Carl. "I can't believe he did that."

"I'm fine. I'll take a few ibuprofen before I go to bed, and everything will be good in the morning." Carl sat back and stretched his legs out. "Do you think Mark will leave you alone now?"

"I don't know. He can be like a dog with a bone sometimes," Jordy said.

"Do you think he'd…?" The thought of anyone hurting Jordy scared me to death.

"He tried to hurt him tonight," Carl said and then got to his feet. "I'm going to go down to the lobby for a while. I can get something to drink and give you two a chance to talk." Carl left the room and gently closed the door.

"You can stay here if you think it will make you safer. I'll set up some cushions on the floor, and you can use my bed. Mark won't bother you here, and tomorrow you can report what he did." I moved closer and slowly ran the tip of my finger over his cheek. "I wasn't sure what was going to happen."

"What? You thought I was feeding you a line?"

"Not exactly. But things can get turned around on a cruise, and I was afraid that when we got back you would go back to the way things were before you left. I couldn't blame you. We aren't at sea anymore...." I wasn't quite sure where I was going with what I was saying, and from the look on Jordy's face, I decided I should probably shut my mouth now.

"I wasn't just saying what I said." Jordy sighed. "I told Mark that things were over between us."

"I hope you didn't do that for me."

"I did it because it was the right thing for me. I don't cheat on people. If I hadn't been serious about ending things with Mark, I would never have done what we did. That would have been wrong for me and you. That's not who I am," Jordy said emphatically.

"I didn't think you were. But getting carried away is easy. Everything seems so romantic with the ocean air, the moon and stars, dancing, all that stuff," I explained.

"Are you trying to tell me something?' Jordy asked quickly.

"Me?" I shook my head. "No."

"Then when you get what you want, don't question it. Just be happy. That's what my mom always told me." Jordy moved closer. "Mark took away the magic. He stifled it most of the time. He didn't want to dance or do anything fun." Jordy kissed me gently. "For the last few months I haven't been in the mood to dance. I haven't wanted to."

"I don't get it."

"Dancing takes everything you have—body, spirit, and soul. I realized that I haven't been in the mood. There was so little joy. Everything I did around Mark was wrong, and he told me so all the time."

I shook my head. "I remember the first time I saw you—actually, heard you," I added with a smile. "It was at the beginning of the semester, and you had gone to the grocery store and were singing up a storm. You exuded joy." I caught his gaze and held it. "The few times I saw you with Mark, in the cafeteria and stuff, that was missing."

"You saw me?"

"Yeah," I felt my cheeks heat. "I've had a thing for you since I first saw you come into the store. You had this exuberance and energy that was very attractive. But like I said, when I saw you with Mark, that energy seemed to be missing."

"My friends Freddie and Kurt told me the same thing when I said I was going to break up with Mark. Apparently, they don't like him much, but kept quiet because they didn't want to interfere." Jordy leaned against me. "I know now he wasn't right for me, but when we started going out, he was nice and we were good together. At least I thought we were." Jordy sighed.

"If you need some time to yourself, I'll understand," I whispered, hoping like hell that Jordy would say no. He straightened up and turned toward me. "I told you when we were on the ship I don't want to be some rebound guy. I really don't think I could take that. If you need some time to yourself to take a break, breathe, just relax, I can understand that."

Jordy scooted back on the cushions. "You're willing to just give me time and wait for me?"

"Yeah. If that's what you need." I swallowed hard. I'd really hoped Jordy would smile and say he didn't need that, but it looked like I was wrong. But I meant what I said. I would wait for Jordy. He was worth waiting for. "I want you to be sure."

"Mark would never have done that," Jordy said softly.

"I'm not Mark."

"No. You aren't." Jordy moved closer once again. "I'm a smart guy, and I know a good thing when I see it. I also know what I want. So for the record, you aren't a rebound guy. You're the right guy, and I'm just lucky to have found you." Jordy moved closer and kissed me.

We both jumped when someone pounded on the door. "I know you're in there!"

"It's Mark," Jordy whispered.

"I saw you come over here!" His words sounded a little slurred.

"Great, he's been drinking," Jordy whispered. "Go away and we'll talk when you haven't been drinking," he told Mark through the door before turning to me. "He'd already started with the beer before I got home."

"I'm not going anywhere until I talk to you and you take me back," Mark said, and then pounded on the door one more time.

"We need to call someone." I had no intention of opening the door.

Jordy pulled out his phone and scrolled through his contacts before making a call. "Kurt, I need help. Mark is pounding on Brad's door and he's been drinking." Mark pounded again, this time more forcefully. "Yeah, that was him," Jordy said after jumping at the noise. "Okay. We're in Taggert Hall 207. Please tell him to hurry." Jordy hung up the phone. "Freddie is on his way over with some of the other players."

"Will it take Freddie long to round them up?"

Jordy shook his head. "They were most likely all watching football, so it won't take long." Mark pounded on the door again, and the sound of other voices drifted through the door. Apparently a crowd was gathering outside. I walked to the door and peered through the peephole. Mark peered back. I jumped back for a second and then looked again. Other people were around him, and I heard voices, but couldn't make out what they were saying.

Mark pounded again. "Jordeeee," he cried. I stepped back and joined Jordy on the sofa. This was a mess. After a few minutes, a soft knock sounded on the door.

"It's me. Kurt."

Jordy got up, unlocked the door, and opened it slightly. A slight man came in, and Jordy closed the door again.

"It's okay. Freddie and the guys are with him, and they won't take no for an answer."

"What a nutcase," I said.

"He's just hurt. It's what some of these guys do. They're strong on the field, but when it comes to stuff like this, they're like kids and aren't prepared for disappointment. They get used to getting what they want, and that extends to people too." I got the impression Kurt had dealt with that firsthand.

"Brad, this is my friend Kurt," Jordy said. Another knock sounded on the door, and Jordy peered out and opened it. "This is his partner, Freddie."

"The guys are taking Mark back to his room. Hopefully he'll sleep it off."

"Guys, this is Brad," Jordy said with a smile.

"This is the guy you dumped Mark for?" Freddie asked, and Kurt smacked him on the shoulder.

"Be nice. Mark is a tool," Kurt said.

"Yeah, I can't argue with that." Freddie extended his hand. "I didn't mean any offense." We shook hands tentatively. "So are you guys okay?"

"Yeah. We're fine." Jordy said. "Mark went a little off the deep end."

"I'll say. He tried to take you out, and he hurt my roommate, Carl," I said. The door opened, and a bunch of the other football players crowded into the room.

"Everyone's okay," Freddie pronounced. "Where's Mark?"

"Johnson is taking him back to the room. He'll sleep it off," one of the huge players said. "Coach Josh will want to talk to him in the morning, and that isn't going to be pretty. He might get suspended from the team. You know what Coach Josh thinks about this stuff." The players all looked at each other and then at him and Jordy.

"Doesn't matter. He should have thought of that before he pulled this crap," Freddie said.

"But we need him," the huge guy said.

"He should have thought of that before he started drinking and hurting people. I'll talk to Coach Josh, and if necessary, you can play his position." These guys were huge, but as soon as Freddie said something, they all nodded. "Let's leave these guys alone, and we can go back to the game." The guys filed out, and Kurt turned to Freddie.

"I'll be over in a few minutes," Kurt said, and Freddie leaned down. They shared a few words, and then Freddie kissed Kurt lightly before leaving the room and closing the door behind him. "So you're both really okay?"

"Yes. Thanks for helping. I don't want Mark to get in trouble."

"I know," Kurt said. "But he did that to himself. The way he acted is his own fault, not yours. Granted, I can understand that he would be upset, like anyone would be when a relationship ends. The guys will get him calmed down, and I think things should be fine. Freddie and Coach Josh will talk to him. None of those guys messes with Coach Josh." Kurt grinned. "He was the one who convinced Freddie to get glasses." Kurt leaned close. "I love him in the glasses."

"Okay," I said, not understanding the reference.

"Kurt was helping Freddie study and realized he was having trouble seeing. It was part of what brought them together," Jordy explained.

"To me they symbolize Freddie's trust. He's been telling me he wants to get contacts, but I've been pretty persuasive up to now." Kurt headed for the door. "Call if you need anything." Kurt left, and I stared at Jordy.

"Those are some friends you have."

"Kurt is pretty amazing."

"I'm not sure Freddie likes me," I said.

"I don't know about that. Part of what makes him a good leader is his concern for the other players, even if he doesn't necessarily like them. He was being protective of Mark, and I can respect him for that. After all, you are the guy I broke things off with Mark for."

"You said you were going to do that anyway."

"Yeah, I was. But meeting you sped up the timeline." Jordy moved closer and pressed to me, hugging tightly. "Don't worry about everything. Mark will get over his hurt and find someone else. He was just angry and had had a little too much to drink."

"If you're sure," I said, because I wasn't. I knew I wanted Jordy, but everything else was a blur. "A week ago I was alone and going on a cruise with my family, and now I've got the guy I've been dreaming about for three months. I keep wondering what I did to deserve all this goodness."

Jordy shrugged. "We don't do anything. If we're lucky, the good things come to us whether we deserve them or not. It's part of what makes love special."

"You love me?" I asked, my mouth hanging open in shock.

"I'm getting there," Jordy whispered and angled his face toward mine. I leaned close and kissed him.

The door opened and I pulled away. Carl came in and closed the door, walked around us, and flopped down in his chair. "I hope you guys had a good talk." We looked at each other and laughed. "What?"

"Nothing, I'll tell you later."

"I should go," Jordy said and picked up his coat from where it had been draped across the bedframe. "I'll see you tomorrow. I usually have lunch at a little before noon to try to avoid the rush. Feel free to join me if you want."

"Thanks." I grabbed my coat and followed Jordy down to the lobby and then out into the night. I kept an eye out as we walked across the yard to Jordy's building.

"You didn't need to walk me home," Jordy told me.

"Yes, I did. I had to make sure you were okay." I continued looking around, half expecting Mark to be hiding in the bushes, which, of course, he wasn't. Mark was most likely passed out in bed, sleeping off the alcohol.

Jordy didn't protest, and he flashed me a smile. "I think I like that." Jordy took my hand and then glanced around before kissing me lightly on the lips. "I'll see you tomorrow. Do you have to work?"

"Not till Tuesday, and then Friday and Saturday night." I had never minded the shift before, but now it was going to put a real damper on the time I spent with Jordy. I could probably put in for a change in shifts, but that would mean working different hours from Helen. "I know it's a pain."

"Don't worry about it. We'll figure things out," Jordy said. "I hear there's a new gift shop opening in town that's looking for help. You could try for a job there. Not that you have to." I smiled. It was a good idea. "Don't worry about it. Things will work out," Jordy added soothingly.

"How do you know?"

Jordy stepped into my arms, sliding his hands and arms around my waist, under my coat. "Because things work out between us—I can feel it. We fit together." Jordy began to rock back and forth, and I swore I heard him humming softly.

"I take it you're happy." A smile broke out on my face. I simply couldn't help it. His mood was infectious.

Jordy didn't pause. "How do you know?"

"You're dancing," I whispered and swayed back and forth along with him. I was happy too, and let Jordy pull me right along with him. We didn't burst into some huge musical number like in the movies, but simply swayed back and forth, the energy and joy from Jordy's movements filling the area around me. The cold seemed to dissipate, warmth seeping in, and for a few seconds he and I were back on the cruise ship, sun warming our skin, the soft tinging of Caribbean steel drums floating on the air. "Jordy," I whispered without stopping.

"Yeah…," he whispered, stepping a little more boldly.

"I think I'm getting there too."

Epilogue

SPRING HAD finally arrived after a hard, cold winter. I was so tired of thick clothes, gloves, and hats I could scream. But now, finally, the trees were budding, and we had the first truly warm day of the season. I had just gotten out of my last class for the day and was walking across campus toward the dorm.

"Brad!"

I turned as Jordy hurried in my direction. I couldn't help smiling.

"Are we all signed up?" he asked.

"Yes. Starting next year, we'll be roommates. I also called my mother, and you're all set to visit us for a few weeks in June and again in August. I think she's accepted the fact that she isn't going to have a daughter-in-law."

"Your mother loves me," Jordy said with a grin. She certainly did. It had only taken Jordy a few hours when he came to visit at Christmas to have my mother wrapped around his little finger.

"I swear she likes you more than me," I joked.

"Well, my mother thinks you hung the moon, and they're looking forward to having you visit in July. So it looks like we're all set."

"Yup." I stopped walking. "How did you do on your chemistry exam?" Jordy and I had spent hours over the last week making sure he was prepared. Dr. Brendon was a good teacher and did a good job of explaining the topics, but he sometimes had a hard time realizing the students couldn't always grasp new concepts at lightning speed, the way he did.

"I got a ninety-seven," Jordy told me, doing a little dance on the sidewalk. "I missed a question about benzene, which was kind of dumb because I knew all about it. I just sort of blanked."

"That's great. See? I knew you could do it." The class had been hard for Jordy. His talents weren't in mathematics and analysis, but in verbal and nonverbal communication. It was the nonverbal communication that he particularly excelled at. When those thoughts entered my head, I blushed and did my best to push them away, but to no avail.

"I never would have gotten through the class without you," Jordy said. But I knew different. He would have plowed through as best he could. But I was glad I could help.

"Are you done for the day?"

I nodded.

"Do you have to go to work?"

"Nope," I said with a smile. "We have the rest of the afternoon."

"Then let's drop this stuff, go for a ride, and then get some dinner." Jordy headed in the direction of his room, and I followed.

Jordy lived in one of the older dorms on campus, which meant it had great woodwork and interesting, odd-shaped rooms with polished wood floors. It was pretty cool and looked very Ivy League. We dropped our books and left again, heading to where Jordy had parked his car. We got in and Jordy started the engine, unlatched the top, and lowered it. The sun felt glorious. Once the top was down, he pulled out of the lot and reached over to flip on the sound system. "If I Could Turn Back Time" pulsed from the speakers—Cher in all her glory. I knew in an instant that if I could, I wouldn't. I had everything I wanted.

Jordy pulled into traffic and stopped at the first light. When the car stopped, Jordy looked up toward the sky, singing in that off-key way he had, at the top of his voice. Then he looked at me and paused for a second. I joined in, and when the light changed, Jordy took my hand and we traveled through the intersection and along the main street of town, singing together. People looked, but we didn't care. Sometimes joy truly knew no bounds.

ANDREW GREY grew up in western Michigan with a father who loved to tell stories and a mother who loved to read them. Since then he has lived all over the country and traveled throughout the world. He has a master's degree from the University of Wisconsin-Milwaukee and now works full-time on his writing. Andrew's hobbies include collecting antiques, gardening, and leaving his dirty dishes anywhere but in the sink (particularly when writing). He considers himself blessed with an accepting family, fantastic friends, and the world's most supportive and loving husband. Andrew currently lives in beautiful historic Carlisle, Pennsylvania.

E-mail: andrewgrey@comcast.net
Website: www.andrewgreybooks.com

CAN'T LIVE
WITHOUT YOU

ANDREW
GREY

Justin Hawthorne worked hard to realize his silver-screen dreams, making his way from small-town Pennsylvania to Hollywood and success. But it hasn't come without sacrifice. When Justin's father kicked him out for being gay, George Miller's family offered to take him in, but circumstances prevented it. Now Justin is back in town and has come face to face with George, the man he left without so much as a good-bye… and the man he's never stopped loving.

Justin's disappearance hit George hard, but he's made a life for himself as a home nurse and finds fulfillment in helping others. When he sees Justin again, George realizes the hole in his heart never mended, and he isn't the only one in need of healing. Justin needs time out of the public eye to find himself again, and George and his mother cannot turn him away. As they stay together in George's home, old feelings are rekindled. Is a second chance possible when everything George cares about is in Pennsylvania and Justin must return to his career in California? First they'll have to deal with the reason for Justin's abrupt departure all those years ago.

www.dreamspinnerpress.com

EYES
ONLY ME
FOR

ANDREW GREY

Eyes of Love: Book One

For years, Clayton Potter's been friends and workout partners with Ronnie. Though Clay is attracted, he's never come on to Ronnie because, let's face it, Ronnie only dates women.

When Clay's father suffers a heart attack, Ronnie, having recently lost his dad, springs into action, driving Clay to the hospital over a hundred miles away. To stay close to Clay's father, the men share a hotel room near the hospital, but after an emotional day, one thing leads to another, and straight-as-an-arrow Ronnie make a proposal that knocks Clay's socks off! Just a little something to take the edge off.

Clay responds in a way he's never considered. After an amazing night together, Clay expects Ronnie to ignore what happened between them and go back to his old life. Ronnie surprises him and seems interested in additional exploration. Though they're friends, Clay suddenly finds it hard to accept the new Ronnie and suspects that Ronnie will return to his old ways. Maybe they both have a thing or two to learn.

www.dreamspinnerpress.com

Noble
INTENTIONS

ANDREW
GREY

Robert Morton is in for the surprise of a lifetime. His mother, a bit of a rebel, raised him away from the rest of the family, and it's not until he's contacted by his lawyer about an inheritance that he learns who he truly is: the new Earl of Hantford. His legacy includes ownership of the historic Ashton Park Estate—which needs repairs Robert cannot afford. He'll simply do what the nobility has done for centuries when in need of money. He'll marry it.

Tech wizard Daniel Fabian is wealthy and successful. In fact, he has almost everything—except a title to make him worthy in the eyes of the old-money snobs he went to prep school with. His high school reunion is looming, and he's determined to attend it as a member of the aristocracy.

That's where Robert comes in.

Daniel has the money, Robert has the name, and both of them know they can help each other out. But their marriage of convenience has the potential to become a real love match—unless a threat to Daniel's business ruins everything.

www.dreamspinnerpress.com

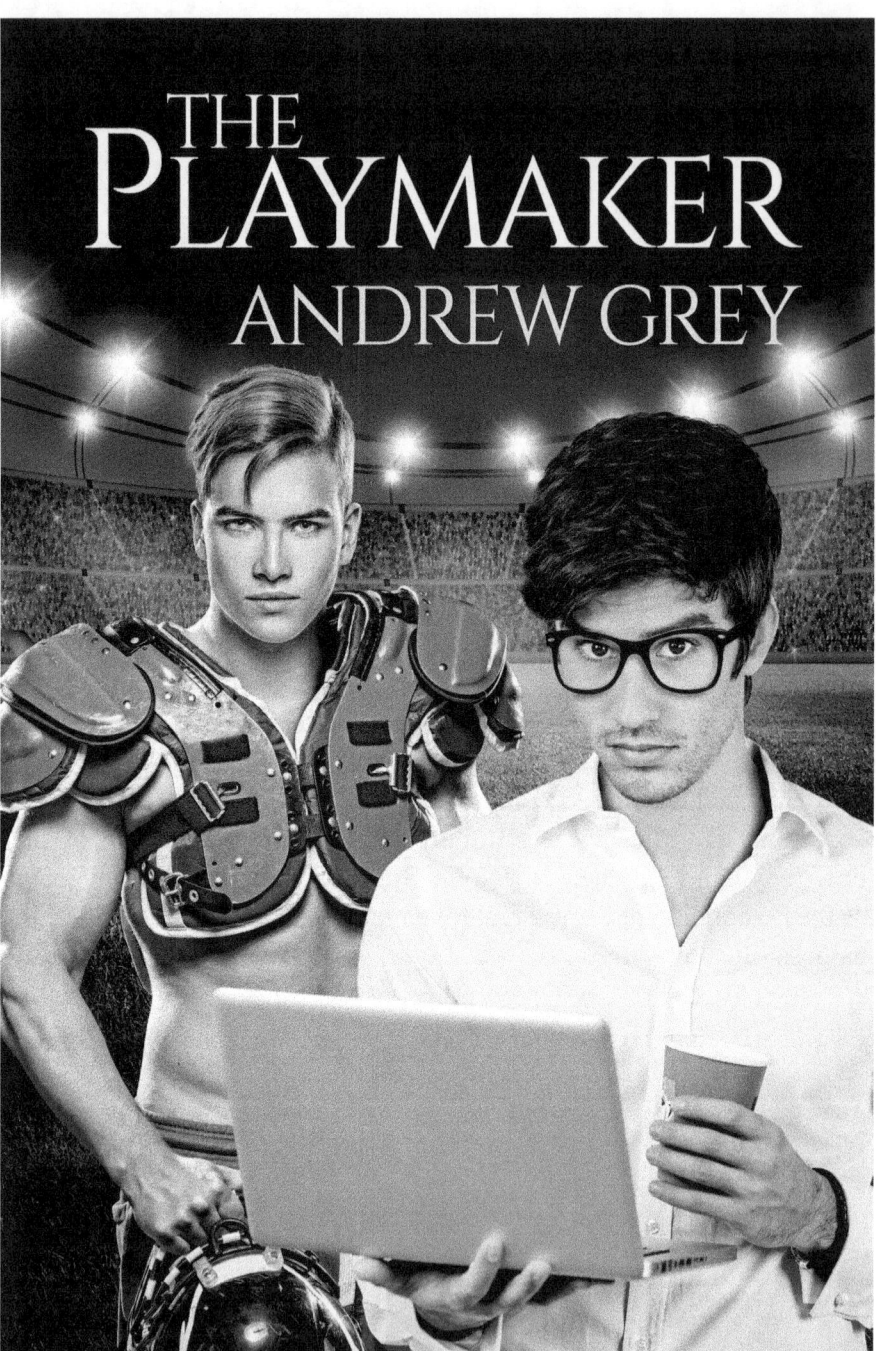

THE
PLAYMAKER
ANDREW GREY

Professional football player Hunter Davis is learning that saying he's gay is very different from actively being in a relationship with another man—especially in the eyes of his teammates and fans. So when Hunter needs a personal assistant to keep him organized, he asks for a woman in order to prevent tongues from wagging.

Montgomery Willis badly needs to find work before he loses everything. There's just one position at the agency where he applies, but the problem is, he's not a woman. And he knows nothing about football. Still, Hunter gives him a chance, but only because Monty's desperate.

Monty soon proves his worth by saving Hunter's bacon on an important promotional shoot, and Hunter realizes he might have someone special working for him—in more ways than one. Monty's feelings come to the surface during an outing in the park when Hunter decides to teach Monty a bit about the game, and pictures surface of them in some questionable positions. Hunter is reminded that knowing he's gay and seeing evidence in the papers are two very different things for the other players, and he might have to choose between two loves: football and Monty.

www.dreamspinnerpress.com

DREAMSPUN
DESIRES

POPPY'S SECRET

Andrew Grey

A second chance born
of love.

A second chance born of love.

Pat Corrigan and Edgerton "Edge" Winters were ready to start a family—or so Pat thought. At the last minute, Edge got cold feet and fled. Pat didn't bother telling him the conception had already gone through and little Emma was on her way. He didn't want a relationship based on obligation. He'd rather raise his daughter on his own.

Nine years later, Emma and her Poppy are doing fine. Edge isn't. He realizes what he threw away by leaving, and he's back to turn his life around and reclaim his family. It'll take a lot to prove to Pat that he's a new man, and even if Edge succeeds, the secret Pat has hidden for years might shatter their dreams all over again.

www.dreamspinnerpress.com